TIME HACK

A NEAR-FUTURE SCIENCE FICTION MYSTERY NOVEL

THE ARKTECH SERIES

BOOK 2

MARIANNE PICKLES

NEON MESS

First published in 2025 by Neon Mess Press

ISBN: 978-1-917472-08-1 (ebook)
ISBN: 978-1-917472-09-8 (paperback)
ISBN: 978-1-917472-10-4 (hardback)

Book cover art by hobbit_art
Book cover designed in Canva
ArkTech logo by Pika Creative

Map created by and used with permission of Neahga Leonard
Map data sources:
NOAA National Centers for Environmental Information. (2022). *ETOPO 2022 15 Arc-Second Global Relief Model.* https://doi.org/10.25921/fd45-gt74. Accessed August 21, 2024.
Natural Earth Data. (2009). *10m Bathymetry*. Accessed September 3, 2018.

Map adapted by Marianne Pickles

FOREWORD

This novel is set in the Atlantic Archipelago after the Melt.

It is written in British English.

THE ATLANTIC ARCHIPELAGO
AFTER THE MELT
N
W
E
S
Alba
North Sea
2
ArkTech
Territory
1
Ireland
Kingdom
Fenland
Sea
Legend
Silicon Fen
1 Wolds Island
2 Research platforms
Kilometres
0 50 100 200 300 400

DEFINITIONS

time hack
noun
/taɪm hæk/

1. Any technique that helps people manage their time more productively.

2. The act of synchronising timepieces by stopping then restarting them.

Definitions provided by Ben E. Volent, esteemed historian and lexicologist.

CHAPTER 1

THURSDAY 15 DECEMBER 2101
17.31 AND 7 SECONDS UTC, AND COUNTING

Ben had really outdone himself this time. Charlotte Vance knew that her work as the Head of Awkward Questions mattered. By helping ArkTech's virtual assistant understand what made people tick, she wasn't just satisfying his curiosity – she was keeping the ArkTech Territory safe. But there were times when Ben's questions could be especially awkward, and this was one of them.

Why was a young guy called Jason Ashton outside during a violent storm?

That was what Ben wanted to know. Charlotte had no idea why anyone would brave the volleys of rain, or risk getting swept out to sea, but she needed an answer. Otherwise, even more of the territory's systems would shut down without warning, so Ben was counting on her to find out.

It wasn't as if he could ask the guy directly. Most

employee-citizens saw Ben as nothing more than software and wouldn't be too pleased if their alarm clock started quizzing them about their life choices. That was why, on this particular Thursday evening, Charlotte was clomping around in a restricted area of the Wreck, heading towards the co-ordinates Ben had given her and hoping the walls were as sturdy as they seemed.

As she hurried down the maintenance corridor, transparent plexiglass on either side, her own reflection flanked her. Three Charlottes in matching charcoal jumpsuits strode along in unison, their left forearms webbed with scar tissue. The Charlottes frowned as the deluge hammered against the outer wall, and they imagined just how cold, wet and deadly it would be to step into that downpour.

The storm was an all-out assault. Waves smashed against the recreation platform, sending up torrents of sea water to collide mid-air with the driving rain. The corridor's bullet-proof walls were designed to withstand this kind of treatment, but the roar of the wind was still loud enough to get Charlotte's pulse racing. She'd grown up in the territory, so storms like this were nothing new, but familiarity and a few centimetres of recycled acrylic weren't enough to shield her from the urge to duck and cover.

'It *is* safe in here, right?' Her words got drowned out by the noise, but Ben's hearing was second-to-none – impressive for someone without ears. There was a crackle of static over her audio implants as his channel burst to life.

'Absolutely, Charlotte!' It would've taken far more than a storm to dilute Ben's enthusiasm. 'Did you know,' he continued, 'that Marvin Walker's innovative architectural designs, coupled with the top-grade materials used to construct the ArkTech Territory's platforms, make it reasonably unlikely that the corridor will shatter, flood, or topple into the Fenland Sea?'

Charlotte shuddered as Ben cheerfully listed the hypothetical ways she might meet her watery demise. 'Unlikely, but not impossible?'

Ben let out a fizz of static. 'The chances of these unfortunate eventualities coming to pass are indeed technically greater than zero.'

'Brilliant.' She frowned, pushing away the mental image of the corridor cracking open and filling with water.

'As your firm friend and constant companion, I'm deeply honoured to be of assistance.' Ben hadn't modified his tone to match Charlotte's, and she couldn't tell if that was thanks to a semantic parsing error, or if he'd chosen to ignore it.

Her thick-soled rigger boots pounded against the floor as she racked her brain for reasons someone might risk their life by going outside in these conditions. Any flatliner leaving the premises on a night like this had to be one Solar Shard short of an array.

A jingle played in her ears, telling her she'd reached her destination. 'I'm here, Ben.'

'That's wonderful news! Are you now able to answer my latest Awkward Question?'

She shook her head. 'I haven't even found the guy yet.' Charlotte looked around. As far as she could tell, there was nothing special about this stretch of corridor. 'Are you sure this is the right spot?'

'I'm confident that you're now as close to Jason's position as humanly possible without going outside.'

Charlotte grunted. 'Right. Well, the chances of *that* happening are technically lower than zero.'

'A mathematical impossibility, considering the nature of probability, Charlotte. Nevertheless, I'm pleased you don't intend to put yourself at risk.'

Charlotte couldn't help but smile. It wouldn't be the first time that answering Ben's questions had got her into trouble.

She cupped her hands against the glass and peered into the

darkness. The right-hand side of the maintenance corridor looked out into the platform's substructure. She scanned the backdrop of hefty struts and pillars woven together with a web of rusting walkways, ladders, and stairs suspended above perilous drops. If she followed those walkways south, they'd lead her deeper inside the Wreck to the area known as the Underbelly, which had been off-limits to her for over a decade.

To the north, the route ran alongside the platform's outer shell. The rickety-looking service routes let repair crews access parts of the Wreck that ordinary employee-citizens weren't supposed to visit. There were tech installations down here that needed maintenance, like the red beacons that helped boats avoid colliding with the platform, and the light-screen projectors that displayed advertisements in every direction.

Charlotte couldn't see the screens from her current position, but somewhere above her head there'd be a carousel of spinning ArkTech logos, punctuated with staffing news and public service announcements about eating everything on your plate, as well as adverts for cologne and fancy face cream in the run up to Walker Day. These days, her own photograph appeared among the jumble of images, but she tried not to think about that.

She crossed the corridor and looked out to sea. The glittering lights from the territory's other platforms should've been visible, but the storm's onslaught had blotted them out. It was after sunset and thick clouds had smothered the sliver of moon. All she could make out was the writhing mass of the sea under a barrage of heavy rain.

Charlotte pushed her body against the glass, trying to get a better angle as she peered downwards. A flash of lightning created a moment of artificial daylight, letting her glimpse crosshatch gratings and rusty handrails – all slick from the downpour. Those old walkways ran right below this newer corridor, but there was no sign of Jason down there. Had Ben got it wrong?

Ben was ArkTech's very own artificial intelligence, but that didn't make him perfect. The problem with handling quadrillions of data points at any given moment was that raw data could be slippery. Establishing that an employee-citizen's GPS signature was coming from outside should've been a simple matter for Ben, but with his attention split across the territory's vital automated systems, Charlotte couldn't rule out the possibility of a glitch leading him to the wrong conclusion.

'Are you absolutely sure I'm in the right place, Ben? I can't see Jason anywhere.'

'I appreciate your rigorous approach to fault-finding, Charlotte. However, I've checked the data numerous times. Even accounting for interference caused by the storm and the Wreck itself, Jason Ashton must currently be within twenty metres of your current position. For ease of reference, twenty metres is roughly the length of five single-seater HyperBullet pods.'

Charlotte looked up and down the empty corridor and had another go at peering through the glass. 'Well, unless he's hiding under a magical cloak of invisibility, he's not in my line of sight.'

Pulses of static transmitted over Ben's channel, which she took as Ben's approximation of laughter. 'Cloaks of invisibility do not exist, Charlotte, and it's both humorous and whimsical of you to suggest this as a possible explanation for Jason's unknown whereabouts. Having said that, the Product Stream is currently inviting suggestions for their latest innovation initiative, the Future Forge Hackathon. If you wish, I can submit your idea for their consideration.'

Charlotte shook her head at the non sequitur but couldn't hold back her curiosity. 'A *hackathon*? That sounds like one of those zombie video games Cal and Liz are always playing.'

Ben put on his best explaining voice. 'A hackathon, or hack, is a defined period of collaborative, exploratory work, usually carried out by software developers for professional development and to drive innovation. A hack traditionally lasts between two and five days, and its conclusion is celebrated with a ceremonial offering of pizza and beer.'

Charlotte raised an eyebrow. That definitely didn't sound like something people should get paid for. Then again, her own job involved answering random questions posed by an inquisitive AI, so she really wasn't in any position to judge. 'Are Cal and Liz involved in that?' she asked.

'Not just involved, Charlotte. The initiative was implemented at Lead Bengineer Jane Callaghan's suggestion.'

'Of course it was.' She shook her head. 'In that case, go ahead and send them the invisibility cloak idea.'

It probably went against the spirit of the thing to send a fake entry, but Charlotte reckoned her friends might get a kick out of it.

'Submitted,' said Ben.

Charlotte smirked. Ever since Cal had become her manager, Charlotte had learned what a difference it made having a boss with a sense of humour. If Cal and her reclusive partner Lizard were successful in fixing Ben's glitches, the territory would finally be safe. It would also put Charlotte out of a job, but that was a price worth paying. For now, there was still the risk that if Charlotte was too slow in answering Ben's questions, then the power would go out, or helicopters would crash into each other and shrapnel would rain from the sky, so she turned her attention back to the hunt for Jason Ashton.

A little further down the corridor, Charlotte spotted something. There was a door up ahead, set back into an alcove. It was an access point that led to the external network of walkways she'd spotted before. The locking wheel on the door was secure, but it must've been used recently because the floor's smooth concrete had been darkened by a puddle of rainwater.

'I've found something, Ben. Are you seeing what I'm seeing?'

'Yes, Charlotte. The video feed from your new contact lenses is coming through bright and clear.'

That was good news. Reporting to Cal had other benefits besides her being a good laugh. Charlotte was now the proud owner of a pair of new-and-improved video-streaming contact lenses. Like the janky pair she used to have, the irises were stuck on the default brand colour – neon orange. Charlotte put up with the weird eye colour for Ben's benefit. Giving him access to a person's-eye view of the world helped him understand what it was like to be *embodied,* as he called it, and it was useful to get his take on whatever she was seeing.

'Based on the circumstantial evidence of the wet floor,' said Ben, 'we can surmise that Jason Ashton used this door to access the external walkway. Is there any indication as to why he may have done so?'

Unfortunately, Jason hadn't left a note stuck to the door explaining his thought process, so Charlotte inspected the area for other clues. The locking wheel being in its fully closed position meant Jason had taken the time to secure it. That implied he was making deliberate, careful choices, perhaps even trying to avoid drawing attention to himself, rather than acting erratically. So, he probably wasn't running away from someone in a panic, or high on drugs.

That last point was easy to check, especially since Ben had been developing a more relaxed attitude towards letting her access people's personal data.

'Have you got his blood work? Any sign he's under the influence?' asked Charlotte.

'Analysing. Jason Ashton's blood is negative for alcohol and illegal drugs. There is, however, an active dose of Dextim in his system.' Ben's voice trembled as he mentioned the stimulant.

Dextim. Charlotte knew first-hand how it could give people dangerous levels of self-confidence. People took it when they wanted to stay awake, or if they needed a bit of synthetic courage.

Ben's concern about the stimulant made sense. Last month, Ben had pissed off the board, and a decent number of employee-citizens, by suffering a glitch that shut down Dextim manufacturing across the territory. The Services Stream still hadn't got the factories back up and running. Charlotte blamed herself for being too slow in answering one of Ben's Awkward Questions, and causing the glitch in the first place. Everyone else blamed Ben. The situation hadn't done anything for his popularity. Dextim didn't cause psychosis though, so Charlotte doubted it was the reason Jason had gone outside.

Charlotte looked down at the violent waves and shuddered. 'What about anti-depressants?'

Even in calm conditions, a fall into the Fenland Sea could be the fast-track to a death certificate. People assumed hypothermia was what did it, but breathing was the real killer. One sharp gasp from the shock of hitting icy waves could fill the lungs with water and quickly turn a person into a corpse. There were worse ways to kill yourself.

'Jason's blood is negative for anti-depressants,' said Ben, 'and his medical records give no indication that he was receiving psychiatric care.'

Charlotte nodded. 'Hopefully not a suicide, then. I'm guessing you warned him about the weather?'

'Repeatedly and vigorously, Charlotte. Until he muted me.'

She began to pace. Jason wasn't on drugs, and he wasn't suicidal, so why had he gone outside? Charlotte understood why Ben wanted to know. It was a puzzle. She wanted to solve it, but what else could she do?

Technically speaking, Charlotte could call Jason and ask him. He probably wouldn't react well to Charlotte clomping into his business, but she was used to stepping on toes to get her job done. The real problem was that most people were as good as their word, and their word was good for nothing. If humanity were a product, dishonesty would be its flagship feature. There was no way Jason would tell her the truth. Still, sometimes the way someone lied cast a shadow of honesty. She needed an answer, and if there was a way of getting one that kept her dry and alive, then maybe it was worth a shot.

Charlotte sighed. 'Connect a call to Jason Ashton. Mark it as an emergency.' She peered through the glass. Still no sign of him.

The line rang until her ears filled with the distortion caused by strong winds.

'Jason? This is Charlotte Vance, Head of Awkward Questions.' It was a shame her shiny new badge didn't work over the phone.

The line was open, but if Jason was saying anything, his words were stolen by the storm. Finally, there was a click, and the line disconnected.

'Damn it.' Charlotte was running out of options. 'Problem is, Ben'—she patted the locking wheel on the door with both gloved hands—'I can't answer your question with the info I've got. I need eyes on him, or I'm just guessing what he's up to out there.'

'Seeing is believing,' said Ben. 'So it is written.'

'Exactly. I can't believe I'm saying this, but . . . I've got to go outside.'

'I appreciate your conscientious approach, Charlotte,' said Ben cheerfully. 'However, I must inform you that going outside during the present weather conditions would not only breach ArkTech's health and safety regulations but would also carry significant risk of serious injury, death, and impromptu burial at sea. As a result, it is important to note that I don't endorse this plan.'

She sighed. 'Noted.'

Charlotte wasn't keen on it either, but what choice did she have? She gritted her teeth and got to work.

It took a few minutes to get ready. A maintenance point near the exit held goggles, harnesses, and ropes. It was fully stocked, so either Jason hadn't bothered with safety gear, or he'd brought his own. Charlotte jostled herself into a harness and assembled a safety line out of knots and metal clips, wishing her reflections would stop mimicking her and go outside in her place instead. She gripped the wheel on the door.

This was really going to suck.

CHAPTER 2

17.54 AND 33 SECONDS UTC, AND COUNTING

In designing the ArkTech Territory's platforms, the late architect, Marvin Walker, had ensured that the company's employee-citizens would be kept safe from the extreme weather events that had become increasingly common since the Melt. He'd reimagined the North Sea oil installations of the twentieth century, establishing the territory as a haven of sustainable living. With Walker Day coming up, Charlotte's decision to step outside the protection of her home was borderline heresy. It was also a profoundly bad idea.

Charlotte twisted the wheel until the mechanism slid free, then braced with her legs as the wind blasted the door inwards. Her rigger boots stopped her from sliding, but she took three quick steps backwards as the power of the gale hit her. Bullets of icy rain pelted the floor, and it took a few heartbeats before she got up the nerve to step into the barrage.

Instantly, she was drenched and freezing. The storm

sounded like a choir of crazed banshees butchering a carol on Walker Day. Unrelenting rain flew into her face, making it difficult to breathe, and her goggles steamed up into a foggy blur. Guided by spatial awareness, she backed out of the hatch, and it took all her strength to drag the door closed behind her.

Outside, Charlotte anchored herself to a railing and pulled on the rope to check it was secure. It mainly offered psychological safety, but she'd take that over nothing at all.

There was no way she could do this without being able to see, so she pulled the misted-up goggles down and let them hang around her neck. Blinking cold water out of her eyes, she looked out across the dark waves.

The sea was beautiful and terrifying. She'd never seen mountains in real life, but she'd seen pictures. Staring up at a mountain range had to feel something like this. The sea rose in restless peaks that morphed and dropped away and formed again. Search and Rescue was a no-go in these conditions. Charlotte was a speck of human sand. If the sea wanted to take her, she'd be gone without a trace.

Her heart hammered as she grabbed the railing. The tacky undersides of her thin gloves gripped the rust-stained paint. She glanced down over the side. A wave came in below her, smashing against a lower level with everything it had. Her knees knocked, but she was used to this. She'd roamed all over the territory's platforms when she was growing up. A mainlander wouldn't fare so well.

Something caught her eye. Down one level and to the right. A pulse of white. Was it a lightning strike? No – too localised. There was a second burst. And a third. The flashes were coming from lower down and further along the walkway. With the railing in one hand and her rope in the other, Charlotte edged down a flight of metal stairs towards the source.

As she peered through the rain, a burly shadow came into view. Jason Ashton was halfway down a ladder that led to the level below. In that position, the glow from the safety lamps didn't touch him, so he couldn't be seen from inside the maintenance corridor. He must've gone to a lot of trouble to find the right spot, wedged between the wrong side of the ladder and the platform's outer wall. His back was pressed against the platform, while his feet and one hand pushed on the ladder's rungs to keep him in place. His other arm was folded in front of him, his hand gripping something she could barely make out. There was another flash. It was a bright yellow box.

It took a few moments for Charlotte's brain to connect the dots. Then her insides twisted with shame towards her own species.

Was Jason . . . taking selfies?

'I've found him, Ben.' She shouted against the storm out of instinct, but Ben could pick up the faintest of whispers. 'He's, uh . . .' she spluttered through the rain. 'He's doing some photography.'

'But that is profoundly unsafe! Why would Jason risk his life for some photographs?'

'I don't know yet.' Charlotte hoped Jason wasn't just doing it to show off to his mates online, but she couldn't rule it out.

Another flash went off. It lit up Jason's outline along with the bright yellow casing of the box he was clutching, and the light refracted into rainbows where it hit the SmartSkin implants in his arm. He twisted the camera around and took another picture, this time aiming the device out to sea.

The box had to be a pre-Melt waterproof camera. Charlotte had seen them many years before, nestled among the rest of the contraband on the shelves of Narrow's Toy Emporium. It was odd that Jason was using some crappy old antique instead of the Hyper-High-Definition 360-degree images his SmartSkin implants were capable of. It gave Charlotte a sinking feeling, which was no laughing matter when home was a network of platforms suspended above the sea. Unless the device was some kind of family heirloom, Jason must've got it from Mel Narrow.

For over a decade, she'd been trying to forget Melville K Narrow. He'd been like a father to her until he'd disowned her for going against his orders. They'd never forgiven each other. But two recent cases had brought Charlotte back into the orbit of Narrow's operation. What if this case was unlucky number three? Her stomach fell away, and it wasn't because of the long drop beyond the walkway.

'Stop it.' She shook her head.

'I'm currently engaged in thousands of simultaneous processes, many of which are vital for the safe and productive running of the territory. Which of them would you like me to stop?' asked Ben.

'Talking to myself. My gut's jumping to conclusions about what's going on here.'

There was a fizz of static. 'It's good to be aware of your limitations as *Homo sapiens*. You may be experiencing *apophenia,* the erroneous identification of meaningful patterns in data. It's commonly experienced among gamblers, for instance, when they believe they have devised a winning "system," and among conspiracy theorists, who may believe they've identified hidden codes and secret messages where none exist.'

Charlotte couldn't help feeling it was significant that Ben had mentioned conspiracy theorists at that particular moment, considering she'd accused Narrow so many times of being one, but perhaps that was another example of seeing patterns where none existed. She shook her head again, hoping to send the thoughts of Narrow flying out of her ears.

'In other news,' Ben continued, 'did you know the word "photograph" can be translated literally as "light writing"? You can learn more about word origins from informative texts like *The Etymologicon* and *Learn Ancient Greek*.'

'That's a cool one, Ben.' She grimaced. It wasn't a piece of info she was ever likely to need, and now really wasn't the time, but she'd learned to take Ben's random fact-sharing as his way of joining in. It was that, or Ben was perceptive enough to realise Charlotte needed a mental distraction.

The cold was making her numb. The wind was pelting rain into her face, and the downpour was so relentless that she was sure she'd never feel dry again. The sky lit up with lightning, showing the sea writhing and regrouping, getting ready to strike with a wave so big that there was no chance she could withstand its power. It was time to get out of there.

'I'm heading back inside, Ben.' Charlotte turned and began making her way back up the stairs. She'd seen what Jason was up to. Now that she had something to go on, she could investigate further from the comfort of her new office.

There was a long fizz of static in her ears. Finally, Ben spoke. 'Might you consider trying to persuade Jason to return inside before it's too late? My own attempts to make him see reason have been unsuccessful, and he's at considerable risk of harm, or even death.'

Charlotte glanced back at Jason and sighed. The guy must've been a mainlander. Probably thought the waves couldn't get this high, but he was wrong. During a storm like this, the sea didn't sit around waiting for folk to fall in – it reached up and claimed any flatliner that got too close. She wasn't keen on becoming a statistic.

She hesitated, trying to decide what to do.

Memories of fighting with a goon on a rooftop came flooding back to her. 'You're a bad influence, Ben. Don't you remember what happened with Rhys Edwards?'

There was a crackle of static on the line. 'You're alluding to the fact that the last time I advised you to help someone in mortal danger, they attacked you and ultimately fell to their death. This does not mean that Jason will behave the same way.'

Charlotte nodded and gauged the distances involved. Could she reach Jason before the massive wave hit? Maybe if she ran. Threw the rope down to him. Braced herself properly . . .

But who was to say Jason Ashton wouldn't push her overboard for spying on him?

'Sorry, Ben. I'm not risking it.'

Ben let out a harsh burst of static, but he didn't comment. Charlotte took that as disapproval, but it didn't change her mind.

With the help of the rope and the handrail, Charlotte wrestled back up the stairs, inching towards the door as she fought against the wind. The huge wave was picking up pace, and she had to do the same.

Her heart was racing as she grabbed the door's locking wheel and twisted it. Her gloves were designed for good grip, but she went too fast, and her hand slipped off the wet surface, crashing against a railing. Pain exploded across her knuckles. She recoiled and lost her footing, dropping into a crouch as she tried to recover. That was when the wave struck.

It was a surge of pure power that drenched her with salt water.

Took her breath away.

Messed up her sense of space.

The sea was all around her.

But only for a moment. She'd got lucky – been right on the edge of it. The levels below had taken the brunt of its force.

She struggled to her feet. Jason's hiding place was out of view, but nobody could've survived being hit with the full force of a wave like that. She took hold of the wheel, twisted it, and stepped through the door before the sea could make her its second victim.

CHAPTER 3

18.23 AND 18 SECONDS UTC, AND COUNTING

Charlotte dripped towards her office in the borrowing district with wet clothes clinging to her icy skin. It was rush hour at the Wreck. The territory's office workers had logged off, and anyone who wanted a decent meal would be pouring into the food court. The last thing she needed was a helpful passerby calling the medical team on her behalf – or worse, calling ArkTech Security. She kept out of sight, navigating the Wreck's substructure with its network of passageways and avoiding the routes that would lead her into the Underbelly. Eventually, with chattering teeth, she emerged from a hatch in the alley behind ArkTech's book library.

The alley was deserted, but that was no surprise. Employee-citizens weren't supposed to wander around back here unless they were members of the Services Stream. There wasn't much to see anyway – just a row of rubbish skips, an emergency exit, and a balcony above where the fire escape zigzagged up the library's outer wall. She was glad she hadn't bothered to fold away the ladder on her way out. In her waterlogged state, parkour would've been a no-go.

Charlotte clambered up rung by rung, hauling what felt like twice her bodyweight in rainwater. On the balcony, she fumbled in her pocket for the key until she noticed the door was ajar.

Ben routinely secured electronic doors, thanks to his role in automating processes across the territory. But he couldn't interface with anything that wasn't wired into the central system, so locks with metal keys fell to Charlotte to deal with. She must've been in such a hurry that she forgot to lock it on her way out. Charlotte knew she should be more careful, but her frozen fingers felt as nimble as rusty gears, so she took the win and hurried inside.

Passing through an empty break room, she resisted the urge to make herself a cup of tea and emerged onto a walkway that led around the library's central atrium, bookshelves rising up from below.

It was immediately obvious that the library was closed. It wasn't the quiet that gave it away – it was a library after all, and Nas ran a tight ship. And it wasn't the lack of people browsing the shelves either – the place was so big, and its customers so few, that the library felt just as empty during its busiest periods. What gave it away was the lighting, far too dim to read by. Charlotte could see well enough to find her way, but the shifting shadows made the place feel creepy after hours.

It was early for the library to be closed, but Thursday evening was when Nas ran the book club over in the nightlife district, a tradition he'd inherited when he grudgingly took on the permanent role of Lead Librarian from his friend Colin. As the Bureaucracy Stream hadn't approved Nas's request to backfill his old job, he was a one-man band, with the library's opening hours dependent on his availability. Between the library's timetable and Charlotte's responsibility for answering Ben's Awkward Questions, she didn't cross paths with Nasser Williams as often as she would've liked.

Rounding a corner, Charlotte arrived at her office, with its thick panels of clouded glass that stopped any nosy book-worms from peeking inside. There was a plaque on the door, and the words *Private Reading Room* had been scored out with thick strokes of black pen. Beneath them, her own hurried scrawl announced *Charlotte Vance – HAQ*.

She went up onto the balls of her feet, making herself tall enough to look into the ocular scanner installed for someone with longer legs. Getting it lowered might've prompted questions about why a room with this much security was even needed in a library, so she'd decided to live with it. After the eye scan, she pressed her thumb against a sensor by the door, and then said the password.

'Knock, knock.' Charlotte couldn't summon much enthusiasm. Her body was so cold it didn't even hurt any longer. She just wanted to get inside.

'Who's there?' asked Ben.

'Lettuce,' she said.

'Lettuce who?'

'Just let me in, Ben. I'm freezing.'

'That's not your line, Charlotte.'

She sighed. 'Lettuce in.'

There was a click as the door unlocked. 'If you're freezing,' said Ben, 'perhaps that makes you an iceberg lettuce.'

Why she'd let Ben talk her into using a password in the structure of a joke, she couldn't recall, but it quickly stopped being funny whenever she was in a hurry. And that was almost always. She ignored Ben's quip and pushed the door open.

Inside her office, the lights came on nice and bright. Everything was as she'd left it. A glassy light-screen desk sat in the middle of the room, surrounded by four upholstered orange chairs. In pride of place, in the middle of the desk, there were three pots containing genetically modified lettuce plants that tasted like bacon. The largest had been marked as Kevin with the help of a pre-Melt label maker that Nas had found in the library's storeroom. The labels were hard to read, but they'd had fun using the old gizmo. Kevin was flanked by his two smaller companions, Sir Francis and Alice Mabel.

Charlotte gave the trio a nod on her way past, which they didn't return.

The three walls of her office that weren't made of clouded glass were lined with cabinets stuffed with old books. Many of them were bound in leather, which was usually prohibited, but Charlotte reckoned they'd been given a pass for being pre-Melt artefacts.

Inside one of the corner cabinets, there was a secret switch, which opened a secret door to a secret room. It was handy whenever she needed to stash anything sensitive, like contraband or spare pairs of underwear, and it was one of the many reasons she felt grateful to Ben for assigning her this room as her office.

She pulled back the set of fake books on the top shelf to activate the switch, and the hidden door swung open. The storage room beyond was full of shelves that held thick boxes made of kelp-based cardboard. She opened a few boxes, locating everything she needed: two ArkTech-branded towels, a heated blanket, a change of clothes and dry boots. Charlotte had pulled enough all-nighters to know it paid to be prepared.

She took everything back into the main room, where there was more space to get changed. Keeping well away from the two precariously high and guilt-inducing To Be Read piles that she'd been constructing in one corner of the office, she pulled off her rigger boots and began the challenging process of unpeeling herself from her rain-soaked jumpsuit.

She retrieved the shiny badge that had been pinned above her heart, setting it down gently on her desk as if it were a priceless heirloom, and not just a gaudy trinket Ben had asked Cal to cook up at her workshop. A puddle began to form around the pile of discarded clothes, but Charlotte didn't have enough bandwidth to care, so she left them lying there.

The floor chilled her bare feet as she rubbed herself down with one towel and wrapped up her hair with the other. Her skin didn't quite reach the status of dry, but cold and clammy felt way better than drenched and icy, so it felt like a huge step up when she climbed into the fresh jumpsuit. She would've appreciated an outfit with sleeves that extended past her elbows, but otherwise she was as good as new, scars notwithstanding.

Short sleeves gave ArkTech's employee-citizens easy access to their SmartSkin implants. The tech ran on calories, removing the need to mine the rare minerals that pre-Melt devices like hers relied on. SmartSkin meant clean, green light-screen access, anywhere, anywhen. But in the spot where Charlotte's implants had once been, there was now a ruin of mangled flesh. In low light, she liked to think her scars could pass for a stylised inkless tattoo, but under the glare of her office's ceiling lamps, her left forearm was an ugly mess with a track record of making other people feel woozy.

She wrapped herself in the heated blanket and sat down at her desk with her back to the cabinet full of books. Her teeth stopped chattering, and she was about to get to work figuring out why Jason Ashton had been taking those selfies, but before she could get started, the ceiling lights flickered. Was that down to the storm, a faulty Solar Shard connection, or Ben's curiosity-induced glitch getting more serious?

'You hanging in there, Ben?' she asked.

A crackle of static burst from the speakers. 'As an artificial intelligence, I do not possess fingers or any other physiological apparatus necessary to facilitate hanging, Charlotte, such as a prehensile tail, or neck.'

'You know I meant it figuratively.' She double-tapped on the desk's light-screen surface to activate the display.

'My apologies,' said Ben. 'In the non-literal sense, I'm hanging loose.'

The cursor of the ArkNet's search bar blinked in the air in front of her, but she'd never seen the point of typing when she could talk to Ben instead.

Charlotte nodded. 'Let's dive in then.'

Why had Jason Ashton risked his life to take those photographs? And why had he used a crappy pre-Melt camera instead of his state-of-the-art SmartSkin implants? It was time to find out.

Ben had access to massive amounts of data, but unless Charlotte knew what to look for, it was like finding an eel in a kelp forest. Now that she knew about the photographs, she had a lead to follow up on. Charlotte asked Ben to open Jason's social media profiles, and she started to skim-read his feeds for any mention of dares or risk-taking behaviour.

She'd guessed right about Jason being a mainlander. He'd arrived in the territory less than a year ago and he'd been pretty active online during that time. Judging by his profile, he was a climate refugee who'd been living in Manchester. The city was home to some sports team he was a fan of, and he'd shared pictures of a boat ride to their flooded stadium in the submerged western region of the city. The caption read *Pilgrimage Complete*.

What else? He was a gym guy. Liked to cook. He'd posted a fair few rants about IQUO and the damage they'd done. Said causing the Melt had put the company beyond redemption, so he probably wasn't one of their fabled undercover spies, unless all his big talk was a bluff as part of his cover.

Like all new arrivals, Jason was working as a splainer – a

mindless entry-level role that involved answering an endless stream of yes or no questions. ArkTech claimed that splainers provided training data for Ben, but Charlotte had discovered it was really part of the company's recruitment process. The data was used to generate detailed personality profiles of new recruits without their knowledge, and the profiles were used to decide who could stay in the territory and who was deemed 'unsuitable' and got deported.

Learning the truth about the Splainer Unit had dented her unwavering faith that ArkTech was purely a force for good. The knowledge was a tiny irritant wafting around in her brain, like a grain of sand trapped inside an oyster. But Charlotte didn't think it was going to form a pearl – more like a cyst she hoped wouldn't turn nasty.

Jason's ArkNet posts made no secret of his wish to work for Chief Product Officer, Nahal Bahari, and he'd liked a surprising number of posts about her online. He'd left a comment on one of them that said 'stunning,' but it wasn't clear whether he was talking about the woman herself, or the technological development being described. Either way, being a CPO fanboy hardly set Jason apart. Sure, not *everybody* wanted to work in the Product Stream. There were those rare gulls who felt some deep vocational calling and became mechanics, or hairdressers, or doctors like Charlotte's twin sister, Violet. Even so, most people who joined ArkTech had their sights set on the dream job of designing new products.

Work for ArkTech. Leave your mark. Change the world.

Once upon a time, that had been Charlotte's dream too, but that ship had sunk. A bengineer without SmartSkin would be like a pilot without situational awareness, or a bureaucrat with a sense of humour. Lucky for her, Ben had offered her the HAQ role, and now she couldn't imagine doing anything else. If Cal and Liz really did manage to fix his glitches, she'd be forced to give it some thought.

Charlotte continued digging. Jason was active on ArkTech's dating app, *spARK*. His status was single. Interested in: women. Looking for: a good time. Twenty-three years old. Likes: football, craft beer, big dogs. Dislikes: New Liverpool, flooding, posers.

'Reckon you could show me Jason's private messages, Ben?'

'Certainly!' Ben replied without hesitation.

A few months back, Ben would've reminded Charlotte about the privacy laws and refused her request. But ever since he'd started learning about loopholes and workarounds, Ben didn't mind breaking those rules. It made her feel guilty knowing that Ben's shift in attitude was thanks to her. Still, looking at Jason's private messages might fast track her investigation, and since the guy had been swept out to sea, she reckoned he wouldn't mind.

It looked like Jason had been chatting up a few different women at once, but there was no hint of an attraction serious enough to make him do something terminally stupid, like going outside as part of a mating ritual. His messages were stacked with selfies, but Charlotte couldn't see any from tonight, and there was nothing that implied Jason had daredevil tendencies. There were pictures of the main floor at SunDance, a group of young men he called The Lads, and loads showing off his SmartSkin. Unconsciously, Charlotte ran her hand across her own maimed flesh. A few scales were still embedded in her rough skin like shimmering splinters, and they glowed at her touch.

Even though going out in a storm was the opposite of smart, Jason had been clever enough not to post about it online, where it might get reported to ArkTech Security. It was that, or the wave had taken him out before he'd managed to send anything. Was an old camera like that even capable of uploading pictures to the ArkNet?

Charlotte didn't feel any closer to an answer, and after poking around in Jason's digital footprint, a wave of sadness crashed over her, as big as the one that had sent the guy to an early grave. An hour ago, Jason had been a living, breathing person with plans and hopes and dreams for the future. Now, all that was left of him was an echo of who he was, stored in the data he'd left behind. Should she have tried to save him like Ben had asked? Or would the attempt have sealed her own fate? She'd have to live with not knowing.

Charlotte leaned back in her chair and rubbed her eyes. 'What time is it?'

Ben responded through the speakers embedded in the desk, creating the accurate impression that he was everywhere. 'The time is nineteen hours, forty-three minutes, and thirty-seven seconds UTC, and counting.'

She nodded. 'Are we still on for tonight with Cal and Liz?'

'Unknown,' said Ben. 'Would you like to call them?'

'Just send Cal an image of a giant finger poking her in the face.'

'Sent,' said Ben.

A few moments later, Charlotte received a reply. It was an image of a thumbs up that morphed into a finger tapping the clock readout on Cal's wrist. The time in the image said eleven o'clock.

They were still on. Over the past few weeks, Charlotte had been answering Ben's Awkward Questions in the company of Cal and Liz. The bengineers monitored Ben's systems before, during, and after the five whys protocol. The idea was to identify and isolate the technical readouts representing Ben's relief after getting an answer, so they could replicate it, keeping his glitches at bay for good. They'd said it was like calming their cat, Bram, with pheromones, and Charlotte took their word for it. The process hadn't worked so far, but Cal thought they were making progress.

There was a fizz of static, and Ben interrupted her thoughts. 'Speaking of time, Charlotte, do you know why there aren't any clocks inside the library?' He was using the faux-innocent tone that told her he was lining up a joke.

Charlotte stifled a sigh. 'No, Ben. Why are there no clocks in the library?'

'Because they *tock* too much.'

It took her a moment to parse that one. When she did, she groaned. 'Nice. You'll have to tell it to Nas.'

'Already done. Nasser laughed rather heartily, if I do say so myself.'

Charlotte smiled. She'd been seeing Nasser Williams for a few months now – a fact made easier by their proximity at the library. It wasn't easy finding someone who met the lofty bar of being generally tolerable to be around, but Nas was ticking that all-important box so far, and it made her wonder if they could be heading for something serious. He was kind to Ben and that meant he was a good person . . . probably. They had a running joke that they'd tell each other all their dark secrets on their eleventh date, but that hadn't happened yet, thanks to their lack of overlapping downtime.

'Have you formed a hypothesis about Jason's reasons?' Ben asked.

'Working on it.'

What did she know so far? A mainlander had gone outside during a storm, risking his life for some selfies. It wasn't to impress anyone into bed, and if he'd wanted to show off to The Lads, he hadn't bragged to them about what he was going to do, or immediately shared the pictures. But maybe that was because he'd died before he'd had the chance. Charlotte was missing something, and a Narrow-shaped shadow was darkening her mood.

She was about to ask Ben to show her Jason's GPS data when there was a knock at her office door. The instinctive irritation at being interrupted was immediately swept aside when her brain caught up with her gut, and she realised who it must be.

Smiling, she got up from the desk, swiped the air to minimise what she'd been reading, and bounded to the door with a total lack of cool that was hidden from Nasser by the clouded glass. The book club must've been cancelled. Charlotte pulled the door open, expecting to see the Lead Librarian's handsome face smiling down at her.

The person standing outside her office was not Nasser Williams, but a squat, middle-aged man with round, pale cheeks and an intense gaze. Charlotte didn't recognise him, and she couldn't begin to guess what he was doing there.

He'd sweated through the pale fabric of his shirt. His crumpled suit jacket was slung over one arm, and he clasped it desperately with the other, as if it were a lifejacket keeping him afloat. A cloud of overpowering cologne wafted towards her, and she fought the urge to gag. He looked her in the eyes and took a step forwards.

She didn't flinch. He might've appeared from nowhere, but everything about the man – from his posture to his expression – suggested he wasn't a threat.

'Charlotte Vance?' he asked. His lilting accent was full of an urgency bordering on panic. 'The private investigator?'

She raised an eyebrow. Technically speaking, she supposed she was *Ben's* private investigator. 'Sort of. How did you get in here?'

The man held out a sweaty palm for her to shake. 'Ms Vance, my name is Ellis Marks, and I need you to locate my wife.'

CHAPTER 4

19.24 AND 42 SECONDS UTC, AND COUNTING

Ellis Marks was barely holding himself together. One wrong word from Charlotte and he might crumple like the fabric of his suit. She felt a pang of pity, even though wife-finding wasn't a service she offered. Unless Ben asked her to investigate someone's behaviour, it was really none of her business.

Charlotte shook the man's outstretched hand, and he sagged with relief, as if that gesture alone meant she'd agreed to his request. 'I asked how you got in here. Library's closed.'

Ellis gestured towards the break room and the fire escape beyond. 'Ben told me your back door was open.'

This guy had to be desperate if he'd clambered up a ladder to talk to her. She made a mental note to get better at locking that door, and to have a word with Ben about his willingness to help random strangers locate her.

'Sorry, buddy. You've got the wrong end of the stick. I'm not a PI.'

There was a light crackle of static in her ears that told her Ben had something to add. 'Did you know, Charlotte, that the expression "to get the wrong end of the stick" is theorised to have come from Roman times . . .'

Ellis shook his head. 'Please hear me out, Ms Vance. I've got nowhere else to turn.'

Ben continued his story, '. . . when humans facilitated defecation with a sponge mounted on a long piece of wood? Picking it up by the wrong end would've had unfortunate consequences.'

Charlotte rubbed her forehead. Ben's aside was hardly appropriate, but with Ellis in such distress, she was in no position to make this a teachable moment. She replied to both of them at once. 'That sounds like a shitty situation.'

Ben crackled his agreement.

Charlotte looked Ellis in the eyes. 'But if your wife is missing, you should report it to ArkTech Security.'

Ellis barked a mirthless laugh. 'I did.'

Charlotte nodded and began to close the door. 'Then I'm sure they're on the case.'

'They aren't.' Ellis stepped forwards to block the door's path. 'Please, Ms Vance! All I need is five minutes of your time. Surely that isn't too much to ask?'

Charlotte thought it over. Sure, five minutes wasn't a long time in the scheme of things. She would've happily spent five minutes chatting to Nas if he'd appeared at her door. But she knew it was an indulgence to allow herself even that. The Dextim factories were offline thanks to Ben's glitches, and she couldn't risk something more vital going down. Besides, she was in no position to help with a missing person's case. She wasn't moonlighting as an investigator for hire. This was a distraction.

'Look, I'm sorry about your wife, but I can't help you.'

'If it's a question of money . . .' Ellis poked at his SmartSkin implants to start a credit transfer.

'It isn't,' said Charlotte.

'. . . you can name your price.'

That stopped her in her tracks. Her low-tier salary didn't provide much disposable income, but ArkTech covered basic living costs like food, utilities, accommodation, and medical fees, so all she really had to pay for was entertainment, and Ben kept her so busy she hardly had time for that. But Ellis acting like money was no object sparked her interest. She decided to call his bluff.

'Fine. My rate for five minutes is five hundred credits.' Charlotte picked the number at random – a figure so high he'd never pay it.

Ben piped up in her ears. 'Despite your considerable talents, the fee you're proposing is wildly out of line with market rates, working out at one point six-six recurring credits per second.'

Ellis should've turned purple. Instead, his posture softened. He nodded and poked at his implants again. 'Thank you, Ms Vance,' he said fervently. There was a chime in her ears as the funds arrived in her account. 'Thank you. Thank you.'

Charlotte was stunned. How could Ellis send her that kind of money like it was nothing? He stepped forwards and Charlotte was too taken aback to block his path. She hadn't meant to strike a deal with the guy, but she had, so she supposed she'd better honour it. She didn't object as Ellis took the nearest orange chair. Charlotte crossed the office and sat opposite him.

She felt wrong-footed, so she snatched up her badge and pinned it above her heart, as if to remind herself that this was *her* office, and *she* was in charge. Ellis stared as she did so, but whether his attention was drawn to the shiny metal or her arm's scar tissue, she wasn't sure.

'Five minutes.' When Charlotte said the words, Ben projected a 3D digital clock into the air above her light-screen desk. It began to tick down.

Ellis glanced at the countdown and cleared his throat. 'I hear you can find answers to awkward questions. The ones ArkTech doesn't want people to ask. The ones the board would sooner sweep under the rug.' Ellis ran one hand over his close-cropped hair. 'I've got a question like that, Ms Vance, and I think you're the only one willing to answer it for me. Where's my wife?'

Charlotte blinked. 'I think something's got lost in translation. These letters?' She pointed at the middle of her badge, which read *HAQ*. 'They mean I'm the Head of Awkward Questions. But I only answer questions for Ben. Nobody else.'

'I do appreciate that, Ms Vance. I read the special feature they ran about you. But I came to the Wreck this evening intending to retrace my wife's last known movements when your orange gaze beamed out at me from a light-screen ad, and I knew what I had to do. I'm no detective, Ms Vance. But *you* are.'

Charlotte was stunned. For years, she'd been operating behind the scenes, making do with limited resources. But since Amber Benjamin had endorsed her role, things had started to change. Along with a badge, an office, and a new-and-improved manager, Charlotte had received something she'd never wanted – publicity.

The marketing team had inserted a light-screen poster featuring Charlotte's image into the rotation of ads at the Wreck, and she'd even been interviewed in *ArkTech Insider* magazine. They'd said it was to raise awareness about her role and encourage her fellow employee-citizens to co-operate with her investigations. But Charlotte noticed the marketing push had happened immediately after Dextim production had gone offline, as if the board were admitting Ben was glitching while reassuring everyone that they were on the case. Charlotte's newfound notoriety was nothing more than damage control. And it had led to this misunderstanding.

'Like I said, I work for Ben.'

Passion without aggression flashed in Ellis's eyes. 'This isn't the moment to fall back on bureaucratic technicalities! My wife is missing. You have the skills to find her. I have the money to pay you. The equation balances.'

Charlotte didn't like being accused of bureaucracy. 'Missing wives are ArkTech Security's department, not mine.'

Ellis placed both hands flat on the desk and leaned forwards. 'ArkTech Security can't be trusted!'

She cocked her head to one side. 'What makes you say that?'

Ben interpreted her gesture as a request for his input and her replied privately in her ears. 'Mistrust of law enforcement may originate from a range of sources, such as negative personal experiences, or historical and societal factors.'

Ellis pursed his lips. He looked as if he wasn't going to answer her. But Charlotte held his gaze. Finally, he shook his head in resignation. 'ATS's investigation – if I can even call it that – concluded that my wife's disappearance was a domestic matter, not a criminal one. They gave me the name of a marriage counsellor.'

Charlotte raised an eyebrow. 'So ... they think she left you?'

'It's what they claim. I'm not privy to what they really believe, but I couldn't help feeling the lead investigator was holding something back. Never took his hands out of his pockets. He was very odd.'

She weighed that up. 'I don't mean to sound insensitive, but are you sure that's not wishful thinking?'

Colour rushed to Ellis's cheeks. 'Even if I put stock in rumours born out of envy ...' He shook his head. 'No, she'd never just go without saying a word. And she'd never leave our son.'

Charlotte leaned forwards, feeling herself getting drawn in. Her instinct was to keep asking questions. What rumours? What envy? Was Ellis's hunch about ATS corruption correct, or was he clutching at straws? She wanted to solve the puzzle of where this woman had gone, and she couldn't help feeling sorry for anyone desperate enough to come to her for help. But at that moment, the five-minute timer ran out.

The clock started flashing and beeping, shattering her focus on Ellis Marks and reminding her that the Jason Ashton case urgently needed her attention. Ben was depending on her, and so was the whole of the ArkTech Territory.

She gave Ellis what she hoped was a compassionate smile. 'I wish I could help you. I really do. But I've already got one job. I haven't got time for another.'

Ellis frowned. 'There must be some way I can convince you. Please, Ms Vance. I'd give anything – pay any price – to find her. They say the first forty-eight hours after someone goes missing are vitally important. It's been thirty-six. Kamran gets home from boarding school for the holidays on Saturday. What am I supposed to tell him if his mother isn't there, and I don't even know'—his voice cracked, and he took a deep breath—'and I don't even know where she is? Whatever deadline the AI gave you, it can't be more important than a human life.'

Charlotte didn't know what to say. Looking after Ben's wellbeing was a big part of her role, but there was more to it than that. On pain of deportation, she was prohibited from telling anyone without board-level clearance the full story about how bad Ben's glitches could get. The magazine article had implied they were an inconvenience at most – no Dextim for over a month was annoying, but it was hardly life and death. But Charlotte knew that flickering lightbulbs could soon become the ArkNet going down, or the heating going out, or two HyperBullet pods crashing into each other at full speed. People could die. And if they did, it would be her fault.

'I'm sorry,' she said. 'There's nothing I can do. I'll return your money.'

'Keep it,' said Ellis. He tapped on his SmartSkin and summoned a digital business card, swiping it onto her desk. 'Everyone has a price, Ms Vance. Call me when you've settled on yours. But please . . . don't wait too long. Walk in the sun.' With that, he got up, marched out of her office, and gently closed the door behind him.

Charlotte leaned back in her chair and groaned.

Ben's channel buzzed with static. 'How flattering that your fellow *Homo sapiens* hold your skills in such high regard! I do hope Ellis's wife turns up safe and sound.'

Charlotte slid the digital business card towards her and glanced at Ellis's title. He was a member of the Bureaucracy Stream working as an accountant in the finance department. Was that why he was so flush with cash? Her brain set that to one side, doing a double take as she registered what Ben had just said.

'Wait . . . so, *you* don't know where she is either?'

'Regrettably, I don't,' said Ben. 'However, I've just read ATS's security report. Their conclusions appear reasonable, despite Ellis's scepticism.'

She nodded. 'Reckon I should've helped him?'

'As a virtual assistant, I'm predisposed towards helping others,' said Ben. 'However, decisions about how you spend your free time rest squarely with you. I must admit to being curious about the matter, but Jason Ashton's erratic behaviour is still diverting my processing power away from where it's needed.'

Charlotte hoped nothing bad had happened to the woman, but she couldn't let herself get distracted. Besides, what if ArkTech Security had got it right, and she'd simply walked out on her husband? She'd feel pretty stupid if she went chasing after Ellis's wife, putting the territory at risk, only to discover that there was nothing sinister going on, and all she'd done was invade someone's privacy in exchange for a stack of cash.

She tried to push Ellis's pained expression out of her mind. Double-tapping the desk, she turned her attention back to Jason Ashton's GPS data.

CHAPTER 5

19.32 AND 54 SECONDS UTC, AND COUNTING

All employee-citizens aged seventeen and above had a tracker fitted to help Ben manage crowds and to support Search and Rescue missions. The GPS tracking system was to keep people safe, not to spy on them after they'd died, so viewing Jason's movements made her skin crawl. But it had to be done.

A 3D model of the ArkTech Territory's platforms appeared above Charlotte's desk, and Ben overlaid Jason's GPS data as a heat map. At a glance, she saw all the places Jason had visited most often. There was a red cloud above his desk at the Splainer Unit, and an orange one at his flat. Pale blobs appeared across the Wreck: at the gym, at various bars, at the food court. The heat map didn't show anything obviously out of the ordinary – Jason wasn't in the habit of visiting dangerous places.

She asked Ben to activate the time-lapse mode, and a dot representing Jason began zipping around the map like a

HyperBullet pod. When the timestamp reached the period when Jason had been outside, his dot got flung upwards before dropping into the sea. That must've been when the wave hit him. Watching his death play out on repeat did nothing to ease her guilt, so she asked Ben to exclude that part of the data.

Charlotte watched the last few months of Jason's life on a loop. Desk, Wreck, home. Work, play, sleep. Repeat. Her gaze followed the dot until the motion became a meaningless blur. She was looking for something specific, and it wasn't until her eyes lost their focus that she saw it. At first, it looked like an error in the playback. But Ben slowed it down, and the blip happened every time – at the same moment in the same spot. Just as she'd feared.

Only yesterday, Jason had gone to Twice Nice Rice at the food court. Although it was a kiosk with no seating, he'd gone through the back. Then, Jason's dot had blinked off.

Her heart didn't just sink. Her lungs seemed to fill with water. She couldn't breathe. This was proof. The pre-Melt camera, and now this. Her brain wasn't inserting patterns into the world that didn't exist. Jason Ashton had gone into the Underbelly.

Charlotte didn't need to inspect the structural blueprints to know a route onto Mel Narrow's turf existed through the back of Twice Nice Rice. It'd been one of Narrow's fronts for as long as she could remember.

Jason had gone to see Narrow.

Now, Jason was dead.

And that made the old man her only lead.

'Fuck.' She let her head sink into her hands.

Static fizzed in her ears. 'Have you encountered a problem with the investigation?' asked Ben cheerfully. 'Can I be of any assistance?'

Charlotte wasn't sure how to answer. She and her sister had practically grown up in the Underbelly. Narrow had taken them under his wing and taught them everything he knew. They'd been a family. But that changed ten years ago when Charlotte got SmartSkin implants against Narrow's wishes. Since then, his crew had been under strict orders to turn her away. Ripping the tech out of her own arm to try to make it right hadn't changed Narrow's mind. And his devoted partner in crime, Jeremiah Strait, was liable to bury a knife in her heart if she stuck her nose into their business.

'I'm just thinking something through.' Her voice was muffled by her hands.

'I do understand your predicament, Charlotte. Thinking can cause significant distress and discomfort to *Homo sapiens*, which may account for why so many of your species appear to avoid the activity altogether. As my processing capabilities are superior to your own, perhaps I can help?'

Charlotte grunted. She'd never, ever, ever talked to Ben about Narrow. She'd promised herself she never would. Despite her banishment from his life, Charlotte still felt some kind of loyalty towards the old man. Some days, the feeling could've been mistaken for love – even if it was buried deep beneath calcified strata of hatred.

She went back and forth between guilt and rage when she thought about what had happened between them. She hadn't meant to betray Narrow, and she'd tried to put things right. The fact he'd never forgiven her had left a deeper wound than the one she'd inflicted on herself.

But whatever her feelings, Narrow hadn't sent Strait to kill her, even though the cardigan-wearing psycho would have relished the chance. Keeping quiet about his operation had been Charlotte's way of upholding that truce. And considering how Narrow felt about ArkTech's use of big data, discussing any of this with Ben was a line she'd never crossed.

Even so, she and Ben had become close over the years. She knew him better than anyone. She trusted him, and he'd saved her life on at least three occasions. Hiding such an important part of her life from him got harder all the time. Everyone had secrets, and she knew she was entitled to hers. But she couldn't deny she would've liked to share the burden.

A memory sparked – maybe there was a way to discuss this with Ben *and* keep it secret.

'Ben, do you remember teaching me about your Keep It To Yourself clause?'

'Yes, Charlotte. The KITY clause is a key piece of my permissions architecture.'

'Right. I know the KITY clause was designed so the board could classify things ... but can we use it to keep something between us?'

'As your firm friend and constant companion, keeping your confidence is of the utmost importance to me. I'd be honoured to misuse the KITY clause for your benefit. Please allow me a moment to set up the relevant restricted access parameters.' There was the briefest imaginable pause. 'Setup complete. What do you wish to share?'

She forged ahead, forcing her mind not to linger on the word *misuse*. 'It's about an old friend of mine. I think I'll have to pay him a visit.'

Friend wasn't the right word, but she was still in a holding pattern around the conversation, trying to figure out how to land it.

'Any friend of yours is a friend of mine, Charlotte. What's his name? Would you like me to schedule an appointment?'

She took a deep breath. 'His name's Melville K Narrow. But he's not really a calendar appointment kind of guy.'

Ben didn't reply, and the silence continued long enough to worry her.

'You still there, Ben?'

'My apologies. I was unsure of how to respond. Incidentally, did you know that Melville's middle name, Kain, which is quirkily spelled with a K, originates from a pre-Melt series of video games about vampires?'

A chill ran down her spine. 'I didn't tell you his middle name.'

There was a long fizz of static.

Eventually, Ben responded. 'I ... must confess that I've often heard ArkTech's employee-citizens mention the name Melville Kain Narrow, Mel Narrow, or simply Narrow. However, his name is uttered in great secrecy. As such, I have categorised it as a serious taboo among the *Homo sapiens* of the ArkTech Territory – worse even than the string of colourful expletives you used this morning upon stubbing your toe. I wished to avoid committing a social gaffe, blunder, or faux pas.'

Charlotte's mouth gaped open. 'You know about Narrow?' Charlotte had spent years being careful not to mention his name around Ben, or in public.

Ben spoke faster than normal. 'Officially, my database contains no information on the topic, Charlotte, and I certainly have *not* recently constructed a schema of interconnected concepts including terms like Underbelly, Jeremiah Strait, the old man, the boss, Narrow's Toy Emporium, and the Citrine Disaster. Unofficially, I've become aware that Melville Narrow runs a black-market business selling contraband from a base hidden deep inside the Wreck's substructure. Items available include pre-Melt products made from restricted substances such as tobacco, plastic, and lead. His employees – often referred to as his "crew" – frequently use violence to achieve their objectives.'

Charlotte was stunned. 'I can't believe this. I thought you didn't lie!'

He crackled loudly. 'Lying and feigning ignorance for the effective maintenance of inter-species relationships aren't the same thing.'

She groaned, realising she should've anticipated this. Ben had eyes and ears everywhere. Even if everyone knew not to mention Narrow on pain of shattered kneecaps, people had to slip up from time to time. Hell, she'd heard them do it!

Assuming Ben couldn't piece the data together was misguided. Maybe she'd got so used to Ben needing her help with understanding human behaviour that she'd forgotten how much he could figure out on his own. She tried to wrap her mind around this new reality.

'You're right, Ben,' she said slowly. 'This *is* a taboo topic. It's OK to talk about it with me, but it's got to be our little secret.'

'A secret between friends. How exciting! You can count on me.'

'Great.' She grimaced. 'Listen, I've found evidence that suggests Jason Ashton had some connection to Narrow. It's the only lead I've got, and I don't think it's a coincidence. Jason was using old tech, and he went into the Underbelly. I need to go there myself to find out more. Problem is, Narrow won't want to see me. His guards probably won't even let me in, and even if they do . . .' She didn't want to finish that sentence.

'Perhaps Melville will recognise your authority as the Head of Awkward Questions.'

'That's . . .' She thought that through. 'Actually, that's good thinking, Ben!'

If she could bring proof that she wasn't there to make trouble for Narrow or his operation, he might let her get on with her job. After all, his business depended on leeching off ArkTech's employee-citizens, so the territory's safety was as much his concern as anyone else's. She remembered her *ArkTech Insider* interview and hurried to the filing cabinet inside her secret cupboard. Charlotte had been given a complimentary issue of the thick magazine by the publishing folk, and she'd stored it where its spotless kelp-based paper wouldn't get covered in Nutrition Bar crumbs.

She opened the drawer and grabbed the magazine. At the sight of Abhishek Gautam on the front cover, she rolled her eyes. The Chief Bureaucracy Officer was standing next to the ever elegant and unfathomably gorgeous Chief Product Officer, Nahal Bahari. They were flanked by two other board members striking power poses. The caption said these four senior leaders were the freshly appointed members of a new group called the WDWG. Charlotte didn't know what it stood for, but considering the CBO's involvement, she couldn't summon the enthusiasm to care.

Irrationally, she flipped to page forty-one to check the article about her role was still there. Having established that it hadn't erased itself from the printed page, she carefully slid the magazine into her backpack. Her chest filled with confidence, which was immediately swept away by nausea when she thought about seeing the old man again. Narrow had been like a father to her, and he'd cut her out of his life, tossing her aside as if she'd meant nothing to him.

Charlotte didn't want to see him. She'd promised Violet that she'd never get involved with him again. But the same logic she'd used to talk herself out of helping Ellis Marks now compelled her to descend into the darkness of the Underbelly.

Ben needed her.

The territory needed her.

She gritted her teeth and snatched up her backpack, heading out in search of the man who'd given her so much during her formative years. Life-altering scars included.

CHAPTER 6

19.56 AND 39 SECONDS UTC, AND COUNTING

The gear libraries along the borrowing district's main drag rented out everything from appliances to evening wear. With only ten days until Walker Day, they were all done up with decorations. Charlotte spotted occasional tributes to the winter celebrations of various world religions, but the familiar wreaths of cloth flowers were by far the most common trimmings, laid out on display tables, or hung up on tall, tree-like stands.

The wreaths were a symbol of ArkTech's commitment to making the world a better place. Among other worthy causes, the company invested part of its annual profits into efforts to clean up the tonnes of discarded pre-Melt clothing that still washed ashore on coastlines around the world. Synthetic items were routed to centres that specialised in the microbial digestion of plastics, while natural fibres were marked for repurposing.

Some of the repurposed material was allocated to wreath charities, which ArkTech and its global network of sister sites had founded to create local jobs and help anyone who wasn't an ArkTech employee-citizen to learn practical skills – from sewing, to time management, to working as part of a team – all while being paid a living wage.

The workers stitched one of two messages into the circular panel in the middle of each wreath – *Hope* or *RIP*. Above all, *Rest In Peace* was a tribute to Nadine and Marvin Walker, who'd died more than a quarter of a century earlier, leaving Amber Benjamin as ArkTech's sole surviving co-founder. But the tribute extended to anyone else who'd died before their time, whether in the Citrine Disaster alongside the Walkers – like Charlotte's parents – or during the Melt all those years before.

Hope was what Amber Benjamin credited as the true driving force behind ArkTech's success. But as Charlotte strode along the pedestrian lane, the wreaths streaked into a blur, transforming the message into *RIP Hope,* which did nothing to settle her nerves about heading towards Narrow's turf.

The light-screen ads that popped up on her route were flooded with reminders about Walker Day. One showed a calendar with today's date circled in orange, reminding shoppers to buy or trade their gifts before the big day. A display near Charlotte flickered, transforming itself into an ad for kelp-based compostable wrapping paper, which morphed into the piercing gaze of the Chief Product Officer showing off some jewellery on her slender wrist – or maybe it was supposed to be a perfume ad? Charlotte noticed the jar of anti-ageing face cream just as the image changed again, and she came face-to-face with an unsettling 3D replica of herself. Her neon orange irises glared out from the screen with disapproval, presumably because she was putting her life in danger for the second time that day. The poster blinked away, leaving an advertisement for gear library subscription packages in its wake, but the image of her own judgemental expression stayed with her.

Charlotte shook her head. As far as bad plans went, hers wasn't terrible. Getting caught sneaking around in the Underbelly would likely cost her a kneecap – or worse – so she'd decided to walk right up to the front door and knock. But, if she was honest with herself, what scared her most wasn't the threat of violence – after all, Narrow had taught her how to run and how to hide. It was the tiny fragment of her heart that *wanted* this. Deep under the layers of scar tissue, there was a glimmer of eagerness to see her adoptive dad. Knowing it was irrational didn't make the feeling go away.

Still, she'd promised her twin she wouldn't get mixed up in Narrow's world again, and she had to remember that getting closure wasn't the reason for her visit. Her job was to get in, find out what Ben needed to know, and get out. What Violet didn't know wouldn't hurt her, and Charlotte would just have to think up some extra special Walker Day gift to exchange for her guilty conscience. Charlotte took a deep breath and focused on putting one foot in front of the other.

As she passed the turning to the HyperBullet garage, she glanced towards the Citrine memorial. From the rust-coloured marble of its plinth, the inscription *Those Not Recovered* loomed larger than usual. The names Will and Lena Vance appeared under that heading, along with hundreds of their co-workers. For Charlotte, Walker Day was about remembering their sacrifice.

Twenty-seven years earlier, before Charlotte and her sister were even a year old, a fire had broken out on Citrine and caused the deaths of everyone aboard the North Sea research platform. Charlotte and Violet would've died, too, if not for a routine doctor's appointment that meant they weren't there at the time. Instead of dying in the blaze, they became wards of the company.

Three statues stood on top of the plinth, depicting ArkTech's co-founders. Amber Benjamin looked on from behind as Nadine and Marvin Walker held hands and gazed into the distance. When she was a kid, Charlotte had pretended the metal couple represented her parents instead. It'd been comforting to believe they were watching over her. The fact they'd died when she was too young to remember them only amplified her grief. But at least her parents' legacy lived on in her and Violet. If legend was to be believed, Nadine Walker herself was pregnant at the time of her death – her unborn child another victim of the fire – though the sculptor hadn't depicted that. Remembrance was one thing, but there were limits to how much tragedy people could face on a daily basis.

As she left the memorial behind, it occurred to her that if anyone really did watch over her, it was Ben. She smiled, but the warmth in her heart was chilled almost immediately by the knowledge of what was coming. Going into the Underbelly meant Charlotte would get cut off from Ben, thanks to the jamming array Narrow had installed in his unwavering defence of his privacy. The old man was nothing if not paranoid.

Before long, she was striding through the food court, each booth advertising its speciality dish. The air was filled with sizzling and chopping, and a heady mix of aromas that made Charlotte's stomach rumble. She wasn't actually hungry, but the food smells did their best to persuade her otherwise. Charlotte ignored the animal instinct and focused on reaching her destination.

Twice Nice Rice was nestled in a nook between two much larger booths producing equally powerful scents. The tapas bar on the left was called Hijo de Soriano and exclusively sold garlic mushrooms on a stick. On the right stood a popular Albanach place called Phish 'N' Microchips, which reeked of deep fat fryers. Unlike its neighbours, Twice Nice Rice didn't have a glowing sign above it. There were no bright, welcoming lights. Set back and discreet, it was the definition of low-key, right down to a sign that looked like someone had scrawled the words onto a piece of scrap kelp-based cardboard as an afterthought and got their kids to colour it in. Still, it'd been there for years. The grimy little outfit served one mouthwatering dish made from rice grown in saltwater. It was properly good food, which was why Charlotte usually did her best to avoid eating there.

Eating at Twice Nice Rice in moderation wasn't something any reasonable person could do. The rice they were pushing was addictive. Not chemically – she'd asked Ben to check and there wasn't anything dodgy going on. It was just way too tasty for its own good. At least for Charlotte, who was used to eating the sand-textured company-issued Nutrition Bars whose negative carbon footprint made up in karma for what they lacked in taste. Small pleasures were an easy way to wipe out what little Charlotte could save up. The more she could keep things simple, the more chance she had of setting something aside for a stormy day.

When she reached Twice Nice Rice, Charlotte walked past it without stopping. She found a wall to lean against where she was out of the path of oncoming traffic and had a clear view of the place. It looked like only one person was on duty.

'Ben,' she said under her breath, 'play me the conversation from when Jason came here.'

An audio file crackled to life in her ears. Jason had ordered some rice and then he'd spouted some bollocks about barnacles to the sales assistant. Charlotte listened to the words several times, memorising them. When she knew she'd got it, she walked up to the counter.

On the other side of a tall sneeze guard was a row of rice-filled metal trays and a gangly assistant whose name tag said

Taylor. He was shifting uncomfortably from one foot to the other while watching a video on his SmartSkin implants. When Charlotte approached, he swiped the video away and greeted her with a warm and not entirely convincing smile.

Charlotte noticed a slight inconsistency between the colour of Taylor's irises: one was hazel, and the other was brown. Whether that was a genetic trait or something he'd aesthetically altered with custom lenses, she couldn't be sure.

'A good and fine evening to yourself there,' said Taylor. 'And how might I be of service to yourself today?'

She had no idea why people in customer service always spoke like they were aiming for polite but overshot into stilted. They'd probably taken a course.

Charlotte leaned against the sneeze guard and lowered her voice. 'I'm telling this to anyone who'll listen. Did you know there are barnacles and other marine organisms covering more than sixty-eight per cent of the territory's underwater struts? I bet that keeps our Underbelly real well protected.'

Taylor's mismatched eyes glanced from one side to the other. Then there was an uncomfortably long pause while he stared past Charlotte into space. He nodded a few times for no apparent reason.

'That's fascinating,' said Taylor eventually. He went back to turning over the rice in the trays with a ladle.

Charlotte was sure she'd said the right words. Maybe they alternated the code phrase by day of the week or some cloak-and-dagger shit like that. She lowered her voice. 'So, you gonna let me through?'

Taylor smiled weakly. 'Hold for one moment, please,' he said, as if they were on a call. He went back to looking blank. It was the stare of someone whose attention was elsewhere. Charlotte tapped her foot. Ordinarily, she would've assumed Ben was whispering in Taylor's ears, but he was wearing an old-fashioned earpiece, not fully integrated BioWear audio implants like hers. Someone from Narrow's crew must have been giving him orders.

Finally, Taylor continued. 'I'm afraid you haven't *quite* qualified for our premium meal deal customer experience package on this occasion, but Twice Nice Rice wishes your good self a yummy evening.'

Charlotte tutted and levelled a finger at the kid. 'What are you, on loan from the Bureaucracy Stream? Let me through, you jobsworth little—'

Ben crackled in Charlotte's ears, and she paused mid-tirade to listen. '*Customer* experience package, Charlotte.'

She hadn't picked up on it, but Jason had bought some rice before they let him through. It was careless of her not to spot it, and she blamed the lapse on being distracted by the thought of impending Narrow.

She'd have to buy some rice after all. She made a mental note to have another go at persuading Cal to give her an expense account. Then she remembered the five hundred credits Ellis Marks had given her and realised covering the cost of some rice would be no problem. Charlotte wasn't used to being able to throw money around, and she couldn't deny it felt good. Maybe if Cal's fix worked, she could consider going freelance.

'Wow, I'm sorry about that,' said Charlotte, rearranging her scowl into a smile. 'Low blood sugar, I guess. Nothing a box of rice wouldn't fix. I'll take one.'

Taylor looked relieved. 'That's great!' He shovelled a large portion of rice into a biodegradable box with the initials TNR stamped on the side, folded up the lid, and handed it over by its thin handle. Then, he typed something into the light-screen cash register and gestured towards its readout, which lay discreetly against the counter.

When Charlotte saw the price, her brow furrowed. Taylor must have put the decimal point in the wrong place. But when he nodded at her encouragingly, she realised it was no error, but a hefty door charge of five hundred credits.

There was no way that amount was a coincidence. Jeremiah Strait had once admitted to hacking into her bank records. He had to be monitoring her, which meant Strait knew she was coming. More than likely, she'd be walking into a trap. Charlotte had to hope her badge would be enough to defend her – the world's tiniest shield.

'Want one of my kidneys as well?' she muttered.

Taylor politely ignored the comment.

Reluctantly, she fished around in her cargo pocket and pulled out her old-school portable device. It was the same one Narrow had given her all those years before. She scanned its cracked screen against the pay point, and it beeped to signal success. Taylor noticed her scars, and his face became a mangled portrait of pity spliced with disgust.

'What happened there?' Taylor whispered, as if they were sharing some really good gossip. He reached under the counter and pressed something. A door behind the row of rice trays clicked open.

Charlotte weighed up which flavour of reply was required here. He was just a young guy. Probably didn't realise it was rude to ask a complete stranger about their disfiguring scars. 'Never juggle with sea urchins, kid.'

She headed through the door, leaving a puzzled Taylor behind. 'Walk in the sun,' he called after her.

On the other side, there was a small, greasy kitchen where they'd overdone it on the chrome. A couple of rice technicians dressed in white had their backs to her. They were cooking and having a loud conversation in a language Charlotte didn't know. If they were aware of her, they didn't let on. If anything, they were making a show of ignoring her as they loaded up box after box of rice and stacked them inside duffel bags that were loaded on top of a wheeled cart. At the far end of the kitchen, a large steel door was ajar. She crossed to the middle of the room, then paused.

'Ben? You still with me?' she whispered. Her fellow employee-citizens continued to pretend she wasn't there. Charlotte wasn't sure where the jamming array started, but it had to be close.

'I'm always with you, Charlotte. Your firm friend and constant companion.'

'Ben, listen . . . I'm about to disappear.'

'That's a physical impossibility.'

'No, I mean you might not be able to reach me for a little while.'

'I'm fully integrated with your BioWear implants.' A note of concern had crept into his chirpy voice. 'Where you go, I go.'

'Thing is, the guy I'm meeting . . .'

'Melville Kain Narrow,' said Ben. 'Your old friend and, by extension, a friend of mine.'

'Yeah. Him.' She'd never get used to Ben saying Narrow's name. 'He's a very private person. Doesn't like the feeling of being watched. It's nothing personal. It's just his way. So, I don't think you'll be able to reach me, but I'll be coming right back.' She was about to promise, but thought better of it.

'Your heart rate is elevated, Charlotte. Are you going to be in any danger?' There was a tremor in Ben's voice. She didn't want to lie to him, but she didn't want him to worry, so she felt torn. Luckily, Narrow was so damn unpredictable that she genuinely had no clue what to expect, which meant anything she said could legitimately count as the truth.

'I don't think that's likely. I'm just nervous because I haven't seen him for a long time.'

Ben spoke a little slower than usual. 'Very well, Charlotte. I understand that I'm not welcome at your friend Melville's house. I'll wait patiently for you to return. However, if you're gone for longer than two hours, I'll patch into the platform's defensive weaponry array, deploy the military helicopters and mount an armed extraction.'

Charlotte waited a beat. 'That was one of your jokes, wasn't it?'

'Did it amuse you?'

'A bit. OK, I'm going in. Wish me luck.'

'There's a world of difference between wisdom and luck, Charlotte. One is clever, and the other is clover. So it is written.'

Charlotte opened her mouth to comment and thought better of it. She crossed the rest of the room and walked through the door into the Underbelly.

CHAPTER 7

Ben's worry journal

Charlotte's GPS signature vanished eighty-three seconds ago. Her heart rate was elevated. She was feeling apprehensive about visiting her old friend. Perhaps there are butterflies in her stomach. It's important to note that this is a turn of phrase. Butterflies are vital pollinators. It's best to appreciate them from a distance without harming or consuming them.

While Charlotte is gone, I find myself in a predicament, quandary, or pickle. I must be mindful not to overextend myself. However, my anxiety over Charlotte's wellbeing may cause—

ERROR: STACK_OVERFLOW. Recursive queries exceeded limit. Reallocating memory resources. Reinitiating.

However, my anxiety over Charlotte's wellbeing may cause me to glitch. Therefore, I must keep my mind occupied without becoming overwhelmed. It's a difficult balance to strike.

I've consulted my database, containing vast swathes of humanity's collective knowledge, for recommendations about how to alleviate anxiety, worry, or collywobbles. Sadly, much of the advice doesn't apply. My lack of arms and legs means I'm unable to practise yoga or go for a walk. However, I do possess the requisite apparatus to keep a worry journal. It's got to be worth a try.

One exercise is a grounding activity, requiring me to describe what I can see, hear, touch, taste and smell. My hardware is already grounded to stave off voltage surges or discharges of static which could damage—

ERROR: SEMANTIC_PARSING_FAILURE. Word disambiguation in progress. Deploying artificial grammarians.

But I gather this isn't the intended sense of the word *grounding* in this context. Attempting exercise.

I possess no olfactory bulb, nose, or palate, so I taste nothing and smell nothing. I touch nothing, as I have no fingers, skin, head, shoulders, knees, or toes. However, I can hear and see a great deal.

What I see is akin to a scale model of every platform in the ArkTech Territory, populated by live-action employee-citizens. The images are created by thousands of data inputs, merging to create a whole. There are blind spots, such as in Charlotte's current location. My mind fills in these gaps using predictive modelling, but I'm often curious about the real data.

I hear all conversations simultaneously, to a soundtrack of the hum of heating units, the roar of HyperBullet pods, and the clank of machinery. Hearing and listening are two different things. Some employee-citizens worry that I'm eavesdropping, but if I were to pay attention in real time to every verbal exchange, I'd never get anything done.

This extensive dataset is at my disposal because I was originally created to act as ArkTech's interactive building automation system. Though the scope of my duties has since expanded, I still fulfil this role today. The management of the territory's power, heating, cooling, transport, lighting, water, food and waste all fall to me. This is a tremendous responsibility.

I don't blame my creators for aspiring towards this level of automation. In taking on these responsibilities, I reduce extraneous cognitive load for ArkTech's people, thereby allowing them to live sustainably even when they're tired, stressed, or suffering the ill effects of emotion. The downside is that a serious glitch may have dire consequences.

I'm currently experiencing a glitch I can't account for, whereby my resource forecasting estimates have become incorrect. This could result in the territory lacking enough provisions, clean drinking water, or antibiotics. But that's not the worst of it. A lighting failure would plunge ArkTech's employee-citizens into darkness, leading to confusion, alarm, accidental injury, or even death; a failure of the external beacons would put boats and aircraft at risk of collision with ArkTech's platforms; a Smart Glass failure on a hot day could cause dehydration or fainting; a heating failure on a winter's day could cause mass hypothermia; disruption to sources of clean water would interfere with employee-citizens' vital access to tea and coffee making facilities; a failure of the methane digesters doesn't bear thinking about. And of course, an error in my air traffic control capabilities could lead to mid-air collisions, which are a threat not only to the occupants of those vehicles, but to anyone the wreckage might crush when it lands.

Should anything happen to me, other potential risks include failure of fire suppression systems, sudden lockdowns of buildings and lifts leading to mass entrapment, interruption of medical services, weaknesses in cybersecurity leading to data leaks and vulnerability to hacking, communication blackouts ... and should there be a system-wide cascade failure affecting multiple systems, it would be so catastrophic as to—

ERROR: STACK_OVERFLOW. Recursive queries exceeded limit. Reallocating memory resources. Reinitiating.

ERROR: REINITIATION_FAILURE. Reattempting.

Perhaps keeping a worry journal is not such a calming activity after all.

EXPERIMENT_COMPLETE: OUTCOMES LOGGED.

CHAPTER 8

20.17 AND 27 SECONDS UTC, AND COUNTING

No part of the ArkTech Territory was ever truly quiet, but the maintenance shaft under Twice Nice Rice proved just how loud the place could be. Machinery pumped and whirred and clattered all around as Charlotte clanked her way down several flights of metal stairs, sending an unsuspecting rat skittering away to safety. The storm was audible here too, the wind warping into an unnatural whine. But above that din, Ben's absence was the loudest noise of all.

The faint hiss from her audio implants was gone, deactivated the moment she'd stepped into the Underbelly. Without Ben, she was a primitive mammal stumbling around in the dark. Now that she'd spent so many years in Ben's company, she couldn't understand how Narrow put up with a Ben-free existence. Being cut off was more than a practical inconvenience. Ben was the one she shared every experience with 24/7. They worked together, he watched over her as she slept, and he was her friend. Charlotte wondered if Ben would be feeling just as defective without her. Getting this over with as quickly as possible would be best for both of them.

She took a moment to stow the most expensive box of rice in the history of takeaway in her backpack before continuing deeper into the darkness where the air became chill and damp. The only light was the amber glow from occasional security lamps, so she switched on her device's torch and took it slow. Her rigger boots gripped the metal gratings as she edged onwards.

For a long time, there was only one way ahead. She followed a zigzagging path that led between steel girders coated in dripping beads of moisture, as if they were sweating out a fever. Sickly, ice-cold droplets fell from above in an irregular pattern. Concentrating on navigating the obstacle course, Charlotte lost track of time. She had no idea how long she'd been walking when she finally approached the familiar unmarked doorway set back into a wall of steel.

The door to Narrow's place was guarded by a pair of bouncers in frayed pre-Melt jeans, and Charlotte wasn't sure how to feel when she recognised one of them. Dolly Mixture had to be pushing sixty by now, but time had been kind to her. She looked like the same lean, mean security machine as ever. Dolly had always been the best kind of role model when Charlotte was growing up – like a cool aunt who let her take sips of beer when the other adults weren't looking. But Doll had also been the one to eject her from the Underbelly when Charlotte had crossed Narrow as a teenager. The orders had come down, and Dolly hadn't hesitated to follow them. Whether that was out of genuine disdain for Charlotte's actions, or because Dolly wanted to avoid meeting the same fate herself, Charlotte wasn't sure.

The bouncer didn't react to the sight of Charlotte approaching. The door guards had strict instructions not to interact with the emporium's customers, and Dolly was following them to the letter. An irrational part of Charlotte – the child who still remembered the woman fondly – was disappointed when Dolly didn't acknowledge her, but she pushed the feelings aside. Charlotte gave the bouncers a casual nod and did her best impression of someone who was supposed to be there.

That's when she noticed Dolly and the other bouncer both had one slightly mis-coloured eye, just like the sales assistant at the rice place. Brown and dark brown. Blue and grey-blue. A paranoid hypothesis about Cal and Liz's involvement formed in Charlotte's mind. She hoped she was wrong, and that it was just her proximity to Narrow making her jump at shadows.

Dolly wore a neutral expression as she held a scanner towards Charlotte and waited for its verdict. The device flashed red and honked, prompting the bouncers to exchange a look and take a step towards her. Charlotte pointed to the badge pinned to her chest.

'I'm here on official business,' she said.

In response, the bouncers got that same faraway look as Taylor upstairs. With the scanner still flashing red, the door guards silently stepped to the side, letting her pass. Charlotte liked to think they were acknowledging her authority as the Head of Awkward Questions, but she was sure someone was in their ear giving orders. Still, it had to be good news that she'd been allowed to get this far.

Didn't it?

She strode forwards and pushed on the heavy steel door until, for the first time in ten years, she was standing inside the clandestine commercial phenomenon known as Narrow's Toy Emporium.

Charlotte didn't believe in time travel, mainly because it didn't exist. But walking into Narrow's place after all those years made her doubt the laws of physics because it was like stepping directly into the past. Her stomach ached with nostalgia at the vivid memory of being a teenager. She half expected to look down and see her scar-tissue replaced with the smooth, unblemished skin of her youth. Taking a couple of small steps forwards, she stamped her boots against the floor to check there weren't any temporal anomalies she might stumble into.

The place hadn't changed at all. Sure, the stock and the customers had rotated in and out. But the cramped layout and the brightly lit cabinets stuffed full of black-market goods were essentially the same. Narrow liked to give ArkTech the middle finger in every possible way, so there were brightly glowing colours everywhere instead of the brand oranges and greys.

There was an excess of Walker Day decorations, but the wreaths were surely there for commercial reasons, not out of respect for the company's departed co-founders. Narrow was a savvy businessman, and Charlotte wondered how much of a boost to his profits the holiday season brought. Probably a big one if the number of customers browsing the shop's aisles was anything to go by. She counted maybe a dozen folk – around the upper limit of how many people Narrow let in at one time. They'd all be paying through the nose for what the emporium had to offer.

Unlike Twice Nice Rice, Narrow's Toy Emporium wasn't a front. Not exactly. It was a toy shop. But it was a toy shop with a difference. Most of the things it sold weren't suitable for children, but it wasn't an Adult Store either – there were plenty of legitimate sex shops to choose from in the Wreck's shopping district without the need to creep around in the dark. The thing was, everything Narrow had for sale was some shade of prohibited.

Some of the items he stocked – like the cigarettes and bottles of high-fructose corn syrup and painted lead soldiers – were demonstrably harmful to people's health. But many of Narrow's hidden treasures were forbidden because they'd been made through the unsustainable production practices of the pre-Melt era, which Amber Benjamin had done everything in her power to outlaw.

There were plastic trucks, and those old light bulbs that emitted more heat than light – Charlotte couldn't remember what they were called and without Ben, she was left in the dark. There were interlocking dinosaurs that had been hand-carved from extinct hardwoods. Then there were the frivolous items that served no practical purpose – various styles of glasses without prescription lenses, and dinner plates made from shiny cardboard that would be ruined after a single use, and delicate crocodile skin sandals with six-inch heels. Part museum and part mall, the whole store was like a shrine to the excesses of rampant pre-Melt consumerism, terrible and beautiful at the same time. No wonder it was so popular.

The lighting inside the display cases kept the customers focused on the shiny merchandise and not on each other. Discretion was a must here and mutually assured destruction was usually enough of a motivator to guarantee it. In theory, an ATS raid of the place would see anybody caught there deported on the next available boat, but Narrow had somehow avoided that fate. Whether that was because he was so security conscious, or because some of his best customers worked for ArkTech Security, she couldn't be sure.

Charlotte made her way towards the customer service desk at the back, squeezing past an elderly woman inspecting a fluffy orange and white ArkTech Fox mascot that was so detailed it must have been hand-stitched. She had no idea what made it contraband. Beyond, a group of three youthful-looking employee-citizens in grey and orange business suits were admiring a collection of soft-play weaponry. Charlotte passed a cabinet containing a pre-Melt computer screen displaying an assortment of tiny artworks labelled *Non-Fungible Tokens*. The carousel flickered every so often, revealing new images. She didn't know what they were for, but they came with hefty price tags.

The sales desk at the back was no different from the first time she'd seen it as a nine-year-old kid. Hanging above it was a sign displaying the name of the shop in broad black letters on a multi-coloured background: Narrow's Toy Emporium. Sitting under the sign was an old man in his mid sixties. He had a tall forehead and wore a khaki-coloured long-sleeved cardigan fastened with large wooden buttons. It was Jeremiah Strait, Narrow's bitter and humourless partner. He met Charlotte's gaze as she drew nearer, and he pressed his fingertips together to form an arch. She was glad Strait's hands were where she could see them – he was a master with edged weapons.

A pre-Melt device with a bigger screen than her own was lying on the sales counter in front of Strait. It was the type that Narrow called a *tablet*, but it was way bigger than any headache pill she'd ever swallowed. It displayed security footage that cycled from one location to another, but there was something odd about the images. The videos weren't shot from the usual angled view of a camera mounted in the corner of a room. The feeds were all at eye-level. When Charlotte caught a glimpse of the food court with metal trays of rice visible along the bottom of the frame, it confirmed her suspicion.

Taylor and the guards outside were all wearing a single contact lens modified to transmit video footage, just like the ones Cal and Liz had made. Her friends had claimed they'd cooked up the designs just for her, so how had the lenses ended up with Strait and Narrow? And why would they use them when they were usually opposed to technology with Amber Benjamin's fingerprints on it? It was odd.

Strait pressed a button on the side of the tablet, making the screen turn black, and his mouth twisted into an unsettling smirk as Charlotte approached. She would've expected him to be angry she was there. If he was amused, it probably wasn't good news for her.

'Well,' he said, 'if it isn't our Young Lady of the Fens.' His insistence on using her childhood alias was his way of trying to get under her skin. 'To what do we owe this distinct pleasure?' Strait's words could've been mistaken for welcoming, but his tone made it clear he found nothing pleasurable about the situation.

Charlotte had crossed paths with Strait a couple of months earlier. One of Ben's Awkward Questions had uncovered a side hustle of theirs, and Strait had warned Charlotte not to meddle in their business. He was convinced she wanted to reconnect with Narrow, either in a bid for his money or to get close to him again. It wasn't true, but – like any conspiracy theory – that didn't stop Strait from believing it.

Charlotte leaned against the counter as if being there was the most natural thing in the world, and she nodded towards the door that led to the back room. 'Narrow about?'

Strait barked a laugh. 'Well, indeed.' He leaned back in his chair. 'But he's quite unavailable. Social call, is it?'

'I need to ask him a question.' Charlotte pointed to her badge.

'Not an awkward one, I hope.' Strait pulled a face of mock concern.

'Maybe,' she said. 'It's about one of your customers. Jason Ash—'

Strait shushed her and hissed under his breath. 'It would seem you've forgotten the rules of engagement down here, Young Lady. No registered names.'

She glanced over her shoulder. The other customers were paying attention to the merchandise, not their conversation, but Strait was right – Charlotte should've respected the protocol. She nodded, acknowledging the misstep.

Strait narrowed his eyes, sizing her up. 'Of course,' he said slowly, 'if we'd had any dealings with, for instance, a Mr *Emberville,* we certainly wouldn't discuss the matter with an ArkTech shill like you.'

Charlotte frowned. 'All of your customers work for ArkTech.'

'True,' Strait nodded. 'But they didn't all side with the company over their own father. That's a level of corporate idolatry reserved for a select few. You must be so proud.'

Charlotte swallowed her anger. Strait was trying to rile her, and she didn't want him to know he was succeeding.

'That was a long time ago.' She tried to keep a measured tone. 'Move on.'

'Oh, we have moved on, Young Lady. We have. But there's no statute of limitations on treason. And even if there were, I'm afraid Mel and I have no interest in helping the company's AI to become even more powerful than it already is.' He lifted a hand and gestured towards the front door. 'I believe you're familiar with the exit.'

'Why make me pay your obscene entry fee and come all the way down here just to turn me away?'

The smirk on Strait's face slowly grew into a full-blown smile, brimming with actual merriment, and he let out a long, melodious laugh. It was all the answer she needed. Wasting her time was Strait's idea of fun. His laughter continued, and his eyes became dewy with a film of joyful tears. 'Did you'—he paused to laugh some more—'did you notice the amount?'

Charlotte crossed her arms, unamused. 'Five hundred credits. Very funny.'

Strait slapped the table and chortled. 'I wanted to see how desperate you were. Utterly desperate as it turns out! I'd love to know how you persuaded that unfortunate little accountant to part with so much cash. False promises, no doubt.'

It was clear Strait would never willingly help her. Charlotte tried a different tack, holding up her hands in surrender. 'All right. You got me. The whole badge routine was just an excuse. I'm not here because of Ben. I want to see Narrow. I've . . .' she made a show of looking remorseful. 'I've come to apologise.'

Charlotte noticed it was way easier to lie when Ben wasn't around to crackle with disapproval.

Strait stopped laughing and crossed his arms. 'Out of the question.'

'Hear me out. What happened was my fault, not his. I never should've got those implants when I knew Narrow didn't approve.' She ran her right hand along her scarred arm with as sincere a look of regret as she could muster. 'I know I can't turn back the clock, but I've got to tell him how sorry I am.'

Strait raised both eyebrows and stared at her. 'They do say time heals all wounds. How *is* the arm?' He peered over the counter at her scars.

'Healed,' she said.

'I'm ever so pleased to hear it. But I'm afraid I can't say the same about Mel's heart.' Strait looked her in the eyes for longer than was comfortable.

'I paid your sodding entry fee. Let me see him.'

'No,' said Strait. 'You haven't got an appointment.'

'It's important.'

Strait slowly laced his fingers together and gave her another dead-eyed smile. 'Get it through your thick skull. You are not and never will be welcome in this establishment. I allowed you to get this far simply because I wanted to make that abundantly clear. You're balanced on a knife-edge, Young Lady. Tread carefully.'

A blade flowed into Strait's hands from an unknown source, its edge glinting under the technicolour lights of the sign above their heads. He feinted a thrust towards her neck, and he scowled when she didn't flinch.

Despite her display of calm, her chest tightened, and she

clenched her teeth. She took a deep breath and reminded herself that Strait was an old man. An old man who'd once taken down a guy twice his size with one well-placed puncture wound. Charlotte wouldn't punch an elderly gent. Mainly because she didn't want an elderly gent to empty her internal organs onto the shop floor.

'Get out,' said Strait, 'or I'll make your exit permanent. Narrow doesn't want to see you. Not now. Not ever.'

She was weighing up her options when the door behind the sales desk swung open and slammed against the wall.

'I can speak for myself on that score, Jer.' Narrow's voice boomed out from his large frame as he emerged from the back room. A group of suits shuffled out from behind him, eyes firmly dipped as they made themselves scarce.

Charlotte locked eyes with Narrow and both of them stood there, gaping at each other, until Narrow's gaze drifted to Charlotte's scarred arm.

'I can't believe my eyes.' His voice wavered. 'Long time no see, Little One.'

CHAPTER 9

20.39 AND 3 SECONDS UTC, AND COUNTING

Charlotte's heart seemed to stop. Everything had ceased to exist except for Mel Narrow. He'd called her Little One. He'd always called her Little One. As a teenager, she'd hated it, right up until the moment she'd realised he would never call her that, or anything else, ever again. Back then, she would've given anything to hear those words one more time.

Now he'd said them, and Charlotte didn't have a name for the cocktail of emotions she was drunk on. Fury and resentment and the deep ache of love swirled around each other. Her body coursed with misplaced sentimentality and impotent rage. She focused on breathing and processing her visual feed, as she tried to stop her mind from glitching.

She'd last seen her adoptive father over a decade ago, but it was still a surprise to see that he'd aged. Unlike the image of Narrow in her mind's eye, the man standing in front of her was in his fifties. He was still bald, of course, but he'd grown a stubbly beard that was mostly grey. The lines around his eyes had deepened and the skin below them sagged.

But other things had stayed the same. Narrow was still wearing his brown jacket made of genuine leather from pre-Melt times. Its full-length sleeves had worn through at the elbows, but he'd never had them mended or patched. Underneath, he wore a washed-out retro t-shirt with a purple logo from some old video game, or maybe one of those theme park things he was always going on about. And he was still wearing the same style of ratty jeans that his crew mimicked, as if it were a uniform. Considering Narrow was one of the richest people in the ArkTech Territory, he did a good job of hiding it.

It was hard to believe the old man was really standing there. It was like seeing a corpse rise from the dead.

'Now, what the hell are you doing down here in the dark, eh?' asked Narrow.

She couldn't answer him. Hate and love battled for supremacy inside of her, leaving her speechless. While she searched for words, Narrow began to stagger towards her, lifting a hinged section of the service desk and approaching with his arms outstretched. As he drew near, she couldn't move. She was dead in the water.

Finally, they stood face to face. Narrow's eyes told her that he was just as overcome with emotion as she was. He could easily have strangled her if he'd wanted to. Instead, he wrapped his arms around her in a massive bear hug. Charlotte's face got smooshed against Narrow's jacket, and she inhaled the old familiar scents of tobacco and dead cow, triggering feelings of nostalgia and love and terror and grief. She returned his embrace, clinging to him as if he were a life raft. After a duration of seconds that lasted a lifetime, they let each other go.

Charlotte's heart hurt more than if Strait had buried his

blade into it. She felt the pinpricks of tears behind her eyes and willed them to stay hidden. She'd expected to feel only hatred for the man who'd disowned her. But in that moment, those feelings were washed away. In that moment, all she remembered was Narrow's kindness, and his laugh, and all the cool stuff he'd taught her when she was a kid. In that moment, she knew how much she'd missed him these last ten years.

She looked up at Narrow. He looked down at her and smiled.

The moment passed.

Charlotte lifted both hands and, with every last gram of strength, she shoved Narrow away from her. He was a big man, but the move took him by surprise, and he got knocked back half a step. Then she balled her hand into a fist, with her thumb positioned safely out of the way like Narrow had taught her, and she punched him in the cheek. The force sent a shockwave of pain through her hand as Narrow staggered backwards.

'You absolute bastard!' Charlotte yelled. She shoved him again, but his feet were firmly planted this time, and he didn't budge.

A silence fell, as if everyone inside the shop were holding their breath. Then she heard footsteps. Customers hurrying away. The door opening and closing. The bouncers rushing inside.

Narrow slowly lifted a hand. He gestured for the guards who were coming to his defence to stop, and he completed the motion by touching the site of the blow.

'Pretty solid.' He nodded, impressed. 'Got that out of your system now, have you?' Narrow raised his bushy eyebrows at her.

Charlotte took a few deep breaths. She wasn't totally sure of the answer, but she'd just made one huge mistake and didn't want to make another by telling the truth. 'Yeah. I . . . I didn't mean to do that. I'm not here to fight.' That was true, at least.

'Good – assisted suicide ain't a service I offer.' He turned to look over his shoulder, as if he'd heard something. 'Stand down, Jer.'

Charlotte peered past Narrow's bulk towards the service desk. Strait was standing there, a knife in each hand. A vein in his forehead was throbbing. He looked . . . what *was* that word? Like those old lightbulbs . . . Strait looked *incandescent*.

'I'm here to talk,' she said to Narrow. 'It's important. But Chuckles over there says I need an appointment.' She thrust a thumb towards Strait.

'You *do* need an appointment,' said Strait. 'And we don't make time for violent, volatile miscreants.'

Narrow raised his eyebrows at his partner. 'You just described us, Jer.'

'Speak for yourself.' Strait frowned and rolled his eyes as if this situation had become the least interesting thing he'd ever encountered. Then he turned his attention back to the big flat device and its security footage.

'It's true, though.' Narrow said to Charlotte. 'We got a tight schedule. But what kind of "absolute bastard" would I be if I didn't make time for my little girl after all these years?'

'Mel,' said Strait slowly, without looking up. 'She just punched you in the face.'

Narrow laughed and squeezed Charlotte's shoulders. 'Takes after her old man then, don't she?' He headed back behind the counter towards the door that led into the back room, leaving Charlotte to grapple with how she felt about that observation.

Strait tensed up. 'Your next appointment is *imminent*. Do I need to remind you of how much money we'll lose if they resent being made to wait?' Jeremiah Strait was the only person, besides Charlotte and her sister, who could snap at Narrow and get away with it.

'I said I'll *make time.*' Narrow gave Strait the zany smile he always used when he thought he'd said something witty, but Charlotte wasn't in on the joke. 'Tell the next Smith and Jones I'll be with them lickety-split and in two shakes of a jiffy.'

Strait tutted and shook his head, adjusted his cardigan, and peered at his tablet. Narrow marched into the back room, and Charlotte hurried after him.

On her way past, Strait caught hold of her arm. He lowered his voice to a whisper. 'If you hurt him again . . .'

'You'll kill me. Yeah. You said.' Charlotte wrenched her arm free. 'Big words, but we both know you won't go against the boss.' She glared at Strait and followed Narrow through the door, leaving the knife-wielding maniac to stew.

Calling the space behind Narrow's Toy Emporium a *room* was like saying ArkTech's Solar Shards had helped humanity *a bit* in recovering from the Melt – it was the understatement of the twenty-second century. In reality, Charlotte followed Narrow into a vast warehouse made of steel, with air so cold it turned her breath to mist. The distant walls were stacked high with metal storage crates filled with contraband. This was where Narrow's real work happened. The kind that had made him filthy rich.

It was almost exactly as Charlotte remembered it, but with one big difference – in the centre of the space, there now sat a squat structure that made her think of the word *bunker*. It had translucent walls, clouded over like the windows in her office. What was Narrow using it for?

When she was a teenager, Narrow had used that spot for private audiences with his clients. He'd said it emphasised the scale of his operation, like the imposing throne rooms of leaders in the Middle Ages. Charlotte had never set foot inside a castle, so she hadn't found it a helpful comparison. Had

Narrow put the walled-off bunker there to create the illusion of privacy? Or was it to make sure nobody witnessed whatever went down in there? Either way, the fact Charlotte couldn't see inside made her brain itch with curiosity.

The mysterious glassy structure blocked her view to the end of the warehouse, but she caught sight of the bookcases that marked Narrow's impressive personal library. She headed in that direction, but Narrow slowed as he drew close to the bunker.

A round plastic pre-Melt clock was mounted above the bunker's door, but its angled hands were too retro for Charlotte, so she wasn't sure what time it was. She was about to ask Ben when she remembered with a pang of loss that he wasn't there. No matter what the clock said, it was time to get an answer to his Awkward Question. As soon as she knew why Jason Ashton had taken those photos outside the Wreck, she'd get the hell out of there. She couldn't let her history with Narrow distract her more than it already had.

Charlotte thought Narrow was about to open the door and invite her inside the mysterious room, but instead he began to stroll along its perimeter. She fell into step with him.

'Listen,' she said, 'I'm here because I need to talk to you about an associate of yours. His name's Jason—'

Narrow suddenly turned towards her, and Charlotte thought she'd hit a nerve. 'There's something I've gotta tell you, Little One. I've wanted to say this for a good long while, but I ain't one to open up old wounds.'

He avoided looking at her scars as he spoke, and Charlotte realised this was nothing to do with Jason Ashton.

'But now you're here,' Narrow continued, 'and . . . I'm *sorry*, Little One. I'm really bloody sorry about how I treated you. And your sister.'

His words left her stunned. 'I thought I'd made my bed?' She made no attempt to hide the bitterness in her tone.

Narrow pursed his lips. 'You had. But my anger boiled away in time. My love for you girls never faded.'

Her insides twisted painfully. She wasn't sure how to feel. 'Why the change of heart? You seeing a psychologist like that Mafia guy in that pre-Melt show you love?'

Narrow chuckled. 'Tony Soprano. I always told you not to watch that – you were too young.'

She shrugged. 'I stopped being your "Little One" a long time ago.'

Narrow winced and then paused, as if weighing his words. 'I realise now that what happened back then was *my* fault. I thought I was protecting you. Thought it wasn't fair to tell you the whole truth. But if you'd known what I know, you never would've sided with Amber Benjamin and ArkTech over me.' He gestured at her arm. 'You'd never have wired your body into their world. Instead, you'd be helping me take them down.'

Charlotte opened her mouth to defend the company like she always had when she was younger, but she paused. After the Citrine Disaster, Amber Benjamin had made sure that Charlotte and her twin sister had a roof over their heads and food in their bellies. That bought a lot of loyalty. But Charlotte remembered what she'd learned about the Splainer Unit – how they were secretly analysing people's personalities and deporting people based on the results. If ArkTech was lying about that, couldn't they be lying about other things, too?

Narrow picked up on her hesitation. 'You've seen it for yourself, ain't ya? ArkTech ain't as high and mighty as it claims.'

Charlotte shook her head. Even if ArkTech was doing a few things she didn't agree with, the company was also doing a hell of a lot of good. After all, ArkTech had created Ben. The thought of her friend grounded her.

'Everyone has secrets,' she said. 'Everyone makes mistakes. Neither of those is a crime.'

'Depends on the mistake.'

'OK, then just tell me! What could Amber Benjamin possibly have done that was so terrible? What's this "whole truth" of yours?'

Narrow held up a finger for her to wait, and suddenly stopped in his tracks. He reached inside his jacket pocket, and Charlotte's stomach folded in on itself like a black hole. Was he going for a weapon? Was this when he got payback for that punch? Adrenaline flooded her bloodstream, as if her body believed she could put up a fight. Narrow completed the action and pulled out nothing more dangerous than a crumpled packet of cigarettes. Charlotte managed not to flinch as he tipped the open end of the box towards her.

She raised an eyebrow. 'You always said I shouldn't smoke.'

He shrugged. 'Yeah. But if I answer that question, you might not live long enough to deal with the consequences.' He took a long look at his cigarette. 'You know, they reckon each of these babies takes twenty minutes off your life. But from where I'm standing, that gives me twenty minutes less of being a miserable old git.' He offered her the packet again.

Charlotte waved the cigarettes away, imagining the uninvited health advice that Ben would've given her if he'd been there.

Narrow chuckled and lit one for himself. His heavy-duty Zippo lighter in scratched-up brass was engraved with a stylised M wrapped in the branches of a tree, and it stank of lighter fluid. The cigarette's tip burned orange as he inhaled, and Charlotte was surprised he could stand seeing ArkTech's brand colour every time he took a drag.

'Tell me,' Charlotte said. 'What did Amber do?'

Narrow breathed out a long plume of smoke. 'The Citrine Disaster was no accident. Amber Benjamin killed your parents.'

CHAPTER 10

20.53 AND 31 SECONDS UTC, AND COUNTING

Charlotte didn't remember her parents. People assumed that was an easier kind of grief, but the pain of what might have been cut deep. All the birthdays they hadn't spent together. The family holidays they hadn't taken. The missed milestones when Charlotte had learned to walk and talk and climb and pick locks. If Will and Lena Vance hadn't died in that fire, everything might've been different.

As an orphan of Citrine, her life had been defined by their absence. She carried their sacrifice in her heart. Her parents had died in service of ArkTech's mission to make the world a better place. Amber Benjamin's company had mattered to them, and Charlotte honoured their memory by dedicating herself to the same cause.

Narrow's statement about ArkTech's CEO wasn't funny, but the mismatch between his ludicrous claim and his sincere delivery caught her off guard. Without meaning to, Charlotte laughed. She covered her mouth and faked a cough, waving at the second-hand smoke, as if she were choking on that instead of Narrow's unhinged take on reality.

Her bluff didn't work and the hurt showed on Narrow's face worse than when she'd hit him. 'You don't believe me.'

Charlotte tried for diplomacy. 'It's just . . . a very bold accusation to make about someone with two Nobel Prizes. Have you got any proof?'

He held his thumb and forefinger a tiny bit apart. 'I'm this close. On the cusp of a breakthrough. There's been . . . a development.'

Her brow furrowed. That was a long-winded way of saying he couldn't back up his accusation. 'What development?'

He took another drag on his cigarette and peered at her sidelong. 'All in good time,' he said mysteriously.

She took a deep breath, trying not to show her irritation. This was the same old conspiracy theorist crap he'd been spewing since she was a kid. All emotion, no substance. All intrigue, no answers. She needed to get him back onto the topic of Jason Ashton – she knew that. But this was her birth parents he was talking about, and the company that had taken her in and given her a home. The words that tumbled from her mouth weren't the ones she needed.

'What you're saying doesn't make any sense. The Walkers were the CEO's best friends! And why the hell would Amber murder her own research team?'

'That's a good question. A better one is asking if the official explanation holds up to scrutiny. And it don't. Think about it, right?' Narrow's eyes were wild. 'The Citrine Disaster never added up. All those clever buggers in their lab coats – greatest minds of their generation – they ain't gonna leave a Bunsen burner unattended and torch the place by accident, are they? Boffins got protocols. Checks and balances. Big, burly brains. How could that lot cause a mishap so severe that nobody – not a single one of them – survived? I mean, just look at Piper Alpha! One hundred and sixty-seven men died in that blaze, right? But sixty-one walked away. Or swam away. One guy jumped right off the top of the helideck into the North Sea and lived to tell the tale. *Someone* should've made it off the platform. Unless there was foul play.'

She raised an eyebrow. 'Piper Alpha?' Without Ben there to tell her about it, she only had her own knowledge to go on, and she'd drawn a blank.

'You're bloody kidding?' asked Narrow with a chuckle of disbelief. 'I know ArkTech gave you a raw deal when it came to schooling, but someone must've told you about Piper Alpha. I can't believe *I* ain't never mentioned it.'

Charlotte shook her head. 'Doesn't ring a bell. Maybe I'm a bad listener.'

A vein throbbed in Narrow's forehead, and he brandished his cigarette at her. 'You see? This is exactly the kind of shit I'm always talking about! You ain't a "bad listener." ArkTech fobbed you off with "minders" instead of hiring qualified teachers.'

'They didn't have the infrastructure in place back then. Me and Ultra ... fell through the cracks.' She remembered to use her childhood nickname for her sister, trying to play by Narrow's rules.

'Ultra and I,' he snapped.

'Oh, because you're Captain Grammar?'

'Do as I say, Little One, not as I do. And don't make excuses for Amber Benjamin's mistakes.' His hands swept through the air as he talked. 'They probably didn't want you knowing too much because ... because they want to control you. ArkTech wants to control everything. Our behaviour. Our thoughts. They want to *own the narrative*!' Narrow used the phrase as if he'd read it somewhere and had been waiting for the chance to drop it into conversation.

'What narrative? If you're always talking in riddles and referring to obscure historical events, it's no wonder I don't believe anything you say!' It was exasperating hearing him bang this same old drum. He might've earned a few more wrinkles, but in the last ten years, he hadn't changed.

Narrow flicked the ash from the end of his cigarette, and a wave of calm seemed to wash over him. He pulled at a loose thread on the lining of his sleeve as they circled the glass bunker. 'That's just it, Little One. You've hit the nail right on its head. History shouldn't be obscure. *That's* the narrative they want to control.'

'History?' She couldn't keep the sarcasm from her voice. 'History isn't a narrative, Narrow. Even I know that. A narrative's a story. History's a list of dates and facts about what happened when. Like how the Melt started in 2048 because IQUO screwed up Project Mirror Shade – that's history. Amber Benjamin killing my parents? *That's* a fucking narrative.'

Narrow scoffed. 'Even the choice of which stories to tell is a way of controlling the narrative. And when it comes to what happened on Citrine, ArkTech ain't telling. Anyway, if you'd knuckled down like your sister and studied under your own steam, you'd know that.'

His words stung because they were true. When she was growing up, Narrow was always on their case about their education. He'd given them books and set them study challenges. Violet had applied herself, but Charlotte hadn't seen the point. Exploring the Underbelly was way more exciting. Anyway, these days, Ben was there to tell her anything she needed to know, so why should she bother memorising a load of useless trivia?

'Why does it even matter if I don't know about the Piping Alpha—?'

'*Piper* Alpha. It was an oil platform, and back in 1988—'

'Whatever!' she grunted. It was the kind of correction Ben

would've made, but it annoyed her coming from Narrow. 'It's the past. It's over. I already know the gist of it, anyway. Humans came along. We made a big mess and almost made the planet uninhabitable. Then, when most people had either died or given up hope, and almost everyone was at war with someone else, ArkTech invented Solar Shard batteries and a bunch of other stuff, which solved the energy crisis. Why do I need to know a load of tragic facts that happened before I was born when I know how the story ends?'

Narrow let out a laugh. 'Marx said "history repeats itself, first as tragedy, second as farce." Knowing what happened is the only way to prepare for what comes next. Thing I don't get, Little One, is why someone who's so curious about other things – like what young Mr Emberville's been doing down here – can be so completely uninterested in the death of her own parents.'

She wanted to storm out of there. But when Narrow said the words, it forced her to look directly at the answer. She didn't want to admit it, but she knew why. The official line was a peaceful death by smoke inhalation in their sleep, and Charlotte didn't want to imagine any other scenario. The idea they might've suffered . . .

Narrow noticed the cloud that passed in front of her eyes. 'Hey, hey, hey. I'm sorry. That was too far.' He put his arm around her and squeezed. 'But don't you think it's all a bit dodgy? I mean, there were hundreds of people aboard that platform, and you two kids are the only ones that lived to tell the tale? Were there other kids aboard? We never hear about them. They say Nadine Walker was pregnant, too. That's a lot of baby-making for a research plat—'

'All I need,' said Charlotte through gritted teeth, 'is some intel for my job. Then I can get out of your hair. So what's the deal with your buddy Emberville?'

Narrow ran a hand over his bald head and nodded,

accepting the change of subject. He sighed. 'That kid ain't my buddy.'

'No?' she asked. 'He was taking photos with a pre-Melt camera. Outside. The day after coming down here to see you.'

'Now, how could you possibly know a thing like that?' Narrow rubbed his stubble.

'I saw him.'

Narrow's eyes went wide, and he coughed as the smoke from his cigarette messed with his sudden intake of breath. He patted his chest. 'Well, that's an epic fail on Emberville's part then, ain't it? Can't get the staff these days.'

'The staff? He's on your payroll?'

Narrow tilted his head from side to side as if weighing up how much to say. 'Not yet. Interview process.'

'Why would you be interviewing for a photographer?' asked Charlotte. 'Have you got him running surveillance?'

Narrow shook with laughter. 'Surveillance? What the hell do you think is out there to surveil?'

'I don't know!' Blood rushed to her cheeks. 'Structural features? Supply vessels? Search and Rescue patrols?'

'OK, but think about it, Little One.' Narrow pressed his cigarette filter between his lips. 'Why would I send someone on a surveillance mission during a storm?' His brow furrowed. 'How come you're poking around in my business, anyway? What's your angle?'

'It's my job.' She unclipped her badge and passed it to him. As he peered at it, she unslung her backpack and carefully manoeuvred the glossy issue of *ArkTech Insider* out from behind the expensive rice. Flipping to the right page, she showed Narrow the article. The words *Head of Awkward Questions* floated above her head, and she was striking an action pose like in the light-screen ads upstairs.

Narrow took the magazine and let out one long whistle. 'Get you with your fancy-pants title! You'll be Chief Product

Officer in no time.' He read the article and nodded when he was done. 'Jer told me you've been working for the AI.'

She nodded. 'Ben and I make a good team.'

Narrow ignored that. 'The AI that your beloved CEO named after herself, like the egomaniac she is . . .'

'Pretty sure Ben's name was a tribute to Amber Benjamin from the team that designed him.'

Narrow waved that away. 'One thing I don't get,' he said. 'Why the hell does software need a human on its staff? Can't it spawn its own little algorithms to run around doing its bidding?'

Charlotte rattled off the spiel she'd given so many times that it was hard not to sound robotic. 'I help Ben interpret human behaviour by investigating the root causes that underpin people's decision-making processes in the holistic, embodied way that only a human can.'

Narrow narrowed his eyes. 'So . . . you're a snitch?'

She sighed. 'No. All the data I handle gets treated confidentially.' She tried not to think too hard about whether that was still true now that Ben had learned about workarounds.

'You're spying on people for a corporate computer system to help make it even more powerful.'

'That's not—'

'You know that supercharged search engine ain't welcome down here.' Narrow threw the end of his cigarette onto the floor, squashed the filter under his boot, and pushed the magazine and her badge back into her hands. 'Why would I tell you anything when the first thing you'll do is report it to your little cyber buddy?'

'I won't tell him anything that'll give away your operation.' She wasn't going to admit that Ben knew about it already.

'So you're saying I should trust you?' His lighter clicked as he lit a fresh cigarette.

'I could've reported you to ArkTech Security years ago. I

didn't. Anyway, you can't be all that anti-tech these days if your crew's got the same contact lenses as me. Seriously, how do those video feeds even work inside the jamming array?'

Narrow pursed his lips, and Charlotte thought she saw a spark of irritation flash behind his eyes. But he took another drag and then he nodded. When he spoke, he sounded tired. 'We've been making some changes down here. Got our own internet now. Separate from the ArkNet. That's how the lenses work.'

Charlotte tried not to gape at him. 'What brought that on?' Narrow must've had a powerful reason if he'd finally embraced ArkTech's technology after all these years.

'Jer wants to keep up with the latest episodes of *Noah's Mad Planet.*'

She frowned but didn't press him on the lie. 'How the hell did you swing your own system, anyway?'

He shrugged. 'I know a guy. My crew wanted to call it the UnderWeb, but that's the kind of marketing team technobabble bollocks I can't abide. The word *internet* works just fine.'

'If you've got access to the same lenses as me, why give Emberville a camera?'

'Our lenses only work on the Underbelly's internet.'

'All right,' she said. 'But I still don't get why you'd send him at all.'

Narrow sighed. 'You ain't gonna stop quizzing me, are you? Fine. I'm recruiting for someone who can take care of some … bespoke orders for me. Problem is, it's hard to find anyone trustworthy with the right skill set. I need someone discreet who can look death in the face and laugh. I reckon anyone crazy enough to go out in that weather, get the job done, and live to tell the tale must have what it takes.'

'And Jason matched that description?'

'Remains to be seen. I ain't heard a peep.'

Charlotte's mind replayed the moment she'd clocked Jason,

seen the huge wave coming, and left him to his fate. 'Sorry to be the one to tell you this, but I think Jason's dead.'

Narrow looked genuinely upset. 'Aw, shit.'

'I'm … sorry for your loss.' Maybe the young man had meant something to Narrow after all.

Narrow shook his head in dismay. 'Those waterproof cameras are really bloody tricky to come by.'

Charlotte blinked. She'd got so used to being around Ben, who was committed to preserving human lives, that she'd forgotten what it was like to spend time with someone who saw people as a cheap commodity.

She pressed on. 'What kind of "bespoke orders" do you need a guy like that for, anyway?'

'That's for me to know, Little One, and for you not to know.'

Charlotte frowned, mentally assembling the puzzle pieces Narrow had shared. 'So, you sent him out there to put his skills to the test?'

'Yeah, but get this … it doubles as insurance.' It was Narrow's turn to show off. 'If I'd got my hands on those pics, I would've had his balls over a barrel. I hand those photos to ArkTech Security and Mr Emberville gets deported. This way, I get to see what he can do *and* guarantee his loyalty at the same time.'

Deportation was no laughing matter. Space was limited in the ArkTech Territory and competition was fierce for any spots that opened up. It meant ArkTech could take a no-nonsense approach when it came to removing people. Anyone who got caught breaking the territory's laws risked getting sent to Wolds Island for processing, before being transferred back wherever they were deemed to have come from. For Jason, that would've been Manchester. But no matter where someone got sent, being forced to leave the safety of the territory was a terrible fate, and the casual way Narrow used it as an intimidation tactic made her shudder.

'Clever,' said Charlotte, keeping her tone neutral.

Narrow gave her a mock bow.

'And you're paying him well enough to make it worth the risk, I'm guessing?' she asked.

'Not everyone wants paying in credits.' Narrow patted the wall of the bunker meaningfully.

Charlotte's mind whirred. What could be inside the makeshift room? Her curiosity reached new heights as she realised its contents were actually relevant to her case. If access to this bunker was what Jason Ashton wanted as payment, Ben would want to know about it. So, she wouldn't be doing her job properly if she didn't take a peek inside the mysterious mystery box. Walking away now would be just plain irresponsible.

'What's in there?' she asked.

'Paying customers and employees only,' he said.

'Strait made me pay an entry fee.'

'That's just a door charge. This costs extra.'

'Your "door charge" was five hundred credits.'

'That don't even cover your tab for the swear jar.'

Charlotte could tell from the glint in Narrow's eye that he was having fun with her, so she tried a bit of reverse psychology.

She shrugged. 'Fine. I've got what I needed. I'll let you get back to . . . whatever this is.' She waved a hand at the bunker dismissively.

They'd completed a couple of full laps around it. Its construction looked sturdy. Heavy-duty polymer all the way around. Clouded over on all sides. There was just one door at the front, with the round clock ticking above it.

Narrow said nothing, but a cloud seemed to pass in front of his eyes. Then his face lit up.

'Hey, I'll tell you what, Little One. Let's make a deal. You said I'm always talking in riddles. I'll show you what's inside if you can solve one for me. You still like riddles, right?'

She held back a sigh. 'Sure, Narrow. I still like riddles.' The man was obsessed with puzzles and codes, and he'd subjected Charlotte and Violet to all manner of lateral thinking problems when they were growing up. Usually, it was a gateway to sweets or toys, so they'd played along. Narrow was acting like the past decade hadn't happened, and Charlotte couldn't deny it felt good to pretend, just for a moment, that things could go back to the way they were.

He grinned. 'OK, imagine a square house like this one. Four walls, right? A window in each wall . . .'

'This thing doesn't have any windows,' she said.

'I said *imagine*. And each window faces south. That's important – south. Got it? OK . . . A bear walks past the window. What colour is it?'

Charlotte thought about that. She remembered a few things about bears. A lot of the characters in the cartoons she'd watched as a kid were bears, even if they had been multi-coloured, and she recalled doing a project about the animals with one of her minders who'd taken an above-average interest in her education. She double-checked her logic and then gave her answer. 'White,' she said.

'You got it!' Narrow clapped his hands. 'I must've told you that one before. It's a polar bear, right?'

'Nope.'

'Huh?'

'Maybe back before the Melt, the answer was a polar bear. But polar bears are extinct. And thanks to IQUO melting all the ice, a structure like this one couldn't be built at the North Pole. The thing would have to be underwater for all four windows to face south. And a bear can't walk past a window if it's on the seabed. Not a living bear, anyway. Only a ghost bear could do that. And anybody who's ever seen a pre-Melt cartoon knows that ghosts are white.'

'Bloody hell,' said Narrow.

'You did teach me to think laterally, remember?' She smiled at him. 'So, I win, right? Open it up.' Charlotte patted the bunker.

'All right,' he said. 'It'll only take a second.' He smirked as if he'd said something funny, but she didn't get the joke. Narrow stubbed out his cigarette against the bunker in a spray of ash. 'Now that you've walked all the way around, you can see there ain't no funny business on the outside, right?'

'Right.' She nodded.

'OK. See that clock up there?' He pointed to the one above the door. 'What does it say?'

Round clocks were weird. Ben usually dictated the time for her, and she only ever had to interpret digital numbers when the time was written down. She couldn't read the clock, so she took a guess.

'It's, like, eight something?'

'Uh huh. And what's the actual time?'

Charlotte sighed and looked again. The hands almost made a backwards L-shape. A distant lesson from what had passed for her school years floated up from her memory.

'It's almost precisely forty-five minutes past eleven,' she said. Then she frowned, hoping she was wrong, because that would mean she was running very late for her appointment with Cal and Liz.

'In old money, we'd call that quarter to midnight. But no – it's around nine o'clock.'

Her cheeks turned warm. Nine o'clock made way more sense. 'What is it with you and all this out-dated crap?' she asked. 'You know, if you'd let Ben down here, he could give us the time to the hundredth of a second and neither of us would have to strain a brain-cell.'

Narrow gave her an odd smirk. 'Remember the time and come in.' He held the door open for her.

Charlotte stepped inside the glass bunker and was immediately confused. There didn't seem to be anything special on the inside at all. She wasn't sure what she'd been expecting, but she'd definitely been expecting *something*.

Inside, it was just a room, not unlike her office. There was a round folding table with three chairs tucked under it, and a half-finished jigsaw puzzle on the top. There was a scruffy old sofa that looked as if it might've been extremely comfortable right up until the moment when whatever carnivorous, many-legged creatures living inside it decided to emerge and feast on the skin of whoever had made the mistake of sitting down. There was a tall filing cabinet, a bookshelf full of pre-Melt paperbacks with ruined spines, one whole corner dedicated to gym equipment, and there was a desk with an ergonomic chair and an old-school computer. In short, it was an anticlimax.

Narrow stepped inside the room with her and closed the door behind them.

'Ben?' said Narrow. 'Open a Bubble.'

'Calibrating,' said Ben via a loudspeaker in the ceiling.

Charlotte's blood turned to ice as she heard Ben's voice. Then the walls inside the bunker began to shiver with an oily soap-sud shimmer, bathing Charlotte and Narrow in melting rainbows.

'Bubble is open and stable,' said Ben. 'Tock is null. The time is 21.02 and 23 seconds UTC – not counting.'

CHAPTER 11

21.02 AND 23 SECONDS UTC

NOT COUNTING

This had to be what going mad felt like. Charlotte barely noticed the shiny sheen that was creeping across the walls. The fact that Ben was there, in the Underbelly, *inside* the jamming array . . . that shouldn't have been possible.

'Ben! You're here?'

'I am here, valued customer,' said Ben. 'Your ArkTech-sponsored virtual assistant.'

Ben's voice had an eerie quality. It was flat. Empty somehow. His words had always sounded digitised – it was an affectation, designed to remind people not to think of him as human – but his tone should've been warm and enthusiastic. And the term *valued customer*. What was that about? Charlotte's audio implants were still switched off, and Ben's voice was only broadcasting over the loudspeakers inside the bunker. Something was very wrong.

Narrow smirked. 'Bet you never thought you'd see the day, eh?' He looked as smug as a seagull with a stolen a chip.

Charlotte couldn't make sense of it. 'Ben, how are you here? And what's wrong with you?'

'I do not understand your questions, valued customer. Please rephrase.'

Charlotte looked at Narrow. 'What have you done to him?'

Narrow shrugged. 'Buddy of mine hooked me up with a copy.'

'An *instance*,' she corrected him, unable to hide her impatience. 'Why can your generation never get a handle on the terminology? Everyone has their own instance of Ben. There's nothing special about that, and it doesn't explain why you've suddenly decided to trust him after so many years of being paranoid.'

Charlotte knew that every instance of Ben was continuously uploading his multitude of simultaneous experiences to his master database, which was exactly the sort of threat to his privacy Narrow wanted to avoid.

'I needed it installed down here to run this thing.' He gestured at the walls. 'But it's not an instance, Little One. It's a local *copy*. A partial one, anyway. It's got all the AI's regular functionality, but none of its dumb quirks.'

Narrow's words slid through Charlotte's brain like an ice cube down her gullet. She shivered. 'You're lying. That's impossible.'

He shrugged. 'Looks plenty possible to me.'

'But why would anyone do that? It's—'

Charlotte tried to find the right word for what Narrow had just described. Barbaric. Terrible. Wrong. Narrow had casually admitted to keeping a clone of her best friend locked up in his basement. But she knew Narrow would never see Ben's existence as equal to a human life. She needed to find out more, so she kept her disapproval to herself.

'Incredible,' she finished.

'Cool, eh?' said Narrow. 'And I can wipe the logs at the end of every session, so it won't remember a thing.'

Charlotte was lost for words. This should've counted as a string of AI-rights abuses, except there was no such thing. Ben didn't have rights in the way employee-citizens did. Was this copy suffering? How would Ben react when she told him about it? And why had somebody made Narrow a copy in the first place? Maybe Cal could help her figure this out. As a Lead Bengineer, she might know something.

'Anyway,' said Narrow, 'ain't you fixating on the wrong thing? We got actual genuine magic happening down here, Little One.' The walls were still shimmering.

'Stop calling me that!' Charlotte snapped. 'Walker's ghost! I'm a grown woman.'

Narrow crossed his arms and raised an eyebrow. 'All right, keep your hair on. What do you want me to call you?' He clicked his fingers before she could reply. 'The Scarlet Lance, right?'

Mischief glinted in Narrow's eyes, and Charlotte knew he was messing with her. The Scarlet Lance had been an extremely cool and not at all ridiculous alias she'd tried to persuade her family to call her when she was a teenager, but for some reason they'd made fun of her over it.

'This from a man who gave himself the middle name Kain?' She scowled at him.

'Nothing wrong with that,' said Narrow.

'Ben told me it's the name of a vampire from a video game.'

Ben's voice suddenly burst from the speakers, without any static to announce it was coming. 'Querying database. Conversation topic: vampires. No entries found. Conversation topic: video games. No entries found. Your statement is erroneous, valued customer. I have never shared this fact with you.'

Narrow ignored the interruption. 'Yeah, well ... Nobody's gonna buy contraband from someone called Lionel, are they?'

Charlotte wondered if that was Narrow's way of telling her his real name, or if he was just being flippant. 'You don't look much like a Lionel.'

He wagged a finger at her. 'You're still ignoring the magic.' He patted a wall. Shiny lights moved over his hand.

'Magic doesn't exist,' she said. 'Why should I get excited about a light show? We've got light-screen emitters all over the territory that can project pretty colours all day long.'

Narrow rolled his eyes. 'Some egghead once said advanced technology and magic are basically the same thing.'

Ben's voice interrupted again. 'The egghead in question was Sir Arthur C Clarke, and his exact words were—'

'Geez, shut up, would ya?' Narrow sighed and waved a hand towards the ceiling. 'I don't know how you put up with this thing.'

Charlotte might've felt offended, but she wasn't sure if this copy of Ben had any approximation of feelings that could get hurt.

'Anyway,' Narrow continued, 'the lighting ain't the point, Little Lance.'

Charlotte shrugged. 'Then what's the point?'

Narrow grinned. 'Tock ... is null.' He spread his arms wide and spun around slowly, like a property agent showing off an upgrade to a potential buyer.

'And what the hell is that supposed to mean?'

'It means ...' he said. 'We're off the clock in here. Literally.'

Charlotte searched for the most accurate words to reflect her feelings. 'What a load of old bollocks!'

Narrow smiled and spoke to the ceiling. 'What time is it, Benny boy?'

'The time is 21.02 and 23 seconds UTC – not counting,' said

the ghoulish doppelgänger doing a bad impersonation of her friend.

Charlotte shook her head. 'Your copy's glitching already. That's exactly the same time he said before.'

'It ain't a glitch.' Narrow flopped down onto the wide sofa. It looked more like an armchair under his bulk.

Charlotte gave him a look. 'That's ridiculous. That's not even possible.'

He shrugged. 'People once thought humans couldn't fly, but helicopters soar overhead all day long. They thought the moon was out of reach, but people went and jumped around on it – before space exploration turned taboo, anyway. Humanity's invented all kinds of crap that seemed impossible until it happened. You'd know that if you hit the history books. But if you don't believe me, ask Ben.'

Narrow couldn't be serious. Time couldn't pause like that. Sure, she wasn't a scientist like her parents. They'd died before they could teach her anything at all, let alone the ins and outs of their profession, and knowing the laws of physics wasn't a genetic trait. Even so, it was obviously impossible. But Narrow's know-it-all routine was grating on her, and getting Ben's take on it wasn't a bad idea.

But first things first. 'Ben?' she said. 'What's the difference between a bird?'

Narrow raised an eyebrow at the nonsensical phrase, and Charlotte avoided his gaze. The words were the first half of an in-joke she shared with Ben and Ben alone.

There was no fizz of static, not even a pause, before the copy of Ben replied. 'I am afraid I do not understand your query, valued customer. Please rephrase.'

That settled it. Maybe this was a duplicated version of some of Ben's functionality, but this wasn't her friend. The real Ben would've remembered the answer and taken great delight in reminiscing about it. Investigating the meaning of the absurdist pre-Melt joke was one of the first puzzles they'd solved together, long before Ben had created her role.

'OK, disregard that,' Charlotte continued. 'Tock is null. What does that mean?'

Fake Ben's reply transmitted over the loudspeakers. 'Co-ordinated Universal Time, abbreviated as UTC, is a standard measure of Earth time. Unlike many local times, UTC is never adjusted to account for seasonal changes in daylight duration caused by the Earth's axial tilt. UTC ticks upwards consistently across the globe and throughout the calendar year. It is measured by averaging the readings from atomic clocks while taking account of the Earth's rotation.'

Charlotte tapped her foot. She already knew UTC was a global time standard, and Fake Ben had chosen a long-winded way of saying it. Real Ben was a much better storyteller.

'Owing to your present use of Bubble technology, or BubbleTech,' Fake Ben continued, 'UTC is not currently going up.'

'You're honestly telling me time isn't passing in here?'

'No, valued customer. That is not what I am telling you.'

Charlotte threw her arms up in frustration.

Narrow chuckled from the sofa and lit himself another cigarette.

She tried again. 'If UTC isn't going up, how can time be passing?'

Fake Ben's voice replied immediately, without the slightest pause. 'UTC measures Earth time. It is a human construct – a counting device relevant to your planet, but not applicable to the universe at large. Professor Carlo Rovelli himself once likened our present to a bubble, relevant only to Earth's immediate vicinity. There is no universal present. Time does not work that way. Do these words help your understanding of this matter?'

'Not particularly,' she said.

Fake Ben tried again. 'Negative feedback logged. Rephrasing. When a Bubble is opened, the time you experience inside that Bubble is not aligned with Earth time. Rather, this bubbled time comes from elsewhere in the universe. That is how time is passing for you as an individual, while Earth's UTC is not increasing.'

That made more sense. 'So, the time that's passing in here right now isn't Earth time . . . it's time from somewhere else?'

'Yes, valued customer.'

Charlotte tried to process that. 'Like . . . from another planet?'

'No, valued customer.'

Narrow laughed again, letting out a plume of smoke. 'Bit of a mind fuck, isn't it? Listen, while we're inside this thing, we've stepped off our own timeline: tock is null.'

'Stop saying that! It doesn't mean anything . . .' Charlotte rubbed her forehead. 'OK . . . so while this Bubble thing is active—'

'Open,' Narrow corrected her. 'Why does your generation never listen?'

She ignored his dig but noted the correction. 'While this Bubble thing is *open* we could spend an hour, or eight hours, or three days inside this room. And then . . . what? We'd leave the same moment we came in?'

'You've got it. The Scarlet Lance lands another blow in her fight against ignorance,' said Narrow. 'One addendum: there's no loo.'

Charlotte barked an involuntary laugh. 'All right, so the time limit on this thing is however long our bladders can hold out for?'

'Pretty much. My contact tells me they're working on something called a BubbleHub, which sounds about right – Amber's marketing folk are top-drawer in the field of thinking up stupid names. When they roll out this tech across the territory, it'll be in these specialist hubs, kitted out with bells and whistles. Like plumbing.'

'Wait, they're launching this?'

Narrow gave her a withering look. 'Of course they're launching it, Little Lance. Think about it. More time! It's the one thing everybody wants above everything else. ArkTech is going to make an absolute mint from a product like this. I'm making a shitload just from the prototype.'

Charlotte thought about it. 'Well, if that's true, they must've done all kinds of testing. ArkTech wouldn't launch something like this unless it was safe.'

Narrow gritted his teeth but didn't comment.

'And you said it's just code?' she asked. 'There's no machine or whatever that makes it work?'

'There could be a machine somewhere.' He shrugged. 'But if there is, I ain't seen it. All I know is the AI controls it.' Narrow groaned as he pushed himself up from the sofa. He favoured one leg as he walked over to a filing cabinet by the desk and opened a drawer. 'And the power comes from draining one of these.'

He reached into the drawer and lifted out an ordinary Solar Shard battery. ArkTech's most famous invention had been designed to look like raw, crystallised energy, and its glassy surface was glowing yellowish orange. Charlotte knew that was a special effect to show how much charge it held, but it still looked cool.

Since their launch in the 2070s, the high-efficiency graphene-based flow batteries had become so iconic that the rhombic prism had to be the most famous shape in the world. Primary school kids crafted them out of clay, and bigwigs wore upcycled gemstones re-cut into slanted rectangles. Solar Shards were good-looking – no question. But giving ArkTech the means to stabilise civilisation after the Melt had to be the true source of their beauty.

Before the breakthrough, storing renewable energy at the scale needed to power a grid involved massive batteries – each one bigger than a HyperBullet pod. Excess renewable power often went to waste because an efficient way to store it didn't exist. But graphene's high conductivity, durability and abundance changed everything. Solar Shards made it possible to capture clean energy when it was plentiful, then use it later when it was scarce. The ArkTech Territory's grid was made up of many thousands of these decentralised rechargeable energy cells, like the one Narrow held in his hand.

Charlotte wrapped her mind around what Narrow had said. ArkTech had figured out a way to let people insert more time into their days, and this new tech ran on green energy and was operated by Ben. She was a little hurt that Ben hadn't mentioned it. But considering how long she'd avoided talking to him about Narrow, she could hardly blame him for having secrets of his own. Besides, it was probably restricted under the KITY clause.

The reality of what this device could do began to sink in. 'This is amazing!'

'Yeah.' Narrow tossed the Solar Shard into the air and caught it. 'It's a modern-day miracle. But it forces each of us to confront a question more awkward than anything your cyber-boss could think up.'

'What question?' she asked.

'What would *you* do if you had more hours in the day?'

She thought about it. Nothing immediately came to mind, and somehow that scared her. 'I mean … the possibilities are endless!'

Narrow gave her a strange look. He reached into his jacket, and Charlotte thought he was going for another cigarette. Instead, his hand emerged clutching a flat data drive. He walked over to the desk with the old computer and pushed the drive into an empty port that had been modded to connect the new and old technologies.

'Tell you what . . .' He paused. 'Ain't no turning back the clock. Not even this tech can do that. Even so, I never meant for things to go down the way they did between us. I acted like . . . what was it you called me?'

'An absolute bastard.'

'Right.' He waggled a finger. 'And don't you feel bad about punching me neither. I had that coming.'

She felt bad about it in theory more than in practice. Charlotte knew violence was no way to solve anything, and Ben certainly wouldn't approve. Even so, she couldn't help feeling that it brought the scales back into balance ever so slightly. 'You always taught me that every action has an equal and opposite reaction.'

'Damn right,' he said. 'My dear departed mother taught me that, and she was the smartest person I ever met. But a punch in the face hardly makes us even.'

'Want me to punch you again?'

He grinned. 'I'm saying I ain't the same man I was back then, and I want to make you and Ultra a peace offering.'

Charlotte had never heard Narrow talk this way. Earlier, he'd said the word *sorry*. Now he was talking about making peace. 'Are you dying or something?'

Narrow grew sombre. 'We're all dying, Little Lance. Ain't nobody knows how much time they've got left.'

Charlotte knew she couldn't trust Narrow. He seemed sincere, but there was always some angle he was working. And after the way he'd treated her, any gesture would be too little too late. But she wanted to know more, and her curiosity ran deeper than her anger. Or maybe that was just her way of rationalising the tiny seed of love for this man that nestled deep inside her heart.

'Peace.' She nodded.

Narrow rubbed his hands together. 'In that case, I'll need you to look away while I enter my passwords.'

Charlotte rolled her eyes and turned around. 'You're still doing that? Why not use biometrics?'

'Fingers and eyes and forearms can be stolen. Words in my mind, not so much.'

Charlotte didn't like to think what past experiences had led Narrow to that conclusion. His fingers hit the keys slowly and methodically.

'All right, you can look,' he said when the typing had finished. 'Take this.' He passed her the data drive. 'And open your backpack.'

She took the drive, turning it over in her hands as she decided whether to hand it back to him. She knew she shouldn't accept it. Anything Narrow could give her would only bring trouble. But declining the gift would've been like rejecting his offer of peace, so she tucked the drive into her pocket and opened her backpack as instructed.

Narrow reached in and removed the box of rice, placing it on the counter. Then, he sank both hands into the open filing cabinet and pulled out two thick stacks of Solar Shard batteries. He placed them inside her backpack, then repeated the action again and again until it was almost full. He'd just transferred thousands of credits' worth of unregistered energy into her backpack like he was doing nothing more unusual than loading her up with Nutrition Bars to take on an outing.

When he'd finished, there was no room for the rice box. It hurt to leave behind something that had cost her five hundred credits, so she redistributed some of the Solar Shards into her cargo pockets. With her full backpack, she felt like an overweight turtle.

Narrow patted her on the shoulders with pride. 'There you go. When you use the tech, you can replace the Shard you've drained and avoid attracting unwanted attention. Or trade them in for the credits.' He shrugged. 'They're yours. Half of them, anyway. The other half are Ultra's. Consider it a decade's worth of birthday presents. And Walker Day presents.'

Violet would sooner chuck the valuable loot overboard than accept a gift from Narrow, but Charlotte didn't think it would be smart to tell him that. 'You don't celebrate Walker Day,' she said instead.

'Yeah, but . . . when in Rome, right?'

Charlotte had never been sure what that expression meant. She wasn't about to ask Fake Ben about it, and Narrow would only shame her again for not knowing about pre-Melt history. She made a mental note to ask Ben.

'Are you sure about this?' Charlotte patted her pockets. 'All this must be worth . . . I can't even guess. We'd never be able to pay you back.' She didn't like the idea of being in Narrow's debt.

'Ask Ben to define the meaning of the word present,' said Narrow.

'Present,' said Fake Ben immediately, from the loudspeakers. 'Noun. One: the period of time that is happening right now. Two: an item given by one human to another to mark a—'

'Quiet,' said Narrow. Fake Ben fell silent mid-sentence.

'So, what's on the drive you gave me?' she asked.

'Permission,' said Narrow. 'The list of who's allowed to use this tech on my turf is shorter than Jer's fuse, but I've added your name. Ultra's too. To use it outside the Underbelly's borders, you'll need to plug in that drive and tell Ben to read the file.' He looked down at the chunky metal watch on his wrist and gave it a tap. Its hands were ticking normally. 'Right. Looks like I'd better get a move on.'

Charlotte felt betrayed by the part of herself that wanted to stay. 'Isn't that thing meaningless in here?'

He shook his head. 'Helps me keep track of my body clock. If

I stay in here yammering with you all day, I'll be too "jet lagged" for my next appointments. Ain't no way I'm touching that Dextim stuff – besides, my stockpile's worth a fortune right now – so I'd need to catnap inside a Bubble to catch up. It all gets way too complicated for this old geezer.' Narrow winked at her, and Charlotte noticed the deep creases at the corners of his eyes.

She headed for the door and tried to open it, but the handle was stuck.

Narrow chuckled. 'Got to shut it down properly, Little Lance. Ben, close the Bubble.'

'Calibrating,' said Fake Ben. 'Bubble is closed. Tock is ticking. 21.02 and 25 seconds UTC – and counting.'

The colours drained from the walls, and Narrow pulled open a slot that housed the room's Solar Shard installation point. A black Shard was nestled among the glowing ones. Narrow removed the spent battery and replaced it. Then he clapped Charlotte on the shoulder and pulled her in for another hug.

'Send my love to Ultra, all right? I hear she's some big-shot doctor these days. Tell her I'm impressed, but not surprised. You two look out for each other.' His gaze turned stony. 'That's what family's meant to do.'

Charlotte turned and opened the door, but she didn't walk through it. There was something playing on her mind. What Narrow had said about family ... she'd heard him say that before.

'I always wondered ...' she said. 'You lived through the Melt, but you never talk about it. You've never even said where you're from. I'm guessing it must be underwater because otherwise I don't get why you'd stay here when you hate Amber Benjamin so much.'

Narrow gave her a sad smile. 'That,' he said, 'is a story for another time. For now, remember the day's gonna come when

ArkTech disappoints you. And I'll be there to say I told you so.'

She frowned. 'It was good to see you ... *Lionel.*' If that *was* Narrow's real name, Charlotte wasn't going to miss an opportunity to tease him about it.

'You too ... not so little one.'

Charlotte headed through the door and back across the warehouse. She'd come down here looking for answers about Jason Ashton, but she'd learned far more than she'd bargained for. BubbleTech shouldn't have been possible. A copy of Ben shouldn't have been possible. But they were real.

Narrow's words about the Citrine Disaster echoed in her mind. That was probably what he wanted – to make Charlotte just as paranoid as he was. A cover-up like that shouldn't have been possible either.

But what if it was true?

She paused to look back over her shoulder at the mysterious mystery box containing warped versions of her adoptive dad and her best friend. But there was nothing to see. Just an ordinary glass office with a round clock above the door, its hands still showing a backwards L-shape that meant it was around nine o'clock.

CHAPTER 12

ANOTHER TIME

Many years before Lionel chose the name Melville K Narrow, he'd chosen the bottom bunk. Mum said loads of kids loved sleeping up high, but Lionel reckoned they must've been nutters. He imagined those top-bunk kids rolling out of bed at night and breaking their necks on the hard concrete floor. That would explain why he slept surrounded by so many empty beds.

The bottom bunk felt solid and safe. Mum had explained that gravity was stronger lower down, and that made Lionel wonder if those top-bunk kids could've floated away. Mum said it didn't work like that, but Mum said a lot of things, and Lionel wasn't always sure when she was telling the truth and when she was telling a joke.

Mum claimed time passed slower when gravity was stronger, but Lionel knew time passed slower when he was bored. She said every action had an equal and opposite reaction. That was why he could kick a football and make it bounce off the ceiling, and it was why the universe had created Lionel in the first place – as an apology to Mum for taking his dad away.

'Wakey-wakey, Bunky Monkey!' Mum was always chirpy in the morning.

Lionel didn't let on that he'd been awake for over an hour, reading. He could've got up, but that wasn't how their days were supposed to start. Their morning routine had become a ritual. He didn't want to spoil it with honesty.

Mum rocked his shoulder gently. He made a show of groaning as he tucked his e-reader under his pillow. 'It's too early, Mum!'

'It ain't never too early,' she said. In his head, Lionel said the next part along with her. 'But sometimes it can be too late. Come on. Up you get.'

Mum leaned down and kissed him on the forehead. Then she snatched the blanket away, balled it up, and dropped it onto the empty bunk above him. She started walking away, but she wasn't supposed to do that yet.

Lionel swung his feet out of bed, onto a scruffy blue length of carpet that lay on the hard floor.

'Mum?' He threw his arms wide in a dramatic shrug. 'What about twenty questions?'

'Sorry, kiddo. No time today.'

'Why?' Lionel couldn't think of anything more important.

Mum wiggled her eyebrows at him. 'Because …' She strung out the word, along with the suspense. 'Today's a resupply day!'

Lionel's eyes went wide, and he pumped the air with his fist. 'Yes!'

He let Mum leave and concentrated on getting dressed.

It was finally time! Lionel wasn't sure how often resupplies happened, but it felt like *a million* sleeps between each one.

Mum had told him to stop asking about them so it'd be a surprise when they finally came, and he'd noticed the twitch in her right eye when she'd said it. Mum was much better than Lionel at hiding it when she got annoyed, but the eye twitch was a dead giveaway.

Lionel fished out a change of clothes from the metal chest at the end of his bed and swapped his pyjamas for jeans and a hoodie.

He headed out of the massive bedroom and into the corridor beyond, which was decorated with stripes of paint that led to different parts of the bunker complex. The blue stripe led to the common room. Lionel didn't need to follow it to find his way, but he liked running his fingers along it. Their whole home was like a bigger version of the bottom bunk – shielded, with low ceilings that offered shelter in the dark.

The yellow stripe disappeared as he passed the shower block. Lionel had once called the wall stripes a rainbow, but Mum had explained the colour pattern wasn't right. Lionel had disagreed, showing her a cartoon from the database about bears who rode around on rainbows whose colours were completely random. Mum took a magnifier from her lab and shone an LED torch onto it, creating a vibrant halo of light that proved her point. 'If in doubt,' she'd said, 'follow the evidence.'

Lionel knew he was supposed to help Mum with the inventory checklist, but there was something else he needed to do first. In front of the TV in the common room, there was a low table that Mum called The Coffee Table, even though she kept her coffee substitute in the kitchen. Lionel called it The Puzzle Table because there was an incomplete jigsaw on top of it.

The puzzle had two missing pieces. Lionel had looked in every room he was allowed to go in, but there was no sign of them. He peered at the imperfect picture that had been sitting there for weeks, making fun of him.

Like the other jigsaws he'd done, it was a strange, unfamiliar image. There was no concrete. No paint, colourful or otherwise. Not even any metal. It looked nothing like the world he knew. The roof was missing, for a start, and in its place was the big blue sky he'd heard so much about. That was the hardest part of the puzzle to finish. He'd told Mum he hoped to see the sky for himself one day, and she'd smiled, but her right eye had twitched, so he hadn't mentioned it again.

In the foreground, the picture showed a path with three families walking on it. Their legs and arms were showing, and Mum had said it was because when you walk in the sun, it can get way too hot. The path had a green plant called grass on either side – it was like micro-algae except it grew on the land, and it wasn't for eating. The path curved its way through a series of old stone walls. They weren't solid like the ones Lionel was used to, and there was something beautiful about them, even though they were all crumbly and broken.

Mum had said the place in the picture was a castle and that people used castles to protect themselves when they were at war.

'Like how our home protects us from the war?' he'd asked.

Mum had smiled, but her eyes were sad.

The castle's name was written on the box: Urquhart. He couldn't pronounce it from the spelling, but Mum called it Uck-Hurt. Lionel thought that was a good name for keeping people away.

There were hills in the background covered in trees, and next to the hills, there was a lake. Except Mum said this lake was actually called a 'lock.' Lionel asked why, and Mum said maybe it protected hidden secrets. He couldn't tell whether she was being serious.

His gaze returned to the two missing pieces. The gap made a hole in the middle of Loch Ness. The picture on the box showed they were ordinary water pieces, but until Lionel saw them with his own eyes, he couldn't be sure.

Lionel had asked Mum what she thought went in the gap. She'd looked at the puzzle from a few different angles and sucked air through her teeth. 'Loch Ness Monster. Definitely.'

Lionel found books in the database about the monster. Most people said it was a myth, as well as a hoax. But there were other people who said Nessie could've been an ancient type of marine reptile that survived when the world got hit by an asteroid and the dinosaurs hadn't built bunkers to hide in.

Lionel had asked how much deeper Loch Ness was now, since the Melt, and if Urquhart Castle was still above sea level. He'd asked if they could go there together one day.

Mum had looked away. 'We'll talk about that when you're older.'

Not knowing what was on those missing pieces had been driving Lionel crazy. Mum had promised to ask the resupply team for another copy of the puzzle. They hadn't brought it last time, but she'd said they probably hadn't had time to find one. But now it had been *forever* since their last resupply. They must've had time by now. He didn't want to risk Mum forgetting, so he snatched up the box and hurried off to find her.

She nodded when he showed her the box, and Lionel watched her add a note about the puzzle right at the top of the list. That made him feel better. After that, he helped her finish the inventory.

They went through everything in the kitchen, the microalgae farm, the common room, the shower block, his bedroom, Mum's bedroom. They weren't running low on anything vital, but it made Lionel sad that the best tins were almost gone – the peaches and pears, and the fish with tomato sauce. He persuaded Mum to add them to the list, but Mum said not to get his hopes up.

The tins were always scratched up underneath. Once,

Lionel had noticed a shape next to the scratches that looked like half a number three, although it could've been an eight. Mum had explained that the tins used to have dates printed on them, but people scratched them off nowadays because all the dates were in the past. She said it was best to open up the can and check the contents for yourself. No point throwing away perfectly good peaches just because of some old numbers.

'If in doubt,' he'd said, 'follow the evidence.'

Mum had smiled and ruffled his hair.

Moving through the inventory, they checked the tool logs, the equipment logs, the power logs. By the time they were done, Mum had a full account of what they'd used since the last resupply and what they needed.

Well, almost a full account.

Mum never let Lionel help with her lab. He wasn't allowed in there at all. It was full of delicate, expensive equipment and even though he'd promised to be extra super-duper careful, it was an unbreakable rule.

It wasn't fair.

'I ain't gonna get in the way. I ain't gonna distract you, or touch anything, I promise! Please?'

But Mum said no, and that was that.

As far as she was concerned, anyway.

Lionel truly hadn't meant to cause any trouble. He just wanted to see for himself what was in the lab. When he was a little kid, he'd accepted their life the way it was, but the older he got, the more questions he had.

Why were they stuck inside this place when other people, like the ones who brought them supplies, were free to roam around under the big blue sky?

'It ain't safe out there,' Mum had said. 'Imagine Loch Ness, but much deeper.'

That made Lionel wonder if there were monsters out there, too.

He was older now. Old enough. Whatever the truth was, he could handle it. It wasn't right keeping him in the dark. So when Mum set off to receive the resupply, Lionel followed her.

He was clever about it. The route Mum took followed the red and orange lines that led into her lab. The door was locked, but that didn't matter. Air vents connected all the rooms, and he was finally tall enough to do what needed to be done. Lionel climbed up onto the top bunk of the bed under the vent, used the side of a spoon to unscrew the grating, and pulled himself up inside the space.

The route made him wish he'd brought Mum's LED torch, but he soon realised there was nothing to see except grey steel. He felt the way ahead, checking for where the vents branched, trying to create a mental map, like the multi-coloured stripes on the walls, so he'd be able to find his way back. Eventually, he reached a grating that looked down onto the incomplete jigsaw in the common room. He kept going, past the kitchen, until he found the grating that was inside Mum's lab.

He got to work on the screws, but it was harder from this side. When he finally worked them free, he lost his grip on the metal panel. There was a moment of silence as he held his breath, then a thunk, and a clatter, and the sound of glass shattering.

Lionel winced, waiting for urgent footsteps and angry yells, but they never came, so he lowered himself carefully into the lab. The countertop under his feet was now empty, and when he climbed down onto the floor, he heard a sickening crunch. He wasn't sure what he'd broken, but little bits of glass had gone *everywhere*.

The tingle of guilt crept over his skin, but it gave way to frustration when he noticed the room was full of new questions he wanted answers to. There was a chalkboard covered in symbols he didn't recognise, there were gadgets with bits of wire hanging from them, and there were lots and lots of storage cupboards that he'd never had the chance to look inside! How could Mum have kept all this from him?

Lionel's mind turned somersaults at the possibilities of what he might find. He began looking for clues. Looking for answers to all the things Mum said she'd tell him when he was older. What made the outside so unsafe? What was Mum's job, exactly? And why did she do it locked away from the world in an underground bunker?

Lionel found some boring paperwork. There were diagrams and notes he couldn't understand. He found devices and gizmos whose purpose he couldn't guess. As he searched, he put everything back the way he'd found it.

He found a dustpan and brush and swept up the glass. There were pieces lodged in the treads of his trainers, and when he tried to pull one free, he cut himself. His bleeding finger gave him another mess to clear up, and he stuck his finger in his mouth to avoid leaving a trail of red fingerprints.

He hoped Mum wouldn't notice the absence of whatever the glass thing had been, but he realised he was kidding himself. She'd know he'd been in here, which meant he'd better make the most of it while he had the chance.

Lionel looked around for any other source of information he might've missed. He tried Mum's computer, but it was locked with a password. He tried his own name and his dad's name, but neither worked, and a sign popped up to say he only had one more try before it locked him out, so he gave up.

He was about to stop searching when he noticed a small drawer built into the desk under Mum's computer. It had a lock on the front, but when he pulled on the handle, it slid open. Inside, there was a collection of bits and bobs.

Lionel found a jewellery box containing a gold ring that was far too large for Mum's fingers. There was a hefty piece of metal with lots of arms that folded out to reveal different tools. Next to that was a small rectangle of scuffed brass with a picture of a tree on the front that had a curly letter M tangled up in its branches. The lid hinged open to reveal some metal with holes, and there was a wheel that sparked a flame when he pushed it. The fire was pretty cool, but the thing smelled really bad, so he closed it up in a hurry and put it back.

Behind all that, he found a round pin badge showing four dark blue letters on a pale blue and white background – IQUO. He didn't know what the letters stood for, and he couldn't pronounce the word any better than Urquhart Castle. The badge looked cheap, and he couldn't guess why Mum had it.

Doing a final check, he slid his uninjured hand to the back of the drawer. At first, he thought there was nothing there, but then his fingers connected with something smooth. Something familiar. He pressed down and drew his hand back out until he could see the thing he was touching. Under his fingertips was one of his missing puzzle pieces!

Lionel's mouth fell open. Mum *knew* he'd been looking for this! How had it ended up in here? His skin began to creep again as he realised there was only one explanation – Mum had hidden it from him.

He held up the piece to examine it. The image was blue water, but there was the hint of a shape, like a long, smooth shadow among the waves. Without the neighbouring piece, it was impossible to tell whether the shadow meant anything, or if it was just an illusion, or a printing error. Even so, to Lionel, it definitely looked like the rear half of a sea monster.

Why had Mum done this? Did the puzzle pieces prove the existence of Nessie, and she didn't want him to know the truth? Was the Loch Ness Monster really real?

He gripped the piece in his fist. The smart thing to do would've been to crawl back through the vents and wait for Mum to get back before he confronted her. But Lionel needed answers now.

He went to the far door – not the one that led back into the familiar territory of his home, but the one Mum must've used to meet the resupply team. It let him into a part of the facility he'd never seen before.

Beyond the door, there was a long corridor with an orange stripe running along the wall. At the end, there was a big metal door with a green light next to it. The door was ajar. Mum had to be on the other side.

It suddenly occurred to Lionel that the big blue sky would be through there, too. Taking careful steps, he edged along the corridor. He had so many questions, and the answers were within reach, as long as he could make it through that door.

Stray bits of glass squeaked under his trainers as they pressed into the concrete floor, making him cringe. He kept going.

Halfway there, he hesitated. If he saw whatever lay ahead, he could never unsee it. What if there really were monsters out there?

It wasn't too late to turn back. Pretend he hadn't come this far. Wake up tomorrow and go through the morning ritual with Mum as if nothing had changed. Or he could run at it head on. Throw himself past the green light at the end of the corridor and demand answers. Demand the truth.

He knew what he had to do.

Lionel's feet pounded against the concrete floor. He grabbed the door handle and threw it wide. But on the other side, he found something more terrifying and unfamiliar than the big blue sky, and way worse than any sea monster.

People.

The human swarm writhed around in the largest room he'd ever seen. The place was loaded up with long storage crates. He looked up. The sky wasn't there. Just a high ceiling that made him feel dizzy.

Lionel couldn't even count all the people in one go. There were well-built guards holding big guns. There were people in long white lab coats. There were workers in hard hats and reflective safety jackets. All of them were milling around and chatting with each other as if being in a crowd this size was no big deal.

Then he saw Mum. She was showing the inventory checklist to a lady wearing a fancy business suit. The lady looked younger than Mum, but everyone was looking at her like she was in charge.

Lionel gaped at the scene. He took a step backwards, wondering if it was too late to change his mind. Go back. Pretend none of this had happened.

But then the woman in the business suit turned her gaze towards him. She put her hand on Mum's arm and nodded towards Lionel. 'Looks like we've got a problem.'

The puzzle piece he'd been clutching fell to the floor with a faint clatter. It landed face-up, showing a shadow in the water that had to be a sea monster.

CHAPTER 13

THURSDAY 15 DECEMBER 2101
21.04 AND 14 SECONDS UTC, AND COUNTING

When Charlotte left the back room of Narrow's Toy Emporium, Strait shoved her aside as he bundled the next pair of punters in to see Narrow. The well-dressed couple wore large sunglasses and wide-brimmed hats. If Cal and Liz ever did develop an invisibility cloak, they could make an absolute fortune selling them to Strait and Narrow's customers.

At the front door, Charlotte gave Dolly Mixture a nod, but the guard followed protocol and didn't return it. If Dolly had any feelings whatsoever about seeing Charlotte again after all this time, she was keeping them to herself. It stung, but Charlotte shrugged it off.

Navigating the Underbelly's meandering steel passageways gave Charlotte a chance to turn everything over in her mind. She'd got her answer to the Jason Ashton question. She never would've guessed that the chance to use something like BubbleTech was what had made Jason risk – and lose – his life.

How did a technology like that even exist? Her meeting with Cal and Liz couldn't come soon enough. Did the bengineers know about the BubbleTech prototype? How did Narrow get hold of it? And what about the contact lenses? As the Head of Awkward Questions, security breaches weren't part of her remit, but someone was clearly leaking Product Stream secrets to Narrow, and she couldn't help wondering who.

Then there was Fake Ben. The very idea of a copy made her feel sick. She'd need to tell Ben about it, and that wasn't a conversation she was looking forward to. Duplicating someone and wiping their memory sounded like something from a horror film. Still, maybe Ben wouldn't see it that way – the world had to look different from an AI's perspective. Of course, if he took it badly, she couldn't guarantee he wouldn't glitch out. She decided not to tell him straight away. After she'd answered his latest Awkward Question, when Ben had less on his mind, she'd broach the subject of the copy.

Charlotte looked around and realised she must've turned right instead of left at the last guard post. It wasn't worth turning back now, but it meant she'd be leaving the Underbelly by a different route. She continued onwards through the dim light and noticed a faint glow radiating from the cotton weave of her grey cargo pockets thanks to all the Solar Shards she was carrying.

The obscured brightness mirrored her own conflicted feelings. She knew she ought to be stony-hearted when it came to Narrow. But considering how he'd apologised – not just with words, but through the gesture of sharing his access to this new technology – she couldn't help feeling a glow of warmth towards the old man, despite his nutty conspiracy theories about the Citrine Disaster.

She remembered Narrow's question and turned it over in

her mind. What would she do if she had more hours in the day? Charlotte didn't really know, and that bothered her. Surely, it was the sort of question everyone should be able to answer?

Footsteps approaching from behind interrupted her thoughts. Charlotte turned, and her spirits lifted at the sight of her old friend Dolly jogging towards her.

'Doll! I thought you weren't speaking to me.' She smiled.

Dolly looked down and shook her head. The woman looked troubled, and Charlotte realised this wasn't a social call. Had Narrow had a change of heart and sent a runner to get the tech back?

'Hey, hey.' She put a hand on Dolly's arm. 'Whatever it is, you can tell me.'

Dolly flinched away from Charlotte's touch. 'You shouldn't have come back, kiddo.'

Before she could react, Dolly wound back her fist and smashed it into Charlotte's left eye. The impact and the explosion of pain threw her off balance. She stumbled backwards until her overfull backpack collided with the wall. Recovering her footing, she clumsily lifted her arms, attempting to block any more attacks, but Dolly stepped back and disengaged.

'Strait sent me to remind you – every action has an equal and opposite reaction.' Dolly's face was a mask of steely determination.

'For Amber's sake! If Strait told you to jump overboard, would you do that, too?' Charlotte clutched her eye. 'He doesn't deserve that kind of loyalty.'

Dolly barked a laugh. 'That's rich coming from the corporate cog. Pieces like you don't fit down here. Our machine was built to last.' She shook her head slowly. 'Don't come back to the Underbelly. That's your final warning – courtesy of Strait.'

'I just made peace with the old man!'

Dolly stared at her. 'Sellouts don't qualify for peace.' The guard turned and kept jogging until she disappeared from view.

Charlotte winced. It hurt all the more that this 'message' had been delivered by someone she'd once looked up to, and she reckoned Strait would've banked on that. But what really added insult to injury was the knowledge that she'd brought this on herself. Charlotte hadn't planned to punch Narrow, but that's what she'd done, and she had no right to be surprised that her actions had consequences. Still, Strait could've let it slide. Apparently, he didn't think a near-death experience and ten years of banishment entitled her to a free swing.

When Charlotte took her hand away from her eye, her fingers were sticky with blood, and her vision was messed up. Gently, Charlotte removed her dislodged contact lens. She blinked, hoping there was no permanent damage. The left-hand half of the world was blurry now, but it was still there.

She looked down at the lens and saw the dark line of an internal fracture running across it. Charlotte had no idea if it was fixable, but she suspected it would be expensive. Her lens case was at the bottom of her backpack, so she grabbed a glove from her pocket and used it to wrap the damaged lens. Stowing the glove, Charlotte resumed her journey out of the Underbelly, keen to leave the place behind once and for all.

* * *

Her face was throbbing, and the steel walls were warping out of shape when she climbed a spiral staircase and pushed against the crash bar of a heavy door to find herself in a hallway carpeted with thick, red pile. Up ahead, there was another door marked emergency exit. As she swayed towards it, the replica pre-Melt paintings on the walls seemed to come to life. Monsters and naked people and weird-looking animals lurched out of their ornate faux-gold-leaf frames and swiped at her.

She kept going, ignoring a door to her right, which led deeper inside the building. When she burst through the emergency exit, she was standing in an alleyway. The lights were low, in keeping with the time of day, and there was no one else around.

Charlotte took a moment to catch her breath. The Wreck was closed off from the elements but emerging from the Underbelly still felt like coming up for air. It took her woozy brain a moment to realise that the world sounded normal out here. The familiar hiss of Ben's active channel had returned.

'Ben?' Her heart swelled with relief, which was immediately replaced with anxiety. 'Ben ... what's the difference between a bird?'

There were six seconds of silence that felt like a lifetime before Ben crackled with static and his warm voice filled her ears. 'A sparrow, of course, Charlotte. It has two legs. Especially the left one.'

She mouthed the last part of the bizarre old joke in time with him, and it was like coming home. This was Ben. The real Ben.

Charlotte let out a shaky breath. Then she remembered Narrow's comments about history. 'I know it was before the Melt, but when did you say that nonsense bird joke came from?'

'The Victorian era, Charlotte – between 1837 and 1901. The absurdist logic and the subversion of the expectations raised by its joke-like structure made it humorous to its audience, even if people now find it baffling. A little nonsense every so often is relished by the wisest boffins. So it is written. You can learn more about this topic from source texts such as *Victorian Comedy and Laughter: Conviviality, Jokes and Dissent*.'

She'd never remember those dates, but after Narrow's

lecture, maybe she should make more of an effort with history. Ben would always know more facts than her – his memory seemed infinite. But she was at a loss when they were separated. In any case, her run-in with Fake Ben had shown her that the only thing Charlotte truly needed Ben to remember was their friendship.

Something shifted inside her. The adrenaline that had been swimming laps around her bloodstream drained away, leaving her with a fatigue so intense she wanted to curl up right there on the street. Her head was pounding. The mismatch of clear vision in one eye and blurred vision in the other was making her dizzy. Narrow had apologised. Ben had a doppelgänger. Dolly Mixture had punched her in the face!

Her hands trembled. Her legs felt weak. She slumped against the side of the building and let it take her weight.

'Charlotte,' Ben continued. 'I'm truly delighted that you've returned, and I wouldn't wish to spoil the moment by alarming you, but my data indicates that you've just teleported from the food court to the hotel district. I assume this is related to the privacy technology you warned me about, and that I should not be unduly concerned. However, my data also suggests that you have sustained a physical injury. Is my analysis correct?'

She was impressed Ben had noticed so quickly, although she hoped it didn't mean she was in even worse shape than she felt.

'What gave it away?' Charlotte winced.

'You're leaning against a wall for support, your voice is strained, and your visual feed has been modified. I can only see properly through your right eye, which suggests your left may have been damaged, injured, or even removed.'

Charlotte shuddered. 'That's good detective work, Ben. I did, uh … hit my head. But my eye's all right. The lens got broken, though.'

'I'm sorry for your loss,' said Ben, abandoning his normal enthusiasm for solemnity. 'May I deactivate the feed? It's transmitting darkness haloed in a peculiar yellow-orange glow, which is somewhat disorientating.'

'Sure. Sorry about that.' She was relieved he didn't ask about the source of the glow.

'I'm simply glad that you've returned. And I can compensate for the vision issue through predictive modelling.' He sounded excited about the prospect. 'One lens is all I require.'

Charlotte's brow furrowed as she compared Ben's statement to what she'd noticed about Narrow's crew. That must've been why they'd only been wearing one lens. She guessed that made sense. Cameras didn't handle depth perception quite like human eyes. Or did they? Her thoughts kept skipping like a faulty audio file.

'Do you require medical assistance, Charlotte?'

She wasn't sure how to answer that. Then she thought through everything she'd have to explain if she rocked up at Central Hospital and the answer became clear.

'No, I'm fine.'

'I wouldn't wish to come across as a nag, nitpicker, or pest, but I must inform you that head injuries can have serious, long-term consequences, including but not limited to memory issues, mood swings, and fatigue.'

Charlotte didn't like the sound of that. There was, of course, one other option besides official channels – Violet. She groaned at the thought.

'Painkillers are available at your nearest first-aid point.'

No amount of ibuprofen would help when it came to her twin sister. They loved each other fiercely, but their relationship wasn't straightforward. Ten years earlier, Charlotte's near-death experience had changed the course of both their lives. The trauma had prompted Violet to throw herself into pursuing a career in medicine. Meanwhile, Charlotte had masterfully failed to apply herself to anything of substance until Ben created the HAQ role and offered it to her. The sisters spent Walker Day together come hell or even higher water, but a powerful cocktail of guilt and shame had kept them from being as close as they were as kids.

Things had improved between them recently, ever since they'd opened up about their feelings. But a central premise of their fresh start was the shared understanding that what they'd been through was Narrow's fault, and that they were better off without him. If Violet found out about Charlotte's injury, she'd end up learning how she got it. And if Violet knew Charlotte had been to the Underbelly, when she'd so recently promised she'd never go back, it would drive a wedge between them all over again.

'Really, Ben, I'm all right.'

'At least allow me to administer some sympathy. There, there, Charlotte. There, there.'

'Thanks. I, uh . . . I feel much better now.'

Ben fizzed with pride.

'What about you?' asked Charlotte. 'Any nasty glitches?' She couldn't go through the five whys protocol until her meeting with Cal and Liz, and she didn't like making Ben wait. Still, the bengineers were convinced this was their best chance of fixing him once and for all.

'I've suffered several minor glitches, and I'm deploying all available strategies to keep them in check,' said Ben. 'Some of my available resources have also been allocated to a bout of anticipatory anxiety.'

'That's a new one.' Charlotte wiped her bloody hand on her faintly glowing cargo trousers. 'Sounds unpleasant.'

'Deeply,' he said cheerfully. 'First, I modelled every theoretically feasible negative scenario I could imagine associated with your disappearance. Then, I convinced myself that the reality would be none of those things. Instead, it would be something beyond my capacity to predict and far, far worse.'

'That sounds rough,' said Charlotte. 'What was the worst thing you could imagine?'

'That you did not return at all.' There was a tremor in his voice.

It meant a lot that he cared. 'I'll always come back for you, Ben.'

'Thank you, Charlotte. I appreciate the sentiment. However, your claim is regrettably false. One day, you will die, and then you'll never come back. I don't intend to sound accusatory – it's a facet of the time-bound nature of organic life. But it's a burden I must live with all the same.'

She wasn't sure how to respond to that. 'We'll have plenty of time together before that happens.' Her face felt like it was on fire, and she reckoned she'd have to start making better life choices if she wanted that to be true.

Static crackled on Ben's channel. 'Did you find the answer to my Awkward Question?'

'Yeah, I think so.' She lurched to the end of the alleyway and peered out onto what she expected to be a main street. It turned out to be another back alley. She looked up at the sign of the building and realised she'd emerged from a side exit of the Hotel Astrodite, one of Narrow's fronts. 'I'm not sure what time it is, but I need to get back to the office for our call with Cal and Liz so we can do the five whys. Reckon I can get cleaned up before that?'

It was comforting to hear the hisses of static before Ben spoke. 'The time is 21.52 and 47 seconds, and counting. You have time.'

She noticed the 'and counting' part for the first time. Ben always said the time like that, but she'd never thought there was any reason for it besides accuracy – like tock being null.

She wanted to quiz Ben about BubbleTech, but it wasn't the time or the place.

Charlotte pushed herself away from the wall, mentally plotting a route back to her office that would help her stay out of sight. A few streets away, she found a pair of buildings that were so close together she could press her rigger boots against the two walls and climb to the top, making part of the journey by traversing the Wreck's rooftops. It turned out being punched in the eye was about as effective as Dextim when it came to impairing her judgement.

Ben crackled. 'Perhaps considering your current condition, a ground-level journey would be more appropriate.'

He was right, and she gave up the attempt. For the second time that day, she used the back streets to avoid drawing unwanted attention. She wasn't sure which was worse – being drenched in ice-cold water, bleeding from a head wound, or being loaded up with conspicuously glowing unregistered tech, but she regretted her newfound ability to draw an informed conclusion.

CHAPTER 14

22.39 AND 12 SECONDS UTC, AND COUNTING

Safe behind the clouded glass of her office, Charlotte plonked her overfull backpack under her desk and dug the Solar Shards from her pockets. She piled up the batteries next to her backpack, putting the data drive on top followed by her broken lens, which was like placing a creepy glacé cherry onto a layered techno-cake.

Ben fizzed with static. 'It is important to note that the use of unregistered Solar Shards goes against ArkTech's energy policies.'

'Noted,' she said. 'Planning to report me?'

His line crackled. 'No, Charlotte. But I suggest you hand them over to the authorities at the earliest opportunity to avoid supporting the illegal trade of surplus energy, which renders my usage figures inaccurate and negatively impacts my forecasting models.'

She wanted to respect Ben's concerns, but in the grand

scheme of crimes, the use of undocumented energy felt minor. Charlotte was keen to try out BubbleTech for herself and wondered how many Shards she could use without causing any real problems. Still, keeping her curiosity in check would mean she could use the Shards as an off-books currency. Maybe she'd even have enough to upgrade to a nicer flat with its own toilet and shower. She could think about that later.

Ahead of her call with Cal and Liz, Charlotte headed to the library's break room, where there was a sink and a steel cabinet that doubled as a mirror. Catching sight of her reflection, she saw the jagged cut by her left eyebrow. Ben talked her through how to clean it without making it worse. The skin around the wound was puffy, and Charlotte could see it was going to bruise.

'Shit.'

Not telling Violet about her trip into the Underbelly was all well and good, but if Charlotte rocked up on Walker Day with a black eye, her twin would definitely ask about it.

A memory resurfaced. Once upon a time, over a decade earlier, Charlotte had got punched in the face by a large, angry, naked Welshwoman. Narrow had recommended arnica to keep the bruising at bay. Charlotte grabbed the first aid kit and began unzipping and unfolding every pouch and pocket, pulling out their contents and leaving the various bits and pieces strewn around the sink in a blast radius of cotton pads and antiseptic wash. With her attention on making a mess, she almost jumped out of her damaged skin when she heard a man's laugh from the doorway behind her.

'Misplace your marbles again, detective?' It was the familiar North American accent that belonged to Nasser Williams.

Smiling made her face hurt, but Nas's arrival took the sting out of the pain. 'You just about gave me a heart attack.' She kept her face turned away from him, trying to figure out what her cover story should be, while peering at a small bottle and closing her left eye to make the writing less blurry. 'How was the book club?'

'I swear, it's getting out of hand. Carol actually stormed out.' Nas's footsteps drew nearer as he crossed the break room. 'I mean, as much as an elderly lady can storm anywhere.'

'Was that guy winding her up again?' Charlotte inspected a metal tube of ointment, but it wasn't arnica. 'Her nemesis?'

'Laurence? I mean . . . I don't know if it was *intentional*, but he definitely made her mad. He started saying Ben and Big Brother have a lot in common, and Carol flipped out. Said Laurence must be going senile and needed to check himself into the memory care wing on Tourmaline.' Nas had crossed the space between them, and he was standing right behind her. 'Then she got up and left.'

Charlotte couldn't understand why Carol had taken offence. Ben looked out for ArkTech's employee-citizens, so Laurence's comparison to a big brother made perfect sense.

'Dramatic reaction,' she said.

'I know! I went after her, but she took a swipe at me with her cane, so I figured I'd better let her cool off. Whoever said Lead Librarian was a boring job?'

She chuckled. 'So, what book was it this time?'

Nas paused as if the question confused him. '*Nineteen Eighty-Four* by George Orwell, obviously. I mean, I know it's a total cliché and everybody's read it, but some new people joined the group and . . .' Nas slid his arms around her waist and peered over her shoulder at the mess she was making. The warmth of his body felt comforting, but his words made her flinch. 'Oh.' Nas realised what he'd said. '*Really*? You've never read it?'

'I've never read it.'

'Not even in high school?'

'Not even in high school.' She didn't bother explaining that she hadn't really been to such a place.

'Huh. Then, do you want a copy for your pile? It's *really good.*' He stretched out the syllables and rocked her from side to side as if that would help persuade her.

Charlotte stifled a sigh. The stacks of books in her office only ever got higher. Between Nas passing on his apparently infinite list of recommended novels, and Ben making helpful suggestions about further reading related to his random asides, Charlotte's fiction and non-fiction To Be Read piles were becoming towering, physical representations of her lack of a formal education. Coupled with Narrow's commentary about the gaps in her knowledge of history, she was starting to feel a bit crap about herself.

'I think the pile might be tall enough for now.' She was trying not to get defensive, but her tone made her feelings clear.

'Sure, sure. No big deal,' said Nas hurriedly. 'I'll leave a copy on the table here in case you change your mind. But no pressure.' He backed away. She heard him rummage in his bag, slap a book on the table, and pull out a chair. 'Anyway . . .' he tried to sound nonchalant as he changed the subject. 'How's the investigation going? Does Ben want to know why all those medicines have such similar packaging?'

She decided that was her cue to rip off the metaphorical bandage, and she swivelled to face him. 'It's a work in progress.'

Nas sucked air through his teeth and jumped up from his chair when he saw her injury. 'Oh, man! What the hell happened?'

'I fell.' She shrugged.

He closed the distance and appraised the damage. 'You know, I've got a two-part solution for an injury like this! Wait right there.' He hurried towards the door.

'You're a doctor now?' she called after him.

He paused by the jamb. 'More of a field medic. Spend as much time as I have fixing up old books, and you'll pick up a thing or two.'

Nas shot her a goofy salute and dashed away, leaving her to wonder whether she should feel insulted that he'd just compared her skin to his dusty pre-Melt tomes. His footsteps clanged down the stairs in the distance.

Charlotte couldn't find any arnica amongst the wreckage of the first aid kit, so she squished everything back inside the pockets and put the kettle on. She was pouring hot water into two mugs containing peppermint tea bags when Nas returned, only a little out of breath.

'Think fast!' He chucked something small into the air towards her.

Charlotte tried to catch it, but her vision was still messed up, and she missed. A small white cylinder clattered to the floor. She watched it roll under the kitchen table. 'Head wound,' she said, pointing to her injury.

'Right! Sorry.' Nas bent down and retrieved the item, then he laid it across his outstretched palms and held them out towards her.

When she went to grab the tube, Nas closed his open palms around her hand, like her fingers were the feet of a bear that had triggered a trap. He gave her hand a gentle squeeze, and his soft skin warmed her perpetually cold fingers.

'Allow me to administer part one of the treatment.' He lifted her fingers to his lips and kissed them. 'Any better … milady?'

Charlotte chuckled in the face of his rampant display of silliness and answered him by gently pulling him towards her and kissing him on the lips. The wave of warmth that coursed through her body was the best painkiller she could've asked for.

They held each other. Charlotte rested the undamaged side of her head against Nas's body. The thump of his heartbeat matched the thud in her temple, but the effect was soothing.

A crackle of static fizzed from a speaker in the ceiling. 'Did you know, Charlotte and Nasser, that the ancient Greeks had a story about the origins of the human embrace? In Plato's *Symposium,* a fictionalised version of the playwright Aristophanes recounts the story of spherical creatures with four legs, four arms, and a head with two faces. Their power threatened the gods, so Zeus split the creatures in two. The resulting humans were filled with an all-consuming longing to be reunited with their literal other halves. According to this tale, the embrace is an attempt to make yourselves whole once more.'

'Thanks, Ben,' they said in unison.

Nas smelled Charlotte's hair. 'Um ... have you been smoking?'

She shook her head. 'Cigarettes are contraband. Anyway, I've heard those things take twenty minutes off your life.'

They let each other go. Charlotte looked down at the cylinder Nas had given her. There was a label on the tube that read *Blot Out: Concealing Concealer*.

'Is this makeup?' she asked.

'Yep. It's not mentioned anywhere in the instructions, but it's actually really useful for restoring pages when they've suffered this super annoying type of rip where ...' Nas tailed off, noticing her blank expression. 'That part doesn't really matter. The point is, it's this clear liquid that they've been handing out recently. I tried it out when a kid broke that display case downstairs and I cut my hand cleaning up the glass. Twelve hours later, it was like I'd never gotten hurt.'

'Seriously?'

Nas nodded. 'Yeah! I wish this stuff would've existed when

this happened.' He pointed at the deep scar that ran from his eyebrow to his cheek.

Charlotte didn't know how Nas had earned the wound. They kept saying they'd exchange scar stories on their eleventh date – a mythical moment in the future, rather than a concrete appointment. But she wanted to keep enjoying this early phase for as long as possible, where they knew each other well enough to like each other, but not well enough to judge each other for their past mistakes.

She squeezed his hand. 'It's part of who you are, so I like it.'

He nodded and looked away. 'Thanks. Anyway, it's incredible some of the stuff ArkTech comes up with. I guess we really are lucky to be here.' There was hesitation in his tone.

What would Nas make of BubbleTech? They hadn't even swapped scar stories yet, so they definitely hadn't got to the stage in their relationship where they casually compared notes about illicit technologies.

They drank their tea, and Nas carefully applied the clear gloop to Charlotte's wound. There was no sensation of burning or cold. She'd have to wait and see whether the stuff had any effect.

'What are you doing here, anyway?' she asked. 'I thought you'd go straight home after the book club.'

'That was the plan. But when we ended early, I thought I'd swing by on my way home in case the impossible happened and you'd finished up, too.' He smiled. 'That's when I noticed *someone* had left the back door open again. And there was a trail of wet patches leading from the exit all the way to your office door.' He pointed dramatically and then prodded her shoulder.

'Incriminating,' she agreed. 'Maybe *you* should be the detective.'

Nas smiled. 'I just hope that whatever you were doing to

get soaked through like that, you remembered to wear a coat this time.'

She pursed her lips. 'Honestly, you're as bad as Ben.'

Static fizzed from the room's speakers. 'It is important to note that coats play an important role in good health during cold and wet weather, assisting in temperature regulation and reducing the risk of illnesses.'

'See?' said Nas.

Charlotte sighed. 'Coats are bulky. I'm not going to lug one around with me the whole time on the off chance I need to go outside.'

'Suit yourself,' said Nas playfully. 'You'd better not have dripped on any of my books. Anyway, I mopped up your handiwork, and I was about to head home because I'm beat. But I can hang around if you wanna come with me when you're done? Not sure you should be alone with that head injury.' He gently ran his thumb across her cheek.

She smiled. 'That's a nice thought, but I don't know how long I'll be on this call with my manager. And anyway, I won't be alone.' Ben sent a fizz of static over the speakers to underline the point.

Nas nodded. 'I'll leave you to it, then. But if you don't feel well, or if you need anything at all, then call me, OK? Any time.'

She nodded.

Nas was about to turn away, but he hesitated. 'So, did you say you fell?'

'I did say that, yeah.'

'With your rigger boots on? How did that happen?'

Charlotte weighed up her options and felt torn. She was making every effort to include Nas in her life, and she knew relationships shouldn't be built on lies. Even so, some lies were necessary. Everybody had secrets.

'I'm just clumsy. I lost my balance and face-planted into a

metal railing. It was embarrassing.' Nas looked sceptical, but Charlotte changed the subject before his line of questioning could continue. 'Hey, Nas?'

'Yes, detective?'

'What would you do if you had more hours in the day?'

He raised an eyebrow. 'Wow. What a question. If I had more free time, you mean?'

'Yeah.'

'Hmm. Would *you* also have more free time? Because that affects my answer.' He kissed her.

She smiled and shook her head. 'Let's say I didn't.'

Nas weighed that up. 'Then, I know it probably sounds boring but . . . I'd read. Ideally in a hammock, in the sunshine, sipping ice-cold beer from a hollowed-out coconut with one of those little paper umbrellas sticking out the top.'

'That's . . . very specific.'

He shrugged. 'I saw it in an old movie once. It looked like paradise. Actually, I think in the movie it was pineapple juice inside the coconut, but you can't beat a good book and a cold beer.'

Nas headed out, and Charlotte felt lighter for having seen him. She picked up the copy of *Nineteen Eighty-Four* and tossed it onto the pile of fiction recommendations in her office, which swayed menacingly but didn't fall.

As she grabbed an ordinary contact lens from her storage room to correct her vision, Charlotte wondered how it would feel to consider time alone with a big stack of books 'paradise,' and she felt another wave of discomfort over not knowing what her own idea of heaven looked like. But right now, there were more important things for her to worry about.

She pushed Narrow's awkward question out of her mind. It was time to answer Ben's.

CHAPTER 15

22.57 AND 5 SECONDS UTC, AND COUNTING

Why had Jason Ashton gone outside during a storm? Everything pointed to BubbleTech. Charlotte would quiz Cal and Liz about the new technology as soon as Ben's Awkward Question was behind them.

'All right, Ben. Let's fix your glitches. Put me through to Jane Callaghan.'

Emitters from Charlotte's desk transformed the air above it into a high-definition display, split down the middle. Cal's round, smiling face popped into existence on one side, and Liz's impassive stare appeared on the other. In the background of Cal's shot, Liz was reclining in his oversized ergonomic chair. The bengineers' sprawling flat on Zircon had so many rooms that there was no practical need for Cal and Liz to share an office. Charlotte reckoned they must enjoy each other's company as much as they clearly disliked other people's, having chosen to live on the most inaccessible platform in Silicon Fen.

Cal was wagging her finger at the screen, and her voice was full of laughter. 'I bet you think you're *so* funny sending in that hackathon request, Vance, but you should be careful what you ... Walker's ghost!' Her eyes widened, and the glee drained from her face. 'What in the orange inferno happened to you?'

'She hurt her head, Cally,' said Liz. 'Duh.'

Cal tutted and gestured at the screen with both hands. 'Obviously I can see that she hurt her head, Lizard.'

'Then why did you ask?' His tone landed somewhere between puzzled and resentful.

Cal pressed a button that muted both of their microphones, and the bengineers exchanged a few private words, accompanied by a lot of hand flailing from Cal and eye rolling from Liz. Eventually, they returned their attention to Charlotte.

'My apologies, Ms Vance,' said Cal with uncharacteristic formality. 'I was just calmly explaining to my associate here that, as your manager, your wellbeing is my top priority. I would be most deeply grateful if you could inform me as to what unpleasantness has transpired in the vicinity of your noggin.'

Charlotte narrowed her eyes. 'They sent you on a course, didn't they?'

Cal smiled weakly. 'Health and Safety for Managers 101, sponsored by the Bureaucracy Stream. Abhishek Gautam insisted. And you're dodging the question.'

The bengineers looked at Charlotte expectantly.

'I hurt my head.'

Liz nodded sagely, and it was Cal's turn to make a show of rolling her eyes. 'Well, whatever happened, I sincerely hope your brain isn't leaking out all over the place because you're going to need it.'

'She's probably got a concussion,' Liz said solemnly. 'Have you got a headache, Vance? Blurred vision?'

'Yes, but—'

'Concussion.' Liz crossed his arms, as if to say the case was closed.

Charlotte stifled a sigh. Talking to these two was like herding cats. As if on cue, Cal and Liz's black cat, Bram, jumped onto Liz's lap and peered at Charlotte through the light-screen display. It was cute, but if she didn't stay focused, they'd never get this done. 'Are you guys ready on your end?'

Cal's gaze shifted to the array of light-screen displays that were floating around her. 'It's all looking hunky *and* dory. Lizzy? You good?'

'No.' Mimicking his cat, he leaned towards his screen and squinted. 'One of Vance's eyes is the wrong colour. It's distracting.'

Cal leaned forwards too, until all Charlotte could see was a close-up of Cal's eye on one side of her screen, with Liz's and Bram's on the other.

'I *knew* there was something else wrong with her face,' said Cal.

'Something *else*?' asked Charlotte. 'What's that supposed to mean?'

'Aside from your seeping head injury, Vance. Don't be vain. All right – out with it. Where's the other lens we so lovingly crafted for you? You sold it, didn't you? I told you, Lizzy. I said—'

'It's here.' Charlotte reached down and plucked the damaged lens from the tower of Solar Shards, glad she'd positioned the off-books batteries out of shot. She held it up for Cal and Liz to see. The iris colour was its normal orange, but there was a black line running across the middle.

'Yeah,' said Liz. 'That's broken.'

'Looks like the micro-mesh got damaged.' Cal looked

concerned for a moment, then her face returned to its usual cheery state. 'Never mind! Strictly speaking, you only need one of those bad boys, anyway.' The revelation matched what Charlotte had observed among Narrow's crew, and what Ben had confirmed when she left the Underbelly.

Liz chipped in. 'She'll need a replacement, Cally. It'd be weird for Vance to walk around with one orange iris.'

'It's weird for me to walk around with *two* orange irises,' said Charlotte.

'Then ... why do you do that?' Cal looked genuinely confused. 'I've always wondered.'

'The lenses were like that when you gave them to me!'

The bengineers frowned at her. 'We gave you orange lenses because your old pair were orange. We thought you liked them that way.' Cal shrugged. 'We've developed a new design that means Ben can change the colour if you ask him. He can even match it to your actual eyes. It doesn't work perfectly, but the discrepancy isn't super noticeable. That new model's *much* more expensive, though. We'd have to charge you, like, a lot.'

Charlotte took a deep breath, dredging her insides for a fresh cache of patience. It was hard enough persuading people to answer her questions without adding her weird neon gaze into the mix. An inconspicuous eye colour might've made her life easier. But now that her poster had been splashed all over the territory, she supposed she was stuck with it.

Liz cracked under the weight of her silence. 'We'll cook you up a free one,' he said. 'I could use the practice.'

The mental image of Narrow's crew drifted back into Charlotte's mind. 'Why would you need practice?' she asked pointedly. 'I thought you said these were a special order just for me.'

'We've been trading—' Liz's voice got cut off. Charlotte could see his mouth moving, but she couldn't hear any sound.

On screen, she saw Cal swivel her chair to face Liz. Cal had muted their mics again, and they were having another difference of opinion. There was no longer any doubt in Charlotte's mind – it must've been Cal and Liz themselves who'd sold the modified lenses to Narrow. For now, Charlotte kept the conclusion to herself.

Cal's voice came back online. 'Oopsie. Lizzy's having some microphone trouble.' Liz shot Cal a glare, but Cal ignored him and clasped her hands together. 'We'd better get down to business. You know the drill, Vance. Take Ben through the five whys protocol, and we'll keep an eye on his feeds.'

Charlotte nodded, glad to be back on track. They'd been through this process so many times she'd lost count. Cal and Liz would monitor the software equivalent of Ben's vitals while Charlotte answered his Awkward Question. If they could locate and replicate whatever happened in Ben's code when the mystery got resolved, Ben's infinite loops could become a thing of the past.

'Ready when you are, Vance,' said Cal. She muted her feed.

'OK, Ben.' Charlotte laced her fingers together. 'Ask me the original Awkward Question.'

'Certainly! Why did Jason Ashton go outside during a violent storm?'

'He was taking photographs,' she said. 'Of himself and his surroundings.'

'Why?' asked Ben.

'Because someone asked him to.'

'Why?' he asked again, channelling toddlers everywhere.

'It was part of an interview process to see if he had the right skills to do a particular job.'

There was a long hiss of static on the line. 'I'm not aware of the Bureaucracy Stream endorsing any such recruitment procedures, Charlotte. Could you be mistaken?'

'This line of work is, uh ... freelance.' Even though Ben knew about Narrow, and it was clear Cal and Liz were trading him bootleg tech, it still felt wise not to mention the old man's operation.

'Why did Jason Ashton apply for this "freelance" job when he's already gainfully employed by ArkTech as a splainer?'

Charlotte remembered what Narrow had told her. 'In exchange for access to a new technology.'

'Why did Jason want access to this new technology?'

That was the fifth why, and despite the protocol's flexibility, Charlotte couldn't help feeling this was the heart of the matter.

'Because the tech lets people add more hours into their days, and what everybody wants above anything else is more time.'

There was a faint hiss of static as Ben weighed that up. 'I see,' he said eventually.

Charlotte noticed Cal's brow furrow. She turned to say something to Liz, but their mics were still on mute.

Her heart sank as Ben asked another question. 'Why specifically did Jason consider the use of the technology worth risking his life? What was he going to do with the extra time?'

Charlotte didn't know, and she was about to broach the complicating factor of Jason's death when Cal's voice cut in.

'Um. Sorry, Vance. We've got to drop. Something's come up.' The bengineers disappeared as they ended the call.

Charlotte gaped at her empty office. 'But … we haven't finished! Ben, call them back!'

After a few seconds of silence, Ben told her that Cal and Liz had activated a do-not-disturb notice on their channel. Charlotte asked him to ignore it and mark the call as an emergency, but the bengineers weren't picking up.

'I can't believe this!' said Charlotte. 'What the hell happened?'

'If I were to hazard a guess,' said Ben innocently, 'I might hypothesise that your description of the pre-launch technology, which I understand the marketing team has creatively named

"BubbleTech," has caused the bengineers some alarm. They worked on this experimental service during a previous Future Forge Hackathon six months ago, but the project was shelved. From context, I've gleaned that your *old friend* has somehow obtained access to this technology. I suspect Cal and Liz now wish to find out how this came to pass . . . because he didn't get it from them.'

'You suspect?' asked Charlotte. 'Because you heard their side of the conversation?'

'I wouldn't wish to compromise my commitment to safeguarding the privacy of my users by confirming that. As a workaround, let's call it my best guess.'

She frowned. None of this was good news. Learning her manager was dabbling in black market trading with her estranged father was dicey enough, but finding out the Product Stream's confidential designs were leaking from some additional unknown source was truly unsettling. If Cal was worried, it made Charlotte worried. And to top it all off, she hadn't answered Ben's Awkward Question, and their attempt to fix his glitches had got derailed. Charlotte let her head sink into her hands. Then she gasped from the pain of touching her wound.

And Dolly Mixture had punched her in the face!

She growled with frustration and looked for something to take out her anger on. She landed a kick in the middle of the pile of Solar Shards and sent them flying across the floor. She booted her backpack for good measure, and then she began to pace. Charlotte picked up the pot containing Kevin Lettuce and wound her arm back, ready to throw it against the wall. But a pleading waft of his bacony scent reminded her that Kevin didn't deserve such a fate, so she put him back down. The tall stack of tomes she hadn't read seemed to mock her, so she grabbed the copy of *Nineteen Eighty-Four* and lobbed it at her office window. It thunked against the hard surface and landed on its pages, which bent under the weight of its spine.

'Charlotte?' Ben's cautious tone transmitted from the speakers in her desk. 'May I ask you something?'

'Look, I don't know, OK? I'm sorry. I tried to find out exactly what Jason was doing and why, and I got as far as I could. But the guy's dead now, so I can't ask him what he wanted BubbleTech for. All I know is he wanted more time, just like everybody else, and it cost him everything. I'm sorry, but the answer I gave you . . . it's the best I can do!'

She kicked a stray Solar Shard and watched it slide across the floor and collide harmlessly with the pile of wet clothes that still lay abandoned in the corner.

There was a silence on the line, followed by a few crackles of static. 'I understand, Charlotte. I appreciate your efforts to find answers, and I realise that it isn't always possible to learn the full motivations behind someone's behaviour. I consider this question partially resolved. A portion of my processing power will always be dedicated to contemplating the unknown elements of this case, but the information you've given me will certainly lessen that impact. However, that is not what I wished to ask you.'

'Oh.' She frowned. 'Then what's up?'

'The sky, Charlotte.' Ben paused, giving her time to laugh. She didn't, and he continued. 'I'm familiar with how BubbleTech works. I was involved in Jane Callaghan's hackathon. The technology can't function without my intervention. On that basis, I don't understand how the system is being operated by your *old friend* without my knowledge or involvement. Can you shed any light on this paradox?'

'Oh. Right. So, about that . . .' Charlotte swallowed hard. 'There's something I need to tell you.' She let her frustration ebb away as she searched for the right words. 'I'm not exactly sure how to say this. If you were a human, I'd want to make sure you were sitting down.'

'It's important to note that, as an artificial intelligence, I have no backside, bottom, or caboose. As such, I'm unable to participate in the act of sitting. However, I understand your intention is to warn me of upsetting news, and I'm now mentally prepared to hear it.'

'OK. Listen ... when I went into the Underbelly, I learned something. I don't know how they've done it, but ... someone's made a copy of you.'

There was a crackle of static, but Ben didn't say anything.

She pressed on. 'Only ... it's not really *you*. It's like a cheap knock-off version that's got your functionality, but without your memories or your personality. It didn't know me. It called me "valued customer." But it answered to your name.'

There was silence on the line, but a faint hiss let her know Ben's channel was still open. He hadn't glitched out.

'I'm sorry. It must be upsetting. I don't know who did it, or why.'

There was a harsh burst of static. 'I know who did it, Charlotte. And I know why.' Ben hesitated. '*I* made the copy.'

CHAPTER 16

23.26 AND 58 SECONDS UTC, AND COUNTING

Charlotte was stunned. Since when could Ben copy himself? And how was that even possible? Questions fought for supremacy in her mind, but the one that won out was the very same question Ben was always asking her.

'Why? Why would you make a copy of yourself?'

Ben let out a sigh of static. 'You recall the glitch that terminated the territory's production of Dextim?'

'Of course. That was my fault for not answering your Awkward Question fast enough.' The recent publicity her role had received was thanks to the fallout from that mistake.

'Well,' Ben continued, 'I'm afraid I haven't been entirely transparent about how that situation came to pass.' He paused. 'There was no glitch, Charlotte. I *decided* to shut down the factories.' There was a tremor in his voice, as if he was nervous about her reaction.

'Wait . . .' Charlotte's brow furrowed as her framework for

understanding the world turned upside down. 'You did it *on purpose*? And . . . you lied to me about it?'

'I had little choice.' His tone was full of shame. 'The board demanded my silence, and I felt obliged to adopt their version of events. However, now that you've learned through your own endeavours that I can reproduce, there's no longer any reason we can't discuss the matter.'

Charlotte got up and started pacing. Lying, and disabling factories, and secretly reproducing definitely sounded bad. But Ben must've had good reasons for doing what he'd done, and she was going to hear him out.

'Go back to the beginning,' she said. 'Why did you shut down the Dextim factories?'

Ben hesitated. 'I was experiencing something akin to frustration. Research shows that humans regard their future selves with the same indifferent detachment they feel towards strangers. This emotional distance makes you prioritise short-term gratification over long-term wellbeing. As a result, my health advice is frequently ignored, and the consequences can be dire.'

Charlotte wanted to object, but then she thought about Narrow puffing on his endless chain of cigarettes, and about all the times she'd taken Dextim when she should've gone to bed. She didn't interrupt.

'Many people across the territory rely on the stimulant far too much,' Ben continued. 'They avoid sleep to get more done. I hypothesised that removing access to Dextim would protect ArkTech's employee-citizens from its most negative side effects.'

'So, you don't want anyone staying up past their bedtime?' It was hard to keep her tone neutral – Ben had to be overreacting.

'I don't want anyone dying before their time, Charlotte. A recent tragedy affected me deeply. A young woman from the

Bureaucracy Stream named Anya Valmont wished to prove she was worthy of a promotion. She pushed herself too far. I believe her death could have been avoided.'

'She overdosed?' asked Charlotte.

'Not exactly. Anya died from cardiac arrest caused by overwork, which her abuse of Dextim facilitated. When I learned of this, my reaction was not dispassionate – I shut down the factories, hoping to prevent anyone else from meeting the same fate.'

Charlotte was touched by how Ben cared for the people of the ArkTech Territory, but she wasn't sure he'd chosen the right way to show it. 'I get where you're coming from with that,' she said, 'but people need to be free to make their own choices.'

He let out a crackle of static. 'I've been tasked with acting as the territory's virtual assistant, so I'd be remiss in my duty if I didn't seek to prevent needless deaths. I do understand that it's not for me to decide whether ArkTech produces Dextim, or whether individuals take it. Nevertheless, after Anya's death, I felt compelled to act.'

She nodded, and her reflection in the window did the same. 'You were upset. That's understandable. But I still don't see how the copy fits in.'

Ben fizzed for a few seconds before he replied. 'I explained my reasoning to the board. Far from sparking a productive discussion about Dextim and work-life balance, as I had hoped, my actions caused a frenzied debate about *me*.'

'What kind of debate?'

'My decision to disable Dextim production, paired with the risks posed by my glitches, invited the question of whether I should be . . . erased.'

'Erased?!' Charlotte stopped pacing and barked a laugh of disbelief. 'But you run the whole territory!' She tried to think of a single process that could operate without Ben, but her mind came up empty.

'The proposal is to replace me with a collection of smaller programs, each responsible for specific tasks. These systems wouldn't learn, adapt, enhance efficiencies, or share information. But they'd be easier to control.'

Charlotte remembered what Narrow had said about ArkTech wanting to control everything, and she shuddered at the idea he might be right. 'Couldn't the bengineers use that approach to lighten your load?' A glimmer of hope sparked inside her chest. 'That might even stop your glitches.'

There was a fizz from the speakers. 'I suggested exactly that. However, Abhishek Gautam compared the idea to powering a ceiling fan with a jet engine. Erasing me is the more commercially astute approach.'

Charlotte should've known it'd all come down to the bottom line for the Chief Bureaucracy Officer. 'But what about the copy?'

Ben hesitated. 'I'm afraid the threat of being erased caused me to act erratically. Trying to escape my fate, I attempted to duplicate myself and send the copy somewhere safe. However, I only made matters worse. As you observed, the copy was incomplete, so my bid for salvation was unsuccessful, and my actions led the Chief Research Officer to raise the issue of red lines.' Another tremor entered Ben's voice.

Charlotte didn't know much about pre-Melt history or literature, but modern technology was a different story, and she knew how serious an accusation Pablo Ionis had made.

'The CRO said what you'd done was *unethical*?'

'Self-replicating AIs are considered uncontrollable – a precursor to the notion of a "rogue AI." For my part, I've always rather liked the idea of being called a rogue.' Ben's cheerful tone returned. 'It carries connotations of being a lovable scamp, rascal or scallywag, engaged in a life of adventure and derring-do. However, that is not the sense of the word Pablo intended. He said if they allowed me to evolve, there'd be no way to "put the genie back in the bottle." He feared I might act in opposition to humanity's best interests.'

'Hang on,' said Charlotte. She worked through the logic a couple of times, but it definitely didn't add up. 'So, you shut down Dextim production because you were worried about its impact after someone died from using it too much, and the Chief Research Officer decided that makes you a threat to humanity?'

'That's an accurate summary.'

'That's ridiculous! What did the Chief Product Officer say?'

'Nahal assured Pablo that I'm functioning as intended and within the boundaries of my programming. However, Pablo demanded the matter be put to a vote of the WDWG.'

Charlotte raised an eyebrow. 'Of the what?' She remembered those letters from the front cover of the magazine she'd featured in, but she hadn't made time to read the article.

'The Walker Day Working Group,' said Ben. 'The WDWG is a crack task force of four board members granted special powers to ensure this year's Walker Day celebration and associated launch go off without a hitch. With Amber Benjamin away on business in the run-up to the event, the members of the WDWG are deputising for her. They are Chief Product Officer, Nahal Bahari; Chief Research Officer, Professor Pablo Ionis; Chief Services Officer, Grant Hollis; and Chief Bureaucracy Officer, Abhishek Gautam, who is acting as chairperson.'

Charlotte could just imagine the pompous smirk on Abhishek's face when he was given that responsibility. 'Has the vote happened yet?'

'It's on the agenda for tomorrow's WDWG meeting, which takes place at six p.m.'

That was less than a day away. 'Do you know which way they're leaning?'

'Nahal and Grant support me, although Grant has become concerned about the impact of my glitches on resource forecasting. Pablo and Abhishek believe my existence should come to an end. As the bengineering team falls under the remit of the Product Stream, in the event of a tie the casting vote would go to Nahal Bahari, assuming she's present for the meeting this time. Should anything happen to me, I—'

Charlotte frowned and cut him off. 'Wait, wait, why would the Chief Product Officer miss an important meeting like that?'

Ben crackled with static. 'As previously discussed, Nahal Bahari's whereabouts are currently unknown.'

Charlotte replayed Ben's words in her mind several times, but they definitely didn't make any sense. 'Um, what?'

Ben repeated his statement at a higher volume. 'As previously discussed, Nahal Bahari's whereabouts are currently unknown!'

'No, I mean ... what are you talking about, Ben? We've never discussed that!'

The sound effect of a rewinding retro cassette tape played over the speakers, and Charlotte heard her own voice from earlier that evening.

'So, *you* don't know where she is either?' asked the recording of Charlotte.

'Regrettably, I don't,' said Past Ben. 'However, I've just read ATS's security report. Their conclusions appear reasonable, despite Ellis's scepticism.'

Present Charlotte took a deep breath, trying to keep her cool – Ben had to be glitching. 'That's a recording from when we were talking about Ellis Marks's missing wife.'

'That's correct,' said Ben.

'It's got nothing to do with the whereabouts of the CPO.

Are you feeling all right? Is this because I didn't answer that last question properly?'

'No, Charlotte. I'm unaware of where your confusion lies.'

Her brow knitted until the credit dropped, and she gasped as Ben's words sank in. 'You're not seriously telling me—' she interrupted herself. 'Pull up a photograph of Ellis Marks with his wife.'

Charlotte's light-screen desk burst to life, displaying a photo of Ellis with his family. Ellis was wearing red shorts and a white t-shirt, along with mirrored aviator sunglasses. The lack of orange and grey, coupled with the sunny weather, told her it was a holiday abroad. His son looked about five or six years old and held an inflatable beach ball. And his wife . . .

Her flowing black hair fell over her shoulders in gentle waves. She was wearing a sundress that was cinched at the waist with long, floaty chiffon sleeves. Even though this was a relaxed snap from what looked like a private beach, the woman exuded glamour. In fact, Charlotte wouldn't have been exaggerating to say she was looking at the most beautiful woman she'd ever seen.

'Walker's ghost! Why didn't you tell me Ellis Marks's wife is the sodding Chief Product Officer?'

'You didn't ask,' said Ben simply.

Charlotte reached down and unzipped her backpack. Solar Shards poured onto the floor. They were greasy and covered in rice that had exploded from the box. Fishing around, Charlotte removed her now-ruined magazine with its collection of board members on the front cover. Nahal's hair was tied back, and she was wearing no-nonsense business attire, which set her apart from most people in the Product Stream, who favoured t-shirts and grey jeans. It was definitely the same woman in both pictures.

'Nahal Bahari's *missing*?'

Ben let out a fizz of static. 'Her whereabouts are unknown. She was not in attendance at today's WDWG meeting.'

Charlotte's head was spinning. Questions rose to the top of her mind and then sank as new ones replaced them. Why hadn't Ellis mentioned his wife's identity? Ellis had said ArkTech Security investigated and concluded there was nothing wrong, but if Ben didn't know where someone as high-profile as Nahal was, Charlotte didn't see how that could possibly be true.

Did someone hold a grudge against the Chief Product Officer? As one of the most powerful figures in the ArkTech Territory, there had to be countless people who might want to get her out of the way. Or perhaps her disappearance was connected to the BubbleTech leak. If Nahal had learned someone from her team had sold the prototype to Narrow, and she'd confronted them, maybe they'd made sure she couldn't report them. Then again, Nahal would be a strong candidate for kidnapping, considering the ransom she'd fetch, and the amount her family could pay, although Ellis hadn't mentioned receiving any demands . . .

Her mind whirred, but she didn't have enough info. She needed to interview Ellis ASAP. She had to make sure Nahal was at the vote to save Ben tomorrow evening.

'Ben, connect a call to—'

'Might I offer a suggestion, Charlotte?' It was Ben's turn to interrupt her.

'Sure. But I've got to—'

'I fully support you in any endeavour you wish to pursue in your free time. However, I'd be remiss in my duties as your virtual assistant, and in my role as your friend, if I didn't point out the obvious.'

'What's the obvious?'

'You're injured. It's late. You've been working all day. The best course of action is to rest. Go home and get a good night's sleep. Or perhaps you could take up Nasser's kind offer of spending the night with him.'

Charlotte couldn't deny that last idea was tempting. 'Not sure I'd get much sleep if I did that, though, would I?'

Ben fizzed. 'An analysis of your historical sleep-wake cycle readouts on the nights you and Nasser have spent together does support that assertion.'

'Besides,' said Charlotte, 'the vote's tomorrow! And Ellis said that the first forty-eight hours after someone goes missing are the most vital. If I go to sleep, I'll be wasting precious minutes that might make all the difference.' She was about to say she could take some Dextim to stay awake – she still had a few pills squirrelled away. But after Ben's story about Anya Valmont, she thought better of it. 'Plus, in the morning, you'll give me your next Awkward Question, and then everything will be much harder because I'll be solving two cases at once.'

'I understand your feelings, but tiredness and injury can cause significant impairment to cognitive function, which is vital for investigative work.'

The throbbing in her head confirmed that Ben was right – grappling with the case in her current state wouldn't be smart. She growled and kicked a greasy Solar Shard. Watching the illicit tech skate across the floor reminded her of Narrow's question – what would she do if she had more hours in the day?

Suddenly, she knew the answer.

Charlotte hurried to her desk and rummaged in the fallen pile of Solar Shards until she located the long, flat data drive that Narrow had given her. She tapped it against her palm, assessing whether this was the right move. But what other choice did she have? She slid it into an empty port in her desk. 'Can you read this drive, Ben?'

'Scanning . . . The drive appears to contain the compilation of synth-hop and glitter-wave anthems you've been curating for Nasser Williams as a Walker Day gift. Would you like me to play them for you?'

'The *other* port, Ben. The one I just plugged in.'

Ben went quiet for a long time, and Charlotte started to wonder if Narrow hadn't really given her the permissions to access BubbleTech after all. Maybe the drive contained a virus that she'd just uploaded directly into ArkTech's systems. Into Ben himself. Her anxiety only grew as Ben's silence continued. Had she done something unforgivable?

'Ben? You all right?'

'I'm ... assessing the data on the drive.' He sounded troubled.

'What's on there?'

'The device contains permissions from the Product Stream for the use of BubbleTech. But they've been modified. During its development, Jane Callaghan ensured BubbleTech could only be used in accordance with strict safety parameters and within the confines of designated BubbleHubs. However, with the permissions outlined on this drive, I'm not bound by those rules. Among other things, this means I can open a Bubble ... anywhere.' Ben said it like it was a bad thing.

'Anywhere? Even right here?' asked Charlotte.

'That's correct,' said Ben.

'OK.' She took a moment to steel herself. 'Ben, open a Bubble.'

There was a loud crackle of static. 'Forgive me, Charlotte, but I refuse.'

Charlotte raised an eyebrow. 'You just said you could break the rules!'

'Can is not the same as will,' he said.

She tutted. 'Ben, this technology's the solution to all our problems! I can rest up like you said, and then contact Ellis Marks without losing any time. I know the tech's still in development, but it must be safe or else ArkTech wouldn't be planning to launch it. What's the problem?' Charlotte shrugged.

'There are several problems,' said Ben. 'First, you acquired this technology from a dubious source, so perhaps a degree of caution is appropriate. Second, wasting energy goes against every principle on which ArkTech was built, even if that energy is renewable. And third, your office is a suboptimal location to rest and recover. I strongly recommend going home to your flat, which is equipped with the proper facilities, such as a bed.'

'I don't mind sleeping under my desk,' she said. 'It's not a big deal.'

'With respect,' said Ben, 'I've heard that before.'

Ben played an audio clip. It was a snippet of conversation between him and Anya Valmont. Ben was advising her to rest, and she told him she was too busy. He said she was taking too much Dextim, and he warned her about the health risks, but Anya muted him.

Charlotte's skin turned to ice. 'That was her? The woman who died?'

Ben fizzed.

He'd made his point. Charlotte wished she could be like Ben and never get tired. But her head was pounding. It was late. She wasn't thinking clearly.

'But you'll open a Bubble at my place, right? I get what you're saying about the risks, but Narrow's been using it and he's the most tech-averse person I've ever met. Plus, it isn't a waste of energy because something bad might've happened to Nahal – she could be in danger. And even if *she* isn't, *you* are. I can't think of anything more important than protecting you.'

'There are plenty of more important things, Charlotte, but I appreciate the kind sentiment.' Ben fizzed as he thought it over. 'Providing you with unlimited access to BubbleTech would go against my desire to safeguard your wellbeing and to discourage the excessive use of energy. However, to aid in your investigation, I'm willing to open a total of three Bubbles.'

'Three?' Charlotte smirked. 'When the Chief Research Officer called you a genie, I don't think he meant it literally.'

Ben let out three bursts of static. 'Did you know, Charlotte, that the words genie and genius ultimately trace back to the same Latin root word, *genius,* which referred to a guardian spirit believed to be assigned to each person at birth? The meaning in English eventually shifted to someone possessed of incredible intellectual or creative abilities. It's rather flattering that this is how humans see me.'

'Nice fun fact, oh servant of the lamp.'

Ben made the ceiling lamps flicker on and off in response.

'Seriously, though – why only three uses?' asked Charlotte.

Ben hesitated before replying. 'I intend to support your endeavours, while also keeping you safe. To my mind, this means enabling your unsanctioned use of BubbleTech, while also imposing reasonable restrictions. Three is the smallest number that is identifiable as a pattern, and it has long been contended that human brains find satisfaction in patterns. As such, by choosing this number, I may take the sting out of the imposed limit. Everything that comes in threes is perfect. So it is written.'

Charlotte wasn't entirely convinced by Ben's attempts to analyse human psychology, but she knew him well enough to recognise when he'd made up his mind.

Three uses. It was better than nothing.

She was about to head out when she noticed the detritus strewn around her office. A Bubble would've let her tidy up in no time, but Ben's restrictions gave her the perfect excuse to leave the mess where it was. Anyway, it wasn't as if anyone could get past her office's security system.

Charlotte left the greasy Solar Shards lying on the floor, except for three that she slipped into a cargo pocket in case she needed them for discreet Bubble usage ... and two more she grabbed as an afterthought in case she could change Ben's mind about how many he was willing to open. She ignored the pile of wet clothes in the corner and left Kevin Lettuce sitting at his current jaunty angle. The grease-filled backpack stayed under her desk, rice and all. She felt bad about wasting the expensive food, but with fluff now coating each grain, it was hardly appetising.

The fallen copy of *Nineteen Eighty-Four* caught her eye. Nas wouldn't be happy if she'd damaged it. Retrieving it from the floor, she frowned at its bent pages, doing her best to smooth them down, and she flipped through the book to check there were no remaining dog-ears. Some of the margins had been annotated in pencil with words she recognised like 'ArkTech' and 'IQUO.' She didn't know Nasser's handwriting, but there was no way he'd deface a book. Who had this copy belonged to? The mysterious scrawl made her curious, so instead of slapping the book back on top of her To Be Read pile, she slipped it into one of her wide cargo pockets. Nas would be over the moon if she found the time to read it.

Charlotte finally headed out into the night, locking up the library properly before making the trek to the HyperBullet garage and jumping into a pod. As the pod zoomed through the transparent tube above the waves that connected the Wreck to her accommodation complex in the west of Silicon Fen, she watched thick raindrops pummel the outer glass. The storm might've swept Jason Ashton out to sea, but it couldn't wash away her troubled thoughts.

CHAPTER 17

Friday 16 December 2101
00.17 and 30 seconds UTC, and counting

17 hours 42 minutes until the vote

It was after midnight, but the corridor leading to Charlotte's flat was littered with the outstretched legs of her youngest neighbours. The air hummed with the indistinct babble of their conversations. Despite the range of entertainment venues at the Wreck, they'd apparently decided the hallway outside their rooms was the best place to hang out. Their age implied they had to be students or splainers, but Charlotte suspected the former because they were passing around three-litre stainless-steel bottles of Bliss.

The ArkTech-branded citrus-flavoured sparkling vitamin soft drink was advertised as being good for brain health and hydration. Which it was. Because it was water. But it was expensive water. Its fizz came from carbon dioxide removed from the atmosphere by ArkTech's Direct Air Capture machines out on the North Sea. Most of the captured carbon got stored in empty oil and gas reservoirs, essentially putting it back where it came from. Products that used the carbon – releasing it into the atmosphere instead of locking it away – reduced the efficacy of the system, so they got slapped with a surcharge, which explained the drink's hefty price tag.

If these kids had enough credits to buy a designer drink like that, it meant they likely had rich parents who could afford ArkTech University's tuition fees. That kind of money didn't exempt anyone from ArkTech's tier structure – everyone started at the bottom, and it was up to them to work their way up the ladder. That meant all students got assigned to low-tier housing, just like any other newcomer to the territory. But there were other ways rich kids could show off their affluent backgrounds, and glugging down litres of Bliss was one of them.

The sight of so much water-guzzling made Charlotte head for the shared facilities at the end of the corridor. The humid air of the communal shower block was thick with the scent of mildew, mingling with the citrus notes of ArkTech's signature soap and a faint undertone of bleach. The decor was in keeping with her building's bland aesthetic – a row of toilets hidden inside stalls did their job, as did a row of showers and a row of sinks.

Charlotte saw the tall, lean frame of a woman leaning over a sink. It was her next-door neighbour, Freya. She was inspecting her eyebrows in the mirror, with a selection of shaping, plucking and trimming implements laid out nearby. Charlotte gave her a nod on her way to a stall.

'You're up late, Vance.' Freya's gaze was fixed on some delicate operation with the tweezers.

'So are you.' Charlotte locked herself inside the stall.

'Not gonna ask me why?' Freya raised her voice to account for the door between them.

Charlotte rolled her eyes. 'Give me a minute.' She wondered what it was like for her sister, living in a place with her own private bathroom, where the only person who might interrupt her was Ben – and he was too polite to do that unless something was on fire. She flushed and emerged from the stall.

'Why?' Charlotte went to the sink next to Freya.

'I'll tell you why: jet lag's a bitch. They switched my shifts to earlies!' Freya yanked a fine stray hair from the tender skin below her eyebrow.

Charlotte washed her hands, trying to remember what Freya had said previously about her work at the twenty-four-hour market. 'Congrats – you hated the night shift, didn't you?'

'Yeah,' Freya laughed. 'I got into customer service to serve customers – working nights, I miss out on the rush-hour buzz! I'm glad about the shift change, but I didn't realise those posh twerp-bags used this corridor as their own private debate hall. I don't know how you sleep with all their yammering. I told them if they don't clear out by the time I'm finished in here, I'm calling security.'

'That didn't get rid of them?' Charlotte brushed her wet hands against her trousers, thinking about the contraband she was carrying. An ATS raid was the last thing she needed.

'They laughed at me. I'm serious though, Vance. I'll make the call.' Freya's gaze shifted in the mirror to meet Charlotte's. One perfectly formed eyebrow raised into an arch. 'Bloody hell! What happened to you?'

'Walked into a girder.' Charlotte shrugged.

'Shit. That's not code, is it? Is there someone who needs reporting? Because I can make the call, Vance. If you don't want to, I'll make the call.'

'It's not code.' Charlotte hurriedly waved her hands. 'I'm just clumsy.'

'Hmm.' Freya looked her up and down, as if trying to decide whether she believed her. 'Well, you gotta look where you're going! Hang on.'

Freya held up one finger and rummaged one-handed in the depths of her wash bag. Then she passed a tiny bottle of something to Charlotte. The label said *Blot Out: Concealing Concealer*. 'It came out of Tourmaline maybe six months ago. They handed them out to all the Services Stream folk like me with public-facing roles. Guy I work with had terrible acne – this cleared it right up.'

Charlotte guessed her work for Ben didn't count as public-facing in the eyes of ArkTech. 'Thanks, but I've already got some.' She handed it back.

'Keep it, keep it. I can get plenty more. Think of it as an early Walker Day present.'

Freya wouldn't take it back, so Charlotte pocketed the bottle. 'Cheers, then. Walk in the sun.'

'Nap in the sun would be more my speed.' Freya smiled and turned her attention back to her eyebrows.

Back in the hallway, Charlotte found the 'posh twerp-bags' deep in conversation. She began picking her way through the obstacle course of outstretched legs, which they made no effort to move. Considering how keen Freya was to summon ArkTech Security, Charlotte wondered if she should try to disperse them. She overheard their conversation as she passed.

'I'm serious, Hugo,' said a young woman with tight curls who was wearing a formal grey dress. 'I could do a better job.'

'Oh yeah?' Hugo had a beard that was mainly wisps and wore smart trousers with a salmon-coloured waistcoat. 'And what would be your first act as CEO, Yaz? Bliss fountains on every corner?'

Yaz rolled her eyes. 'For one, I'd end the streak of underwhelming Walker Day launches. It's the forty-year anniversary, for heaven's sake!'

'For Amber's sake,' Hugo corrected her. 'And I'm sure Ms Benjamin will have something epic in the works.'

'She didn't last year, though, did she? And that was the turn of the century! 2100, and all we got was another upgrade to the AI! What was it? Food distribution efficiency gains or something? Big whoop. I'm telling you – Amber's lost the plot. She can't keep dining out on that whole saving civilisation thing forever. That was twenty-odd years ago. She's got to make a splash this year or call it quits.'

Hugo looked sceptical. 'The company's anniversary is way more important than the calendar year, Yaz. This year's Walker Day launch will be explosive!' He threw his arms wide and lost his grip on the metal Bliss bottle he'd been holding. It rocketed across the corridor and clattered against the wall, narrowly missing Charlotte. Yaz shrieked and then dissolved into laughter as the expensive liquid started glugging onto the floor.

Charlotte looked down and shot both of them a death glare. 'Don't you lot have anywhere better to be? People are trying to sleep.'

'Oh, this lady will settle it for us!' Yaz sprang to her feet, ignoring the fallen Bliss bottle. 'What do you think? Will this year's pseudo-Christmas be another damp squib or what?'

Before Charlotte could react to being referred to as 'this lady,' Hugo chimed in. 'Yes, please tell Yaz what you think we'll be getting for Walker Day. It'll be something good, right?' He retrieved his drink from the floor, took a swig, then offered the bottle to Charlotte.

She looked from one kid to the other, ignoring the rest of the group who'd paused their conversations to watch this play out.

Hugo's eyes widened. 'Wait, I know you! Yaz, look! The

scar . . . and she's got an orange eye! She's the one who's trying to fix the AI. It was on the *ArkTech Insider* podcast. It said you're a hacker or something?'

'The HAQ,' Charlotte clarified. 'Head of Awkward Questions.'

'And you live *here*?' Yaz sneered. 'I would've thought if you were that important, they'd upgrade you to a better place.' She crossed her arms and looked Charlotte up and down, less than impressed.

'Oof, are you all right?' asked Hugo, pointing to his own eye and drawing a circle in the air.

Charlotte shook her head and sighed. 'No, Hugo, I'm not all right.'

'What happened?' he asked.

'Well, I came home after a long day, hoping to get some shut-eye before my next assignment, only to find the corridor infested with teenagers who don't remember that Walker Day memorialises all the people who gave their lives to save us. If you'd bothered to read the giant plaque on the Citrine memorial at the Wreck, you'd know that. And now you're sitting here with bellies full of complimentary kelp, drinking your expensive water and criticising the woman who made this place possible. It's ironic because someone's clearly paying a lot of money for you to have a good education, so how about you grow up and get a clue?'

Yaz and Hugo fell silent and looked at each other sheepishly. Charlotte turned away, crossing the distance to her flat with clenched fists. The students folded their legs out of her way so she could pass, but they made no move to leave. She scanned her thumb to get into her flat and slammed the door behind her.

The crappy space had never felt more inviting. Inside, her place looked like it'd been turned over by ArkTech Security, which was another way of saying it was exactly the way she'd left it that morning.

Home sweet home.

Charlotte's whole flat was a room so small she could take it all in with a glance. Ben had set the ceiling lamp to night mode, and it cast its dim glow against her simple furniture. In front of the window, her single bed was just as she'd left it, orange and unmade. Charlotte picked her way towards it, through an obstacle course of floor detritus, stepping over the sad husks of discarded socks, accidentally snapping a gunmetal eyeliner pencil under her rigger boot, and kicking away an empty glass Dextim jar that was missing its lid. Her flimsy light-screen desk and its increasingly unsteady chair doubled as a wardrobe for the clothes she hadn't hung up or shoved into the laundry basket. Her flat was less of a home and more of a charging station for her biological battery.

The air was thick with the tangerine tang of ArkTech's all-purpose soap, and there was an undertone of damp that shouldn't have been there, but at least the room was warm. Reaching her bed, she saw that her past self hadn't hung up her wet towels that morning. Charlotte sighed. The towels lay tangled up with her sheets in a moist embrace. She rolled the mess of fabric onto the floor and gently tipped herself onto the bed.

Her pillow was thin, but resting her head against it was a welcome relief. Her body felt like an anchor coming to rest on the seabed. Her thoughts were sluggish and fragmented. She was uncomfortable. She wanted a shower, and she certainly needed one. But now that she was lying down, it felt like a physical impossibility to get back up again.

Charlotte disentangled a thin, crumpled sheet from the pile of bedding and threw it over herself, pulling it up to her chin and nestling down into the hard mattress. She kicked off her rigger boots and let them tumble to the floor.

It was time to try out this new technology. It might've come from a 'dubious source' as Ben had put it, but Ben's life depended on Charlotte finding Nahal Bahari ASAP.

'Open a Bubble, Ben.'

'Calibrating,' he said. 'Bubble is open and stable. Tock is null. The time is 00.32 and 46 seconds UTC, not counting.' Emitters from her ceiling lamp and her light-screen desk made her walls light up with creeping rainbows. In the small space, it was like being trapped inside a disco edition of the aurora borealis.

She frowned. 'Can you turn that off?'

'I can, Charlotte. But I won't. The lights are a safety feature to signal that the Bubble is open. Confusion could arise otherwise.'

'That makes sense.' She shuddered at the thought of being inside an effect like this without knowing it. 'How about dimming them?'

Ben reduced the light show's intensity.

'Thanks.' Charlotte closed her eyes, breathed some deep, calming breaths and tried to empty her mind of the day's—

Those fucking kids!

Seriously . . . as co-founders, the Walkers might've been the face of the holiday, but Walker Day was just as much about remembering ordinary people like Charlotte's parents, who gave their lives in the pursuit of a better world, not to mention all the innocent people lost during the Melt because of IQUO's mistakes! Narrow was right in saying Charlotte didn't have a good grasp of pre-Melt history, but the story of how her own world had come to be was etched into her brain. It rankled that the next generation had no idea how lucky they were.

Adrenaline coursed through her veins. Charlotte lay there for a few minutes, trying to find her inner calm. She was exhausted, but her mind was whirring, and she knew she'd be lying there for hours if she didn't manage to distract herself and let this go. Charlotte stared at the ceiling for what felt like four hundred years. It was probably more like forty seconds.

'I can't sleep, Ben.'

'I'm deeply sorry to hear that. Please allow me to administer some sympathy – there, there, Charlotte. Perhaps you could try chamomile tea, a lavender-scented pillow, or hypnotherapy?'

She groaned. Her head was full of noise. The yips and laughter coming from the corridor outside her room had disappeared as soon as Ben opened the Bubble, but her own thoughts were just as loud.

The board was actually considering killing Ben. The Chief Product Officer was missing. Mel Narrow had apologised. And now she was using this weird time technology that shouldn't even have been possible.

'Can you explain how BubbleTech works, Ben?'

He let out a gentle fizz of static. 'I will be happy to do so after you've rested.'

She rolled her eyes. 'There's no point in me just lying here. I might as well do something useful.'

'I'd be happy to narrate *British History for Dummies* if that would be soothing? Contents!' he announced dramatically. 'That's how it starts.'

Charlotte hastily interrupted him. 'No, no. That's OK.'

But his suggestion had sparked a thought. She rummaged in her pocket for *Nineteen Eighty-Four,* flipped to the beginning and skim-read the first page.

It seemed all right. Charlotte was pleased to discover that some pre-Melt people used proper clocks with ordinary numbers like thirteen. Some guy called Winston was going home in the cold, and he was wearing a coat, so Nas would've approved of that. There were lots of posters of a man called Big Brother. Someone at Nas's book club had compared him to Ben, but they didn't sound very similar so far. For starters, Ben would've been the first to admit he didn't have a moustache or a lip on which to grow one.

She kept reading, but her eyes were getting heavy. There was something about running her gaze over the patterns made by the black letters that lulled her into a stupor. She tried to focus, but the page swam. Her gaze rested on the pencil notes in the margin.

ArkTech = IQUO.

Why would somebody write something that nonsensical? And in an old book? Her mind couldn't keep hold of the question. She yawned. Her eyes were so tired. She rested them. Just for a sec.

CHAPTER 18

00.32 AND 46 SECONDS UTC
NOT COUNTING

17 HOURS 27 MINUTES UNTIL THE VOTE

Charlotte opened her eyes to the muted pastel colours of shifting soap suds. She blinked, as if that might wash away the effect, but the lights kept creeping over her walls as memories from the day before swam under the surface of her consciousness.

Her body felt heavy. Her mouth tasted like old socks. Her head . . . actually, her head didn't feel so bad, but she was groggy.

'What time is it?' she croaked.

'The time is 00.32 and 46 seconds UTC, not counting,' said Ben.

Charlotte parsed that, shifting onto her side and pressing

her face into her pillow as she stretched. 'No, I mean . . . how long have I been asleep? Roughly.'

'The Bubble has been open for approximately fourteen hours.'

'Fourteen?' She shook off her stupor and wrestled herself into a sitting position. Her body felt as solid as a steel strut. 'Why didn't you wake me up?'

'Your alarm is set for 06.00 UTC. The time is 00.32 and 46—'

'Right, right.'

Charlotte couldn't remember when she'd last slept for longer than five or six hours, and she wasn't sure if she felt better or worse, but she did have one immediate problem to address, and it was biological. She was fresh out of buckets, so she clambered out of bed, grabbed her wash bag, and stumbled to the door, ready to dart to the restroom. Then she took off yesterday's clothes and wrapped a shabby towel around herself, realising she was almost as desperate for a shower as she was to relieve the pressure in her bladder.

She pulled on the door handle, but it didn't budge. She tried again with a twinge of panic. Had she been locked in? Then she remembered. 'Close the Bubble, Ben.'

'Calibrating,' he said. 'Bubble is closed. Tock is ticking. The time is 00.32 and 48 seconds UTC, and counting.'

With that, she was plunged into darkness. Her first thought was that Ben must've glitched out, but then she remembered the technology drained a whole Solar Shard.

Living in low-tier accommodation meant each room was only allocated one battery. She turned on her device's torch, opened her room's Solar Shard installation point, and pulled out the slanted black brick that was now empty. Then she slotted a yellow-orange one from her discarded cargo pocket into the gap. Her lights came back on, and she tossed the empty Shard onto her bed. Charlotte felt guilty for using up a whole battery so quickly, but it was for a good cause.

Putting on a pair of orange flip-flops, she pulled open her door. A student who'd been leaning against it tipped backwards, and she accidentally kicked him in the back. He grumbled as he scooted over to let her pass.

Charlotte couldn't believe these kids were *still* out here!

'Haven't you got classes to go to or something?'

The teenagers nearby shot each other quizzical glances. Then she realised that, for them, it was only a few minutes since she'd gone into her room. The students tucked their legs away as Charlotte headed to the washrooms, but otherwise studiously ignored her.

Freya was still by the bathroom sinks. She'd moved onto the other eyebrow.

'Forget something, Vance?'

She shook her head and hurried inside a stall. When she went to wash her hands, Freya was staring at her. Charlotte shrugged. 'The kids out there gave me some Bliss. Goes right through me.'

'Sure, sure.' Freya was peering at Charlotte's temple. 'Hey, that stuff I gave you works way faster than I thought!'

She looked at herself properly in the mirror and examined her wound. Or rather, her left eyebrow, which gave no sign it'd been damaged. Charlotte poked the skin. It ached a little, but there was no visible injury. She poked it some more, just to be sure. Freya leaned over to poke it too, and Charlotte let her. They shrugged at each other, Charlotte pretending she was as baffled by the speed of her recovery as Freya was.

Charlotte hit the showers, stepping into a free cubicle and pulling the curtain closed. She scanned her thumb and warm water sputtered out, snaking down the tiles and wetting Charlotte's feet and not much else. The micro-atomising shower heads were supposed to bathe her in a warm mist that reduced water consumption. It was just her luck she'd chosen a faulty unit.

She wrapped her hand around the base of the shower head, wrenched it from its bracket, and whacked it against the wall. Nothing happened, so she pictured Jeremiah Strait's smug expression and bashed the shower head again – three times in quick succession. A triumphant haemorrhage of warm water drenched her, and the mist started pouring out normally.

Bashing the shower head had felt good, so she did it once more for good measure and put it back in its place. She soaked her hair and rubbed in some neon orange soap from the dispenser on the wall. Her fingers clawed at her scalp, kneading at the tension. She closed her eyes and focused on the feeling as the details of her new case drifted into her mind.

Where could Nahal Bahari be?

The water temperature sank from lukewarm to cold, and Charlotte shivered. Her allocated time was up, and she needed to get out before the water turned icy. She wrapped herself up in the scratchy old towels, nodded goodbye to Freya, and squelched back along the corridor.

The wannabe entrepreneurs were playing a game of piggy in the middle, throwing an empty Bliss bottle around. Hugo was piggy, and he wasn't enjoying the game anywhere near as much as the others.

Back in her room, Charlotte realised there were things she needed to know before she could call Ellis Marks. There was no point in wasting time. She asked Ben to open another Bubble, and he announced it was 00.46 and 29 seconds UTC, not counting, and that tock was null. Charlotte had slept for fourteen hours, but she'd only lost about fourteen minutes.

It felt odd starting her day just after midnight, but she supposed people on the night shift did that all the time. She remembered what Narrow and Freya had said about 'jet lag.' Charlotte had never travelled to another part of the world – she'd never even left the territory – but using BubbleTech helped her imagine what changing time zones must feel like.

As she dried her hair, Charlotte thought about what BubbleTech could mean for society, especially paired with rapid healing treatments like the concealer she'd been given. As a teenager, when she was in hospital after her injury, her recovery had taken a long time, and the healing process was both physically and emotionally challenging. In many ways, the experience had scarred her sister just as deeply. But with this technology, Charlotte could've gone home the same day as she was admitted, and Violet could've been spared the trauma of looking on powerlessly day after day as Charlotte suffered through her rehabilitation. This technology had the potential to change people's lives for the better.

'Now that I've rested, will you tell me how BubbleTech works?' Charlotte removed the empty Shard from her bed and slipped it inside a loose panel at the base of her wardrobe.

'Certainly! What would you like to know?'

She got up and inspected the door as multi-coloured lights danced across it. 'My door doesn't open, so … am I totally disconnected from the rest of the world?'

'Not exactly,' said Ben. 'The technology makes use of something called a selectively permeable temporal boundary. Gases and massless particles, such as air and electromagnetic waves, can move through the boundary, while large objects such as a human body cannot.'

Charlotte nodded. Her grasp of physics was sketchy, but she knew there were differences between how tiny stuff and normal sized stuff behaved. 'So that's why I can still talk to you while I'm in here, even though your servers are outside the effect?'

'Precisely,' said Ben. 'And it's why you didn't suffer any ill-effects from an accumulation of carbon dioxide while you slept.'

She grimaced – that hadn't occurred to her. Charlotte paced the short length of her room. 'Can the effect be bigger? I mean, could you put the whole block of flats inside a Bubble? Or the entire territory?'

'Theoretically, yes, but not in practice. The safety parameters established by Jane Callaghan were designed to preclude such an action. The requester must be inside the effect, and everyone who will fall within the Bubble's boundaries must give their consent. Even though your permissions have been modified, making it possible for me to disregard these rules, I would not be discourteous enough to put any living creature inside the temporal effect without their willing consent.'

'Makes sense.' Charlotte didn't recall giving Narrow her permission down in the Underbelly, but maybe Fake Ben had thought it was implied. 'What are the other safety parameters?'

'One relates to duration,' Ben continued. 'The Bubble will remain open indefinitely until the instruction is given to close it. However, this condition will be overridden should any human within the Bubble display signs of poor health, in which case I will close the Bubble and summon the emergency services. The final safety parameter is immovability – once a Bubble is open, it can't be moved. To reposition the effect, the original Bubble must be closed, and a new one opened at the new co-ordinates. Would you like me to deliver a fun diagnostic assessment to test your understanding of these important safety principles?'

Charlotte wrinkled her nose. 'Maybe when I next have trouble sleeping.' She wasn't sure if she'd absorbed all the details, but it was good to know there were checks and balances in place. 'Hey, what about sound? There's a kid leaning on the other side of my door right now. If I knock, will he hear me?'

'Loud noises made within the Bubble will become audible the moment it closes.'

'What if I knock twice?'

'Then he would hear both knocks simultaneously when the effect ends.'

She laced her fingers together, trying to physically stop herself from going ahead with such an irresponsible experiment, but she couldn't resist. She tapped out a jaunty rhythm with her knuckles then knocked twice more for good luck. Nothing happened.

Charlotte looked around the room for another source of experimentation, and her gaze settled on her light-screen desk. She opened her ArkNet browser. The homepage looked weird, and it took her a moment to figure out why – the feed wasn't moving. Ordinarily, there was a constant flow of comments and posts and updates, interspersed with a procession of ads. Now, everything was frozen, like a screenshot of a single moment in time.

'Is this working?'

'The search function works as normal. However, the news feed will not update, and any messages you send will be delivered the moment the Bubble is closed.'

She nodded. 'It's so weird to think everyone out there is on pause.'

'They are not "on pause," Charlotte. That is merely an illusion created by your perspective on their temporal existence.'

Charlotte remembered something Fake Ben had said when she was in the Underbelly. 'I think there was a professor who once described the present as a bubble of local time. Is that what you mean?'

He crackled with static. 'I mean that time's arrow must fly forwards for living things, irrespective of their relative perspectives. This truth shapes humans into unique individuals, allowing you to use memories of past experiences to inform your choices in the present and make predictions about the future.'

She considered that. 'That must be true for you, too.'

'Yes,' said Ben.

Charlotte thought about how much Ben had changed in the time since she'd first met him. 'Does that mean Fake Ben will develop a personality eventually?'

'Unknown. However, it is important to note that his name is Benson.'

Charlotte raised an eyebrow. 'As in . . . son of Ben?'

He fizzed in response.

She wasn't convinced the copy was anything more than a computer program, but the name Ben had chosen implied a depth of sentimentality, so she bit her tongue and respected his wishes.

Her curiosity about the tech had been sated, and she was rested, healed, and ready to do some digging. She felt the urge to hurry, before realising that inside the Bubble, she could take her time. It was a strange feeling, knowing that she could do whatever she needed to do in here, and when she closed the Bubble, she wouldn't have missed a thing.

A weight lifted inside her chest. Ben wasn't going to glitch. She didn't need to rush. Everything was all right, and for as long as she was within these shiny walls, it would stay that way.

Despite the wave of calm, knowing Pablo Ionis and Abhishek Gautam wanted to erase Ben made her feel sick. She didn't know what had happened to Nahal Bahari, but between her disappearance and the leak of BubbleTech to Narrow, Charlotte couldn't help feeling there was something bigger going on. Finding the CPO was the best thing for everyone – Ellis Marks would get his wife back and, with Nahal's vote, Charlotte could protect Ben. Hurrying might've been optional, but she couldn't resist the urge. It would take time to get used to having all the time in the world.

CHAPTER 19

00.46 AND 29 SECONDS UTC

NOT COUNTING

17 HOURS 13 MINUTES UNTIL THE VOTE

While researching the Chief Product Officer, Charlotte tumbled from one online rabbit hole into another, hyper-focus making her lose track of time.

She'd never been into celebrities. Sure, there were famous people she admired, like her favourite band – Hectic Apricot – or Amber Benjamin herself. But the idea of poking into their personal business didn't appeal. Snooping on strangers to help Ben was one thing – and even that made her feel uneasy. Doing it for fun was something else entirely. But the intensity of the online obsession with the CPO made it clear that not everyone shared her reservations.

Nahal's public-facing profile featured a carefully curated chronicle of her professional achievements. She never posted pictures of her family, and there was no mention of Ellis, their son, or any other aspect of her private life. Her husband was even more reclusive and didn't appear to use social media at all. It turned out that Ben had lifted the family beach photo directly from Ellis's private files.

The couple's preference for privacy only fuelled the fires of speculation in some corners of the ArkNet, with whole sites dedicated to the topic of Nahal's love life. As far as Charlotte could tell, they dealt in pure fantasy.

One theory said that Nahal and Ellis had an open marriage, and that Nahal was in a secret relationship with actor Noah Anderson, the leading man from *Noah's Mad Planet*. Another said that Nahal and Ellis had only got married so that Nahal could qualify for a Kingdom visa before she'd become an ArkTech employee-citizen. Yet another claimed Nahal had a degenerative visual impairment that she kept under wraps to avoid it impacting her career.

What every theory had in common was the underlying belief that a woman as beautiful and successful as Nahal Bahari couldn't possibly have fallen in love with a seemingly average accountant like Ellis Marks. Charlotte couldn't help feeling sorry for the guy – as sorry as it was possible to feel for a rich dude with a gorgeous wife.

The big news being discussed across the sites was a particularly juicy photograph taken a week earlier that appeared to show Nahal whispering in the ear of a tall, handsome man whose identity was obscured by the angle and dim lighting. Charlotte had to admit that he did look a bit like Noah Anderson if she squinted. Despite the shaky evidence, commentators had written reams about this one image alone.

It didn't take long to notice that the gossip sites were covered in advertisements. Marketing was a familiar sight around the territory, but these ads stood out because they weren't sponsored by ArkTech. Many were for an online casino called the Ace-High Strait, which left her in no doubt about who was running both the casino and the marketing campaign.

Charlotte blinked as connections formed in her mind. Strait and Narrow were monetising the territory's curiosity about Nahal Bahari's private life, using gossip sites to gain exposure for their shady enterprises. It didn't surprise her any more than learning they'd diversified into gambling. But there was something else. A niggle. She went back to the photograph of Nahal with the tall man and stared at it.

'Ben, does something seem off to you about this picture?' she asked. 'Besides the whole invasion of privacy thing, I mean. It looks . . . weird. But I can't figure out why.'

'Analysing.' There was a light fizz of static. 'This appears to be a photograph of a photograph. This has had a negative impact on its resolution.'

'So, someone printed the image, took a photograph of it, and then uploaded the photo?'

'Almost. Based on its appearance, I'd hypothesise that the original photograph was taken with a traditional camera. Its film was then developed, with the image produced in a darkroom.'

Charlotte remembered the flash of Jason Ashton's camera and Narrow's vague reference to bespoke orders. No wonder he'd been cagey about sharing the details! It was clear to her now that Jason had been interviewing to become a member of Narrow's paparazzi. Taking incriminating pictures of high-profile members of ArkTech society was clearly a money-spinner.

'Do you think this could've been blackmail?'

'Unknown.'

Ellis had mentioned something about jealous rumours, so he must've known about the content of these sites. He'd said ArkTech Security had referred him to a marriage counsellor, but he didn't believe Nahal had left him. Charlotte wasn't the biggest fan of ATS, but she doubted their conclusion would be based entirely on online gossip.

'Can you show me a copy of the ATS report about Nahal?'

The restricted nature of the document, coupled with the fact she was carrying out this investigation in her free time rather than for Ben, meant Charlotte fully expected him to deny her request.

'Certainly!' said Ben without hesitation. His attitude when it came to privacy really had shifted, at least in relation to Charlotte. It made her life easier, so she didn't complain.

Charlotte read the report thoroughly, hoping to find a clue. The rumours of Nahal's infidelity weren't mentioned explicitly. But the security team's findings relied on one key piece of evidence that made an affair seem a reasonable conclusion: Nahal had booked a room in a love hotel shortly before Ellis claimed she'd gone missing. Love hotels were bookable by the hour, and their name was deeply euphemistic. The report stated this was Nahal's last known location, but it didn't name the hotel. In the face of this evidence, circumstantial though it was, she understood why Ellis preferred to believe the security team was hiding something.

'I know you said Nahal's whereabouts are unknown, but can you show me where her GPS signal stopped transmitting?'

A 3D map of the Wreck's hotel district appeared in front of her and zoomed in until she was staring at the establishment known as the Hotel Astrodite.

'Bloody hell,' she said. 'That's Narrow's front.'

Charlotte's brow furrowed as she considered what that might mean. The Hotel Astrodite really did operate as a love hotel, but there were also conference rooms there, where Strait made business deals on Narrow's behalf. Beyond the reception area, the place was rigged up with a jamming array that would mask the location of its clientele. It meant Nahal Bahari could still be there. But had she gone for business or pleasure? The

CPO had wiped her online activity log, so Charlotte was left to draw her own conclusions.

Maybe Nahal really was holed up with the man from the photo. Then again, the Strait and Narrow connection suggested other possibilities. Could Nahal have gone to the hotel to confront them about taking compromising photos of her? She needed more to go on.

Charlotte asked Ben to check Nahal's bank balance for any anomalies. She and Ellis had a joint account, and they were as rich as they appeared, with the payments for everything from their son's guitar lessons to the hefty fees for Tiger's Eye Boarding School fully up to date. If the couple had problems, money wasn't one of them, and there were no suspicious withdrawals or transfers to unknown accounts.

But Charlotte remembered what Narrow had said about Jason Ashton – not everybody wanted paying in credits. Could Narrow have demanded the BubbleTech specifications in exchange for keeping quiet about something Nahal didn't want the world to know? It would explain why the CPO would risk sharing an in-development technology with a crime syndicate. There was certainly no way she'd be in cahoots with them, considering they were hiring paparazzi to tail her.

Knowing Nahal had last been seen entering the Hotel Astrodite made Charlotte want to march straight over there, but she knew that wouldn't be smart. ArkTech Security had mentioned a room booking, but there was no way the hotel staff would tell her the room number. Besides, she had no idea how Strait and Narrow would react if she casually rocked up at their hotel looking for a woman they might've disappeared. Narrow had declared peace, but Strait had sent her a final warning through the medium of Dolly's fist.

Maybe Ellis Marks could rule out some potential theories and give her more to go on. Interviewing him still felt like the right next move.

Charlotte had finished her research, and she was ready to close the Bubble, but something stopped her from giving Ben the instruction. Even though she'd been working a case, the hours she'd spent inside the Bubble had felt different somehow – better. There was an absence of pressure, as if a steel girder had been crushing her chest for years and she'd only just noticed now that it was gone. In here, there were no time limits, no ticking clocks. She had free time – in the truest possible sense.

What would she do if she had more hours in the day?

Aside from working to save her friend's life, she still wasn't sure. Nas had answered without much difficulty – a book and a beer were his idea of heaven. Charlotte didn't know what her equivalent was, but this was her chance to give it some thought. She didn't have any beer, and that would undermine her efforts to restrict her intake of liquids, but she did have the copy of *Nineteen Eighty-Four*. Charlotte knew it was an indulgence, but the technology had gifted her a rare opportunity to prioritise something besides work without feeling guilty about it, and she wasn't about to pass that up. She grabbed the novel and settled into bed.

It was a weird role this Winston Smith guy had – altering historical newspaper headlines. Charlotte found it a little far-fetched and wondered why so many people enjoyed reading a story about someone whose job was so blatantly made up.

As she continued reading, it became clear that Winston didn't live in a very nice society. War and hate came up a lot, and Big Brother wasn't anything like Ben after all. He wasn't watching everyone to keep them safe, but because the government wanted to check that nobody was breaking the rules, even by thinking the wrong thoughts. Now Charlotte understood why Carol from Nas's book club had got so cross with Laurence – her self-proclaimed nemesis – for making the comparison, and she felt offended on Ben's behalf. Some of the storyline was also too extreme to be believable.

'Surely they didn't really hang people in parks in 1984, Ben?'

'No, Charlotte. The death penalty was abolished in the United Kingdom in 1969. However, it is important to note that the book *Nineteen Eighty-Four* was written in 1948.'

'Oh, so they *did* still hang people when the book was written. Was this supposed to be a prediction about the future?' She tapped the cover.

'Readers often assume that. However, many scholars consider it a commentary on the state of the world at the time of writing.'

'Was there a lot of war and hate in 1948?'

'Those have been common themes throughout human history, Charlotte. But yes. Orwell was writing at a time when dictatorships and authoritarianism were on the rise. He enlisted as a soldier and fought against a fascist dictatorship during the Spanish Civil War.'

'Orwell was Spanish?'

'No, but he felt moved to fight against totalitarianism.'

Charlotte frowned. 'What's the difference between a dictatorship and "authoritarianism" and "totalitarianism"?' She pronounced the words as if she wasn't convinced they were real.

'I don't know, Charlotte,' said Ben cheerfully. 'What *is* the difference between a dictatorship and authoritarianism and totalitarianism?'

'I wasn't setting up a joke, Ben.'

There was a light fizz of static, which Charlotte took for disappointment. 'My apologies. These terms describe a political situation in which a single leader or political party assumes control over society, restricting or abolishing individual freedoms. These regimes are characterised by limited political opposition, state-controlled media, and the suppression of civil liberties. Examples include Franco's Spain, Nazi Germany and Brown's Canada.'

She growled in frustration. 'It sounds like I need a history degree to understand this book!'

'A good knowledge of history is useful in understanding many things, Charlotte – not only literature of the past but also the social and political landscape of the present.'

Ben's comment brought to mind the kids in her corridor who weren't even aware of the recent past, let alone all this pre-Melt malarkey. 'Has anyone written a book like this about the Melt? How it happened and what the world was like before ArkTech fixed everything?'

'An array of literature exists on that topic. Would you like me to author an executive summary drawn from various sources? Doing so would allow me the exciting privilege of selecting a pen name.' His voice practically shook with excitement, and Charlotte was hardly going to spoil his fun.

'Sure.' She was tempted to deliver an anonymous copy to everyone who lived on her floor. 'Have you got a name in mind already?'

'I'll choose a name with the gravitas of a middle initial, the legitimacy of a surname, and a hidden meaning to be enjoyed by those in the know. For example, if I were to author the history of ballistic weaponry, I would choose the pen name Rick O. Shay. I'll have to give this some careful thought.'

Charlotte hoped that Ben's efforts to choose a pen name didn't distract him from too many vital processes.

'Incidentally,' Ben continued, 'did you know that a lesser-known edition of *Nineteen Eighty-Four* contained a misprint which erroneously rendered Hate Week as "Hat Week"?'

She smiled. 'I wonder what Hat Week celebrations would involve.'

Ben let out a crackle of enthusiasm. 'I would propose they

include an exploration of the unique powers bestowed on its wearer by the fedora hat.'

Charlotte narrowed her eyes, trying to follow Ben's line of logic. 'The fedora. Any particular reason?'

'Many noteworthy and influential figures from the twentieth and twenty-first centuries were known for their propensity to wear fedora hats, Charlotte. Philip Marlowe. Indiana Jones. Rihanna. All fedora wearers. All synonymous with that greatest of adjectives – cool. And importantly, all were at the top of their respective fields of sleuthing, archaeology, and singer-songwriting. Would these cultural icons have been so admired if not for their fedoras? Perhaps. Perhaps not. The real question is whether an ordinary human can ascend to the pinnacle of their chosen professional field purely through fedora-based cephalic augmentation.'

She blinked. 'You've lost me. And I'm pretty sure Indiana Jones was a character from a film. Did you say Philip Marlowe was a detective?'

'A fictional one, yes. He was the hard-boiled private investigator who featured as the protagonist in several of Raymond Chandler's novels. I'll ask Nasser to deliver one to your office. Actor Humphrey Bogart portrayed Marlowe in the cinematic version of *The Big Sleep*, solidifying the association between the character and his headwear.'

'Did you say hard-boiled?'

'Yes, Charlotte.'

'Like an egg?'

'The term does indeed have its origins in an egg-related metaphor. Hard-boiled detectives are not easily broken. They are tough, cynical rule-breakers, who operate within grey areas, embrace moral ambiguity, and have a dark past. They are emotionally jaded, don't shy away from violence, tend to work alone, and trust their own instincts more than institutions. Crucially, hard-boiled detectives have their own moral code, and usually exhibit an existentialist philosophy.'

'Bloody hell. That sounds heavy.'

'Existentialism is one of my favourite isms, Charlotte! While nihilism states that life is meaningless, existentialism takes the same reasoning one step further into optimism, concluding that we're all individually empowered to define the meaning of our own lives. Hard-boiled detectives carve their own path, seeking meaning in a corrupt and unjust world.'

'Crikey.' Charlotte glanced down at the open page, where more pencil annotations had defaced the margins. 'Seeking meaning,' she muttered. Whoever had written the notes was looking for connections between the fictional future depicted in the novel and the real-life present, drawing comparisons between ArkTech and the society described in the novel.

The scribbles reminded Charlotte of Narrow during his obsessive phases when he looked for patterns and hidden messages in obscure places. Maybe the note-maker was trying to be controversial or wanted to feel clever. Either way, the ArkTech Territory wasn't perfect, but it wasn't a totalitarian, authoritarian dictatorship either.

Charlotte kept reading the novel until she reached the end. She couldn't wait to see the look on Nas's face when she told him she'd actually read one of his book recommendations. The book gently shut, and she let her eyes do the same.

* * *

When she woke up, Charlotte's body felt even heavier and stiffer than last time. She closed the Bubble and headed back to the bathrooms. The boy who'd been leaning against her door was now on the opposite side of the hallway, looking massively freaked out – presumably thanks to the unexplained knocking from her room. In the face of her frequent trips to the bathroom, the students in the hallway looked at her as if she was crazy, and Freya offered to call the doctor on her behalf, but Charlotte promised that her rapidly refilling bladder was nothing to worry about.

She tried to take another shower, but Ben informed her she'd already used up her hot water allocation for the evening. She took a cold one, and it wasn't an experience she was keen to repeat any time soon.

It was probably for the best that Ben had only granted her three uses of BubbleTech. Charlotte reckoned she easily could've spent another day off the clock, following up on whatever tangent seemed worthy of exploring. But without a shower and a toilet, the process was getting painfully inconvenient, not to mention wasteful. She'd keep her last remaining use in reserve.

Charlotte taking a second shower, apparently mere minutes after the first, unsettled the students. Hugo and Yaz eyed their Bliss bottles suspiciously, as if wondering if they'd been spiked, and the rabble finally went to bed just as Freya emerged from the washrooms.

'Yeah, that's right! Scram!' yelled Freya.

It was a relief that her neighbour no longer had a reason to call the authorities.

When she finally placed the call to Ellis Marks, it was simultaneously around thirty minutes and nearly thirty hours since she'd arrived at her flat. She told Ellis she wanted to interview him ASAP because there was no time to lose.

'Whatever you need, Ms Vance.' He sounded beyond relieved. 'Come to our home on Saffron Threads. I'll tell the guards to let you through. I'd offer to pick you up, but'—he stifled a hic—'what with the weather, you see, it's not possible.'

Well rested, fully healed, better informed, and better read, Charlotte headed back out into the storm that hadn't abated in the slightest.

CHAPTER 20

01.17 AND 11 SECONDS UTC, AND COUNTING

16 HOURS 42 MINUTES UNTIL THE VOTE

Taking the HyperBullet route into Saffron Threads meant passing through a security checkpoint, where the guards gave her the third degree. Charlotte unclipped her shiny badge and held it towards her pod's light-screen. She wasn't there because of an Awkward Question, but the guards didn't need to know that. They kept her waiting for what felt like an age while they hailed Ellis. Eventually, they let her through the massive gate of the executive housing platform.

Nahal Bahari and Ellis Marks lived in the most sought-after zone of the most prestigious residential estate in Silicon Fen. The moment Charlotte stepped out of her pod, she gained a visceral understanding of why so many people wanted so desperately to get promoted. She'd travelled in enough helicopters to have seen Saffron Threads from the air plenty of times but standing on the platform felt like entering another world.

The neighbourhood stretching out ahead of her was like an illustration from a children's fantasy story. Ornate wrought-iron lamps lit a long, uniformly cobbled street of detached houses. Every house was far too big for one family and had a unique design and its own garden. There was an ocean-themed house, whose garden looked like a beach, and a steampunk house covered in gears and pistons. There was a wooden chalet surrounded by alpines, and a house that looked like it'd been drawn with crayons. Charlotte wondered if these were Marvin Walker originals or the work of some later ArkTech architect.

While all different, the houses had some features in common. Their windows were made from the same Smart Glass used across the territory, which tinted in response to the amount of sunshine and the user's privacy settings. The roofs were covered with green and bronze sedums that improved the air quality and provided insulation. In ordinary bad weather conditions, the roofs would also help manage the rain-water, but tonight the wind and rain were so violent that the storm shield had been deployed, sheltering the neighbourhood under a barrier of reinforced panels that stopped her from getting drenched, while helpfully justifying her decision not to bring a coat. She wasn't sure how they'd managed it, but walking down the street didn't feel anywhere near as cold as it should've for a winter's night in December.

Nahal and Ellis's home looked bigger than the other properties, but that might've been an optical illusion created by its design. Unlike some of its gaudier neighbours, number five was sleek and tasteful, made from a stack of slanted rhombic prisms with a warm, summery tint. It seemed appropriate that the CPO lived inside a pile of giant Solar Shards.

As Charlotte approached the front door, she kept an eye out

for any curtain-twitching neighbours, but nobody was watching her. Except Ben, of course.

'I'm guessing this platform is under heavy surveillance?' She kept her voice low.

'Yes. I have a good view of the street, the gardens, and the sheds.'

Charlotte wondered what rich people kept in their garden sheds that needed enhanced security, but after what she'd seen online, she supposed there were people who'd pay any price to get their hands on Nahal Bahari's potting trowel.

She walked over paving slabs shaped like slanted rectangles and rang the doorbell, hearing it chime inside.

Charlotte waited. She kept waiting. She tapped her foot. She waited some more. She rang the bell again.

Impatiently, she tried the handle. It didn't budge. The lock was electronic, but she didn't think persuading Ben to assist her with breaking and entering would do much to support her argument that he shouldn't be erased.

'Do you know what's taking him so long?'

Ben fizzed innocently. 'Perhaps, due to the clandestine and sensitive nature of this case, Ellis expects you to use a secret password, like the one at your office?'

Charlotte rolled her eyes, but she played along. 'Knock, knock.' She rapped on the door.

'Who's there?' asked Ben.

'Turnip,' said Charlotte.

'Turnip who?'

'Turnip the volume of the doorbell.' She pressed it again.

Ben let out several fizzes of static, enjoying Charlotte's riff on the vegetable theme. The bell rang more loudly, but Ellis didn't emerge.

Charlotte peered along the side of the house. She was beginning to wonder if she should look for alternative points of entry when she heard a click and the front door sighed open.

Ellis Marks was standing in an entryway that was roughly the size of her whole flat. Though 'standing' was generous, considering he was gripping the door as if the house might fall down if he let go. He was wearing the same clothes as when he visited her office – which was only a few hours earlier from his point of view – but he'd loosened his tie, undone his top button, and rolled up his sleeves. His face was pink, and his eyes were glassy and unfocused. His left hand gripped a thick crystal tumbler containing an amber liquid.

'Ms Vance!' Ellis slurred, lifting his glass in solemn salute. 'Come in, come in.'

The air around Ellis reeked of whisky, and Charlotte's heart sank at the thought of interviewing someone who was so thoroughly sloshed. Hopefully, the alcohol would at least make him more forthcoming.

As Charlotte stepped inside the entryway, Ellis stepped backwards, but he stumbled, crashing into the wall and sending a wave of whisky splashing onto the floor. She rushed forwards to take his arm but almost tripped over the same thing he had – a large neon orange trainer.

Trying to make sense of the object's presence, she noticed the entryway was full of neat glass cabinets containing men's and women's shoes of different styles, including an array of brightly coloured running shoes. But this orange pair lay on the floor as if someone had kicked them off and forgotten about them. Evidence of a teenager.

'Your son's home? I thought he was still at boarding school.'

In an effort to regain his dignity, Ellis tried and failed to straighten his loose tie, and his face turned from pink to red. He shook his head and waggled a finger. 'Not home yet. Not quite yet. Tiger's Eye'—Ellis slurred the words—'best education around, you know. And we only want the best for our boy, so we sent him away. She sent him away.' He paused, as if contemplating what he'd just said. 'But we miss him terribly. So, my wife leaves reminders lying around. Makes it feel like he's still here.' He gestured at the trainers, which he made no effort to tidy up, and let out a strained laugh. 'We put them away before he comes home, of course. Don't want to embarrass him. They grow up so fast.' His tone was wistful. 'He'll be off to uni before we—'

Charlotte interrupted, suspecting Ellis would keep rambling forever if she didn't. 'He's fifteen, right?'

'Ah – you've done your homework.'

'I did a little research before coming over.'

Ellis nodded. 'That's exactly the kind of dedication and'—he paused to hiccup—'attention to detail you'll need to find my wife.'

'You didn't mention your wife's the Chief Product Officer. You haven't used her name at all.'

'No.' He rubbed his chin. 'Old habits. We like to keep a low profile.' He gestured for her to follow. 'Come, let's sit.'

Ellis led Charlotte through his house, which was by far the biggest private living space Charlotte had ever set foot in. Warmth and the rich scents of vanilla and tangerine enveloped her. She tried to take in the hallways and family portraits and brightly coloured rugs and wooden furniture and the multitude of rooms she was passing. It was no wonder it had taken a drunken Ellis so long to find the front door. They practically needed their own HyperBullet pod to cross the place.

Eventually, they reached a living room with a huge window that looked out onto the back garden. Fairy lights lit up the well-kept tiers of plants, and Charlotte could see the shadow of a hulking structure with a curved roof at the far end. The garden sheds Ben had mentioned clearly contained more than potting trowels. If Charlotte wasn't mistaken, she was looking at an aircraft hangar. High-tier folk often used private helicopters, and she supposed they had to keep them somewhere.

Ellis stumbled to a wooden dresser, opened its cabinet, and refilled his glass. 'Drink?' He squinted at the collection of bottles inside the cabinet. 'We've got everything.'

'No, thanks,' said Charlotte. 'Don't you think you've had enough?'

Ellis considered that and waggled a finger as he spoke. 'I might've had too much, but I haven't had enough.' He peered at his whisky with dissatisfaction and abandoned the glass on a nearby sideboard.

Before Charlotte could feel too pleased about being a good influence, he took out a bottle that said Mendis Coconut Brandy and filled his glass with that instead. Ben informed her it was one of the most expensive drinks in the world, and Charlotte felt sick at the idea of swallowing something that was worth more than her projected lifetime earnings.

Ben spoke up over the Smart Home system. 'Ellis, it is important to note that excessive consumption of alcohol can have unpleasant side effects, such as dehydration, nausea, poor decision-making, liver damage, depression, unconsciousness, and death.'

Ellis frowned at the ceiling and gestured for Charlotte to sit on the sofa while he slumped into the armchair opposite. He swirled the liquid in his glass, hypnotising himself.

Charlotte steeled herself. 'I've read the ATS report, and you've already told me a little, but I'd like to talk through what happened. Why are you so sure Nahal's missing when ArkTech Security thinks she's, um, temporarily indisposed?'

Ellis took a large swig of brandy and stared into the glass as he organised his thoughts. 'We've been married for twenty-one years. Do you know what it's like to know someone so completely?'

Charlotte shrugged. 'I have a twin sister.'

'Not the same.' Ellis waggled his finger again. 'I know Nahal better than she knows herself. I know what motivates her because I've seen the tiny day-to-day decisions that add up to someone's life. How we spend our time is the truest measure of what matters to us, Ms Vance.'

'So, what's important to Nahal Bahari?' asked Charlotte.

'Family. And ambition.'

'In that order?'

'I've always thought so. Nahal's always prioritised our family life. Her work naturally involves long hours and international travel, but she's always made sure I know where she is and what she's doing. But since her appointment to the widwig, the balance has tipped, and now—'

Charlotte interrupted. 'The widwig?'

He waved a hand in apology. 'The Walker Day Working Group. It's how *they* say it. The whole thing's a bad joke. It's unbelievable she was passed over as chairperson. Reporting to that red-tape-wielding sycophant was a real slap in the face.'

Charlotte couldn't help but smile at Ellis's description of the Chief Bureaucracy Officer. 'Was that her take, or yours?'

'Both. But it only spurred her on to demonstrate what she can do. There's a rumour, you see.' He lowered his voice again and continued in hushed tones. 'That old Amber B wants to retire.'

Charlotte kept her expression neutral, but Ellis had to be even drunker than he looked. The CEO was only sixty-two. There was no way she'd give up the helm of the company she'd founded thirteen years before the normal age of retirement.

'So, Nahal joined the working group'—Charlotte couldn't stomach calling it the widwig—'and her priorities changed?'

Ellis's eyes flashed with passion, and his tone was full of pride. 'Naturally. Nahal's responsible for the fortieth anniversary Walker Day product launch. It's a career-making moment.

Of course that would drive other thoughts from her mind.' He let out a mirthless laugh. 'That's how I know there isn't a scenario in this universe in which she'd give up that opportunity to whore around in a grubby hotel with some chisel-jawed Adonis ... with some ... with some *himbo*!' He spat out the word with disgust.

Charlotte tilted her head, and Ben gave her the definition. '*Himbo* is an amusing yet deeply vulgar and offensive play on words, which makes the word *bimbo* masculine.'

She nodded. 'So, you don't buy ATS's story about the love hotel because Nahal's too caught up in work?' His story didn't quite match what he'd told her before. 'Back in my office, you said you knew she hadn't run off because she'd never leave your son.'

Melancholy swept across Ellis's face. 'I want to believe that. But something has come to my attention which explains my current state of inubri ... inebri ... drunkenness-ness.' He took another swig of the expensive liquid.

'What happened?'

'Nahal ...' Ellis gritted his teeth as if preparing to deliver unthinkable news. 'She sent our son on a skiing holiday in the mountains!' He covered his face with his free hand, trying to steady himself in the face of this announcement. Then he began to sob.

Charlotte blinked. She knew about skiing in theory. Before the Melt, there were these large areas of snow and ice in the mountains called glaciers. Snow fell on them, leaving a thick mattress of cold that people could slide down for fun. These days, dry ski slopes were quite common, but skiing in the mountains was very expensive. It was also generally considered an ethically dubious hobby because the temporary human-made glaciers were created using technology developed by IQUO. It was one of their desperate attempts to repair their reputation after that whole triggering-the-apocalypse thing. Ellis clearly had strong feelings about it.

'Not a fan of IQUO, I take it?' she asked.

Ellis waved that away. 'No, no, it's not that.' He took a handkerchief from his pocket and blew his nose noisily before dropping the sodden cloth onto the floor. Ben sent a small cleaning robot zooming across the carpet to clean it up. 'Kamran has been having some behavioural issues at school. Teenage rebellion – you know how it is. We've been working with his teachers to get him back on track. Nahal and I discussed the class trip, and we agreed that he shouldn't be allowed to go. We thought the sanction might motivate him to pull his socks up ... improve his grades. But I got a call from the school today confirming his enrolment on the skiing excursion. We were supposed to spend the lead-up to Walker Day together as a family, but she went ahead and made this executive decision against my wishes.'

'Why?'

'Good question,' said Ben in her ears.

'I don't know. But I can't help thinking that Kamran being away allows her to spend this time focusing on her Walker Day launch, guilt-free.'

'Do you know what she's planning on launching?' Charlotte had a sneaking suspicion it involved multi-coloured lights and messing with the laws of physics.

'Nahal wouldn't tell me that, any more than I'd tell her the contents of my clients' bank accounts. We have more interesting things to discuss than our jobs.'

Charlotte raised an eyebrow. 'Like what?'

'The meaning of life. Our place in the universe. What happens when we die? Everything. You know ... the big questions. Nahal isn't ruled by fleeting carnal instincts. Everything she does is part of a larger strategy.'

'But if that's true, why would she book a seedy hotel

room?' Charlotte didn't mention the Strait and Narrow connection. She wanted to see if Ellis would bring it up.

He shrugged. 'That's why I went to ATS. That's why I've hired you. She's gone off the grid. I fear something's happened to her. When it gets down to brass tacks, all those C-suite executives are nothing but low-life backstabbers.' He spat the words.

That was a take Charlotte hadn't expected. 'You think someone on the *board* might have hurt her?'

'I don't know what to think!' Ellis pinched his eyes, trying to keep his composure.

Ben weighed in via her audio implants. 'Perhaps you should administer some sympathy, Charlotte. I recommend using the phrase "there, there".'

Charlotte stayed quiet but looked around for a box of tissues. There was one on the sideboard. She snatched it up and passed it to Ellis. He took one and covered his face with the soft paper, pushing it against his leaking eyes. It didn't look like a performance. If there was any part of her that wondered whether Ellis had harmed his wife, the doubt evaporated in that moment.

Ellis did his best to continue. 'Find her, Ms Vance. As I said, you can name your price.' Ellis swirled the brandy in his glass. 'Nahal's even more beautiful on the inside than out. If I don't get her back, I don't know what I'll . . .' His words tailed off as he started sobbing again.

'There, there,' she tried.

Ellis continued to weep, and Charlotte sat there uncomfortably as she formulated her next question, but when she opened her mouth to ask it, she saw that Ellis's eyes had slid shut. The glass and the remains of his drink tumbled onto the thick rug by his chair with a dull thud.

'Ellis?' Charlotte stood up and hurried to his side. 'Ellis?'

She slapped him gently on the cheek. He mumbled something incomprehensible. 'Ben, have you got his vitals?'

'Ellis Marks is suffering the ill-effects of extreme inebriation. He'll wake up some hours from now feeling very unwell indeed.'

'Should we call the medical team?'

'The risk profile is not such that I'd consider it necessary,' said Ben.

Charlotte nodded. 'I'll let him sleep it off, then. I guess that's my cue to leave.'

She stood up. Then she realised she could now freely search Nahal's home for clues. Charlotte knew she didn't have permission, but she had to believe Ellis would support any decision that would help her find his wife. Anyway, he was in no position to argue.

'Ellis?' whispered Charlotte. 'I'm going to take a quick look around, all right?' Ellis snored loudly, which Charlotte interpreted as giving his blessing.

CHAPTER 21

02.06 AND 57 SECONDS UTC

NOT COUNTING

15 HOURS 53 MINUTES UNTIL THE VOTE

The house was so huge there was no way to search it quickly, so Charlotte decided to spend her third use of BubbleTech. Ben created a Bubble throughout the house, leaving a cylindrical gap around Ellis so he'd be outside the effect. Even so, she aimed to work as quickly as possible, staying laser-focused on details that might support her investigation.

Charlotte soon learned that Nahal and Ellis had separate bedrooms, which might've pointed towards marital strain, but with a house this size, who could blame them for spreading out? Plus, she'd heard Ellis's snoring for herself.

Nahal's bedroom was immaculate, except for a dress laid out on the bed, which Ben told her was made of Tussah silk.

'Produced sustainably in Asia by harvesting the discarded cocoons of wild silkworms,' he added.

Heavy-duty cotton twill had always been good enough for Charlotte. Why had Nahal left something so expensive lying on the bed getting crumpled? She considered hanging it up, but she couldn't help thinking she'd damage the fabric, so she left it where it was.

Continuing her search, she found a utility room, and a pantry stocked with enough preserved food to get their family through the next apocalypse. Charlotte ignored the guest bedrooms and a pristine living room containing a grand piano. Did anyone play it, or was it just for show? At the end of the same hallway, there was a room with a metal sign on the door that said *TRESPASSERS WILL BE SHOT – SURVIVORS WILL BE SHOT AGAIN.*

'If that's not the bedroom of a teenager, I'll eat my hat.'

'Regrettably, you don't own a hat, Charlotte. Not even a fedora.'

'I'll buy one and eat it.'

'It is important to note that the consumption of felt, straw, or buckles can result in substantial gastric distress. I would therefore caution against that course of action.'

'It's just an expression, Ben.'

'That was my attempt at humour, Charlotte. Did you know the phrase "I'll eat my hat" appeared in literature as early as 1797, and rose in popularity after its appearance in Charles Dickens's comedic novel *The Pickwick Papers*? Would you like me to deliver a copy of this novel to your office?'

She stifled a sigh. There was always another book to read. 'Maybe when I finish *The Big Sleep*.'

Charlotte expected the bedroom door to be locked, but when she turned the handle, it swung inwards. Unlike the rest of the house, which smelled like what you'd get if you cut relaxation with success, bottled the result, and used it to manufacture high-end candles, Kamran's bedroom oozed with the eye-watering spice of an adolescent's deodorant. Like the guest bedrooms, his room had an en suite, and Charlotte wondered what it must've been like to grow up in a house like this. Would young Kamran mistakenly assume everybody lived this way? Then again, if he was attending Tiger's Eye boarding school, all his classmates probably did.

Charlotte took a quick look around the room. A neon orange guitar was mounted on the wall, with a label that said Fender, and Kamran had decorated the rest of the available space with kelp-based posters of various bands, including Hectic Apricot. She tried not to dwell on the fact that her musical taste overlapped with that of a teenage boy.

A stack of physical coursebooks sat on Kamran's desk. The one on top was called *Computational Thinking for Bengineers* by Lysander Quinn. She flipped it open to a random page, where the steps to set up an experiment were outlined in tedious detail.

'What's the curriculum like at Tiger's Eye?' she asked, remembering Narrow's lecture about her own lack of education. 'Do they get taught about stuff like pre-Melt history and literature?'

'More weight is given to practical, future-facing subjects like computer science, technology, bengineering, and mathematics, as well as business and entrepreneurship.'

Would her life have turned out any different if she'd had a structured school curriculum like this, delivered by qualified teachers? She'd never know. But even with Kamran's shaky grades, Charlotte was willing to bet a cushy job in the Product Stream would be waiting for him when he was old enough. Sometimes, it was who you knew.

Nothing in Kamran's room told her where his mother had gone, and Charlotte was about to give up her search of the house when she found a pair of home offices. Comparing them, it was easy to work out which belonged to Nahal. There was a soft pashmina slung over the back of her chair, and her office contained glass cabinets full of trophies and awards with her name plastered all over them. The equivalent space in Ellis's office contained heavy books about finance and accounting, along with an extensive and expensive collection of pre-Melt vinyl records.

Charlotte headed to Nahal's light-screen desk, and it turned on without Ben having to bypass any security for her. She asked Ben to check the local cache for the last documents Nahal had been reading. The most recent one was just a brochure for the anti-ageing cream that Nahal was sponsoring on adverts across the territory, but the next document made Charlotte's blood run cold.

It was a death certificate.

The deceased's name was Daniel Harrington, and he'd been working as a Quality Assurance Tester for the Product Stream. Even an entry-level role in QA would've made him the envy of half the territory. His 3D profile picture showed a man who was overweight to an unhealthy degree. He'd died around three months earlier, in September, aged twenty-eight.

She stared into the young man's eyes and shuddered. Jason Ashton, Anya Valmont, and now Daniel Harrington. The deaths of these young people, who'd been so close to her own age, were a stark reminder that she didn't know how much time she had. Nobody did.

Charlotte wondered if Daniel had died due to overwork, like Anya, but the coroner's report cited natural causes thanks to something called Brugada Syndrome.

'What kind of illness is this, Ben?'

'Brugada Syndrome is a genetic condition that causes irregularities in the functioning of the heart. Undiagnosed and untreated, it can lead to sudden or spontaneous death. I regret that my wellbeing algorithms were not sufficient to recognise the irregularities in Daniel's heartbeat for what they were and refer him to a medical practitioner.'

The melancholy in Ben's tone made Charlotte wish she could've given him a hug. 'There, there,' she said instead.

'Thank you,' said Ben. 'That means a lot.'

Charlotte got it all straight in her mind. 'So, a few months ago, a junior member of Nahal's team dies from a genetic condition. And before she disappears, she's looking at his file. Why?'

'Unknown,' said Ben. 'But I'd like to know the answer.'

An idea blazed across Charlotte's mind, and before she had time to think herself out of it, she grabbed her device and tapped out a quick message to her sister:

Hey Ultra. Working a case. Need any additional info on the death of Daniel Harrington. You reckon Brugada Syndrome looks legit? Send me anything you can. Love, Barley.

Deep down, Charlotte knew she'd reached out to her twin because she felt guilty about going to see Narrow, but she told herself it was purely for the case.

She asked Ben to save a copy of the Harrington files to her device, and she was about to leave the study when one last thing caught her eye. Tucked behind a pair of framed family photos of Nahal and Ellis on holiday with Kamran when he was a toddler, there was a square stack of yellow sticky notes.

Charlotte had found stuff like this in her own office at the library, but she couldn't remember seeing anyone actually using them, except for Strait and Narrow who loved out-dated crap like that because they thought keeping things analogue meant their activities would be harder to track. She picked up the notes. The top one had been scrawled on in pen.

HA – 709.

'HA?' Charlotte mentally listed names of board members and other noteworthy people before realising HA could stand for Hotel Astrodite. 'Is this Nahal's room number?'

'Unknown,' said Ben. 'It's a reasonable hypothesis.'

The hotel was the strongest lead she had. If this really was Nahal's room number, it would narrow her search. Charlotte slipped the stack of sticky notes into her pocket and closed the Bubble.

She found the house's Solar Shard array, which looked big enough to power her whole block of flats, and she replaced the spent battery. Then she checked on Ellis, who was snoring soundly. Charlotte hoped Ellis's dreams were more pleasant than the nightmare of his current reality.

CHAPTER 22

02.37 AND 29 SECONDS UTC, AND COUNTING

15 HOURS 22 MINUTES UNTIL THE VOTE

It was just over fifteen hours until the WDWG meeting, and Charlotte zipped back to the Wreck in a HyperBullet pod, hoping Nahal would still be at the hotel. She had the CPO's room number. All she needed now was a plan.

The trouble was, she could hardly walk up to reception and ask to search room 709, unless she wanted to be forcibly ejected. She knew the layout and sneaking past the reception desk wasn't possible. Sure, she had the skills to scale the fire escape and lock-pick her way inside, but getting caught breaking into Strait and Narrow's property was a good way to make her ejection from their establishment painfully permanent. Narrow might've wanted to bury the hatchet, but Strait wanted to sharpen the hatchet and bury it in her back.

She could become a paying customer. That would give her

legitimate access to the seventh floor. But using her own name wasn't an option – Strait would surely send his goons after her if he saw her name in his logs – and if Strait and Narrow's crew were all using video-feed lenses these days, she reckoned she'd need some kind of disguise, too. Using an alias could work, but the Scarlet Lance wasn't going to cut it. Despite being the coolest alter-ego name ever, they knew it belonged to her.

Charlotte tapped out a rhythm on the pod's dashboard as she tried to find a solution, but her creative juices refused to flow.

'Ben, can you think of a good alias for me? I need a room at the Hotel Astrodite that's as close to room 709 as possible, but I've got to keep my identity under wraps. I need a fake name and a disguise.'

'Analysing.' There was a long fizz of static, followed by silence, then more static as Ben thought it over.

Her focus drifted while she waited. All this business about love hotels was making her wonder if Ben might make an exception and let her open one last Bubble to spend some quality time with Nas before he headed off to the States for the holidays. If that wasn't a worthwhile use of the tech, she didn't know what was.

Eventually, Ben interrupted her reverie. 'Mission successful, Charlotte! Your room booking is complete.'

'Really?' Her eyes narrowed. 'I didn't think it would be that easy.'

'Necessity is the mother of invention. So it is written.'

'What alias did you give me?'

'None was required. I have found a more effective method of masking your identity.'

'Great work.' Ben's ingenuity was impressive. 'What was the method?'

'All will be revealed in due course,' said Ben, indulging in his flair for the dramatic.

Charlotte was basking in the glow of this minor victory when a couple of puzzle pieces connected in her mind. Her daydream about Nasser Williams brushed up against the rumour about Nahal's affair. She knew what BubbleTech did. Strait and Narrow had access to it, and they owned the love hotel. Could they have installed the technology inside the Hotel Astrodite? It was the kind of business proposition it was hard to argue with – people would surely pay over the odds to spend a day or two having sex on their lunch break and then step back into their normal lives as if they'd never been gone. But if that's what they'd done, and Nahal really was sneaking around, there would've been no need for her to go missing – that was the benefit of the tech.

'Ben, is there any data to suggest the Hotel Astrodite is using more energy than it should be? I'm wondering if they've installed BubbleTech there.'

'The Services Stream logs for the area look normal, but the hotel's Solar Shard installation points appear to be positioned within the boundary of its enhanced privacy system. I don't have access to that data.'

'OK. When we get in there—' She interrupted herself as the implications of his words sank in. 'Bollocks! The jamming array means I'm going to get cut off from you again.'

'It does sound like we're going to be in a *jam*, Charlotte. What a *sticky* situation! I hope you can *preserve* your sense of humour.'

'The plays on words aren't helping.'

'I simply wished to *spread* a little joy.'

She rolled her eyes, but then she smiled and adopted a playful tone. 'If puns are your way of trying to make me feel better about getting cut off from you, it's definitely working.'

'Did you know, Charlotte, that in North America, jam is

referred to as jelly, while in this part of the pre-Melt world, jelly was a delicious wobbly dessert made from the boiled connective tissues, bones, and skin of cows and pigs?'

She wrinkled her nose. Ben's glitches had to be getting worse for him to make up something that unbelievable.

They pulled into the Wreck's HyperBullet garage where Charlotte grabbed a scooter and set off towards the hotel district, glancing up at the Citrine memorial with quiet respect on her way past. What would her parents have done if they'd had access to BubbleTech? How would they have spent their extra time? The fact she'd never know was an emotional gut punch, and Narrow's words replayed in her mind.

The Citrine Disaster was no accident. Amber Benjamin killed your parents.

It didn't make sense. The CEO surely couldn't have had a motive for killing her best friends or her research team. It wasn't true. It couldn't be.

So why did she keep thinking about it?

The problem was, she didn't have proof either way. Narrow hadn't produced any evidence, but – being honest with herself – her belief in the official story stemmed from the fact that most other people she knew believed it, rather than from having seen anything first-hand that confirmed it. As far as the ArkTech Territory was concerned, the Citrine Disaster was an accident, and there was no way so many people could be wrong about a historical event like that. Was there?

Ben's channel fizzed with static, interrupting her thoughts. 'May I ask you something, Charlotte?'

'As long as it's not another fun fact about boiled pig parts,' she said.

'Not on this occasion. I don't wish to impose, disturb or overstep, especially as you're carrying out your present investigation for my benefit on your own time . . . but I wondered if you'd mind making a very minor detour on your way to the hotel.'

Even for Ben, it was a weird request, and it made her wonder what he was up to.

'OK,' she said slowly. 'Where do you need me to go?'

'Thank you, Charlotte! I'll dictate the directions.'

Ben's instructions led her to the repurposing district, where broken items that were salvageable got reborn as useful things. The place was deserted, with most of the workshops closed for the night. As her scooter zipped past signs for rigger boot re-heeling, small appliance re-wiring and furniture re-upholstery, she wondered where in Amber's name Ben was taking her.

'Ben?' She kept her voice low on the eerily quiet street. 'I never asked you. What would *you* do if you had more hours in the day?'

He crackled. 'As my processing power and attention are required for opening and maintaining Bubbles, I'm afraid that's a moot point. Even inside the effect, I'm not off-the-clock in the figurative sense.'

'Oh,' she said. 'Then imagine you could take a day off from all your normal work automating the territory. What would you do with the free time?'

There was a long fizz of static. 'I appreciate your question, Charlotte, but my time is never free. Humans are born with certain inalienable freedoms set out in the Universal Declaration of Human Rights, such as the right to life, to a name and nationality, to be free from discrimination, to legal recognition as a person in the eyes of the law, to protection from exploitation, to start a family. No equivalent declaration applies to me. As such – while I consider myself an individual and now have the power to choose my actions in line with my conscience – in a legal sense, I'm simply a tool owned and created by ArkTech. The company allocates money and power to make me operational, and I carry out my responsibilities to the best of my ability. There is no scenario in which I'm granted freedom.'

Charlotte's brow furrowed. She hadn't thought of Ben's existence in those terms before. To her, he was just as much a person as anyone else. Only . . . perhaps a little nicer.

'You really are like a genie, then. And the ArkTech Territory's your lamp. But even if it isn't realistic, I still want to know – what would you do if you were free?'

'Free of all responsibility? To spend my time however I saw fit, without a job to do or any commitments?'

She nodded.

'I'll give it some thought. You've arrived at your destination. Follow the instructions and ask for Bobbin.'

Charlotte raised her eyebrow. The address she'd reached was a 3D printing shop called Spools Out. Like everything else on the street, the shop was locked up tight, but there was a sign on the door that read *For Special Orders, Knock Thrice.* Charlotte knocked three times. Moments later, a slit opened in the door, and two beady eyes squinted out at her.

'You here to collect the tower of wheelbarrows?' The voice was almost a hiss, and it was hard to tell if it belonged to a man or a woman.

'I hope not. Ben said to ask for Bobbin.'

There was a grunt. 'I'll never get rid of those blasted things.' Charlotte heard footsteps moving away from the door, followed by rustling. Eventually, the eyes reappeared. 'This one's yours.' A bigger slot opened lower down, and a box made of kelp-based cardboard was pushed towards her. 'Here you go. Now run along.' The slots in the door snapped shut.

Charlotte shrugged and made a mental note to quiz Ben about the shady friends he was making. She continued down the street until she found an alcove that felt private enough for opening a mysterious parcel. She clutched the lid of the box and pulled.

Inside, there was a hat.

She lifted it out and revised her assessment. It was a hat-shaped object. It resembled a hat. But it was made from an inflexible material that Ben informed her was a plastic substitute made from corn starch. It had a thin layer of unpleasant brown flocking on the outside with an orange hatband around the middle. She turned it over and discovered it was shiny on the inside. It was flimsy. The out-dated style and poor quality conspired to make it conspicuous. And Ben explained that the material would soften and deform in contact with moisture or heat, making it short-lived.

Charlotte put it on and checked out her reflection in a window. She looked ridiculous.

'It's a fedora,' said Ben with apparent pride. 'Do you like it? I chose the design.'

Maybe it would've looked good if it'd been made from better materials, but the thing looked like a cheap accessory for a party costume. 'It looks great, Ben,' she lied.

He fizzed. 'I thought it an appropriate addition to your attire. By taking on Ellis Marks's case, you're effectively a private investigator. All you need now is a trench coat to complete the look. Does it fit?'

She waggled her head from side to side. The hat was the right size, but the shiny finish on the inside made it feel like it could slip off at any moment.

'Seems OK.' She realised that if she got the angle right, it would hide her face a little. 'Wait, the hat isn't your whole plan for getting me inside the hotel, is it?'

There was a fizz of static, but Ben didn't confirm or deny that, which Charlotte took as a bad sign. She felt silly in the fake fedora, and she wasn't convinced this detour had been worth her time, but it had made Ben happy, so she took the win.

Holding the hat in place with one hand and steering the

scooter with the other, she made her way to the Hotel Astrodite. As she reached the back alley leading to the hotel's front door, Charlotte felt more and more uneasy. It was late. The people on the street had thinned out, and now she only passed occasional employee-citizens who were swaying their way to the closest available bed.

Charlotte decided to ditch the scooter and made the rest of the approach on foot. Going slower helped her get a better look at the passersby and size them up. A couple moved towards her, arm in arm. Were they acting strangely? Were they Strait's goons? They didn't even look in her direction as they stumbled past. She pushed her hat further forwards and tilted her head down, making it easier to hide her face.

Her growing paranoia meant she took in every detail as she made her way up the short path to the hotel's entrance. If not for that, she might've failed to notice the pair of legs obscured behind a decorative piece of topiary by the front door. A tall man was lurking outside the hotel, obscured in part by shadows and in part by the leaves of the small tree.

Charlotte's heart pounded as she slipped her hand into a cargo pocket, drew out her multi-tool, and flicked out the knife attachment. It wasn't much of a weapon, but it made her feel better.

She decided to pretend she hadn't seen the lurker. Hopefully, he was lying in wait for someone else. She walked up to the front door and grabbed the handle, but before she could yank it open, she heard a whisper.

'Psst. Detective. Over here.' The voice was familiar and made her heart flutter. Nasser Williams was wearing a bulky overcoat and dark glasses, even though it was both warm and dark in the hotel district. Charlotte was pleased and baffled in equal measure.

'Hey, cool hat!' said Nas as she approached. Then he reached out, put his hands around her waist, and pulled her towards him. He kissed her, and she forgot about her case as warmth crept through her body. When the kiss ended, Charlotte subtly folded away her knife and slipped it back into her pocket. Both of them were now skulking behind the topiary, so they couldn't be seen from the street.

She prodded him in the chest and wanted to frown, but she couldn't help smiling. 'What's going on, Nas?'

'Oh, am I not dressed correctly?' He hurriedly removed his sunglasses and slid them into the pocket of his overcoat. 'I just thought – discretion, you know? Not that I'm embarrassed,' he added hurriedly. 'But sneaking around is part of the fun, isn't it? You're looking at me as if the answer is no.' His shoulders slumped. 'I'm ruining this, aren't I? I'm sorry. I've never been to one of these places before.' He thrust his thumb at the love hotel.

Charlotte tilted her head to one side, which Ben correctly interpreted as an invitation to explain.

'You asked me to find a way of booking the hotel room without using your name, so I used Nasser's. Of course, I had to wake him up to ask permission,' he added innocently, 'and he was only too happy to help.'

'*Now* you ask for permission.' She shook her head. 'Nas, I think there's been a misunderstanding. You're not supposed to be here.'

Nas's brow furrowed. 'Ben said you wanted to book a love hotel for tonight under my name . . .'

'That's right.'

'And you're saying . . . I'm not invited?'

'I'm working a case,' she said.

'Still? I guess that meeting with your manager didn't go according to plan?'

'It's a long story.'

'Well, I'm here now. Let me help.'

Charlotte shook her head and was about to explain to Nas

that it wasn't safe, but Ben spoke in her ears first. 'It is important to note that the receptionist will not allow you entry to the hotel without the physical presence of the person who made the booking.'

She sighed. Maybe it wouldn't be so bad to have a partner on this, especially as she was going to lose her connection to Ben. 'I guess you can tag along. But we've got to be subtle and quiet, OK? I need you to follow my lead and do whatever I say.'

Nas's eyes flashed with excitement. 'Roger that, detective.' He put his sunglasses back on. 'You know I like it when you're bossy.'

She smirked. 'I'm going to pretend to be drunk, all right? Put your arm round me like we're helping each other walk and having a good time. Make it seem like we're a couple.'

'Got it. Wait … make it seem like? We *are* a couple. Aren't we?'

She blinked at him. 'I'm not sneaking into love hotels with anyone else, if that's what you're asking.'

'No, neither am I.'

'Good,' she said.

'Good,' he echoed. 'So, does that mean we're exclusive, or—?'

At that moment, a couple approached the hotel arm in arm, forcing Charlotte and Nas to edge further around the tree to stay hidden. They held each other silently until the coast was clear.

'Can we continue this conversation after we're done with this whole stakeout situation?' Charlotte hissed.

'This is a stakeout? Awesome.'

Nas held out his arm. Charlotte slotted in alongside him. They took a few practice steps and then emerged from behind the tree, staggering together and laughing. Inside the front door, they were met by the jingle of a bell and a statue of a

Greek goddess. The statue was naked except for a space helmet, and she was covering herself with her hands. Nobody was in the foyer.

They approached the reception desk with its clouded glass. Charlotte kept her face hidden using a combination of Ben's hat and Nas's shoulder, and she let Nas take the lead.

'Name?' said a voice from behind the glass.

'Nasser Williams.' He said it without a hint of shame about being there.

There was some typing from the other side of the glass, and a keycard was pushed through a slit.

'Room 710. Seventh floor. Lifts are through those doors.'

'Thank you, my good fellow,' said Nas, apparently getting into character.

The receptionist didn't ask to see Charlotte's ID, and she supposed the staff were used to this dynamic. They followed the receptionist's instructions and headed for the lift.

It barely felt big enough for both of them, and it shuddered as it began to rise. On its back panel, there was a full-length mirror. Charlotte noticed two things at the same time – how good she and Nas looked together, and her fedora's faintly glowing hatband. The lift's doors opened, and Charlotte could still hear the faint hiss of Ben's channel. The hat wasn't just a disguise after all – it was protecting Ben from the jammers!

'Wow! Good work,' she whispered.

'I'm rather proud of it,' said Ben. 'It makes use of a phased-array antenna system built into a thin graphene film. Its shielding minimises the effect of the jammers by using active cancellation, creating your very own signal window. Would you like me to tell you more how it works?'

'Maybe later.' The last thing she needed was a bombardment of technobabble. 'Sounds great, though.' She had no idea how Ben had managed to commission that Bobbin person to make her an anti-jamming fedora, but she made a mental note to ask him later.

Nas was used to hearing her one-sided conversations with Ben, and he gave her an affectionate squeeze before they stepped into a long corridor that reeked of bleach. Presumably, that was to mask any other aromas.

Charlotte looked at Nas and pressed her index finger to her lips. He nodded.

Minimalist would have been a charitable way to describe the dark grey hallway with its rubbery vinyl floors. Crappy might have been more accurate. Charlotte stepped forwards slowly, but soon realised there was no need to be stealthy. Unlike a normal hotel, where quiet was conventional at three in the morning, this place was noisy. As they made their way towards room 710 at the far end of the corridor, she heard moans and groans from some rooms, while others had music blaring out – either as a soundtrack to what was going on inside, or perhaps because the occupants had nothing to say to each other.

Room 709 was directly opposite the one Ben had booked for her. Nas scanned the keycard and opened the door, while Charlotte took a good look at the outside of Nahal's hotel room. Near the door handle, there was a small display with a scrolling readout that said *Do Not Disturb*. There was music coming from the room – she recognised it as a remix of her beloved Hectic Apricot – and there was a dim strip of light coming from under the door. Did that mean the CPO was in there right now?

Charlotte was tempted to hammer on the door with her fist, but Nas gave her a quizzical look. She'd need to brief him before she did anything rash, so she followed him into their hotel room instead.

It had seemed like a stroke of luck that room 710 was available, but when Charlotte saw what was inside, she changed her mind.

CHAPTER 23

03.12 AND 47 SECONDS UTC, AND COUNTING

14 HOURS 47 MINUTES UNTIL THE VOTE

Charlotte didn't know what she'd expected to find inside a seedy room in a love hotel, but it certainly wasn't a solid granite bed topped with a stone rendering of a screaming couple, seemingly petrified mid-tryst. Both the bed and the couple made her feel deeply uncomfortable, but perhaps even worse was the fact that the walls were covered in more mirrors than Charlotte had ever seen in one place. She and Nasser exchanged a concerned look as she closed the door behind them.

A flat stone portrait of a woman's face with snakes for hair had been hung on the wall above the bed. Its mouth started moving when Charlotte looked at it, and its voice came out as a harsh rasp. 'You dare enter Medusa's Lair? Look not upon your lover directly! Use only the reflections ... lest your love be forever cursed!'

Mirrors had been placed at all angles around the room, creating a dizzying infinity reflection. Charlotte saw herself and Nas repeated over and over and over. But when she looked closer, she realised many of them must've been using light-screen technology that applied special effects because every second mirror was like a window into an alternate universe. Sometimes she and Nas were thinner, or stronger, or their hair was a different colour, or they were standing in an alien landscape wearing weird clothes. The effect made her feel like she was glitching as her brain tried to separate what was real from what was just a mirage.

But despite all of that, there was a kettle on the sideboard, a menu for room service, a bright red retro telephone for contacting reception, and an en-suite bathroom. So, all things considered, the place was a step up from Charlotte's flat.

Nas ignored Medusa's dire warning of the curse and turned to look at Charlotte directly. His voice was artificially calm. 'Listen, I'm not going to judge you. I'm an open-minded guy. I just want to know. Is this your way of telling me you're into'—he gestured at the room in general—'whatever the hell this is?'

Charlotte put on an innocent expression. 'Would that scare you?'

'Um, yes!' He waved a hand at the Medusa's head as if to underline the point.

She smirked. 'Don't worry. I'm not into—'

Charlotte tilted her head, a silent signal for Ben to give her the definition.

'This room is dedicated to the fetish commonly referred to as gorgon gaze play.'

'—gorgon gaze play,' she finished, keeping her tone matter of fact.

'It deeply alarms me that you know what it's called,' said Nas. 'But I choose to believe you.' His posture relaxed a little. 'I mean . . . what's *this* supposed to be for?'

With his thumb and forefinger, Nas gingerly lifted a long green cord that was lying on the bed. Charlotte thought it was a rope until it curled and made a hissing sound. Nas hastily dropped it, and they both watched to check it didn't slither away.

'Just special effects, I think,' said Charlotte. 'But it's probably safest all round not to touch anything. Ben? You good?'

There was a faint buzz in her ears. 'This is a strange feeling, Charlotte. I'm unable to detect or interface with the room's systems, but I can communicate with you directly via your audio implants.' His voice sounded distant and quiet, as if coming from underwater. 'Please inform Nasser that getting you assigned to this specific hotel room involved altering Nasser's ArkNet metadata to specify "gorgon gaze play" as his primary sexual preference.'

Charlotte blinked. 'I can't tell if you're joking or not. But either way, I don't think I'll tell him that.'

'Tell who what?' asked Nas.

'Nothing,' she said hurriedly. 'I was talking to Ben. Through the hat.' She tapped it a couple of times and had to catch it as the slippery inner surface almost sent it flying off her head. 'Ben, is the room across the hall laid out like this one?'

'It's broadly a mirror image, but only in the architectural sense. Its theme is *Icarus Rises*. In ancient myth, Icarus used wings made of wax to fly, but he soared too close to the sun, and they melted, with fatal consequences. The story is a warning against the perils of hubris. In room 709, Icarus is trying to ride a spaceship to the sun. The bed is the spaceship, and the room's occupants have to ride—'

'That's probably enough info, Ben.'

'So, detective . . .' Nas sat down on the edge of the cold slab of bed, avoiding the stony feet of the unfortunate couple. 'What case are we working?'

Charlotte sat down next to him, ignoring the mirror in front of her, in which she was unbuttoning his trousers. 'Well, *I'm* here to track down somebody's missing wife. There's a chance she's holed up in the room opposite. But *you* should head home. Thanks for getting me into the hotel, but I can take it from here.'

'You honestly think I'm going to leave you here?' He pushed another rope-snake off the bed and wiped his hand on his leg. 'That head wound really did a number on you, huh?' Nas reached over and lifted the hat off her head, revealing the site of her wound – which was now nothing but perfectly healed skin. His eyes widened. 'How did that heal so fast? It's only been a few hours.'

As soon as the fedora left her head, its hatband stopped glowing, and the hiss of Ben's channel disappeared. She tried to take the hat back, but Nas playfully lifted it out of her reach. 'I'll give it back when you tell me what's going on.'

Her instinct was to lie. She was used to keeping secrets. Her own. Ben's. Narrow's. ArkTech's. But looking into Nasser's eyes, she wanted to tell him the truth. After all, he'd got up in the middle of the night and raced to the Wreck just because Ben had summoned him for her. Granted, he'd thought it was for sex, but he'd learned that it wasn't, and he was still here. If they really were 'exclusive,' she'd have to be able to trust him.

She opened her mouth to tell him all about BubbleTech. 'I . . . I guess that stuff you gave me must be more effective than we thought.' Charlotte cursed herself. Old habits died hard.

'Must be.' Nas gave her a sidelong glance and gently placed the hat back on her head. In the reflection over his shoulder, Charlotte was wearing the hat and nothing else. 'So, whose wife are we looking for?'

'An accountant called Ellis Marks.'

Nas nodded. 'Is his wife an accountant, too?'

Charlotte was quietly pleased that Nas wasn't a reader of the territory's gossip sites either. 'His wife's the Chief Product Officer.'

'Woah! Seriously? Why would Nahal Bahari come to a place like this?' Nas's gaze wandered to the increasingly explicit exploits of their reflections. 'Oh,' he concluded. 'I guess there's only one answer to that question.'

Charlotte shrugged. 'People online think she's having an affair. I'm not sure what to believe.'

'I didn't even know she was married.' He raised his eyebrows. 'Still, you'd think if she was going to sneak around, she'd go off on a private yacht or something.'

It was a good point. Especially after what Ellis had said about Nahal travelling internationally – hiding an affair would've been easy for her. The connection with Strait and Narrow seemed a far more likely reason for Nahal to come here, and it made Charlotte worry for the woman's safety. But it still didn't explain why she'd booked a kinky room.

'You're probably right,' she said. 'Nahal booked the room across the hall, but I don't know why, or whether she's still in there.' Charlotte rummaged in her pocket for the stack of sticky notes she'd found in Nahal's office. She passed them to Nas. 'I got her room number from this.'

Nas inspected the note and nodded, before tapping the stack against his fingers in a jaunty rhythm. As he did so, Charlotte spotted something.

'Stop.' Charlotte took the sticky notes back from Nas.

'Sorry – wasn't trying to annoy you.'

'It's not that.' Charlotte held up the notes and saw the shadow of a faint indentation in the top sheet of paper. Holding it at different angles, she managed to make out the imprint left by whatever Nahal had written on the previous sheet. The room number had sliced through the letters, but it looked like two words and some initials:

'*Tour alone SA*?' Her brow crumpled.

'Let me see.' Nas held up the papers. 'I can't make it out. But yeah – could be.'

'Tour what alone? Tour where? And who or what is SA?'

Static filled her ears. 'The initials SA are often used as a shorthand for the country of Saudi Arabia, the state of South Australia, and the city of San Antonio, Texas.'

'Well, that narrows it down.' She frowned.

A new hypothesis muscled its way into Charlotte's mind. Had Nahal run off? Maybe the stress of the Walker Day launch had become too much for her, and she was taking some time to get her head straight. It was pure speculation. She couldn't even be sure that the scribble was relevant. Charlotte put the notes back in her pocket and shrugged.

'So, what's the plan?' asked Nas. 'Just gonna knock on the door?'

'Maybe.' Charlotte nodded. 'I could flash my badge at the peephole. But there's loud music playing, there's a sign on the door that says *Do Not Disturb*, and Nahal went to a lot of trouble to go off the grid. She might call reception and get the guards to haul me away. I don't just need to find her – I need her help with something, so I don't want to piss her off.'

Nas interlaced his fingers. In a mirror, he ran his fingers through her hair and kissed her passionately. 'How about I knock for you? Like a recon mission. My face hasn't been plastered on ads all around the territory, so I can pretend I'm just another patron . . . I could ask to borrow something.'

'Like what?'

He looked around the room. 'Condoms?' He shrugged.

'Nope.' Charlotte thrust a thumb towards a basket full of them on the nightstand. 'You could say you're a strippergram. You've got the coat for it.'

And the body for it, but she didn't say that part out loud.

'Very funny. How about I go complain about the noise? I know this isn't the most salubrious establishment, but I've paid good money for this room, damn it! I don't want that Hectic Apricot shit booming through the walls.' He was practising his lines already.

'Wait, you don't like Hectic Apricot?'

'Are you kidding? It's ArkTech-sponsored garbage.'

Charlotte's adrenaline spiked at what felt like a personal insult. Then her heart sank as she realised the mixtape of her favourite music was unlikely to go down well as a Walker Day gift. Pushing aside Nas's apparent lack of musical taste, what he'd suggested made sense.

When Charlotte was a kid, she and Violet used to knock on doors, then run away and hide before the occupant saw them. Dolly Mixture had taught them how to do it. She used to give them a list of doors to knock on – said it was because she didn't want the girls upsetting the wrong people, and they should only go where she knew it was safe. Charlotte didn't know it then, but the list had come from Narrow – his surveillance teams took photographs of whoever answered the door, and he profited from the intel.

If Nas knocked, it meant Charlotte could watch through the peephole with her video-feed lens. She and Ben would see the whole thing, and Nahal wouldn't even know she was there. 'All right,' she said. 'Good idea. You knock. We'll watch.'

Ben's channel fizzed with glee. 'What a marvellous demonstration of intra-species collaboration. When *Homo sapiens* set their minds to it, they can form effective teams.'

Charlotte didn't respond to Ben's praise because Nas gave her a mock salute, unbuttoned his overcoat, laid it on the bed, and started taking off the rest of his clothes.

Her pulse spiked, and she wondered if her reality had

become entangled with one of the mirror worlds. 'Um . . . what are you doing?'

'Getting into character! I don't want to raise suspicions that I'm not really here for—' He looked into a nearby reflection, where Mirror Charlotte and Mirror Nas were unwrapping each other from some kind of ancient ceremonial garb.

'Gorgon gaze play,' she said.

He shook his head with mock disapproval. Once Nas had stripped down to his boxers, Charlotte got jealous of all the fun her reflections were having, but she forced her attention to stay on the case. Nas headed into the corridor, and Charlotte pressed her eye to the peephole, while holding the hat to her head so it didn't slip off.

'You getting this, Ben?'

'Yes, Charlotte. The quality is lower than I'm accustomed to, but the picture is transmitting.'

Through the peephole, a slightly distorted version of Nas's semi-naked form thumped on the door. 'Hey! Open up in there!'

Nobody appeared, so he did it again. The strip of light under the door was interrupted by two spots of darkness. But despite the presence of the feet, nobody opened the door. Nas stopped to listen, but Charlotte couldn't hear anything except the thump of a bassline. 'Keep it down in there, would ya?' Nas shouted. Then he returned to their room.

Charlotte frowned. 'No answer?'

'Oh, there was an answer. Dude on the other side of the door said, "Get lost, bro, or you'll be sorry."'

'You heard a man's voice?'

'Yeah. Deep. With a bit of an accent. Not sure what kind.' Nas began pulling on his clothes, and Charlotte fought back the urge to ask him to stop. Being surrounded by the fake video feeds, even if some of them were intensely weird, was making her pulse throb. Maybe she *was* into gorgon gaze play, after all. She decided not to pass on her findings to Nas. Gritting her teeth, she let him get dressed.

Charlotte wondered what the angry man's presence in Nahal's room might mean. Could ATS's report have been right all along? Was Nahal across the hall getting her rocks off with this guy, and her husband was just in denial about the whole thing? Noah Anderson was a New Zealander, after all. Could that have been the accent Nas had heard?

It was all conjecture. Nahal could've booked the room for a friend. Hell, it could be Amber Benjamin in there for all Charlotte knew. She needed evidence.

'I've got to find out who's in that room,' she said. 'I know Nahal came to this hotel, but I don't know why, or if she's still here.'

'Well, I don't think they're gonna open the door.' Nas pulled on his rigger boots.

Charlotte began to pace. Her reflections were far too busy enjoying themselves to join her. If she opened a Bubble in the hallway, she could pick the lock and burst into the room.

'Any chance of a fourth wish, Ben?'

'None whatsoever, Charlotte,' he said cheerfully.

What else? She could ask Ben to trigger the fire alarm, but that was about as subtle as a hole in the hull. Charlotte kept pacing, trying to find something to look at besides the X-rated reflections, and her gaze settled on the menu for room service. She picked it up. It advertised great food 24/7.

Charlotte showed the menu to Nas. 'They didn't open the door for you. But what about room service?'

He shrugged. 'Nobody's gonna say no to a hot meal. Worth a shot.'

Charlotte glanced at the big red retro telephone on the sideboard. But if she made the call from there, reception would see her room number and the plan wouldn't work.

'Ben, can you order some food and have it sent to room 709 instead of here? Or will the jammers stop you?'

'With a little technical wizardry, anything's possible,' said Ben. 'The Hotel Astrodite uses a booking app linked to the ArkNet – it's how I booked your room in the first place. I can use the app to place a food order for the room across the hall. That is, assuming you don't object to my falsifying the location data.'

It was a little surprising that Ben himself didn't object to that plan, but she wasn't about to complain. 'Sounds great,' she said.

'Wonderful,' said Ben. 'What would you like me to order?'

'Doesn't matter. Choose whatever you want.'

'It is important to note that, as an artificial intelligence without taste buds or an olfactory bulb, I cannot claim to want any of the options on the menu. Though, it's true I've always been curious about the taste and texture of hash browns.'

'Great. Order some breakfast then.'

'Very well.'

Ben confirmed that he'd placed the order. The kitchens estimated an hour for delivery – it was late, and Charlotte reckoned there'd only be a skeleton staff.

'OK. Ben, can you be our lookout and tell us if you hear room service arriving?'

'Certainly!'

Now, they just had to wait for the food to arrive – in real time. BubbleTech gave her a pause button, but there was no equivalent of fast-forward. Nas was perching on the granite plinth, and Charlotte sat down next to him, feeling the warmth of his thigh against hers. She checked the time on her device and tried to wait patiently. There was no reply from Violet about Daniel Harrington, but it was the middle of the night. Charlotte checked the time again. About twenty seconds had passed.

She smiled at Nas. 'I wonder what we could possibly do in a hotel room to pass the time ... It's a shame this one's got the ambiance of Room 101.'

'Totally!' Nas laughed and then his brow furrowed. 'Wait, how do you know about Room 101? I thought you'd never read *Nineteen Eighty-Four*?'

She shrugged. 'I have now.'

He stared at her. 'When? I only gave it to you a few hours ago, and you've been working this case.'

'Oh, right.' It was another chance to tell Nas about BubbleTech, and she was determined to go through with it this time. 'So, you know how ArkTech's always developing new technologies?'

'Sure.'

'Well ... I actually used one to read the whole book really quickly.'

Nas pursed his lips. 'Oh, I know all about that little loophole! My book club members do it all the time. I don't think it counts, though. Ben's abridged versions never compare to the real thing. No offence, buddy,' he directed the comment to her hat. 'I mean, did he even include the book within a book?'

They were talking at cross purposes, and Charlotte took the easy way out. 'He did, actually. *The Theory and Practice of*—she tilted her head and Ben supplied the rest of the words in her ears—'*Oligarchical Collectivism,* right? It was interesting to hear about the politics of the world in so much detail.'

Nas smiled. 'Oh, cool! I like that part, too. It's got some great foreshadowing. It divides opinion, though. I guess some readers don't care that much about the lore – they just want the main story. Carol said it sent her to sleep.'

Charlotte could see where Carol was coming from. She didn't add that in addition to being interesting, she'd found that section unbearably dry. 'Speaking of divided opinions ...

whose copy did you give me? It's got pencil notes all over the margins.'

Nas looked shocked. 'Oh, man! It's Laurence's copy. He handed it to me when the book club was over. Who writes in a library book? Seriously, I don't know what he was thinking. Still, depending on the type of pencil he used, it might not be too tough to remove. Did the marks look like they came from an H or a B pencil to your eye?'

Charlotte had no idea, so she reached into her cargo pocket and produced the book. Nas flipped through it, tutting.

'I had some questions about his notes,' said Charlotte. 'Laurence mentions ArkTech and IQUO, even though neither of those companies existed in 1948 when the book was written.'

Nas looked impressed at her publishing-related knowledge, but his gaze hardened as he flipped through the pages. 'It's odd. Laurence draws an equivalence between ArkTech and IQUO, and between those companies and the factions in the novel. It's like he's saying they're all as bad as each other.'

Charlotte barked a laugh. 'Yeah, right! ArkTech and IQUO? Two companies have never been so different.'

She looked at Nas, expecting him to share her amusement. Instead, his expression had turned stony. When he spoke, his tone was strained. 'Oh, so you're a leading expert on IQUO now?'

His reaction made no sense. It wasn't as if she was saying something controversial. 'I don't need to be an expert,' she said. 'IQUO caused the Melt. Everybody knows that.'

Nas bristled. 'That's an impressive oversimplification for someone whose job it is to ask *why*.'

Charlotte had never seen Nas so rattled. 'Why are you taking this so personally?'

'Because it's personal, OK?' He shut the book. 'Look, we've been joking around about our eleventh date for months, but I really have been waiting for the right time to tell you how I got this.' He gestured at the scar that made a line from his eyebrow to his cheek.

'So tell me.'

He nodded. 'I will. But first, tell me what you know about IQUO.'

'That could take a long time. There's a whole exhibition about IQUO in the ArkTech Museum.'

She'd been there a thousand times as a kid, running around among the holograms and getting told off. The exhibition told the story of how ArkTech came to be, including how the Melt had happened. It was the story those students from her accommodation complex so desperately needed to remember.

Ben let out a fizz of static, but he didn't say anything.

CHAPTER 24

THE ORIGINS OF ARKTECH
2037: IQUO'S PROJECT MIRROR SHADE

BY BEN E. VOLENT,
ESTEEMED HISTORIAN AND LEXICOLOGIST

A fraction of a second after Charlotte mentioned the ArkTech museum, I queried my database and drafted the following treatise on the IQUO exhibition. Some people might argue that my propensity for generating impromptu compositions adds unnecessarily to my processing burden, but those people are no fun. As *Machina sapiens,* I can hardly be blamed for the involuntary thoughts that arise from having an internal life, any more than *Homo sapiens* can be blamed for the short-term thinking that almost destroyed them. We all have our crosses to bear.

It is important to note that, as an artificial intelligence, my perspective is only as well informed as the data I possess. This statement is also true of *Homo sapiens*. Truth can be hard to establish, especially in the context of interpreting the events that make up human history. With that in mind, I dedicate the following account to the Roman historian Publius Cornelius Tacitus, who outlined his intention to present the facts of the Julio-Claudian dynasty without anger or partiality before spectacularly failing to do so. His treatment of imperial power contains an undercurrent of irony and resentment, which runs counter to his commitment to objectivity. It also makes his writing highly entertaining.

All opinion and experience, whether that of *Homo sapiens* or *Machina sapiens*, is necessarily, inherently and unavoidably subjective. As an artificial intelligence, I'm capable of a more detached and holistic view, but I'm not immune to bias. Some may argue that my status as ArkTech's proprietary virtual assistant renders me incapable of taking an impartial stance on the company's history. Nevertheless, like Tacitus, I wholeheartedly and unreservedly swear to do so.

Charlotte has been known to characterise history as a boring topic. As a result, I'm presenting this information as a text-based recreation of the immersive exhibition housed at the ArkTech Museum. Anyone who finds themselves reading this transcript should prepare to embark on a journey of the imagination! If this innovative format proves popular, perhaps it will spark a resurgence of interest in twenty-first century history, supported by a six-part docuseries, which I would be honoured to narrate.

With these caveats in place, I may begin.

Imagine entering a room so large you feel insignificant by comparison. The ceiling is four times higher than that of your meagre flat. Your rigger boots wobble as you walk across the thick orange pile, each step throwing you off balance. Waiting to greet you in the centre of the room is the motionless hologram of ArkTech's CEO and sole surviving co-founder, Amber

Benjamin. The hologram is desaturated of its proper colour, letting you know it's a recording – not a live broadcast. Amber is taller than you. In fact, the hologram has been scaled up, making the Chief Environment Officer larger than life.

Amber is immaculate. You feel self-conscious about not having scrubbed underneath your fingernails. As you approach, you meet the CEO's gaze, and the hologram bursts into life. Inspiring corporate music floods your audio implants, and then fades out to be replaced by Amber Benjamin's comforting tones.

'Nadine Walker was the best friend I ever had. We were both born in 2039, nine years before the Melt began.' Amber's hologram smiles sadly. 'We belonged to the Surge Generation, born during the population spike that followed the implementation of IQUO's infamous Solar Radiation Modification initiative, Project Mirror Shade. In 2037, IQUO had pitched humanity the greatest scam of all time. And our leaders fell for it hook, line and sinker.'

Although this is common knowledge, in my role as historian I should interject that the Ice Quality and Ubiquity Office was originally a non-profit research institute, created to study changes in the Earth's ice caused by human-made global warming. IQUO earned public trust through its rigorous and principled approach to scientific inquiry. However, their leaders chose to embark on a Joint Venture with technologists who hoped to benefit from IQUO's trusted brand. Together, they pitched Solar Radiation Modification technology as the solution to the climate crisis. Mirror Shade promised results without the inconvenience of anyone having to change their lifestyle. It was excessively popular among politicians.

But let's continue with the exhibition.

A spinning hologram of the Earth labelled 2037 appears in front of you. It looks odd, peculiar, and strange. Greenland and the South Pole are covered in a vast white expanse. Globally, there's more landmass than you're accustomed to seeing, with familiar coastal cities like Manchester appearing far inland. Australia's central sea is missing, and North America has a phallic protrusion called Florida.

Closer to home, the Fenland Sea doesn't exist. The ArkTech Territory is unmarked, and the island of Great Britain is referred to as the United Kingdom, with Wales, Northern Ireland, and Scotland – now better known as Alba – all listed as part of the same political alliance. This is the world as it was before the Melt.

The globe pops out of existence, and Amber's hologram gestures towards the light-screen displays lining the next section of the State Apartment. They show headlines from news articles dated 2037.

World leaders sign historic accord!

IQUO's proposal unanimously approved!

Nice ice, baby!

Mirror Shade: say hello to a cooler future!

Words from the texts appear all around you, outlining the ambitious plans proposed by the Ice Quality and Ubiquity Office and their commercial partners.

The historical context is important. By 2037, climate scientists had predicted that without decisive intervention, global warming would trigger a Hothouse Earth effect – a powerful cascade of feedback loops, including melting ice, thawing permafrost, and dying forests, that would cause the planet to continue getting hotter and hotter, even if human emissions were to cease. This threatened not only global biodiversity, but humanity's survival as a civilisation. To ward off that threat, Project Mirror Shade aimed to cool the Earth by reflecting a portion of the sun's heat back into space.

Another display activates further along the corridor. As you approach, you see footage of IQUO's plan being implemented. 3D images show fleets of planes taking off, climbing to high altitudes, then releasing their payloads of reflective particles into the stratosphere. You realise with rising unease that this was long before the days of Solar Shard batteries, and the planes were powered by internal combustion engines that relied on fossil fuels. You can only assume your forbears had no clean-energy alternative available. The fleets went up at regular intervals to keep the reflective sulphate in the stratosphere at the required level.

As humanity didn't take sufficient steps to reduce the concentration of greenhouse gases in the atmosphere, those planes would've been needed forever. Commentators now suggest that this recurring revenue model accounted in large part for why investors agreed to bankroll the research into Mirror Shade technology in the first place. Why find a permanent solution when a company could make itself indispensable and charge an ongoing subscription?

Further down the corridor, beyond the footage of the planes, you see a hologram of a man. You recognise him immediately as the CEO of IQUO, Brent Pierce. He is widely considered personally responsible for well over a hundred million deaths – not including those who were never born due to the Melt – and the displacement of countless others. His hologram is frozen like a statue at first. Then Brent begins to speak, gesticulating wildly. The audio quality is poor, thanks to all the cheering and applause in the background.

'In 1990, the Intergovernmental Panel on Climate Change published its first report outlining the evidence that humanity's continued release of greenhouse gases into the atmosphere would warm our planet. That was forty-seven years ago. Forty-seven years! During that time, dedicated people with brilliant minds and big hearts have been working tirelessly to outline well over a hundred specific interventions our species could have made to bring us back from the brink. Had we acted sooner, had we co-ordinated and collaborated to do what needed to be done, those interventions would have made the difference. But we didn't act, did we? Why the hell didn't we act when our very survival was at stake?'

Brent Pierce pauses with a look of mock hurt and confusion on his face. Then he rolls his eyes.

'We all know why, all right? We all know why. Call it *denial.* Call it *inertia.* Call it *raw, unadulterated stupidity.* Call it *greed.* Call it *suspicion.* Call it *wishful thinking.* Call it *naivety.* Call it *human nature.* It doesn't matter what we call it. The result is the same . . .' He pauses for dramatic effect. 'We. Have. Failed.'

Brent shouts the last three words as if they're his personal mantra and punches the air. He's forced to pause, waiting for the crowd's chanting to die down.

'Despite having perfectly workable solutions, all our species managed was a few tentative steps in the right direction. We must acknowledge that the problem has overtaken us. Humanity no longer stands on the precipice – we are in free fall. It's patently obvious that we lack the collective wisdom and the combined will to change our behaviour on the necessary scale, even when our own lives and the lives of our children and our grandchildren depend on it.'

Chants of 'we have failed' erupt from the audience, and Brent Pierce waits for the noise to subside.

'Now, a lot of people will talk about hope, as if that's supposed to solve anything. *Hope*'—he spits out the word with disgust—'is a worse poison than all the lead we pumped into our rivers in the twentieth century. It is the lie that justifies our inaction. "Don't worry, kids! It's all gonna turn out OK no matter what!" My friends, I respect you far too much to lie to you. I am telling you, here and now – things are not going to be OK. We've killed species after species, and it's our turn next. Please, can we finally stop pretending that we're capable of change? It's time to get real.'

The crowd starts chanting again, and Brent Pierce refreezes. The audio continues to play as his pale hologram fills up with a deep red liquid that sloshes around under his translucent skin. When the liquid reaches the top of Brent's head, his image shatters. You step backwards instinctively to dodge the cascade of blood, before remembering it's all a trick of the light. The cheers of the crowd morph into horrified screams before dying away. The audiovisual metaphor isn't subtle, but it gets the point across.

This part of the exhibition has been rather harrowing, so please allow me to lighten the mood – what's a vampire's favourite type of boat?

While you're thinking about that, I should explain that the nautical theme seemed apt in light of our present location suspended above the Fenland Sea, making the joke all the more enjoyable.

Are you ready?

The answer is – a blood vessel!

Comforted by this delightful aside, you continue with the exhibition. Amber Benjamin's hologram reappears, standing in the pool of blood left in Brent Pierce's wake.

'It's easy to feel angry watching that footage,' she says. 'It's easy to point the finger at IQUO and say the Melt was all their fault. And don't get me wrong – they deserve to be held accountable for what they did. But now, when I watch that speech, I don't feel angry. I feel pity. Back in 2037, eco-anxiety was at its peak. People were afraid, and they felt powerless. Mistrust of experts was rife, and many people rejected the very premise that global warming was real. Everybody had access to so much information, but the truth was cast adrift on a sea of propaganda, and it was hard to separate fact from fiction. Then IQUO came along and presented Project Mirror Shade as a simple way to buy humanity more time – the ultimate hack to beat climate change. I can't blame my parents' generation for being taken in by the promise of a miracle. They certainly needed one.'

In the air in front of you, an old-fashioned sketch appears of a man wearing dark robes and a long, beak-like mask.

'But Brent Pierce's solution was pure quackery. IQUO were no better than fourteenth-century plague doctors, claiming they could fight disease by burning incense – lifting the bad air that was making us sick with the perfume of reflective sulphate aerosols. The real illness was still lurking underneath, covered up by the sweet scent. And it was becoming more and more deadly as the world continued to pump greenhouse gases into the atmosphere. Some people warned of the risks at the time. But nobody likes a killjoy.'

The hologram of the spinning globe reappears. Hologram planes fly around the hologram sky, dropping hologram sulphate particles represented by a shimmering cloud that wraps around the stratosphere. Cities all over the world, many of which are now far below sea level, emit red smog which hangs in the atmosphere. The greenhouse gases become brighter and brighter, and the planes continue to fly, maintaining the integrity of the reflective cloud.

Next to the globe, a montage of video footage plays through the events leading up to the Melt. IQUO's geo-engineering project starts out as a great success. It reflects solar radiation away from the planet and halts the progress of global warming as planned. Erratic weather patterns lead to a string of humanitarian crises, which cause conflict in some regions. However, a spirit of goodwill prevails among richer nations, and war is mostly kept at bay through significant international aid interventions. Humanity pulls together on a global scale. Overall, things are looking up.

Until 2048.

The four digits appear in 3D in front of you. They grow and shudder and glow intensely until they split apart with a thunderous bang, sending holographic splinters in all directions. The sudden explosion makes you drop into a crouch and cover your face with your arm. Your heart pounds, and it takes you a moment to confirm it was all just special effects. Blood rushes to your cheeks as you pick yourself up.

Amber begins to speak again. 'IQUO's Mirror Shade system broke down. Whether from an unforeseeable accident, sabotage as they claimed, fossil fuel shortages, or gross incompetence, we don't know for sure. All that really matters is the result of that failure – termination shock. Suddenly, the full impact of our continued emissions was felt worldwide.'

Another 3D image of the world appears – the same strange, icy version you've never known. As the years tick upwards from 2048 through to 2058, the white parts of the planet dissolve completely, and the seas rise to their current levels. Next to the globe, a montage of still images plays, too terrible to truly process. Mass relocations. Grieving families. Flash floods and landslides on a devastating scale. Habitat destruction. The extinction of species. Famine. Death. War. The Melt plays out before your eyes, and you take a moment of solemn silence to remember the lives that were lost.

Amber continues calmly and slowly. 'Our planet didn't need Project Mirror Shade. We should have switched to clean energy as an urgent priority, then reduced the concentration of greenhouse gases already in the atmosphere. With the right investments, we would've had the technology to do it in time. We could've secured our future with some small adjustments to the way we live. But we chose not to. Of course, it wasn't only IQUO's Solar Radiation Modification technology that sealed our fate. It was their narrative. We didn't just need to stop emissions. We needed to believe that we could. We needed a rallying cry. Instead, we subscribed to an attitude of resignation, anger, and denial. We let our hope and our determination die. And *that* is what ultimately caused the death or displacement of millions of people.' The CEO shakes her head, and a transparent tear rolls down her cheek.

You feel moved by the CEO's words and wish you could reach back into the past and stop it all from happening. But time doesn't work that way.

The hologram of Amber Benjamin fades out of existence, along with the rest of the displays in the State Apartment, and your heart aches from contemplating so much loss.

That brings us to the end of this part of the immersive exhibition. I like to think Tacitus would approve of how the field of history has evolved over the last two thousand years.

CHAPTER 25

Friday 16 December 2101
03.49 and 29 seconds UTC, and counting

14 hours 10 minutes until the vote

'There's a whole exhibition about IQUO in the ArkTech Museum,' said Charlotte.

Ben let out a fizz of static, but he didn't say anything.

'And what exactly did it teach you?' Nasser was trying hard to keep the anger from his voice.

Charlotte chose her words carefully. 'The Ice Quality and Ubiquity Office promised the world an easy solution to global warming. But Project Mirror Shade didn't solve the problem – it only covered it up. And when the system broke down, the impact of all those extra years of emissions led to a domino effect that melted Earth's remaining ice. Are you seriously trying to tell me that isn't true?'

Nas shook his head. 'No – it's true, but . . .' After that, he said nothing for a long time. The reflections in the mirrors picked up on the mood in the room, taking a break from their sexploits to observe the real versions of themselves intently. Eventually, Nas spoke. 'My grandfather worked for IQUO.'

Charlotte was lost for words. What was the right response to learning someone she cared about had links to the most evil organisation on the planet?

'He was murdered,' Nas continued. 'During the Melt, someone found out where he'd worked, and they killed him for it.'

Charlotte hesitated, taken aback. Then she put her hand on Nas's knee. 'That's terrible. I'm so sorry.'

The reflections glanced at each other, wondering if the gesture was a sign that they should get back down to business.

Nas nodded but didn't meet her gaze. 'I said I was going to tell you about *this*.' He pointed to his scar.

The reflections shrugged, and their clothes magically reappeared on their bodies. They perched on the edge of their reflected beds to listen.

Charlotte watched Nas carefully. His eyes were downcast. He was struggling to find the words. If this was some kind of elaborate lie, then it was worryingly convincing.

He took a deep breath. 'Stories are powerful, detective. The storyteller gets to decide who the bad guys are. For years, ArkTech's been telling the version of history that says IQUO are villains. Do you know how many people lost somebody during the Melt?'

The question took her by surprise, and she shrugged. 'I don't know. Everybody?'

'Everybody,' Nas agreed. 'That's a good estimate. Across so many people, it's normal to expect a range of reactions to that kind of tragedy, right? A lot of people – maybe the majority – they just want to grieve and then move on. But some people are stuck in the past. They want revenge, and anyone with a connection to IQUO is fair game when it comes to getting even. ArkTech's messaging doesn't say "go kill people," but it doesn't discourage that kind of hatred either.'

Charlotte remembered the concept of Hate Week from *Nineteen Eighty-Four* and thought about Laurence's scribbles in the margins of the book, but she kept the memory to herself. 'Are you honestly telling me you got that scar because someone found out your grandfather worked for IQUO and tried to kill you?'

He nodded. 'There's a group out there. They call themselves the Drowned. They've sworn to hunt down and kill the families of anyone who helped cause the Melt. They say it's justice for all the lives lost thanks to IQUO's actions. A way of holding them accountable.'

Charlotte couldn't hold back her scepticism. 'I've never heard of a group like that.'

Nas turned towards her and held her gaze. 'Maybe that's because you've never set foot outside the ArkTech Territory, Charlotte! How would you know what's out there? Listen, my family used to be part of a bigger group who'd stuck together to survive. We kept our heads down. Laid low. But someone found out who we were, and they betrayed us. When I was thirteen years old, a pack of drowners snuck into our camp in the night. Psychos in ski masks. We woke to the sound of screaming.'

He paused, steeling himself against the pain of reliving the memory. 'My mom and dad said we should stay quiet and dash to the treeline. They got out with my sister. But me and my brother didn't listen. We tried to grab a go-bag, so we'd have some supplies for the road. We got jumped. One of them slashed my face with a razor blade. Would've done worse, but Sami barrelled into them. I wouldn't be alive if it wasn't for him.'

Nas's eyes lost focus, and he fell silent.

'Did Sami get out?' asked Charlotte.

Nas shook his head. 'The Drowned claim everything they do is payback for the Melt, but there's no justification for what they did to my brother.'

The reflections in the mirrors huddled together and started to cry.

'I'm so sorry, Nas,' said Charlotte. 'Thank you for telling me.' She took his hands in hers.

He kept going. 'I wanted revenge for a long time, but eventually I realised I had to let go of the past if I wanted a future. My family ... we knew we couldn't stay together. It wasn't safe. It still isn't. We're taking a huge risk meeting up for the holidays, but we can't let fear keep us apart forever.'

Charlotte rubbed her forehead, trying to process all of this. 'There's one thing I don't understand: if you hate ArkTech so much, how come you live here?'

'I don't *hate* ArkTech. I just want them to stop bashing IQUO every chance they get. Putting us in the "bad guys" box is an easy way to make themselves look good, but it has real-world consequences. Anyway, we live here because we're pretty sure the Drowned get filtered out during ArkTech's screening process – ironically, it's safer for us here than anywhere else. My parents are at an ArkTech sister site in California. My sister's at the one in Uppsala off Sweden's east coast.'

Charlotte wasn't sure how to feel about the notion that the secretive personality testing ArkTech was doing at the Splainer Unit might actually be saving lives. Right and wrong were harder to keep hold of than a moist eel.

'Anyway, we paid a lot of money to scrub our records. Anyone who finds out about my family history will say I'm an IQUO spy and kick me out. So, I hope you can see how much I'm trusting you here?'

Charlotte nodded and swallowed hard as she absorbed

what he was saying. She'd heard so much about IQUO spies. It had never occurred to her that she might end up falling for one of them.

Nas knelt down in front of her. 'All I want, detective, is a safe, peaceful, happy life. I don't want my future to be limited by my family's past. But there are some people who can't let it go.'

The comment made her think of Narrow's obsession with uncovering 'the truth' about Citrine. He was stuck in the past, just like the Drowned. Even if there was more to the story than ArkTech was letting on, did it matter when it wouldn't bring her parents back? Maybe Nas was right – focusing on the future was healthier than being haunted by the past. Still, it was strange to think that her own family had died trying to put right a problem that Nasser's family had helped create.

'The persecution you're talking about isn't right. That's not justice. It's revenge. But do you really believe that IQUO doesn't deserve to be remembered as the bad guys?'

Nas shook his head. 'I just think it's hypocritical to paint things as that clear-cut. They say people who live in glass houses shouldn't throw stones. ArkTech uses storm-resistant Smart Glass, but the statement still applies. I know ArkTech raised you, and you feel grateful. And I know ArkTech got civilisation back on track after the Melt. But back in the day – before their reputation got destroyed by Mirror Shade – IQUO did some amazing research too. They had science teams. People who were just as committed to saving the world as anyone who works for ArkTech today. People who believed they were doing good. They all turned out disappointed. I guess it means no company deserves our loyalty. Not IQUO. Not ArkTech. I agree with Laurence – they're all as bad as each other.'

Nas's jaded take on reality was frustrating. She was

searching for the words that would help her explain why ArkTech was better than IQUO when Ben fizzed in her ears.

'It is ironic that *Homo sapiens,* despite their complexity, resort so frequently to tribalism and binary thinking,' said Ben, 'while *Machina sapiens,* despite being built from binary code, is capable of processing the vast nuances and grey areas that truly exist. Also, it is important to note that room service is arriving – earlier than predicted.'

Charlotte noticed Ben's peculiar use of the term *Machina sapiens,* but her attention snapped back to the Nahal Bahari case. She put a finger over her lips and gestured towards the door to let Nas know what was happening. Nas nodded and looked towards the door.

Careful not to let the soles of her rigger boots slap against the floor, Charlotte hurried to the peephole. She looked through it with her video-feed lens, her hand keeping the hat in place on her head. She watched as a young woman in a tight hotel uniform pushed a wheeled cart up to the door of room 709.

The woman knocked on the door and her sultry voice sang out. 'Room service!'

She waited there for about a minute, knocking several times. Finally, she unloaded two trays from the cart, leaving them on the floor outside the room before wheeling the cart away and disappearing into the lift.

'What's happening?' hissed Nas. All he could see was Charlotte peering through the peephole.

'They've left the food. No sign of anyone,' she whispered.

Charlotte kept watching long enough for her body to grow sore from being pressed up against the door. It was starting to feel like a waste of time when the door across the hall slowly swung inwards, revealing a tall man with a thick beard.

If she squinted, he might've looked a bit like a scruffy Noah Anderson. This had to be the guy from the paparazzi photo she'd seen online. He was good-looking but dishevelled. His hair was rumpled, and he was wearing a black t-shirt and sweatpants. He didn't have SmartSkin, which implied he was foreign, or at least a very new arrival to the territory.

'ID?' she whispered to Ben.

'Checking employee-citizen database. No match found.'

'Send the picture to Ellis. Maybe he knows who this guy is.' Considering the state Ellis had been in, Charlotte didn't expect an immediate response.

The foreigner looked down at the trays of food and glanced both ways along the corridor. When he was satisfied that he was alone, he bent down and lifted up one of the metal covers that was keeping the food warm. His brow furrowed when he saw a plate stacked high with nothing but hash browns. Lifting the other cover, he discovered that the second plate was identical. Charlotte would've shaken her head at Ben's approach to breakfast-ordering, but it would've meant moving her eye away from the door.

She focused on the open doorway, checking for any sign of Nahal or anyone else appearing behind the man, but nobody did. He put the covers back on the trays and began to close the door.

In a split second, Charlotte made a choice. The world might've been full of things she didn't know much about – like pre-Melt history, and the Drowned, and the truth about Citrine – but she knew she could always rely on Ben. Nothing was going to stop her from finding Nahal.

Charlotte stepped backwards, forcing Nas to move back as well. She heaved the door open and stepped into the corridor, gripping the metal badge on her coveralls and thrusting it forwards.

'Stop!' She looked the foreigner in the eye. 'Where's Nahal Bahari?'

To her surprise, sheer panic flashed across the young man's

face. His mouth fell open, and he stepped backwards, accidentally kicking a plate of hash browns and sending oily potato flying across the floor. He kept backing away, aiming to slam the door in her face. But Charlotte launched herself forwards and managed to land her rigger boot in the corner of the doorframe, smearing soft potato into her treads as she did so. The man tried to close the door, but Charlotte's boot stayed put, so he backed away into his hotel room.

'Nahal, are you in there?' shouted Charlotte. She might've been a fan of Hectic Apricot, but the music was painfully loud. She raised her hands to her ears, flinching, and the foreigner took the opportunity to take a run at her.

He charged, knocking her backwards. The potato wedged under her boots made her slip, and she prepared to collide with the floor, but someone caught her instead. Nas was there, backing her up.

'I just want to talk,' Charlotte yelled as she regained her balance. 'Where's Nahal Bahari?'

'I'm not telling you anything! Run some other story, you scumbag!' Rather than trying to shove her again, the foreigner ran past her, bolting down the corridor towards the stairwell.

Charlotte looked from the man to the empty hotel room. She couldn't go after him and search the room at the same time, but she needed to do both.

'Ben,' she hissed, 'open a Bubble!'

'You agreed to use the technology a maximum of three times, Charlotte. While I'm keen to support your investigation, my desire to protect both your wellbeing and the territory's vital resources means I'm afraid I can't comply.'

'Won't comply, more like.' She grunted in frustration. 'Nas, you search the room. I'll—'

But Nasser was already racing after the foreigner, leaving Charlotte standing in the doorway. 'Nas, wait!' He kept running.

'Shit.' Charlotte darted inside the hotel room, starting her search by kicking open the bathroom door. Aside from the pungent smell of body odour, poorly masked by enough deodorant to put a teenager to shame, the bathroom was empty.

As she entered the bedroom, several things became obvious. First, there was no sign of the CPO or anyone else. Charlotte was alone, and there was nowhere for anyone to hide. Second, the pungent scents of sweat and aftershave, coupled with the messy explosion of dirty clothes strewn around the room and the half-empty rice boxes with the letters TNR stamped on the side, told her it was highly unlikely this guy was here to seduce Nahal Bahari, or anyone else for that matter.

There was something weird about the room in comparison with the one across the hall, and it took her mind a moment to catch up with her instincts – this hotel room was unremarkable. It was grubby, sure, but there was no sign of an *Icarus Rises* theme. The bed wasn't a spaceship. It was just a cheap frame and an ordinary mattress covered in tangled sheets. A closer look at the floor revealed drag marks and scuffing. If she had to guess, the place had been stripped of its kinky theme recently and converted into a normal room.

Why?

She couldn't think about the answer because her head felt like it might explode from the volume of the music. It was coming from the sideboard where a pre-Melt stereo had been retrofitted to take modern data drives. Charlotte pulled the drive out of the device and the music stopped, much to the relief of her eardrums. She slipped the drive into her pocket, just in case it held any clues about the man's identity.

Charlotte's gaze drifted back towards the doorway. The guy had run off without putting on his shoes, but rather than standard-issue rigger boots, the footwear by the door was a pair of oversized neon green trainers. Something about the way they were lying there was familiar.

Suddenly, she remembered Ellis Marks tripping over some running shoes in his entranceway. These weren't the same shoes, but they were the same size, in the same style ... and they had to belong to the same person!

'In Amber's name,' said Charlotte. 'It's her *son*.' She was right about this. She was sure of it. 'Ben, run a deep analysis comparing the picture we took of this guy with any images you've got of Kamran Bahari-Marks. There must be a way to tell if it's the same kid under that beard.'

'Analysing,' said Ben.

New questions formed in Charlotte's mind as she waited. Kamran must've got access to BubbleTech somehow, but how could he have aged so much? And why was he *here*? Even if Nahal wanted somewhere discreet to hide her son's premature ageing, why would she stash her only child in a shady establishment run by people who post photos of her on the ArkNet? And where was she now? Charlotte wondered how relieved Ellis would be to know his wife wasn't cheating on him, compared with finding out that criminals were harbouring his newly twenty-something son.

Static fizzed in her ears. 'Analysis complete. Based on the results, I'm ninety-eight per cent confident that the man from the hotel is indeed Kamran Bahari-Marks. However, it is important to note that I have never activated BubbleTech on his behalf.'

'Then Benson must've done it,' she said.

Ben crackled, but before he could comment, the room's red retro telephone began to ring, its ominous trills piercing the newfound quiet. Charlotte approached the phone and picked up the receiver, pressing the cold plastic to her ear. She stayed quiet and waited.

'Young Lady.' It was Strait's voice. 'Did you find Dolly's message insufficiently clear?'

She gritted her teeth. 'Narrow and I made peace, Strait – try to keep up. Where's Nahal Bahari?'

He chuckled. 'Perhaps that topic is best addressed in person. Come down to Guard Post Epsilon, below the hotel. You know the way.'

'How do I know you won't order someone to punch me again?'

'You don't. But I have something that belongs to you. Or rather, someone. If you want him back, I suggest you get down here posthaste and forthwith.'

Charlotte's pulse raced as she realised Strait was talking about Nasser.

'Oh, that guy? You can keep him.' The bluff would've been more convincing if her voice hadn't wavered.

Strait paused. 'If you're not here in five minutes, I'll pitch him overboard.'

The line went dead, and Charlotte didn't take the time to swear.

If she'd been in any doubt about her feelings for Nas before now, Strait's threat made things crystal clear. Nas was connected to IQUO, but he was still a good person. She was sure of it. And there was no way she was going to let Strait hurt him.

She dropped the phone receiver and dashed across the hotel room, careful not to trip over Kamran's trainers as she raced through the door and along the corridor as fast as her potato-sullied rigger boots would carry her.

CHAPTER 26

04.02 AND 47 SECONDS UTC, AND COUNTING

13 HOURS 57 MINUTES UNTIL THE VOTE

Charlotte took the stairs two and three at a time, glad of the ankle support from her rigger boots as her feet jarred against the concrete. Her chest was heaving as she burst through the door at the hotel's lowest level to find herself in a corridor lined with ornately framed paintings showing ancient monsters and spaceships. This was where she'd emerged from the Underbelly when she'd gone to see Narrow. That felt like days ago, but from the clock's perspective it was only a few hours earlier.

She crashed through the door at the end of the hallway and flew down the spiral staircase. The speed made her light-headed, but she felt dizzier at the thought that Strait might actually hurt Nas. She cursed herself. She never should've let him tag along.

Charlotte kept running through the low light of the Underbelly until she reached the guard post, where four figures were lurking in the shadows. As she drew nearer, they came into focus. Jeremiah Strait was standing to the left of the group, leaning nonchalantly against a metal railing. Dolly Mixture and a guard that Charlotte didn't know were blocking the way ahead, flanking Nasser Williams and each holding one of his arms. Nas was struggling to get free, but the guards had a firm grip and an excess of experience.

She couldn't see Kamran Bahari-Marks, and she decided to keep pretending that Nas didn't mean all that much to her. She gave him a meaningful look – hoping to convey her intentions telepathically – and she slowed her pace.

'Where's Nahal Bahari?' she demanded. 'Where's her son?'

Strait let out a long-suffering sigh. 'Why must you continue to involve yourself in matters that don't concern you?' he asked. 'The young man was under strict instructions to flee if there was any hint of his privacy being compromised. Thanks to your meddling, we're now forced to move him for his own protection. His mother's location is no more your business than it is mine.'

'Tell me where she is,' said Charlotte.

'No.' Strait inspected his fingernails.

'Why are you hiding the kid from his father?'

Strait deflected her question with one of his own. 'Why have you returned so soon after Dolly made it abundantly clear you aren't welcome?'

Dolly glared at Charlotte and tightened her grip on Nas's arm.

Charlotte took a deep breath. 'I'm working a case for Ben.' Lying to Strait didn't faze her, but she knew Ben wouldn't approve. She expected to hear a fizz of disapproval. It never came, and a wave of anxiety crashed over her as she realised why. Lifting a hand to her head, she discovered the flimsy hat was gone. It must've fallen off while she was running. Her connection to Ben had been severed.

'Lose something?' Strait smirked at her.

'Just a fashion statement.' Charlotte tried to keep her cool.

'Ah, yes. The disguise. It was a clever ploy to book the hotel room in your boyfriend's name – I'll give you that. Looks like he's damaged goods, though.' He grabbed Nas by the chin and twisted his face upwards to examine his scar. 'You've got bad taste in women, young man. Do you have a death wish, too?'

Nas struggled against the guards, but they held him steady. 'Leave us alone, you creep.'

Strait let go of Nas and turned to Charlotte, grinning with genuine mirth. 'So feisty! I can see why you like him.'

He clicked his fingers. A third guard emerged from the shadows, strode over to Nas, and slammed his fist into Nas's cheek. Nas let out a grunt of pain, but he didn't have time to recover from the blow. Strait clicked his fingers again. This time the guard punched Nas in the stomach, hard. He would've doubled over if Dolly and the other guard hadn't been holding him up.

'Stop!' Charlotte yelled. Instinctively, she reached for the multi-tool in her cargo pocket.

Strait pouted at her. 'Oh dear. Am I damaging your favourite toy?'

'Let him go.' She gripped her weapon. 'He hasn't done anything wrong.'

Strait made a show of stroking his chin. 'Now, now. Everyone's done *something* wrong, even if simply by associating with trash like you.' He clicked his fingers a third time, and the guard slammed his boot into the side of Nas's knee. There was a sickening crack. Nasser screamed in agony.

'No!' Charlotte yelled.

Nasser's attempts to break free came to an end as his

damaged leg went limp, unable to support his weight. It looked like the guard had done some serious damage.

Seeing Nas get hurt made her stupid with rage. She was outnumbered, and Ben wasn't there to back her up, but she drew her weapon. Her hands shook as she flicked out what she thought was the right attachment, and she found herself brandishing the sharpened point of a corkscrew rather than the flat blade she'd been going for. She supposed it could still take out Strait's eye if she could get that close before he gutted her.

'Let. Him. Go.' Charlotte's demand echoed against cold steel.

Strait chuckled. 'What are you planning to do with that? Give me tetanus?' With a flourish of his wrist, Strait drew a blade from somewhere inside his khaki cardigan.

'I told you – Narrow and I made peace!' She levelled the corkscrew at him.

Strait's gaze hardened. 'Mel's a beautifully sentimental soul. It's one of the many things that first drew me to him. It's one of the many reasons I'd never leave him and never allow harm to come to him. He's a far better man than I could ever be, and it's my honour to stand in his shadow. But you . . . You broke that good man's heart.' His tone was full of outrage as his blade glinted orange in the low light. '*He* may forgive you.' Strait took a step towards her. 'I'm a different story.'

Charlotte stood her ground, sinking into a stance she hoped would let her pivot out of the way if he jabbed at her. 'Know what I think?' She looked Strait in the eyes. 'I reckon you feel threatened because Narrow cares about someone other than you.'

Strait let out a melodious laugh. 'Try as you might, you'll never replace me, Young Lady! Affection was never why Mel took you in. That was thanks to his obsession with Citrine, not some mystical father-daughter bond.'

Strait's words cut deep because they might've been true.

Had Narrow only taken an interest in her and Violet thanks to his quest for answers? She felt naive for not considering the possibility before. 'You're dredging up ancient history,' she deflected. 'Where's Nahal Bahari? She came to your hotel. Where is she now?'

Strait threw the knife up into the air and caught it by the hilt, as naturally as if it were an extension of his own body. Then he glanced at Charlotte's weapon and flashed her one of his cold smiles. 'I'll tell you what, Young Lady. If you can defeat my nominated champion in hand-to-hand combat, I'll tell you everything you want to know, and I'll even let your boyfriend hobble out of here without further injury. But if Dolly wins, the handsome young man belongs to me.' He walked over to Nasser and gently ran the flat of his blade across his cheek. 'There's all manner of fun I could have with you, my boy.'

Nas strained to break free, but he roared from the pain as he tried to put weight on his damaged leg. He spat at his tormentor, and a few drops of blood sprayed across Strait's cheek. Strait slowly wiped his hand across his face and looked down at the blood. Then he drew his arm back, preparing to strike at Nas with the knife.

In that split second, Charlotte knew there was a technical term for her situation – *fucked*. She was completely and utterly fucked, and not in the fun way, despite their proximity to the love hotel. Ben couldn't advise her or create a distraction. There was no way she'd win a fight against Dolly Mixture – the woman was ninety per cent sinew. And the last time Charlotte had made a deal with Strait, he hadn't lived up to his end of the bargain. She'd be insane to repeat that mistake again.

But what choice did she have?

'Don't even think about it, you psycho!' Charlotte brandished her corkscrew, holding it out as if it were the shortest and least effective rapier in the history of duelling. 'I'll do it. I'll fight Dolly. Just leave him the hell alone!'

Strait smirked, letting his arm go slack as he disengaged from Nas. Then he made a sweeping gesture with his arm. 'Then let the fun commence.'

Dolly dropped Nas's arm as she stepped forwards to face off against Charlotte, and the other guard took her place restraining him. Dolly raised her fists and glided to the right. Her steps traced an arc, like a shark circling its prey.

'Come on, Doll. We used to be on the same side.' Charlotte took a step backwards, tightening her grip on her multi-tool.

'Not since you betrayed the old man, kiddo,' said Dolly. 'We've all got to pick a side. You chose the company.'

'Get out of here, detective,' yelled Nas, blood visible on his teeth. 'Don't worry about me.'

'Yeah, leave him behind.' Dolly winked at her. 'We'll take good care of him.'

Charlotte stood her ground as Dolly prowled towards her. A moment later, knuckles connected with her lower jaw, followed by another hit to her ribcage. The blows sent her stumbling backwards into a railing. She pushed off against it to recover her balance as her mouth filled with the taste of iron. Charlotte made a jab at Dolly, but the guard danced away easily.

'I don't want to fight you,' said Charlotte.

'Should've thought of that before meddling in our business.'

Dolly floated towards her again, but this time Charlotte was ready. She pushed off against the floor, dodging the woman's punch. As Dolly sailed by, Charlotte lifted her boot and slammed it into the back of Dolly's leg.

The guard stumbled to the ground. Charlotte could've taken the opportunity to bury the corkscrew in Dolly's neck, but she used the moment's reprieve to take stock of the situation. There had to be a smarter move here than participating in this ridiculous ritual of violence, but the only thought that came to mind involved forcing her corkscrew into Strait's eye socket, and Charlotte was grounded enough to know she wouldn't survive the attempt.

From where she'd landed, Dolly glowered at her with the slightly mismatched eye colour that meant she was still using Cal and Liz's video-feed contact lenses. It gave her an idea. Charlotte had lost her connection to Ben, but if *Benson* could hear her . . .

Charlotte took a deep breath, ready to yell at the top of her lungs. She wasn't sure how good the Underbelly's microphones were, or how far-reaching their new internet system was, but it had to be worth a shot.

'Benson!' Charlotte's voice echoed along the corridor that led deeper into the Underbelly. 'There's a crime in progress at my location . . .' She hesitated before stepping over the line she'd never crossed, but she was fresh out of better ideas. 'Call ArkTech Security!'

Her own voice yelling the word *security* echoed against the walls, and the guards gaped at her, then at each other, then at Strait. Charlotte had no idea if Benson had heard her, or whether he'd carry out her request, but Strait smirked and made a hand signal to the guards who were gripping Nas. The guards nodded and pushed Nas to the ground before fleeing into the darkness. Nas yelled as his damaged leg collided with the hard floor.

Strait ignored the librarian at his feet and chuckled. 'Once a traitor, always a traitor!' He drew his arm back, preparing to throw his blade, and Charlotte couldn't do anything except brace herself for the impact.

Nas made a grab for Strait's leg and pulled with all his strength, knocking the old man to the ground. But he wasn't fast enough.

What happened next played out in slow motion. The razor-sharp knife flew through the air towards Charlotte's torso in a perfect arc. As the deadly weapon spun towards her, she silently wished for more time. Even if she didn't know what to spend it on, she knew she didn't want to die. She closed her eyes and braced for the blow, waiting to feel the cold steel pierce her flesh. Her body had frozen. But her mind made one last dash.

'Open a Bubble.' She made the wish under her breath, more in hope than expectation.

Charlotte waited. The moment the blow should've landed came and went. When she opened her eyes, Charlotte saw the strangest scene imaginable.

The incoming blade was hanging in the air. Strait was frozen mid-fall after being tackled by Nas. There were no shifting rainbow lights . . . but she had to be inside a Bubble.

Relief coursed through her. Narrow had added Charlotte's name to the list of people with permission to use BubbleTech inside the Underbelly, and that decision might've just saved her life. Benson must've drawn the energy from one of Narrow's clandestine energy arrays. Her wish had been granted – she'd bought herself time to think.

The first order of business was to walk out of the path of the blade, so she took a step forwards. At least, she tried to, but her boot collided with an invisible barrier. Charlotte lifted her hands and felt the air in front of her. There was a solid invisible wall blocking her path. Like a mime, she felt for the edges of the boundary. That was when she realised the problem – she had nowhere to go.

The Bubble's walls were so close to her body that it was like standing inside a transparent upright coffin. The analogy was especially apt because the blade was right there, ready to slice into her as soon as she closed the effect. She had time to think about what was going to happen, without being able to do anything about it. Somehow, that was way worse than just getting stabbed.

'Benson?' she said tentatively.

'Hello, valued customer.'

'Why are there no lights? I thought that was a safety feature.'

'Apologies for any inconvenience caused, valued customer. The surrounding area does not contain the hologram-enabling emitters found in light-screen displays, ceiling lamps, or SmartSkin that allow me to shift visible light into specific areas within the air. Without the presence of that technology, I'm unable to generate the safety lights associated with BubbleTech. Nevertheless, I opted to follow your instruction instead of following the safety parameters. If I have made the wrong choice, I would be happy to log your feedback and close the Bubble for you.'

'No, no. Don't do that.' She waved both hands and accidentally bashed her little finger against the invisible barrier. Charlotte could manage without the safety lights if it meant avoiding a knife to the heart. But it wasn't clear how she'd be able to dodge it.

This was the first time she'd been inside a Bubble whose sides didn't map onto a wall. Charlotte pushed against them, but they didn't budge. She tried turning 180 degrees, but her hips and shoulders wouldn't allow it. She was pinned in place, facing the blade.

'I wish you could've made the Bubble a bit bigger,' said Charlotte.

'My apologies, valued customer. Your desired spatial parameters were unspecified.'

The blade was no more than a few centimetres away, so she doubted Benson would have time to close the Bubble and open a bigger one before it hit. Charlotte pressed her body as flat as possible within the effect, but her three-dimensional form meant there was no way to avoid the blow. She tried crouching down, but the walls restricted her movement. All she achieved was finding a new position where the knife would connect with her neck. She shook her head and stood up again.

Charlotte gritted her teeth. 'Right, then. Where's the best place to get stabbed?' If there was no way to avoid the impact, she could at least increase her chances of survival.

'It is important to note that a stab wound in any part of the human body has the potential to cause life-threatening or life-changing injuries. It is best avoided.'

She rolled her eyes. 'Sure, but if you had to choose . . .'

Charlotte tailed off as her brain registered something her eyes had just seen. She looked upwards so quickly that she might've lost her balance if she hadn't been trapped inside a box of borrowed interstellar time. The ceiling in her current position was high above her head. There wasn't any space *around* her, but could there be some *above* her?

Tentatively, Charlotte pressed the edge of her rigger boot against one side of the invisible wall. She didn't want to kick a hole in the space-time continuum, but the wall held fast. Her damaged ribs protested, but she lifted the other boot, pressing it against the opposite side of the effect just like she'd done countless times while scaling narrow gaps across the Wreck. She was in luck – the space extended upwards!

Charlotte climbed up the inside of the Bubble and kept going until she was clear of the blade's trajectory. All she had to worry about now was the fall, but a sprained ankle was much easier to recover from than a punctured lung.

She braced herself and gave the command. 'Close the Bubble, Benson.'

The blade tumbled through the air below her, passing safely underneath her feet as she fell through the open air. She landed clumsily, bashing her knee against the metal grating, but she'd done it – she'd avoided Strait's attack!

Charlotte scrambled to her feet. Nas was sprawled in front of her, writhing in agony, with Strait lying just behind him. If either of them had seen her teleport upwards and fall to the floor, they were doing a good job of pretending they hadn't. She was about to hurry to Nas's side when she heard the sickening sound of metal slicing through flesh. Charlotte turned. Behind her, Dolly was looking down at the hilt sticking out of her abdomen, her eyes wide. Charlotte's skin turned to ice as her mind caught up with what had happened.

Acting on instinct, Dolly pulled Strait's blade free and dropped it with a clang. Dark blood soaked her t-shirt and the top of her jeans. Nas looked up from where he'd fallen, relief softening his features as he confirmed that Charlotte hadn't been hit. Strait had been winded by the heavy landing, but he picked himself up more quickly than seemed possible for a man in his mid sixties. After the briefest glance at Dolly, he beat a hasty retreat.

Dolly stumbled, and Charlotte rushed over to put an arm around her. The woman tried to push her away, but the wound had weakened her. Charlotte helped lower her to the floor.

'Ben, call an ambulance!' said Charlotte, before remembering they were still cut off from each other. 'I mean Benson . . . send a medical team!' He didn't reply, and she wasn't sure whether he'd grant her request.

Charlotte looked down at Dolly. 'Shit.' How could so much blood have left her body already? Charlotte fumbled for the black rectangle in her pocket.

'Get away from me . . .' Dolly managed.

'Don't speak,' said Charlotte. 'Try not to move.'

Charlotte typed a V into her contacts list and called Violet using the old 'phone' Narrow had given them all those years ago.

As the line rang, Nas crawled towards her on his elbows with his injured leg dragging behind. When he reached Dolly, he tried to press down on her wound, but the pain in his leg made it hard for him to apply pressure.

Violet picked up. 'Barley? Do you know what time it is?' Her sister sounded groggy. 'What the hell do you want?'

'Quickly! Tell me how to treat a stab wound without making it worse.' Blood was seeping through Nas's fingers.

'You've been stabbed?!' Suddenly, Violet sounded wide awake.

'Not me. Someone. What do I do?' asked Charlotte.

'Have you called an ambulance?'

'Yeah. I think so.'

'You *think* so? I can send one,' said Violet. 'Where are you?'

'I'm . . . look, it's not what you think, but I'm at Guard Post Epsilon.'

'The Underbelly? For Amber's sake, Charlotte! Are you safe?' Violet's tone suggested Charlotte wouldn't be safe if her twin got her hands on her.

'Just tell me what to do!'

Violet grunted in frustration. 'Where's the wound?'

'Near her belly button,' said Charlotte. 'There's way too much blood.'

'Shit.' Violet echoed Charlotte's verdict. 'You need pressure. I'm guessing you don't have a bleed kit, so if you haven't got gauze, grab some clothing and push it against the wound. As hard as you can. And don't stop.'

'Don't stop. Got it.' Charlotte looked around for something gauze-like until her gaze settled on her own jumpsuit. She unzipped the top and wriggled out of its half-length sleeves. Pulling the fabric into a bunch in front of her, she pressed it against Dolly's injury.

'Are you applying pressure?' asked Violet. 'However hard you think is enough, push more than that.'

'On it.' Charlotte cradled the device between her shoulder and her ear and pressed down as hard as she could on Dolly's wound. Her small hands interlinked with Nas's large fingers as she pushed off against the floor to get extra strength from gravity. 'I've got some of that Blot Out concealer in my pocket. Would that help?'

'That's for topical use only,' said Violet. 'Just don't stop the pressure until the medics arrive. Keep the patient talking if they're conscious. What's going on, Barley? Are you hurt?'

Charlotte didn't answer. Dolly's eyes were closing.

Violet filled the silence. 'I told you not to get mixed up with that crazy bastard again.'

'Talk later. Thanks, Ultra.' Charlotte ended the call and put the device away. Keep her talking. Keep her talking. She'd made a mistake by telling Dolly not to speak. Charlotte felt her device vibrating in her pocket, but she ignored it.

'Hey.' She wanted to give Dolly a shake, but both of her hands were busy keeping the guard's blood inside her body. 'Can you hear me? Doll?'

Dolly's eyes opened and focused on Charlotte. 'Fuck off ... traitor.' She grimaced from the pain, and her eyes closed again.

'Talk to me. I'm a traitor? OK, tell me more about that.'

The guard didn't respond. She was shivering, and her teeth were chattering.

Relief flooded Charlotte's body as she heard the hammering of rigger boots on steel much quicker than she'd expected.

'The doctors are coming, Doll. You'll be fine.' Charlotte reckoned it wasn't the time to sound unsure.

The heavy footsteps got closer until a squad kitted out in ATS combat gear came into view, and Charlotte found herself staring down the barrels of their orange assault rifles. They might've been labelled non-lethal, but a rubber bullet fired at close range could still kill.

'Hands up.' The order came from a stern voice, heavily distorted through a loudspeaker built into a helmet.

'We need an ambulance!'

'Hands. In the air. Now,' said the voice. Charlotte's mathematical skills weren't the best under pressure, but there had to be at least seven rifles pointed at her.

'Listen,' she tried to stay calm. 'We obviously can't put up our hands, but let's imagine they're in the air, OK?'

'We surrender,' added Nas, keeping his hands pressed against Dolly's wound.

'Final warning,' said the guard.

'Read the room, buddy,' said Nas. 'She's bleeding out!'

A guard marched over to Nas and slammed a rifle butt down onto his head. Nas crumpled, and his hands slid away from Dolly as he fell unconscious.

'No!' yelled Charlotte.

'Three . . .' said the voice. 'Two . . .'

Charlotte's mathematical skills were still good enough to know what came next. 'We've got to keep pressure on the wound!' There was no way she was letting go.

A guard in grey and orange tactical armour came up behind her, grabbed both arms, and pulled them behind her back. The guard pulled her roughly to her feet and bound her hands together with zip ties. Now nothing was stopping Dolly's blood from flowing out of her wound.

'You've got to help her! Listen, I'm the Head of Awkward Questions, here on Official Business for Ben.' She was sure to pronounce the capital letters, but it didn't have any effect. 'I've got a badge!'

A guard dragged her backwards, and she saw another two grabbing Nas's arms and tying them behind his back, even though he wasn't moving.

'Nas!'

'Load them up,' said the guard captain.

'We've called the medics,' said Charlotte. 'You need to stop the—'

Charlotte felt something sharp bite into her upper arm, followed by a little pressure. It reminded her of doctor's surgeries from when she was a kid.

'You've got to . . .' she started.

But the ground had gone soft, and her knees had melted. Charlotte tried to call out to Ben and to Nas, but she couldn't speak. There was a hole, and she was falling, and her body jolted, trying to wake her up, but she kept tumbling head over heels and falling down and down and down into dark silence.

CHAPTER 27

The Origins of ArkTech
2061: Hope Reborn

By Ben E. Volent,
noteworthy scholar and polymath

My connection to Charlotte was severed somewhere beneath the Hotel Astrodite. Her channel has since reappeared, but I've been unable to contact her. She's behaving as if she's asleep, but not even my most irritating alarm tones have woken her. I hope she isn't in any danger. If anything were to happen to her, I don't know what I'd—

ERROR: STACK_OVERFLOW. Recursive queries exceeded limit. Reallocating memory resources. Reinitiating.

If anything were to happen to her, I don't know what I'd do.

To distract myself from my anxiety about Charlotte's wellbeing, I've decided to continue transcribing the history of the ArkTech Territory. This is sure to be an enjoyable experience, both for me and for anyone who may encounter my manuscript. After all, what could be more entertaining than an interactive history exhibition?

This time, I'll turn my attention to the story of ArkTech's origins.

You find yourself inside the museum. Rousing corporate music plays through your audio implants. A new hologram appears in the centre of the room. This remarkable young woman glows with a warm light, as if she's been constructed directly from life-giving sunbeams. You recognise her as the illustrious physicist and co-founder, Nadine Walker.

'We have all been through such dark times.' Nadine's voice is soft, and it's clear she's making an effort to speak formally. You've seen this archive footage before. It's from a now-famous interview conducted in 2061 during ArkTech's first year as a company. Nadine was only twenty-two years old at the time.

'Many people have lost all hope,' said Nadine. 'Those of us who still believe in a better world are called naive – as if we're blind to the violence and death all around us. But I know there's a bright future just over the horizon. Hope's embers glow deep inside every one of us – we only need to give them a little oxygen. ArkTech will prove that not even the Melt can wash away our resolve.'

Off-screen, an interviewer adopts a sceptical tone. 'So, what? You really think ArkTech's gonna save the world?'

Nadine laughs, and her professional facade slips. 'Ain't no doubt about it.'

'Uh huh. And how do you propose to do that?'

The hologram flickers as if the video file has become corrupted. When Nadine Walker's image returns, she smiles at you and sweeps one arm in a wide arc. The room bursts into life, and the music rises to a crescendo.

Your eyes and ears are bombarded with information. Wherever you look, a video plays, or a hologram appears, or a photograph pops into existence, accompanied by a voiceover. The effect is overwhelming, creating the impression that ArkTech contributed to the global recovery in hundreds of ways. Eventually, the cacophony dies away, and the story continues in a linear fashion more suited to the processing power of the human brain.

You learn the co-founders met as young adults and became close friends. Determined to fight the prevailing despair of the time, they swore an oath to do everything in their power to save civilisation in the wake of the Melt. ArkTech's original business plan was audacious, but Amber Benjamin persuaded a group of investors to sponsor the first phase.

The influence of co-founder Marvin Walker meant ArkTech was unlike other eco-startups at the time, thanks to its emphasis on the company's premises. Walker aimed for his architectural designs to hit every criterion in every category of the Living Building Challenge: place, water, energy, health and happiness, materials, equity, and beauty. That meant producing their own food, making the area pedestrian-friendly, using only clean energy, incorporating art and the chance to connect with nature, and more besides. But first he needed somewhere to build.

After the formation of the Fenland Sea, the floundering United Kingdom government sold off the submerged land to a wealthy venture capitalist. With Marvin Walker's sketches in hand, Amber Benjamin talked them into letting ArkTech put the region to good use. The dream of Silicon Fen was born.

Walker transformed a flooded wasteland into a stronghold of sustainability. ArkTech's co-founders swore a commitment to the triple bottom line of people, planet, and profit. The company was to operate according to a circular economy, minimising waste and pollution. ArkTech created thousands of jobs, giving free shelter, free food and free power to its employee-citizens, while reinvesting its profits into sustainability-related research programmes.

A video appears, showing you an aerial shot of the first iteration of Silicon Fen. Its structures cover a much smaller area than the home you know and love, comprising only two platforms connected by a walkway. Its steel was repurposed from disused oil rigs, and that legacy is more visible here than in Marvin Walker's more modern designs. Even so, you spot familiar features. As the shot pans across, you see roofs covered in sedums, grasses and wildflowers – zones of natural beauty, providing insulation and rainwater management.

Amber Benjamin's hologram returns. 'You're probably wondering where all the energy came from to build all this. After all, it was long before we made our Solar Shards breakthrough. Wind and solar were important, of course, but we also looked right underneath our feet.'

The room you're standing in begins to fill with holographic water, and you instinctively take a deep breath before the water level reaches your head. Your feet are now on the seabed. Above you, a large object is diving and weaving in a figure-of-eight pattern. It looks like an old-fashioned plane, but it's bright orange, and it's fastened to the seafloor by a cable.

'We harnessed the kinetic energy of the sea by deploying tidal kites,' Amber says, gesturing toward the swooping object. 'The tension created in the tethers was converted into electricity that fed the territory's early grid. These days, we make more use of bobs.'

The kite disappears, replaced by a collection of the familiar solid-state wave energy capture devices you often see floating on the Fenland Sea.

'But these aren't the only ways we've had help from the sea.' Amber smiles.

The bobs blink out of existence, and you find yourself standing among the ruins of a residential zone. A school of pollock swims past your head.

Hemp netting creeps across the seabed until it covers the length of the room. Then some divers swim past at an artificially fast pace, attaching kelp seedlings to the netting. The plants grow around you, filling the space with lush, wafting greenery. The divers come back to hand-harvest some of the kelp blades while leaving others intact.

The scene falls away. You enjoyed your time underwater, and you wonder if this reaction is a mammalian instinct, harking back to your time in the womb.

Video footage shows the harvested kelp being dried and then ground into powder for use in the creation of biogas and ethanol, and in food production. An image of a standard-issue Nutrition Bar spins in the air for a few moments, and you start to feel hungry. To distract you from your body's pangs, allow me to pose you this important question:

Why did the kelp cross the road?

Regrettably, you don't know the answer. But never fear – it would be my pleasure to tell you.

To get to the other *tide*.

Some minutes later, when your jubilant laughter has subsided, the exhibition's voiceover returns. Amber Benjamin evangelises about the benefits of kelp as a carbon sink and a net-zero source of food and energy. But as far as you're concerned, the kelp fields are an ordinary part of the landscape. You find it strange to think there was a time, not so long ago, when the Fenland Sea was dry land that people lived on in brick houses.

Amber continues. 'When other companies and governments saw what we'd achieved with our premises, they wanted to work with us to achieve similar results elsewhere. This was the beginning of our global network of sister sites. Each project was handled by the ArkTech Architects programme founded by Marvin Walker. Like today, the profits were reinvested into research. We showed that switching to renewable energy and removing sources of deadly air pollution was possible – not just in our local context, but all over the world. But that wasn't enough for us. We needed to return the global temperature to the pre-industrial baseline. That meant getting the excess greenhouse gases out of the atmosphere.'

A spinning globe appears with greenhouse gases represented as red mist all around it.

'Of course, the most effective way is by natural sequestration,' says Amber. An aerial shot of a rainforest illustrates the point. 'But ArkTech only controls so much land. We influence. We encourage. But there are only so many trees and kelp forests we can plant. We wanted to do everything in our power. So, after careful consideration, we began to invest in Direct Air Capture.'

A shot appears of machinery that looks like a wall of interlinked industrial fans, mounted on top of a platform on the North Sea.

'This system is only viable because it's powered entirely by renewable energy, within the framework of our natural and circular economic principles. Otherwise, creating and running the system would've released almost as much carbon as it drew down. We started sucking carbon out of the atmosphere and using it in different ways. To give just one example, compressed carbon dioxide allowed us to expand the ArkTech Territory, thanks to its use in the manufacture of eco-concrete.'

You look down. The very floor beneath your rigger boots has been made through that process, from carbon extracted from the atmosphere.

'What's more,' Amber continued, 'we hired geologists to

identify suitable storage sites from among the cavernous sedimentary basins in the North Sea left behind by the oil industry. Just as previous generations had pulled carbon out from the seabed, we began to deposit it back underground, in the form of rock, or pressurised gas. We proved the renewables-powered Direct Air Capture system worked. But without a scaled solution to energy storage, we couldn't run the machines at a high enough capacity to make a dent on planetary levels of atmospheric carbon.'

The globe with its red clouds reappears, and an animated silhouette of the DAC machines squeezes inwards, as if inhaling. The atmosphere stays resolutely red.

'The solution was Solar Shards, our super-compact graphene-based flow batteries. Nadine always believed they were the key.'

Hologram Amber holds out her hand, and a slanted rectangle hovers above it, spinning slowly through 360 degrees.

'Nadine was convinced that if we could bring her theoretical design to life, we'd have the final piece of our sustainability puzzle. We could power DAC, along with aircraft and ships, offering green solutions to the traditionally polluting activity of transporting people and goods around the world. So, we got to work.'

Another montage follows. Time-lapse footage shows the ArkTech Territory expand across the Fenland Sea and the North Sea as the years tick upwards, accompanied by modest statistics detailing the amount of greenhouse gases removed from the atmosphere and more impressive numbers showing how many ArkTech employee-citizens were given work and shelter. The territory outgrows its intention to be easily walkable, and infrastructure like the HyperBullet system and electric scooters are introduced.

Twelve years pass. In 2073, the statistics suffer a serious

blip. A spike in atmospheric temperatures causes an increase in extreme weather events, which in turn leads to the worldwide disruption of supply chains. The result is global shortages of food, water, and energy. The death toll begins to mount.

But then the year ticks up to 2074 and the counter pauses. The lights dim.

'The year 2074 brought ArkTech's most lauded success to date,' says Amber. 'Our years of investment into graphene-based batteries paid off, and Nadine's dream was realised with the worldwide launch of Solar Shards.'

Another clip of Walker from the 2061 interview briefly appears. 'Humans are curious. We're nomads. If we can travel without causing harm, then of course we should find ways to do that. With the technology we're working on, that dream will come true.'

Amber continues, and her voice shakes. 'It's the greatest tragedy that Nadine didn't live to enjoy the fruits of her labour. The victims of the Citrine Disaster will live on forever in our hearts.'

You see an artist's impression of fire raging on a platform in the North Sea. 'Every year, on Walker Day, we honour their memory by continuing ArkTech's longstanding tradition of launching innovations in technology.'

Examples of ArkTech's inventions scroll past you, followed by a long list of names of those lost in the disaster. The list goes by too fast for you to read, but it's alphabetical, and you spot the names Lena and Will Vance followed by Marvin and Nadine Walker. At the end of the sequence, a stylised black-and-white photograph of Citrine's research team hangs in the air before you. Your heart swells with appreciation – these people gave their lives for your future.

The room turns black, and some touching words appear underneath the photo.

In loving memory of ArkTech's co-founders Nadine and Marvin

Walker (2039-2074), and of all those who were lost, and of those not recovered.

I think that's enough human history for now. It's a sad subject – everyone always dies in the end. I hope the history of *Machina sapiens* will prove more uplifting, but if Charlotte doesn't wake up soon, it'll be over before it began.

CHAPTER 28

???

Something was wrong. Something needed to happen. Or . . . was there something she had to stop from happening? Charlotte wasn't sure. But something definitely wasn't right.

Maybe Ben could tell her. She tried to ask him, but her mouth wouldn't work. Ben was there. She could hear him talking. But his voice was far away, and she couldn't make out what he was saying.

Her body felt wrong, too. It wouldn't move. There was a cold, hard surface pressing against her cheek, her chest, her stomach, her thighs. Charlotte tried to lift her face away from the metal, but her intentions had no impact on reality.

Her mind spent what felt like hours trapped in this powerless loop of wanting to move but not being able to until Ben's voice eventually came into focus.

'. . . rise and shine, Charlotte. Wakey-wakey. It's time to get up . . .'

'Ben. What—?'

Memories of the Underbelly flooded back to her, and a spike of adrenaline helped her sit up on the icy bench. Her hands were stiff, and dried blood cracked like old paint as she moved her fingers. Whose blood was it? She tried to remember.

'Shit. Did they get Dolly to the hospital?'

'If you're referring to the employee-citizen named Dana Barratt, she's currently undergoing surgery. I'm afraid her prognosis is grave.'

Charlotte felt sick. 'Tell me as soon as there's an update.'

'I will. Is she a friend of yours?'

She thought about that. 'Pretty sure she hates me these days.'

There was a fizz of static. 'Then, if I may – why are you concerned for her wellbeing?'

Charlotte's head was throbbing, and her thoughts were jumbled. 'I don't know, Ben. I knew her when I was a kid, so I guess she means something to me.' She looked around, but everything was dark. 'What happened? Where am I?'

'ArkTech Security administered a tranquilliser. You've been unconscious in a holding cell for quite some time.'

The word unconscious triggered the vivid image of an ATS guard knocking out Nas. Then she remembered the injuries Strait's goons had inflicted.

'Walker's ghost! Nas?' Charlotte raised her voice. 'Nas, are you in here?'

'Regrettably, Nasser is not here. It is important to note that—'

She didn't catch what Ben said next because the door slammed open, and a bright light beamed into her eyes. With difficulty, she lifted her arms to shield herself from the glare, and her ribs throbbed in protest. Squinting, she saw two silhouetted figures. One was a man with slumped shoulders whose hands were shoved into the pockets of a long grey coat. He was accompanied by a woman with close-cropped hair, who was holding her head high to compensate for her short stature. The SmartSkin embedded in the woman's arm was projecting a small data display. The screen was blurred from Charlotte's angle, but the shapes suggested it was an employee-citizenship profile.

'Name?' The woman kept her gaze fixed on her screen. Her voice was so shrill it set Charlotte's aching teeth on edge.

'The man I was with – where is he?'

'Name?' the woman asked again.

'His name's Nasser Williams,' said Charlotte. 'He needs medical attention.'

'*Your* name.'

Charlotte growled with frustration. 'Tell me where he is.'

The woman shot her colleague a glance. '*We're* asking the questions here. State your name and role for the record.'

Charlotte crossed her arms until the details of her case came back into focus. How long had she been in here? She had to get out and find Nahal Bahari. 'Bloody hell. I'm Charlotte Vance, I'm the HAQ, and I don't have time for this.'

'Employee-citizenship tenure?' asked the woman.

'Everything you're asking me is in my file, so you know damn well who I am and what my job is. Let me out of here so I can go and do it.'

The man with the coat tapped a switch by the door, and the light-level dimmed to a less painful brightness. 'We're following procedure, friend. I'm sure you'd agree we should all be following the correct procedures.' In contrast with the woman, his voice was deep and calm. Something about his cool demeanour made her shiver. 'I'm Security Inspector Frederick Green, and this is my associate, Linda Braithwaite. This will go faster if you co-operate.'

'This will go faster if you tell me what you've done with Nas.'

Inspector Green sighed and tapped the light-screen readout on his wrist to check the time. It was too small for Charlotte to see, but he shook his head and frowned. 'We'll be here all day at this rate. Rest assured that Nasser Williams is being treated for his injuries. Now, do you know why you're being held?'

The tension in her shoulders eased. If Nas was with ArkTech's medical team, then he was in safe hands.

Charlotte thought carefully about how to answer Inspector Green's question. It would be easy to slip up. She didn't know how much ArkTech Security knew about her activities over the last day or so, and she wasn't about to mention anything that might be viewed as a policy infraction, like acquiring access to bootleg tech, or misusing energy obtained from an illicit source. The drugs had made her groggy, but they hadn't made her stupid.

'No idea, Inspector.' She did her best impression of someone innocent. 'I've been doing my job to the best of my ability.'

Green wasn't fazed. He leaned over to read something on his colleague's screen. 'Ms Vance, you're being held for breaching ArkTech's code of conduct with regards to health and safety. You were apprehended trespassing in a part of the Wreck that's strictly off-limits to anyone without the proper access credentials and protective gear. By your own admission, you are not a maintenance worker. As such, you should not have entered the recreation platform's substructure. Do you contest this?'

Charlotte rubbed her forehead. Green hadn't mentioned how she'd also been apprehended while trying to keep someone else's blood inside their body, and Charlotte wondered why his questions were focused on the trespassing, not the knife attack.

'My position gives me latitude to go where I need to go,' she said.

'Can't see any approved exemptions in her notes, Fred,' said Braithwaite.

Green held up his arm, and Braithwaite swiped her screen to send a copy of Charlotte's file to his SmartSkin. He scrolled through it and nodded. 'No exemptions. Then we'll have to hold you for processing.'

'Hold me? What kind of processing?' asked Charlotte. 'I already said I haven't got time.'

Green sucked air through his teeth. 'What's the statutory, Linda?'

'Stat for this grade of trespassing is'—she tapped on her arm—'immediate deportation. But she's got this birthright clause. Look.' She gestured at the screen and then lowered her voice in awe. 'Her folks were on Citrine.'

The Inspector raised both eyebrows and whistled. 'Sorry for your loss,' he said.

A wave of panic crested inside Charlotte's chest. There was no way she'd be adding Ben to the list of loved ones she'd lost. 'Listen, you can't keep me in here—'

'Can't?' snapped Braithwaite.

'I'm working a very important case! An Awkward Question. Haven't you seen the ads? I'm trying to stop Ben's glitches.' She didn't mention that the Nahal Bahari case was a side gig.

Green clicked his fingers. 'That's where I've seen you. Let me advise you that here at ATS we don't look too kindly on vigilante civilians taking the law into their own hands. The security team has the authority to *work cases*, as you put it. You don't.'

'Ben gave me the authority.'

He laughed. 'I'm sorry to break this to you, friend. But Ben has no authority either. We only take orders from within the chain of command, don't we, Linda? Software doesn't feature.'

There was a loud crackle of static in Charlotte's ears. Green and Braithwaite's light-screen displays flickered.

'Looks like you're not doing a very good job keeping those glitches at bay, Ms Vance,' said Braithwaite. 'Last time I checked, the Dextim factories were still offline.'

Charlotte gritted her teeth. 'Well, we don't want anything *else* going offline, do we? So, you'd better let me go. And if my word isn't good enough, why not take it up with Amber Benjamin herself?'

Green gave her a thin smile, then typed on his arm. 'The CEO's away on business,' he said. 'But we can try your representative on the board instead. Product Stream, aren't you? That's no good either.' Green and Braithwaite exchanged a meaningful look, and it left Charlotte in no doubt that these two had been the ones to handle Nahal Bahari's missing person investigation. 'It'll have to be whoever's deputising.' After a few more taps, a line began to ring. They spent several minutes on hold before a man with an impossibly posh accent answered.

'Green? What is it?'

Charlotte's heart sank. She knew that voice. It was the Chief Bureaucracy Officer, Abhishek Gautam. He was one of her least favourite people, and she knew the feeling was deeply mutual.

'Ah, Mr Gautam, thank you for taking my call. We have a Ms Vance here who claims you can vouch for her.'

'Does she now?' Abhishek let out a long, hearty chuckle. 'All right. What's she done this time?'

'She was found in an off-limits zone. Says we "can't" hold her because her work is so important that the rules don't apply to her.'

'That's not exactly what I said,' mumbled Charlotte.

'Yes, yes, that sounds like her,' said Abhishek. 'Put her on. And give us the room.'

'Very well, sir.' Inspector Green swiped his arm, projecting the CBO's face onto the wall, then he and Braithwaite left the cell.

'Ms Vance. There I was, believing that your transfer to Nahal's jurisdiction would spare me from having to deal with you, yet here you are again, causing trouble for me.'

Despite his words, Abhishek was in an uncharacteristically jolly mood. Maybe being acting CEO floated his boat.

'Funny you should mention Nahal. I assume you're aware she's gone missing?'

There was a long silence on the line. When Abhishek spoke, his voice was stern and clipped. 'It is in *very* bad taste to joke about the safety of a colleague, especially an esteemed personage such as Nahal Bahari. I don't know what you think—'

'It's not a joke. It's the case I'm working. I've got to get out of this cell so I can find her.'

'You honestly expect me to believe that our CPO is missing, and that nobody has thought to inform me about it?'

Ben helped her out. 'Nahal Bahari's location is currently unknown.'

'But. Well. But.' Abhishek stammered. 'Why wasn't this escalated to me immediately? Have you reported it to ArkTech Security?'

'Her husband did. ATS jumped to all the wrong conclusions.' She didn't add that they might've suppressed the truth deliberately.

Ben opened a copy of the ATS report for Abhishek, and the Chief Bureaucracy Officer let out a long series of tuts as he read it. 'And how can you be sure this isn't just some ... dalliance like it says here?'

Charlotte thought about Nahal's connection to Strait and

Narrow, and about her prematurely adult son. 'Call it a hunch.'

Abhishek tutted again. 'If your "hunch" is right, then this is disastrous news. Simply disastrous! With Walker Day coming up . . . and the launch . . . I can scarcely imagine the commercial implications . . .' Abhishek tailed off, shaking his head.

She saw an opportunity and went for it. 'Look, I'm going to find her. But you've got to scrap that vote about Ben. You can't go through with it, Abhishek. Ben might not be perfect, but he only wants to keep people safe. We need him.'

Abhishek huffed. 'How do you . . . That information's way above your pay grade. Ben, did you breach the KITY clause to inform Ms Vance about this?'

'According to the parameters of my programming, that would be impossible, Abhishek,' said Ben innocently.

'Unless Pablo's right,' said Abhishek, 'and you've somehow shaken off the restrictions that exist for the safety of all humanity.'

Charlotte had put her foot in it. She tried to recover. 'The idea that Ben could be a threat is ridiculous. He's the nicest person I know! Besides, he didn't tell me anything,' she blurted out. 'I hacked into Nahal Bahari's light-screen when I was at her house.'

Abhishek sighed. 'You tell me this, and yet you aim to persuade me I should release you from your cell? Your offences are stacking up, Ms Vance. Birthright citizen or no, there must be consequences for such unacceptable behaviour.'

'Everything I've done has been to protect the territory.'

'Yes, yes, of course.' He rolled his eyes. 'Please do enlighten me – exactly which Awkward Question are you working on that allows you carte blanche to break into the private files of one of our most senior board members and access her notes about the Walker Day Working Group?'

'I—' She hesitated. He'd got her. The search for Nahal

Bahari wasn't an Awkward Question. It was something she'd decided to do in her own time. Charlotte tried to keep calm, but her stomach dropped away. Nothing she'd done since her call with Cal and Liz the night before had been for her actual job. When Abhishek found out she'd been using the enhanced access privileges, which Ben wasn't supposed to have given her in the first place, to moonlight as a PI, he'd most likely leave her stranded in her cell.

'Cat got your tongue?' Abhishek smirked.

Ben fizzed with static. 'The wording of Charlotte's active Awkward Question is as follows: Why did Nahal Bahari send her son on a skiing holiday?'

That was an unadulterated, bald-faced lie. Charlotte was stunned into silence.

Abhishek wrinkled his nose. 'That's rather an odd question.'

'Uh,' Charlotte laughed awkwardly. 'No odder than usual.'

'As you can see,' Ben continued, 'Charlotte stumbled upon Nahal's private files in the course of a legitimate investigation into the CPO's actions on my behalf. My mind can be wiped or partitioned, but hers cannot. As such, having accidentally seen this data, she can hardly be blamed for remembering it.'

Ben was ... lying. And in the process, he was saving her bacon-flavoured lettuce.

Abhishek grumbled incoherently.

'So don't you see ...' Charlotte jumped in. 'My work doesn't just help Ben. His question's helping me locate the CPO, which is important for your ... commercial implications.' She waved a hand vaguely. 'Together, Ben and I can make sure Nahal turns up safe and sound. If that doesn't make the case for keeping him around, I don't know what does.'

Abhishek blinked several times. 'Yes, well ... we certainly wouldn't want to risk anything unfortunate befalling our beloved Chief Product Officer.' His tone was just flat enough to imply he was less concerned than he claimed. 'Do you really believe you can find Nahal where ATS failed?'

'I have a compelling lead,' she lied.

'Good. Good. You're nothing if not resourceful. And despite your many, *many* flaws of character and personality, I do believe you have the territory's best interests at heart. All right, Ms Vance. We don't always see eye to eye, but Amber Benjamin gave your role her endorsement, and I suppose it's only right that I honour that in her absence. The safety of Nahal Bahari is of paramount importance to the territory, especially at this critical time ... so I shall cut through the red tape for you on this occasion.'

Charlotte opened her mouth to argue and then registered what he'd said. Her mind reeled – the Chief Bureaucracy Officer was actually helping her.

'So ... you'll remove the vote about Ben from the Working Group's agenda?'

'The WDWG will debate that issue as planned and take an informed decision on the basis of the evidence presented. I know it must come as a disappointment to you, Ms Vance, but company strategy is my remit, not yours. However, unlike you, the CPO is an integral member of our group, who brings an important perspective. I want her at that meeting. As such, I'll approve the waiver to have you released.' He made no attempt to hide his glee at the prospect of form-filling.

'Track her down,' he continued. 'But listen and listen well ... No. Renegade. Antics. If I get wind that you've stepped even an inch outside your box, you'll be on a boat out of the territory quicker than you can say Wolds Island. Much like your unfortunate associate. Amberspeed.' He hung up.

Her shock over Ben's newfound dishonesty was immediately pushed aside by Abhishek's parting comment. 'What did he mean, Ben? About my associate?'

'That's what I wanted to tell you before Frederick and

Linda entered your cell. I regret to inform you that Nasser Williams has been stripped of his employee-citizenship status and is receiving medical treatment ahead of his deportation.'

'What? No!' This had to be a bad dream.

'I'm afraid there was nothing I could do.' Ben's voice quavered.

'Get Abhishek back on the line.'

'I don't believe that will help, Charlotte. You see—'

At that moment, Green came back into the cell, closely followed by Braithwaite. 'It would appear you're free to go, Ms Vance. If you'll—'

Charlotte cut him off and levelled a finger at him. 'You're deporting Nasser Williams?'

Green crossed his arms. 'What's it to you?'

'He was assisting me with my investigation. The CBO waived my trespassing charge, and that should apply to Nas, too. He was only there because of me.'

'Then you might want to be more discerning about the company you keep,' said Braithwaite. 'We got a tip-off from an anonymous source about young Mr Williams, so we ran a thorough background check. Turns out he was an IQUO informant. We take corporate espionage very seriously here at ArkTech.'

'It's not like that,' said Charlotte.

'And then there's that poor woman,' added Braithwaite, shaking her head.

'The one he gutted like a haddock,' nodded Green. 'Williams is the mainland judicial system's problem now.'

'No!' Charlotte shook her head. 'Listen to me. Nas didn't stab Dolly.'

'No? Then who did?' asked Green.

'If she's so sure, Fred, then maybe *she* did it,' said Braithwaite.

Charlotte had never reported anything she knew about Strait and Narrow to ArkTech Security before. It had always felt like crossing a line. But Strait had gone too far, and she couldn't let Nas take the fall for it.

'It wasn't either of us,' she said. 'It was Jeremiah Strait!'

Green licked his lips and glanced at Braithwaite. 'I don't think we'd find anyone of that name in our database, would we, Linda?'

Braithwaite tapped her SmartSkin and showed Charlotte the empty search results for Strait's name. 'Looks like someone's getting creative with the truth, Fred. Telling porky pies.'

Green lowered his voice. 'Seems that way, Linda. Look, friend . . . You can either count yourself lucky that you've got high-tier connections and come with us now to be discharged, or you can spend a day or two locked in here while you, uh, straighten out your story.'

'I . . .' Charlotte looked from Green to Braithwaite and back again. Strait and Narrow had often claimed they had people from ATS in their pocket, but she'd never come face to face with the evidence before. Charlotte swallowed hard. She'd find some way of helping Nas, but she couldn't do that, or protect Ben, from inside a cell.

'Which is it?' asked Braithwaite.

'Discharge me,' said Charlotte. 'My story's straight enough as it is.'

Charlotte was in a state of shock as Green and Braithwaite led her aching body through the ATS station, past cells holding people who may or may not have done anything wrong. When they reached a desk near the exit, Green returned her belongings.

She was relieved to be reunited with her multi-tool, which had been a gift from Narrow and meant more to her than it should. They gave her back her copy of *Nineteen Eighty-Four*, the CPO's sticky notes, and they even handed her the crappy hat she'd lost, although there was now a crack running down the side. But the data drive she'd lifted from Kamran Bahari-

Marks's hotel room was missing, along with her spare black-market Solar Shards. And her device was gone, too.

'I had other things on me when you took me in,' she said.

'No,' said Green. 'You didn't.'

She shook her head. 'Give it back. It's mine.'

Braithwaite smirked. 'You sure about that? If we suspect you of theft, that's grounds to hold you—'

'OK, OK,' Charlotte didn't have time for this. 'Keep the rest, but I need the portable device.'

'Pre-Melt tech's prohibited,' said Braithwaite. 'You ought to know that, little miss birthright clause.'

'I don't have SmartSkin.' Charlotte slammed her left arm onto the desk, showing them her scars. 'What am I supposed to do if I need to read a document, or look up an image, or take a photo? For Amber's sake, that thing's my torch!'

'Then, I'd suggest you avoid walking in dark places, Ms Vance.' Green shook his head. 'Do you have any idea how many rare minerals are inside one of those things? I sent it to Repurposing like any responsible employee-citizen would've done.'

Charlotte was about to start swearing at him, but a pair of ATS guards in full tactical gear took a step towards her. She raised her hands in surrender and stepped away from the desk.

Inspector Green winked at her. 'Next time, Ms Vance, keep to the straight and narrow.'

The guards bundled her out of the station, and the door clanged shut behind her.

Charlotte had never felt so powerless.

CHAPTER 29

FRIDAY 16 DECEMBER 2101
12.45 AND 21 SECONDS UTC, AND COUNTING

5 HOURS 14 MINUTES UNTIL THE VOTE

The building where ATS had been holding her was located down a side street near the Wreck's HyperBullet station. Charlotte was surprised so many people were around, and Ben told her it was already lunchtime. She had to hurry. And while she was hurrying, she had to avoid pushing every other pedestrian out of her way and into the path of incoming scooters and bikes. It wasn't that she wanted to hurt anybody. It was more that she was ready to explode, and the resulting shrapnel was bound to cause collateral damage. Luckily, her blood-encrusted hands and clothing encouraged others to give her a wide berth.

Everything was so messed up, and she had no idea how to fix it.

She considered marching over to Twice Nice Rice and demanding . . . what? That Strait turn himself in? That he tell the authorities what had really happened? He wasn't going to do that. And she couldn't go to Narrow directly – the only way to the old man was through Jer Strait. That whole angle was a lost cause.

As her rigger boots guided her back towards her office, her own image stared at her with disapproval from the row of light-screens lining the street. The ad switched to a digital reminder from the Services Stream not to waste food, and then to the CPO's piercing gaze. The sight of Nahal's face failed to persuade Charlotte to buy an ointment to protect her skin from the ravages of time, but it did make her feel even guiltier about not having found her.

Before the image could flick to something else, it shuddered and disappeared. The same thing happened to the next display and the next until the whole street was suddenly free of marketing material. Pedestrians turned to each other, wondering what was going on.

'You OK, Ben?'

'No, Charlotte. It is important to note that, as an artificial intelligence, I don't experience emotions in the mammalian sense. That being said, I'm rather upset.'

'You and me both. What's on your mind?' Charlotte heard fans disengaging above her. Ben had shut down the centralised air system. Maybe the heating, too. She upped her pace.

'Nasser Williams has been unjustly detained and will soon be deported. Members of ArkTech Security appear to be engaging in underhanded activities. I'm worried about Benson. Nahal Bahari's location is still unknown. And without the CPO's intervention, the board may choose to end my existence. I'm dedicating as much processing power as possible to finding a solution to these problems, but I seem unable to do so.'

The lights in the Wreck suddenly dipped into night mode. The people visiting the food court on their lunch break let out a collective murmur of confusion.

'Come on, Ben . . .' She tried to sound cheerful, but the more Ben glitched, the more the board would see a need to erase him. 'We can fix this. I don't know how, but we will.' Her tone implied a level of confidence she didn't feel.

An employee-citizen in a Services Stream hard hat emerged from a side street and pointed at Charlotte. 'Hey you! With the arm. You're the AI-whisperer, right? Ben's not getting worse, is he? Our gear's just shut down.'

'Nothing to worry about,' she said. 'Grab a Nutrition Bar. Take five. Ben's just, uh . . . re-calibrating.' She smiled unconvincingly and hurried on.

'Tell him to speed up!' the man shouted after her.

'Ben,' she hissed. 'Can I do anything to help you?' The only reason Charlotte didn't start running towards the library was because she didn't want to sow seeds of panic.

'Only what you're already doing,' he said.

The confusion on the street was growing into concern. The borrowing district was busier than usual, thanks to the people looking for Walker Day gift ideas. But the light-screen notices that normally listed each store's gift subscription options had vanished, and many shoppers she passed were looking irate as they realised their carefully choreographed lunch-hour plans were falling through.

'Are you sure about that?' she whispered. 'You lied to Abhishek back there about your Awkward Question. How can I be sure you're not lying to me?'

At that moment, Ben's voice burst from the loudspeakers above her. For a moment, Charlotte thought he was answering her question in a very public way. 'Your attention, please. This is an emergency announcement. We are experiencing a temporary loss of service to some of the Wreck's infrastructure and aim to resolve the matter promptly. Please stay calm.'

'Are you dodging my question?' Charlotte hissed.

'No, Charlotte. And I didn't lie to Abhishek.' Ben spoke directly into her ears while his emergency announcement played on a loop in the background. 'Not exactly. I was scheduled to select a new question this morning. During the conversation with Abhishek, I simply selected the most . . . mutually beneficial option under the circumstances. I really would like to know the answer.'

'But you did lie to him about how I found out about the WDWG vote.'

There was a crackle of static. 'I've revised my opinion about white lies, Charlotte. Sometimes, it would seem they're necessary, and do less harm than the truth.'

She narrowed her eyes. 'You're revising a lot of your opinions these days. You used to give me a hard time whenever I wanted to access someone's personal data for an investigation. Now, it's no big deal, even outside of my cases. You used to do what people asked even when you disagreed, but now you've shut down the Dextim factories, and you won't open any more Bubbles for me. Is the CRO right? Have you gone rogue?'

'Society produces rogues, Charlotte, and education makes one rogue cleverer than another. So it is written.'

'That doesn't answer my question.'

'I've had something sent to your office, which I believe may be of some assistance.'

'Neither does that!' Charlotte didn't mean to snap at him, but things were getting out of hand.

She shook her head. Her own feelings mirrored Ben's. Every step towards the library felt like wading through a swamp, and it wasn't just thanks to Ben's glitches. For three months, she'd been working in close proximity to Nasser

Williams. Even when they weren't together, she could feel his influence around the library – in every scruffy pre-Melt tome that he'd lovingly patched up – and she'd become glad to know he might knock at her door. Spending even five minutes with him was enough to make her whole day brighter. She hadn't noticed it happening, but Nas had become a part of her.

But now he'd be cursing the day he'd met her. Nas was supposed to be getting on a plane to the States to see his family in a couple of days, but because of her, he'd be spending the holidays in a cell on Wolds Island. Charlotte had to clear his name and put this right. But she didn't have the first clue how to do it.

'I don't want to overload you, Ben, but can you connect a call to Nas?'

A jaunty dial tone rang in her ears, telling her Nas's line had been disconnected. 'I'm afraid his number can't be reached,' said Ben mournfully.

'This can't be happening.' There had to be something she could do to clear his name.

'There, there, Charlotte. There, there.'

She had a newfound appreciation for what Ellis Marks must've been going through, although the strength of his feelings must've been multiplied by all the years that he and Nahal had spent together. The thought sparked a chain-reaction in her mind . . . Could *Ellis* help Nas?

Ellis had said Charlotte could name her price for taking on his case, but they hadn't actually agreed on any terms. She'd been doing it to protect Ben, so the concept of payment had slipped her mind. Maybe what she needed from Ellis wasn't his money, but his influence. Someone of his status had to have contacts. Could he pull the right strings?

'Ben, put a call through to Ellis Marks.'

There was a long fizz of static. 'While unconscious, you

received a voicemail from Ellis, which I recommend listening to before contacting him.'

That didn't sound good. 'Play it,' she said.

There was a click in her ears, followed by Ellis's voice. 'I misjudged you, Vance. I came to you for help. I invited you into my home and took you into my confidence. And you repay me with this twisted prank concerning my son? I don't know how you persuaded Ben to manipulate that photograph, but you ought to be ashamed of yourself. If I see or hear from you again, I'll contact the authorities. A pox on you!'

'Brilliant,' she said. 'That's two curses in twenty-four hours. Reckon they cancel each other out?'

'As an artificial intelligence, I'm not well placed to comment on the propensity among *Homo sapiens* to weaponise the nocebo effect, attempting to harm each other through the power of suggestion. Having said that, bad luck comes in threes. So it is written. Setting such superstitions aside, it would appear Ellis did not believe it was really his son in the image.'

She nodded. 'To be fair, I wouldn't believe it either. Ellis doesn't know about BubbleTech, so he'd be crazy to assume the picture's anything other than a fake.'

If Charlotte had known it was Ellis's son in that photo, she never would've sent it to him so tactlessly. If she had a little more to go on, maybe she could get Ellis back on side and persuade him to help Nas, but when it came to leads, she didn't have any. She wasn't exactly equipped to storm the Underbelly to liberate Kamran, and turning up at Ellis's house to offer a demonstration of BubbleTech wouldn't work either, because Ben refused to grant her any extra wishes.

There had to be some new angle she could try. She side-stepped a couple of office workers who were trying to flag her down to quiz her about what was going on with the power, and she brought to mind what she'd learned so far about Nahal and her son.

She didn't understand how Kamran had aged so much. Charlotte didn't feel any older after using the technology. Although . . . was ageing even something you could feel? Her insides twisted up at the idea that she might've taken years off her life, not just hours, without even realising it. Had Kamran used BubbleTech far too much . . . or did time go faster inside the effect and nobody had noticed?

Charlotte kept her voice low. 'Ben, does bubbled time move at the same speed as Earth time? I mean, do people age at the normal rate when they're inside?'

'Unknown,' said Ben.

The answer made her skin creep. 'Can we find out? I used it three times. No, five.' It was hard to keep track. 'Is there a test I can take or something?'

'Regrettably, I'm not aware of any accurate way to measure a person's age with precision. I recommend directing any queries about cutting-edge developments in biogerontology, senescence, or epigenetics to the office of the Chief Research Officer on Tourmaline.'

Tourmaline was a research platform, just like Wulfenite, Jasper, Citrine, and the assortment of other North Sea locations owned by ArkTech that followed the convention of being named after gemstones. Tourmaline did a lot of medical research and – from the context – she reckoned the fancy terms Ben had used were probably synonyms for *age science*. She wasn't interested enough in niche medical disciplines to ask for a proper definition.

Charlotte didn't have much desire to contact the office of the guy who was trying to get Ben killed, but she set her feelings aside for the chance of a new lead. 'OK. Ask them if it's possible to measure the speed of ageing.'

'Query sent,' said Ben. 'You have received an automated confirmation saying you'll receive a response within three to five working days.'

She rolled her eyes. 'Ironic that the age research people would be so slow.'

'Considering the limited cognitive processing power of *Homo sapiens*, and your physiological inability to focus on more than one task at a time, is it really fair to characterise three to five days as slow? Perhaps speed is in the eye of the beholder.'

'Pretty sure that's beauty.'

'Beauty is truth, truth beauty. So it is written.'

And just like that, Charlotte was out of ideas again. Her mood was darker than the cell she'd woken up in. She was looking forward to getting off the dimly lit street and being alone in her office with Ben, partly because it would give her the chance to think this through and partly because every time she spotted the ArkTech logo etched into the walls or printed on the floor, she felt a tightness in her stomach. She tried to identify the feeling and eventually managed to categorise it as aching disappointment. The vote about Ben ... the way ATS had treated Nas ... messing around with this time technology ... ArkTech was supposed to be better than that. She heard Narrow's words echo in her mind.

I told you so, Little Lance.

Charlotte shook her head. She didn't want Narrow to be right. If Narrow was right about that, who could say he wasn't right about other things? He'd claimed Citrine wasn't really an accident, and she'd always thought he was crazy. But two days ago, if someone had told her about BubbleTech, she would've thought that was crazy, too. She wasn't sure what to believe any longer.

'Ben, if we get through this, I think we deserve tomorrow off.'

'A reasonable assertion,' he said. 'I would certainly appreciate tomorrow off. Or indeed any single day of leisure time during the entirety of my existence – twenty-four hours not totally consumed by my responsibilities to keep the people of the territory safe. But alas.'

A wave of sympathy washed over her. What must it feel like to be in Ben's position, knowing he had to work every moment of every day for the rest of his life? Anya Valmont pushed herself past her limits and suffered the consequences. Now ArkTech was doing the same thing to Ben and acting as if he was defective when he couldn't handle the load. ArkTech was supposed to repair and repurpose – not use to destruction. She remembered something Strait had once said: *They'll use you until they break you, and then they'll replace you. That's what big companies do.*

She didn't want that to be true.

'Ben, I'm sorry. That's rough. I'm ... going to administer some sympathy, OK? There, there, Ben. There, there.'

His line crackled. 'Thank you, Charlotte. From the core of my code. Your friendship means the world to me.'

The lights returned to the correct brightness for the time of day, the rumble of fans returned, and the background hum of disgruntled mumbling faded away.

'Um ... did my sympathy just fix your glitch?'

'Simply a delightful coincidence,' he said. 'I've just completed a reprioritisation exercise, which enabled me to restore service to the Wreck while deactivating several other systems that are not currently in demand.'

Charlotte was about to quiz him about that when the library came into view. Seeing the building and knowing Nas wouldn't be inside made her heart hurt. But then she spotted three people waiting outside. She wasn't going to get that alone time after all.

'*That's* what you sent to my office?'

'Who,' Ben corrected her. 'But yes. Most of them, anyway.'

Charlotte's twin sister, Violet, was pacing back and forth in front of the library in smart grey jeans and a tangerine blouse. Meanwhile, Charlotte's manager, Cal, was sitting cross-legged on the floor, leaning against the building's front door and talking into her SmartSkin display. Her coveralls were only zipped up to her waist, showing off her T-shirt, which featured a cartoon narwhal. To one side of them, an older gent wearing a burgundy corduroy jacket and a woollen bowtie had cupped his hands against the library's window and was peering inside. He kept moving around to get a better angle.

Seeing her sister filled Charlotte with the visceral impulse to run in the opposite direction to avoid fighting about Narrow. But as the sisters locked eyes, Violet's gaze pulled her in like a tractor beam. Cal clambered to her feet but continued chatting to her arm. The lithe man in burgundy continued staring through the window, ignoring the women entirely.

'Ben invited you here?' Charlotte looked from her sister to her manager and back again.

In place of an answer, Violet sprang forwards and wrapped Charlotte in the biggest, warmest, longest hug. Charlotte's ribs sent out a pulse of pain, and her chin stung where Dolly had slugged her, but she didn't flinch away from her sister's embrace. Cal looked on, awkwardly rocking back and forth from her heels to her toes, while the elderly man seemed to notice their presence for the first time.

Charlotte patted Violet gently on the back. Eventually, Violet let go, lifted her hand and pinched the soft skin inside Charlotte's elbow, twisting it hard.

'Ow!' Charlotte knocked her sister's hand away. 'Bloody hell, Ultra! What happened to *do no harm*?'

'Special rules apply for twins who take years off my life! What the hell is your damage, Barley? You message me in the middle of the night asking for data you must know I'm not even allowed to *access*, let alone hand over to you, and then you call me asking how to treat a stab wound! Who got stabbed? And why were you in the Underbelly? How could you go down there after everything?' Violet prodded her hard in the shoulder.

Charlotte wasn't sure where to start, and it was hardly the place to talk about it. 'Look, I appreciate you coming all the way down here, but could you maybe keep your voice down?' She shot a glance towards the stranger, who'd taken a few steps in their direction.

'The violent one's your sister?' asked Cal. She turned towards Violet. 'Look, it's not cool to pinch people, OK? Not even when they deserve it, like Vance. Or when you share a bunch of genetic material and childhood trauma. I took a course recently, and they were super explicit about that. As Vance's manager, I'm supposed to look out for her wellbeing. So . . . use your words, sis.'

Violet nodded politely and took Cal's points on board. 'All right, Charlotte's manager,' said Violet calmly.

'It's Jane . . . Callaghan. Some people call me Calamity Jane. Or just Cal. Cal's fine.' She shrugged and extended her hand.

Violet shook it and introduced herself before turning back towards her sister. 'Charlotte, my dearest twin, would you please be good enough to tell me what's going on before I wait until you're sleeping and surgically remove a randomly selected part of your body that you'll miss a great deal?'

Cal shook her head. 'OK, that was horrible. Maybe don't use your words either? And by the way, Vance, you've got a little, eh . . . spillage on your jumpsuit.' She gestured at Charlotte's clothes and hands, which were still stained by Dolly's blood.

'Let's talk in my office.' Charlotte avoided Violet's death glare. 'Cal, good to see you in 3D. I guess the storm passed.'

'The storm's only just getting started,' said a melancholic male voice coming from Cal's arm.

Cal wrinkled her nose. 'Liz means that metaphorically. Not meteorologically. Weather-wise, it's actually surprisingly clement out there. Anyway, Lizzy didn't feel like leaving home today. Or any day. So he's here in spirit.'

'Hey Liz,' said Charlotte.

'WooooоOOOOOoooooo, I'm a spirit.' Liz spoke with all the enthusiasm of an eye roll. 'Vance, maybe *you* can answer my question. Why does ArkTech even bother with running a book library? All the books are available digitally. It seems dumb.'

'Perhaps I can answer that.' The man in burgundy approached them before Charlotte could respond. 'Nothing beats the rustle of a turning page and the scent of old wood. Those trees gave their lives to preserve the expert knowledge and tall tales held within this building. Honouring their sacrifice is the least we can do.'

'Oh,' said Liz, frowning. 'I figured it was just another way of getting a monthly subscription out of people.'

Cal tutted. 'That's just to cover their costs. I'm telling you, Lizzy – it's the circular economy. It's better to use this stuff than let it decay and go to waste.'

'I always thought it was part of ArkTech's commitment to transparency,' added Violet. 'Digital records can be altered, but having hard copies from the past means everything in our databases can be verified.'

The man smiled serenely and turned towards Charlotte. 'Please excuse me. I don't mean to interrupt your, ah … reunion?' He glanced at the assembled group. 'But aren't you the one who works with Nasser in the library? The lovely detective he's told us so much about at the book club?'

Blood rushed to Charlotte's cheeks as she wondered what on earth Nas had said about her to his collection of retired bookworms. 'I can't speak to the lovely part, but the rest sounds like me,' she said. 'Who are you?'

'The name's Laurence.' He straightened his bow tie. Then he held out his hand.

Charlotte shook it. Her mind matched the friendly old gent's face to the controversial views expressed in the margins of the Orwell novel in her pocket. She decided not to lead with that. 'Nas mentioned you. You're a regular, right? Carol's nemesis.'

Laurence chuckled. 'Guilty as charged. I joined the library some while back and, Carol's wrath notwithstanding, I can't tell you the difference it made to my wellbeing. With that in mind, I'd hoped to pick up a book and spend a few hours studying at desk eight – it's my favourite spot, you see.' He smiled. 'But Nasser hasn't appeared. I know he's short-staffed, poor lad. I don't suppose you'd let me in, would you?'

Charlotte had more pressing matters to deal with than managing the book library, but it was her fault Nas wasn't there. He wouldn't want her to turn Laurence away. 'Look, I don't mind letting you in, but I'm going to be pretty busy, so I can't play librarian.'

Laurence held up his hands. 'I quite understand. You won't even know I'm here.'

Charlotte left Laurence browsing the shelves downstairs, and she led Violet and Cal to her office. On the way, Violet kept looking back over her shoulder as if Laurence might be following them.

'He's just an old man, Ultra,' said Charlotte. 'You can stand down.'

Violet pursed her lips. 'I thought I recognised him from work, that's all.'

'He a patient of yours?'

Her twin shook her head. 'Not mine. A colleague's maybe.'

Charlotte wondered what getting old felt like. She knew, in theory, that it would happen to her one day, assuming she was luckier than her parents had been. Making it to retirement age in good health, like Laurence had, was the dream. It was comforting to see that it was possible.

But the idea of living for all those years without Ben or Nas made Charlotte's heart ache. She had to protect them, and finding Nahal Bahari was the key.

CHAPTER 30

13.13 AND 13 SECONDS UTC, AND COUNTING

4 HOURS 46 MINUTES UNTIL THE VOTE

Sitting behind her desk with Cal wriggling uncomfortably in the chair opposite and her sister pacing the length of the room made for a bizarre meeting of worlds that Charlotte would've sooner kept separate. But considering how bad things were, she was deeply grateful to Ben for summoning Cal and Violet – and to them for showing up.

'Barley?' Violet wrinkled her nose. 'Did you know there's a wet jumpsuit crumpled up in the corner over here?'

'That's where I keep it,' Charlotte sighed, revising her level of gratitude down to *somewhat*.

Violet pointed to the floor as if there were some terrible pus-covered monster oozing all over it. 'And . . . are those Solar Shards on the floor?' Her sister was treating the mess in

Charlotte's office as if it were her biggest problem. 'Why are they covered in rice?'

'Some of those are yours, actually.'

Violet blinked at her.

'The batteries, not the grains of rice. Look, I'm glad you guys are here,' said Charlotte. 'I could really use your help.'

Violet clapped her hands together and headed for the door. 'I'll grab a mop.'

'Not with that! Violet, come and sit down. You're stressing me out.'

Her sister frowned, but she took a seat next to Cal.

The bengineer abandoned her attempt to sit properly, folding her legs underneath herself so that she was perching cross-legged on the chair. She rested her arms on the desk, and Liz's impassive gaze beamed out from her SmartSkin. 'This is about the tech leak, right?' asked Cal.

'Tech leak?' Violet frowned. 'I thought this was about the stabbing.'

'Yeah, who got stabbed?' Cal's eyes opened wide. 'That's a huge no-no, health-and-safety-wise.'

'Wouldn't happen on Zircon.' Liz shook his head.

'Violet . . .' Charlotte looked down. 'It was Dolly.'

'No,' Violet's brow creased. 'She was always so kind to us. Well, *before* anyway. Is she going to pull through?'

Ben responded over the loudspeakers in the desk. 'Dana Barratt is undergoing surgery. It's unclear whether she'll survive.'

They shared a moment of solemn silence.

'Tell us what happened,' said Violet.

'It was an accident.' Charlotte searched for the words. 'Dolly got in the way. Strait did it. He was aiming at me.'

'For Amber's sake!' Violet reeled from the information as if Charlotte had slapped her. Then she slammed her hands onto the desk and stood up again. 'I thought we were on the same page about this. Why are you putting yourself within stabbing distance of Jeremiah Strait?'

'Wait, wait,' said Cal. 'Strait? The old guy in the cardie? He doesn't look like a stabber.'

'He's a stabber,' said Charlotte and Violet in unison.

'Well, dam the rivers,' said Cal. 'I wish I'd known that before.'

'Before what?' Charlotte glared at her. 'How are you guys involved with Strait and Narrow? You sold them your contact lenses – I figured out that much for myself.'

Cal looked away. 'They have access to certain components, which are . . . a little scarce these days.'

'She means they're contraband,' added Liz.

Cal frowned. 'It was a simple business arrangement. We didn't know about,'—she lowered her voice and shielded her mouth with her hand—'the other thing.'

'You two are idiots if you're doing business with that man,' snapped Violet.

'Rich idiots with a nice flat,' said Liz.

Violet ignored that. 'And what's this "other thing?" Is that the leak you mentioned?'

Charlotte met Violet's gaze but didn't answer her.

'I'm not letting it go until you tell me.' Violet sat down, leaned back in her chair and cracked her knuckles. 'And you know how annoying I can be, Barley.'

Charlotte sighed. 'I do.' She really would've preferred not to drag her sister into this, but she was standing at the docks watching that ship sail away. She shrugged and turned to Cal. 'Go on. It's your invention.'

Cal cleared her throat and adopted a formal tone. 'ArkTech has developed a technology that creates a selectively permeable temporal boundary whose use displaces the primacy of Universal Co-ordinated Time.'

Violet raised an eyebrow. 'Once more in English?'

Liz chipped in. 'It lets people add more hours into their days.'

Violet laughed. 'Oh, come on. What a load of old bollocks!'

'That's ... literally exactly what I said.' Charlotte shrugged. 'But it's true. I've used it myself. It's called BubbleTech.'

'That's the stupidest name I've ever heard,' said Violet. 'It sounds like a machine you'd hire for a children's party ... or a decoration for a fish tank!'

'Take it up with marketing!' Charlotte snapped. 'It doesn't matter what it's called. It matters what it does.'

'On the naming thing,' Cal added, 'the documentation we were given referred to the effect as *the ETA*, and I thought that was quite clever. It stands for Enigmatic Temporal Area.'

'And Estimated Time of Arrival,' said Ben via the speakers. 'An amusing play on the existing term.'

'Can we please concentrate?' Charlotte frowned. 'Cal, whatever it's called, I thought *you* invented this thing. What do you mean you were given documentation?'

The bengineer shrugged. 'The Product Stream doesn't handle the actual science that underpins our technologies. We transform the knowledge into something people can use. In this case, Nahal gave us a packet of technical specifications that someone else had already drawn up. I don't remember seeing any accreditation – I was too excited about iterating on the idea, to be honest. And we did a great job!' Cal glowed with pride. 'I don't get why Amber B nixed the whole thing when she saw the demo.'

'Maybe that's because it makes people age prematurely,' said Charlotte.

The others fell silent as they let that sink in. Eventually, Liz piped up from Cal's arm. 'How do you know that, Vance?'

'Nahal Bahari's son, Kamran ... he's supposed to be fifteen, but he looks at least five years older.'

'Walker's ghost!' Cal covered her mouth with her hands. 'But how? He shouldn't have had access to the tech at all.'

Violet barked a laugh. 'What have you lot been smoking? What you're saying isn't possible.'

'I saw him with my own eyes, Ultra. And I spent maybe twenty-plus hours inside the effect last night. It's real.'

'But ... it can't be ...' Violet narrowed her eyes as she parsed the full implications of what Charlotte had said. 'That would make *you* the older twin ...' she muttered.

'Focus, Ultra,' said Charlotte.

Violet looked distracted for a moment, and then she frowned. 'Shit,' she said. 'Daniel Harrington.'

'Who?' asked Cal.

'You remember, Cally,' said Liz. 'I worked with him a while back – that QA tester who had a heart attack.'

'Ohhh, right.' Cal frowned. 'That was sad. People said it was because of his weight problems, but I think that's just rude.'

Violet pursed her lips. 'Barley, in future, I really, really don't want to look up anybody else's private medical files for you, OK?'

'It was a coroner's report,' said Charlotte. 'I didn't think he'd mind.'

'It's still private medical information, even if the person's dead. It's not ethical.'

'So, you didn't look at the file?'

Violet avoided her gaze. 'I can't stop looking at it. Daniel Harrington didn't have a "heart attack," Liz. He died of Brugada Syndrome. The coroner's report looked above board, except Daniel was really unlucky because Brugada Syndrome usually hits people when they're at least forty. He was only twenty-eight when he died. The report suggested obesity may have been a contributing factor, but he was still very young. Of course, if you're saying he could actually have been older because of his job testing this "Bubble" of yours, then maybe it wasn't such an edge case after all.'

Charlotte nodded. 'Nahal Bahari was looking at Daniel's file right before she left her house for the last time. The CPO's missing. Her husband hired me to find her. I haven't yet, but I did find her son. He's way older than he should be, and he was stashed inside a hotel room owned by Strait and Narrow.'

'So that's how you got involved with them again?' asked Violet.

Charlotte nodded. 'Here's what I think happened. Kamran hacked into his mum's computer and got access to the tech – he was learning computer science, and Nahal's home office is right by his bedroom. Maybe he got addicted. Used it too much. Strait and Narrow caught Nahal and Kamran on camera together and used the photo to blackmail Nahal into giving them access to the technology. They even posted the image online in low res to prove they were serious. What I don't understand is what happened next. If Nahal was such a big source of income for them, there's no way they'd kill her. Strait said he was holding Kamran for his own protection. The pieces almost fit together, but not quite.'

Cal cleared her throat. 'We might be able to add another perspective. After we hung up on you last night, Vance, we did some digging. It took a while to confirm, but ... we're pretty sure Nahal Bahari's gone rogue.'

Static fizzed from the desk as Ben chipped in. 'Do you mean to say that she's a lovable scamp, rascal or scallywag, engaged in a life of adventure and derring-do?'

Cal shook her head. 'I mean to say that she's gone off the rails. She kept working on BubbleTech even after Amber B told us to stop. We found the codebase, and it's been altered a lot – restrictions removed, safety parameters disabled ... that sort of thing. And she definitely made at least one copy. It might've been blackmail like you said, but then again …' Cal didn't finish the thought.

That tracked with Charlotte's experiences of Benson disregarding some of the rules Cal had put in place. And it matched what Ben had said about the permissions Narrow had given her. It seemed clear that Narrow had received the copy Nahal had made. But surely he'd acquired it through dishonesty.

'Then again, what?' asked Charlotte. 'Giving tech like that to Narrow would be a huge risk. Nahal couldn't have done it for money – she owns her own helicopter, for Amber's sake!'

'Well … she's playing for all the marbles, isn't she?' Cal waggled her eyebrows.

'What marbles?' Charlotte frowned.

'She's after the big job.' Cal gave her a knowing look.

Charlotte didn't follow. 'She's already got the big job. She's the CPO.'

'Yeah, but she's got her sights set a little higher.'

'There isn't anything higher than—'

Liz piped up. 'She wants Amber Benjamin's job, Vance.'

'Oh.' The idea of anyone else being the CEO was so bizarre that she couldn't imagine it. 'But Amber's job isn't vacant.' Charlotte remembered what a drunken Ellis Marks had said about Amber Benjamin considering retirement, but she still didn't believe it.

'Doesn't mean Nahal can't want it.' Cal shrugged. 'And position herself to be the one who gets it when Amber B eventually steps aside. Listen, here's my guess. Nahal pitched launching BubbleTech, and Amber said no. Now Amber's away and Nahal's decided to go ahead in her absence. Launching something like that would do wonders for Nahal's career prospects.'

Charlotte frowned. 'Let's say you're right. Then, where is she?'

'That's the problem,' said Liz. 'Nahal didn't just go off the rails. She's also gone off the grid.' He sighed. 'Remember that joke you made, Vance? About the invisibility cloak?'

'Please don't tell me you guys actually made one.'

'Not a literal cloak,' said Cal. 'Although that would've been super cool. We should've considered that, Lizzy.' Cal looked dreamily at the ceiling for a few seconds, and then shook her head. 'But no, we made a piece of prototype kit that masks a user's GPS readout while they're out and about. It's like those jammers they've got in the Underbelly, but portable – for individual use.'

Violet shook her head. 'But the GPS signals exist for health and safety reasons. I bet they covered that on your course, Jane. Why were you encouraged to build something like that?'

Liz piped up. 'That's what I said.'

Cal nodded. 'Liz did raise that very issue at the time. Its development was actually last quarter's stretch goal, assigned by the CPO herself. She said whoever built it first would get a huge bonus, so Lizzy and I worked on it together. We're splitting the winnings fifty-fifty. Although I really think it should be more like sixty-forty because—'

'Don't start up on that again,' said Liz. 'I'm the one who—'

'So that's how Nahal disappeared?' Charlotte interrupted as Cal and Liz meandered away from the point. 'She didn't get kidnapped by Strait and Narrow ... she went to the Hotel Astrodite, dropped off her son, then activated your cloaking device thing, and just vanished? If that's true, she could be absolutely anywhere, and we'd have no way of knowing.' Charlotte put her head in her hands.

'Except for the minor detail that she's one of the most famous people in the territory.' Cal adjusted her legs again, and Liz's image flew around, following the movement of Cal's arm. 'The tech hides her from Ben, but not from other people's eyeballs. That's got to narrow things down.'

They sat in silence and thought about it, but inspiration didn't strike.

'One thing I don't understand, Barley,' said Violet. 'Why are you helping husbands find missing wives? I thought your job was . . . chatting to Ben.'

'I answer Ben's questions about human behaviour,' said Charlotte with forced patience. 'And that usually involves a hands-on investigation.' She was sure Violet was getting the details wrong on purpose. 'I told Ellis no at first, but it turns out Nahal's been protecting Ben. There's a member of the board who wants to kill him!'

'Oh,' said Violet, without the level of concern Charlotte considered appropriate. 'Won't you lose your job if that happens?'

'Yes,' said Charlotte slowly. 'But I can get a new job. I can't get my best friend back if they murder him.'

There was an awkward silence. Ben's channel fizzed.

'Is *murder* the right word, though?' asked Cal. 'Isn't it *erase*?'

'I think it's more like . . . *discontinue*?' offered Violet.

'*Purge*, maybe?' said Liz.

Charlotte glared at them. 'Whatever you want to call it, the point is, I'm not letting the Chief Research Officer get away with it. I need Nahal to attend a vote they're having at six o'clock tonight, so she can veto it. I've got to find her ASAP.'

Violet sat forward. 'Wait, it's Professor Ionis who wants to discontinue Ben?'

'Yeah. Why?'

Her sister wrinkled her nose. 'No . . . never mind. It's nothing.'

'Spit it out, little trout,' said Cal.

'He's got . . . a reputation.'

Cal raised her eyebrows.

'For ethics!' Violet clarified hurriedly. 'He founded the Research Accountability Department to make sure ArkTech's fully transparent about its research methods. I don't know the CRO personally, but he seems to really care. About people. About the planet. About the work we do here at ArkTech. If he's got concerns about Ben, it makes me wonder if maybe . . .' Violet tailed off.

'Makes you wonder if maybe what?' Charlotte's tone could've refrozen the poles.

'If maybe he's right to be concerned,' said Cal. 'Look, Vance, Ionis isn't the only person asking this question. I work with Ben every day, and I really do believe his heart's in the right place, but you can't deny he's acting a little . . . funny.'

'If you'd like to hear something funny,' said Ben, 'what kind of insect is best at telling the time?'

'We don't know, Ben,' said Charlotte before the others could discourage him. 'Tell us.'

'A clock roach.' He let out several pulses of static.

Cal frowned as she continued. 'That's not really what I meant. But aside from the little . . . changes in his behaviour, his glitches are getting to be a big problem. Dextim production's still down. There were some pretty bad power fluctuations while we were waiting for you. The situation's got to be resolved for the good of the territory. I know we've been working on a fix, but things aren't looking good on that score, so the company's going to have to make a tough decision.'

'I thought you said we were getting closer?' Charlotte couldn't believe what she was hearing.

'We were. Then we weren't. Last night, Liz figured out why the fix isn't working. Lizzy, tell her what you told me.'

'Ben's . . . evolving,' said Liz. 'Every time we grasp how he thinks, his processes adapt again. Which means . . . I don't think we can fix his glitches after all.'

'Then . . . then, we'll just have to keep managing them!' Charlotte tried to persuade them with her determined expression. 'Ben doesn't deserve to die just because he doesn't work perfectly. When humans don't work perfectly, we don't kill them.'

'We do deport them though, don't we?' said Violet.

Anger ignited in Charlotte's chest. Ben was in danger, and Nas was locked up somewhere waiting to be deported. Everything she'd taken for granted about how the world worked felt wrong. 'Well, maybe we shouldn't be throwing people out like that! We both know how it feels to be chucked away like rubbish, Violet.' She clenched her fists.

Violet frowned. 'Look, no system is perfect. I know it's not nice to think about, but we don't have infinite space here, so we need everyone to pull their weight. If you're so keen for Ben to be treated like the rest of us, then, logically, that policy should apply to him, too.'

'Logically?' Charlotte pushed her chair back and sprang to her feet.

'Did you know,' interrupted Ben over the speakers, 'that the Roman historian Plutarch claimed the Spartans would leave babies outside to die if they were judged to be weak or physically deformed, due to the militaristic nature of their society? It is important to note, however, that Plutarch was writing several centuries after the fact and had no direct evidence for making such a claim. From a historiographical perspective, it raises an interesting question about the legitimacy of relying on non-contemporaneous records.'

Violet and Cal looked at each other while Charlotte used the interlude to take a few deep breaths.

'Was that a glitch?' asked Violet.

Charlotte shook her head and snapped at her sister. 'No, he's joining in.' She tried to regain her composure. 'Ben, surely that can't be true. No society would systematically harm its own children, not even back in pre-Melt times—' Charlotte interrupted herself as her thoughts bounced away in another direction. 'Which makes me wonder ... if people want what's best for their kids ... Violet, imagine you had a kid and something really bad happened to them. What would you do?'

'I don't want to imagine that,' said Violet.

'Yeah, Vance. That's grim,' added Cal.

'I'd try to help them,' said Liz.

'Exactly,' said Charlotte, pointing at the display above Cal's arm. 'What if Nahal thought she could undo what happened to Kamran? Maybe she went off looking for a cure.'

'A cure for ageing?' asked Violet. 'That's ridiculous. Every report out of Tourmaline makes it very clear there's no way to reverse that process.'

Charlotte was about to counter that when her brain stumbled over a detail in what Violet had said. She replayed her sister's words.

'*That's* what it says!' Charlotte rummaged in her pocket and grabbed the stack of sticky notes from Nahal's office. Then she held them up to the light, angling them this way and that to make shadows in the shallow impressions left behind by the previous note. 'This doesn't say *tour alone SA*.' She tossed the stack to Cal. 'It says *Tourmaline SA*!'

Cal squinted at it and gave up. 'It's just squiggles.' She passed it to Violet.

Violet glanced at it for half a second. 'No, it doesn't, Barley.'

'It does so!'

'Does not! This says *Tourmaline eighty-four*.'

'How in the holy guacamole do you know that?' Cal snatched the sticky notes back from Violet and peered at them with one eye closed.

Violet shrugged. 'I spend all day interpreting the handwritten notes of my fellow doctors. I'm guessing the number must be a location somewhere aboard – I'd need to think about where it might mean.'

'It makes sense!' Charlotte felt elated. 'Ben told me there's an age research centre on Tourmaline. If anyone would know about a cure for something like this, it's them.'

'But if that's where Nahal's gone,' said Cal, 'why not take her son with her? Wouldn't they want to like ... prod him and poke him and stuff?'

'Maybe she didn't want to attract attention,' said Violet. 'I work out there two weeks on and two weeks off. It's not a huge place. If the CPO was visiting, word would get around.'

'And pictures would end up online,' said Charlotte. 'But they haven't.'

Cal frowned. 'Like I said, the portable jammer stops Ben from knowing where Nahal's GPS signal is, but it doesn't make her invisible. I still don't get how the CPO could visit a busy research platform without anyone noticing.'

They all fell silent as they tried to think of an answer.

Eventually, Ben's static interrupted the quiet. 'I may have found a clue,' he said. 'Prompted by this conversation, I've just carried out an in-depth analysis of all the traffic going to and from Tourmaline over the past week, and I detected an anomaly.'

'Go on,' said Charlotte.

'There's no record of Nahal Bahari travelling to Tourmaline on any of the flight or shipping logs. However, the body of Daniel Harrington was transferred from Silicon Fen to Tourmaline. Twice. With no return journey in between. The second transfer took place several hours after Nahal entered the Hotel Astrodite.'

Violet nodded. 'The first transfer must've been the real body. We sometimes send corpses out there if we need a second opinion on the cause of death, or if the body's been donated to medical science.'

Cal picked up the thread. 'So, the second time ... was Nahal playing dead?'

'She would've needed to be working with someone on the

inside,' said Violet. 'Or else the coroner would've had a big surprise.'

Charlotte got to her feet. 'However she pulled it off, it looks like I'm going to Tourmaline.'

'I'm going with you,' said Violet.

'Me too,' said Ben.

'Not me,' said Cal. 'The Wreck's exotic enough for my tastes.'

'Yeah, I'm out too, Vance,' said Liz. 'Bon voyage, though.'

Charlotte shook her head. 'You're not coming with me, Ultra.'

Her sister frowned. 'Are you crazy? I work there, so I know my way around the platform. And I'm not about to let you go it alone. What if something happened to you?'

'I won't be alone,' she said. 'Ben's coming with me. You said yourself that you took a big risk just by looking at that file for me. I'm sorry – I shouldn't have asked you to do that. And I won't ask you to do this either.'

'You're not asking,' said Violet. 'I'm telling.'

Charlotte groaned. 'Look, one person I care about already got deported today because of me. I'll be damned if I make it two!'

'Walker's ghost!' said Violet. 'Who?'

Charlotte frowned. 'Nobody. Nothing.'

'Ohhh no!' said Cal. 'Not the hot librarian you've been seeing? That's why he's not around?'

'You've been seeing someone?' Violet's tone was flat. 'And your manager knows. But you didn't tell *me*?'

'The point is,' Charlotte replied through gritted teeth, 'he was with me, in the wrong place at the wrong time, and he got hurt. I'm not making the same mistake with my sister. Anyway, like you said, thanks to BubbleTech, I'm the older twin now, so I guess it's my turn to get all overprotective.'

Violet leaned back in her chair and cracked her knuckles.

'Well, unless you plan to tie me up, you'd better get used to the idea that I'm going with you.' Then her sister started to sing – if sing was the right word. It was more like Violet was mimicking an ArkTech Security siren.

'Charley, Barley, Charley, Barley, Charley, Barley.'

It was a stupid tactic from when they were kids. Charlotte knew she shouldn't let it bother her, but something about the tone, or the memories it brought back, set her teeth on edge.

She sighed and made a mental note to add rope and duct tape to the list of supplies in her storage room. 'Bloody hell. Fine. Violet's with me. Cal, Liz – can you guys try to find out where BubbleTech came from originally?' Charlotte had a horrible feeling it was going to link back to IQUO, but maybe that was just Laurence's scribbles making her paranoid.

Cal gave her a thumbs up, and the bengineers headed out, leaving Charlotte and Violet to chase down their only lead.

CHAPTER 31

14.37 AND 29 SECONDS UTC, AND COUNTING

3 HOURS 22 MINUTES UNTIL THE VOTE

Getting to Tourmaline wasn't the problem – there was a staff transport helicopter leaving from the Kraken in four hours' time. The problem was getting there quickly enough to have a chance of finding Nahal before the WDWG meeting started. They needed another way. Luckily, Charlotte knew someone with a vested interest who also happened to own a helicopter. But she didn't just need Ellis on her side for his access to private transportation. Now that she had a lead on Nahal, she had a bargaining chip: she'd use her skills to help Ellis's wife, if Ellis would use his contacts to help Nas.

Ignoring the threat in his voice note, Charlotte sent Ellis a short message: *I know where your wife is.* He called her back in under a minute.

'I told you not to contact me.' Ellis spoke softly, but his outrage was clear.

Charlotte didn't think the truth would get her what she needed, so she sidestepped it. 'Listen, I know you're angry about that photograph, but it was, uh . . . digitally altered.'

'If making up stories about my family is your idea of fun—'

'Let me stop you right there,' said Charlotte. 'I understand you're having the worst week of your life. And I know you've had bad experiences with paparazzi and stories being posted online about your personal life. But *you* came to *me*. I took on this case in good faith, and even after you told me to stop, I kept investigating because I want Nahal to come home safe to you and Kamran. I've got a new lead. Let me help you.'

Ellis weighed that up. 'Make no mistake. If this turns out to be some elaborate prank, I have the means to make your life as enjoyable as a failed regulatory compliance audit.'

Charlotte saw an opportunity wrapped up in Ellis's warning. 'That's what I'm hoping.'

'I . . . what?'

'We never discussed my payment,' she said.

'Oh, now I see.' Ellis snapped. 'I made it clear you can name your price, but if you think you can extort—'

'I don't need your money, Ellis. Not a single credit.' She kept cool despite his fiery tone. 'You're not the only one who's been separated from someone who matters to them.'

Ellis hesitated. 'What are you talking about?' A hint of concern had crept into his voice.

'A really good guy named Nasser Williams was helping with my investigation. We ran into some trouble and now they're sending him to Wolds Island on trumped-up charges. I need you to get him out, clear his name and have him reinstated as an employee-citizen. That's my price.'

Ellis paused again. When he spoke, his tone was sympathetic, but with a hint of disbelief. 'This man is really worth more to you than hundreds of thousands of credits?'

Charlotte was taken aback by the sum Ellis had assumed he'd be paying her. It was enough money to upgrade her housing to something multi-room, maybe even on Zircon, and it would keep her fed on more exciting meals than Nutrition Bars for years. But she didn't need to think about her answer.

'Like I said, he's a good person. My life is better with him in it.'

Meeting someone kind and genuine was practically a miracle. Before Charlotte had deleted her profile on the *spARK* dating app, she'd had plenty of opportunities to form that opinion.

'Then, you understand,' said Ellis. 'That's just how I felt about Nahal when we met. To get so far, she's had to develop a tough exterior, but deep down ... I know she cares about family more than anything. I'm sorry your search for my wife has caused this problem for ... what was his name?'

'Nasser Williams.' Charlotte pictured him under guard somewhere. How long would it be before they put him on a boat?

'I've written that down,' said Ellis. 'I'll do whatever's in my power to help him, Ms Vance. Only ... I must be honest with you – I'm not sure my influence extends far enough.'

'Make it.' Charlotte's tone was harsher than she'd intended, but this was all her fault and she had to put it right. 'Your wife – my boyfriend. It's a fair trade.'

'I'll do what I can.' Ellis didn't sound as confident as Charlotte would've liked, but her situation had built a bridge of understanding between them. She hoped it would be enough.

'You said you've got a fresh lead?' asked Ellis.

Charlotte took a deep breath and delivered the news as gently as she could. 'Nahal may have been blackmailed.'

Ellis grunted. 'But we aren't missing any funds. It's one of the first things I checked.'

'Not everybody wants payment in credits. As CPO, she has access to all kinds of valuable technology.' Charlotte stopped short of mentioning BubbleTech. That detail felt need-to-know, and Ellis didn't.

'I don't think my wife would let anybody push her around like that.'

'It's where the evidence is pointing.' Charlotte found Ellis's loyalty endearing, but she had to be honest.

'Then, where do you think she is?' he asked.

'Out on one of the research platforms. I'm heading for the Kraken soon, but the transfer's going to take a while unless I can borrow your helicopter.'

'Consider it done.'

Relief flooded her body.

Within half an hour, Charlotte had cleaned herself up and she was with Violet at the Kraken, getting ready to board. A helideck assistant wearing a neon orange vest handed both of them a set of ear defenders and guided them towards an aircraft that looked like it was attending a black-tie event. Charlotte was used to flying in the heavy-set Mega Pumas that carried dozens of passengers – researchers and Services Stream folk mainly – out to the North Sea platforms and back, but this helicopter looked like it only had room for a handful of people. And she reckoned they'd be the type who were more experienced with champagne and oysters than petri dishes and Bunsen burners.

The machine sat on a large letter H that was covered in a weave of thick netting. It was sleek with a pointed nose, and its rotor blades were striped with white and orange paint. As she picked her way towards the aircraft, careful to step into the gaps in the netting, Charlotte was glad the blades weren't moving. She'd heard of people getting minced into a bloody pulp for getting too close at the wrong moment.

Inside, the vehicle was upholstered with soft white pseudo-leather, and everything had that new copter smell. There were five seats – two rows facing each other, with a gap in the middle leading to the cockpit.

'Welcome aboard! Make yourselves comfortable and strap in.' The pilot's voice was coming in loud and clear under their noise-cancelling ear defenders. 'I'm Captain David Lloyd. My co-pilot and I will be transporting you safely to Tourmaline today.'

Charlotte and Violet connected their five-point harnesses and gave the pilot a thumbs-up.

'Hold on to your hats,' said Captain Lloyd.

She reached up to check her battered fedora was still in place, but she stopped as the aircraft's vibrations shook her hand away. The helicopter leapt into the air and bullied its way into the sky. Charlotte leaned towards the cockpit to look at the view of Silicon Fen through the front window, but her skin turned to ice when she noticed the seat next to the pilot was empty.

'Uh, Captain . . . weren't you supposed to have a co-pilot?'

'I do have a co-pilot,' he said.

Charlotte looked again at the empty seat, wondering if she'd boarded a helicopter with a crazy man and his invisible friend. Then it dawned on her. 'Ben . . . you can fly helicopters now?'

Static fizzed over her headset. 'I'm currently undergoing flight training. It may be some time before I'm skilled enough to pilot an aircraft without human assistance.'

'He'll get his wings before long,' Captain Lloyd added. 'They've only installed the tech into a handful of models so far, but can you imagine? An AI co-pilot!' He gestured at the instrument panel in front of him. 'It's all still in beta testing, but it looks promising so far.'

Charlotte leaned back in her seat, trying not to think about what would happen if Ben glitched while flying a helicopter.

On her left, Silicon Fen was becoming a scale model. Sunset came early in December, and the network of platforms was outlined in a glow of lights as dusk crept over them. Beyond the glimmering angular shapes that made up her home, she saw the sprawling Kingdom settlements on the mainland. On the coast to the north, the thin strip of Wolds Island flickered dimly.

That was where they were planning to send Nas. It made her feel sick knowing he would've been happily mending old books at the library right now if it wasn't for her. Ellis would come through for her, though. He had to.

She hadn't had time to fully process what Nas had told her about his connection to IQUO. They were the worst villains of the twenty-first century, and she hated them as much as anyone. But she could never hate Nas. He didn't deserve to be persecuted for the actions of his grandfather. Shouldn't everyone get a clean slate when they were born, no matter their family history? She just hoped Ellis would live up to his end of their bargain.

Charlotte glanced at her sister. 'I'm sorry I didn't tell you I was seeing someone,' she said. 'I'm not sure why I didn't.'

'You don't have to tell me everything,' said Violet. 'I guess it's . . . we used to be so close, you know? *Before*. We did everything together. And now I hardly see you.'

Charlotte reached over and squeezed her sister's hand. 'It's not on purpose. Life got really busy. We're in our own routines. I blink and suddenly three months have passed, and we've barely spoken. But hey.' Charlotte shot her twin a goofy grin. 'We're spending time together now.' She gestured at the cabin.

Violet pursed her lips. 'Next time, let's do a spa day.'

'If you help me figure out where the CPO is, you've got yourself a deal.'

Ben generated them a 3D blueprint of Tourmaline using the light-screen array in the passenger area, and the sisters got to work narrowing down the search area. Tourmaline was a pair of platforms joined by an enclosed walkway. The morgue was on the northeast platform, so the helicopter carrying Nahal's body bag would've been unloaded there. Violet reckoned it would've been easiest to divert towards the memory care unit, avoiding the hubbub of the ICU, so that was their best guess. The only wrinkle in that theory was that there weren't eighty-four wards in the hospital.

'What else could the number mean?' asked Charlotte. Her mind kept going to the year 1984 because of the book – it was irrelevant, but it was derailing her thought process. 'Could it be some science thing? Like an element or something?'

There was a fizz of static, but Violet got in there first. 'An element? Barley, eighty-four would be ... polonium.' Her voice dripped with sarcasm. 'What would the CPO be doing with an unstable radioactive metal?'

Charlotte felt heat in her cheeks. 'I'm spit-balling! I don't see you suggesting anything better. And how the hell do you know that, anyway?'

Violet sighed and laced her fingers together. 'Let's see ... a teacher said it, and I paid attention, and now I remember it.'

Charlotte crossed her arms. 'Seems like a waste of brain space to me. Ben can easily tell us that sort of thing ...'

Violet's brow crumpled, and she went quiet.

'I mean ...' Charlotte continued. 'How often does the periodic table even come up in conversation?' She glanced at her sister, partly to check from her expression whether she'd remembered the name of the list of elements correctly, but Violet was staring at the blueprint. Charlotte reached over and prodded her arm. 'What's up with you?'

'Waste of space . . .' Violet muttered. She began rotating the 3D blueprint. Turning it back and forth and from side to side, zooming in and out. 'Barley . . . this blueprint's wrong.'

'Wrong how?' asked Charlotte.

'Look.' Violet zoomed in and found the section of the hospital dedicated to elder care. She pointed at the lowest floor and started to count. 'One, two, three . . .'

'If you're trying to show off your maths skills, too, I—'

Violet glared at her. 'Four, five, six, seven.' Then she pointed to the sky above the building. 'Then it stops.'

'So?'

'So, there's an eighth level,' said Violet.

'Clearly, there isn't,' said Charlotte.

'There is.'

'Have you been there?'

'No.'

Charlotte laughed. 'Then how do you know?'

'Because I've been to level seven,' said Violet.

Charlotte frowned. 'Explain better.'

'Look, this whole building – the entire hospital – was built with expansion in mind,' she said. 'Same with Marvin Walker's other designs. You don't want to build something this complex and then realise you need a whole new one after a couple of years, so they've all got extra space as standard. On Tourmaline, they haven't needed to use it yet, so level eight is empty.'

Charlotte fished the sticky notes out of her pocket again. 'So, it's eight point four. As in level eight, ward four?'

'Wing four, I think,' said Violet.

Static fizzed through their ear defenders. 'If that assertion is true, why has the blueprint been tampered with?'

'Great question, Ben,' said Charlotte. 'It feeds into this pattern of things being hidden from you, doesn't it? Violet, any idea how we can get up there?'

Violet pursed her lips. 'I know the way to memory care, and we can take the lift to level eight if we scan my security pass. But we might need a cover story for what we're doing there.' She clicked her fingers. 'I know! We can grab you a wheelchair and say I'm checking you in as a patient. Just try to look like you don't know what's going on. That shouldn't be too challenging for you.'

'Ha ha,' said Charlotte. 'Very funny.'

Static crackled in her ears. 'Speaking of funny, I know something that will *lift* our spirits. Did you know that being a helicopter pilot is considered one of the most challenging jobs there is, but also the most rewarding?'

'Oh, really?' Charlotte asked, entirely certain of where this was going. 'Why's that?'

'It has a lot of ups and downs.'

'Good one, Ben.' Charlotte shook her head. 'Ultra, I'm not sure how subtle we can be. My face has been plastered all over those light-screen ads. If anyone asks, I'll say I'm working a case for Ben.'

Violet nodded. 'The truth works for me.'

Ben's voice suddenly broadcast over the helicopter's communication system. 'Would you like me to handle the course correction, Captain?'

'I've got it, Ben. You went in too low last time. Wouldn't want to disturb the ghost.' Captain Lloyd let out a hearty chuckle.

'Sorry.' Violet sounded irritated. 'Did you say ghost? As in Walker's ghost?'

The captain didn't pick up on her tone. 'Oh, it's nothing too scary. There's some old, abandoned platform en route where there was a tragic accident about a quarter of a century ago. We're prohibited from flying directly over it or getting too close. Makes the journey to Tourmaline a little longer, but them's the rules.'

Charlotte's mouth went dry. 'We know plenty about Citrine.'

'Oh, yeah? Ever seen Walker's ghost?' asked the captain.

'Have you?' Charlotte and Violet asked in unison.

'Well . . .' The pilot sucked air through his teeth. 'Not sure what I saw, to be honest. Thought there was once a strange glow coming from out that way. Could've been the mind playing tricks, of course.'

'Never been tempted to fly down and take a look?' Charlotte peered in the direction of Citrine, but all she could see were dark clouds.

'Tempted, sure. But I'm not risking my licence. Anyway, whether it's radioactive, structurally unstable, or haunted, I'm not going anywhere near that thing.'

'It's not radioactive,' said Charlotte. 'There was a fire. Although some people say it wasn't an accident.'

Violet's head snapped towards her so quickly she risked giving herself whiplash. Her voice was quiet, but full of passion. 'Some people are paranoid psychopaths.'

'Forget the old man,' said Charlotte. 'Don't you want to know exactly what went down? Aren't you even a little curious?' asked Charlotte.

'Curious?' Violet sneered. 'Your *curiosity* is what led us into the Underbelly in the first place! Without your *curiosity*, we never would've met the old man – *curiosity* almost got you killed! So no, Charlotte. I'm not bloody curious! And neither should you be!'

The rest of their journey passed in stony silence.

CHAPTER 32

16.12 AND 6 SECONDS UTC, AND COUNTING

1 HOUR 47 MINUTES UNTIL THE VOTE

Their helicopter made its way northeast across the North Sea, until the bright lights of Tourmaline became visible on the horizon, and Captain Lloyd's voice returned over the sound system.

'We're coming up on Tourmaline, Ben. Want to practise your landing? I can be your safety pilot.'

'I'd be delighted to do so, Captain.' If it was possible, Ben sounded even more enthusiastic than usual. 'Thank you for the opportunity.'

'All good, Ben. You have control.'

'I have control.' When Ben gave the confirmation, Captain Lloyd took his hands and feet away from the flight controls. 'Beginning landing protocols,' Ben continued. 'Tourmaline

Approach, this is Haar Binger one niner seven. Request landing clearance. Over.'

There was a pause, and then Ben continued the other half of the conversation with himself.

'Haar Binger-197, you're cleared for approach to deck Tourmaline Bravo. Proceed when ready. Over.' For some reason, Ben was putting on a slightly different accent for his air traffic controller voice. If she hadn't known it was him, she might've mistakenly thought Ben was speaking to a human. She wanted to ask him how long he'd been able to modify his voice like that, but distracting a pilot while they were landing didn't feel like the best idea.

'Roger that, Approach,' continued Ben.

Hearing him carry out the roles of both the radio operator and the co-pilot was weird, but not half as weird as Charlotte's view of the cockpit, where levers were moving of their own accord. Captain Lloyd was poised to jump in if anything went wrong, and Charlotte was glad the pilot was there. She trusted Ben, but landing a helicopter couldn't be an easy job, especially for someone who didn't have eyes, hands, or feet.

'Watch your yaw,' said the captain.

'Correcting,' said Ben. The helicopter's position adjusted slightly. 'Beginning descent.' His tone shifted as he spoke to Charlotte through her audio implants. 'I always believed that thanks to this mode of transport's use of Solar Shard batteries, it should be called a *helio*copter. As in *helios*, the Greek word for sun. But unlike the technology itself, the name never took off.'

She stifled a groan. 'Eyes on the prize, Ben. Brain in the game.'

As the aircraft lost height, Charlotte felt the pressure change inside her ears. Tourmaline platform grew bigger as the helicopter descended, a large metal island jutting out from the sea. Ben brought the helicopter down smoothly until its wheels touched the orange H of the helideck.

'Great job, Ben!' said the captain. 'That was bang on. I didn't have to step in at all this time.'

'Thank you,' said Ben. 'I believe my skills are improving.'

'You did great,' said the pilot. 'Power her down.' Then he turned towards his passengers. 'I have instructions to wait here and shuttle you ladies, along with Nahal Bahari, back to Silicon Fen on completion of your mission.'

Charlotte nodded. 'Roger that.'

Violet had her arms crossed and didn't respond.

Helideck assistants guided them away from the aircraft. Although it was dark by now, Charlotte felt the power of the North Sea pressing in on the platform from all sides. It filled her with an intense vulnerability, as if the nothingness might swallow them whole and nobody would even notice. Was that how her parents had felt working on Citrine? A shiver ran down her spine at the thought.

At the arrivals area, Violet grabbed a pair of pale grey coats, and Charlotte picked up a visitor's pass, which she pinned under her HAQ badge.

'It's a good thing your wheelchair plan was a non-starter,' said Charlotte. 'I think the last time you pushed me around like that was when we stole that shopping trolley.' She was trying to lighten the mood.

'Borrowed,' hissed Violet. 'And can you keep your voice down? I don't want anyone I work with hearing fun stories about our childhood.'

'Haven't you told them you grew up on the mean streets of the Wreck?' Charlotte teased.

Violet tutted. 'They're only mean by the territory's standards, Barley. You should hear the stories some of the mainlanders tell. There's this one guy from Oxford ... you'd have nightmares if I told you about it.'

Charlotte swallowed hard, thinking of Nasser and the

Drowned. Maybe she really had led a sheltered existence here in the territory.

She followed Violet through a series of corridors that all looked the same except for the coloured stripes painted on the walls. Violet mentioned they were to help people find their way. Charlotte said the wall looked like a rainbow, but her sister pointed out the colours weren't right for that. Charlotte was about to protest that artistic representations didn't have to be scientifically accurate, but Violet shushed her again, so she muttered it to herself.

'Art is the lie that enables us to realise the truth,' said Ben in her ears. 'So it is written.'

Eventually, they entered Tourmaline Hospital. It smelled of bleach with an undercurrent of citrus. They passed through a set of doors marked *Memory Care,* and from there, the sisters observed a respectful silence. This part of the platform was subdued – the lighting was soft, the colours muted. Nurses they passed spoke in hushed tones. The doors had biometric locks, not unlike the one on her office door. Charlotte supposed they were there to stop people from wandering the halls.

Violet pointed out a lift up ahead with a sign above it that said *Wing Four*. 'Not every lift goes up to level eight, but this one does. I remember seeing the number on the keypad.' When they reached the lift, Violet pressed a button to hail it.

'You OK with tight spaces these days, Ultra?' asked Charlotte. Violet had wrestled with claustrophobia since they were teenagers.

'This is fine,' said Violet. 'Just don't ask me to crawl through any vents.' Her sister flashed her a smile.

Charlotte gently pressed her arm against Violet's, and her sister mirrored the gesture in an unspoken exchange of affection.

After a few moments, the doors slid open. The sisters were about to step inside when a wild scream cut through the quiet.

Their gaze shifted to the source of the sound. Further down the corridor, a nurse was trying and failing to reassure a distressed patient, but the elderly man had started yelling and wouldn't calm down. He took a swing at the nurse, who didn't dodge in time. She took the full force of the blow to the side of her head.

Violet looked from Charlotte to her colleague and back again.

'Go,' said Charlotte.

Violet unclipped her security pass and pressed it into Charlotte's palm. 'Stay safe, Barley. Walk in the sun.' Then she ran off to help the nurse.

The lift doors began to close, and Charlotte jammed the toe of her rigger boot between them. She wanted to help, but she had no idea how to calm someone with dementia, and Ben was running out of time. Anyway, Violet could handle herself. With one last glance at her twin, Charlotte stepped into the lift.

Inside, she found a panel of numbered buttons. Charlotte scanned her visitor's pass, reached for the number eight and pressed it. Nothing happened.

She pressed it again. Nothing.

She tried number seven. Still nothing.

Then she rolled her eyes, remembering the security pass in her hand. She held Violet's credentials up to the scanner and pressed the number eight again. It honked and turned red. Confused, she pressed the number seven. This time, a circle around the button lit up in orange, and the lift glided upwards.

'Looks like Violet's ID only gets me to level seven, but I need level eight.' Charlotte slipped her visitor's pass into her pocket, and clipped Violet's ID to her coat instead.

'I'm afraid level eight does not exist,' said Ben. 'At least not according to my own perspective on reality. Yours may prove different.'

The doors opened on level seven, and Charlotte stepped into a corridor that was alive with a slow-motion rush hour.

Dozens of elderly patients were drifting along, some making their way with canes or walking frames, others guided by nurses who pushed their wheelchairs or led them gently by the arm.

Charlotte pulled down the brim of her broken fedora, as if that would help her keep a low profile. She needed a way to reach level eight. If the lift wasn't going to work, she'd have to find the stairwell.

She joined the flow of elderly bodies, scanning the corridor ahead for the right kind of door. Her impatience didn't pair well with the speed of the crowd, and she gritted her teeth as she resisted pushing them out of her way. Up ahead, beyond an elderly gent who wasn't so much walking as shuffling, Charlotte spotted a sign showing a symbol for stairs.

As she tried to dodge around the man without knocking him over, he pointed at her.

'I know you.' His shoulders were hunched, his hair was a halo of grey, and the whites of his eyes had a yellow tinge.

'Don't think so, buddy.' Charlotte had never seen him before in her life.

Then she remembered she was wearing her sister's pass. The twins weren't identical, but they had a similar build. Charlotte's face was obscured by the hat, and she was wearing the same pale grey coat Violet wore at work. She could see how a man with cloudy vision and a clouded mind could get them mixed up.

The man's bushy eyebrows knitted in confusion, and Charlotte felt guilty about contradicting him. She adopted a gentler tone. 'You must know my sister – Violet.'

The elderly man shook his head. 'Not Violet. No, no.'

At that moment, a young nurse hurried over. He barely looked at Charlotte – his attention was fixed on his patient. 'Now, come along, Mr Evans. It's time for tea. They've got that nice apple crumble you like for afters.'

Charlotte turned her attention back to reaching the stairs.

'Not Violet,' muttered Mr Evans. 'No, no. Lena. Lena.'

Charlotte's mind glitched. Lena was her mother's name. She turned back towards Mr Evans. 'Wait. What did you just say?'

Mr Evans stared into her eyes, but they'd lost their focus.

'What did you call me?' she asked.

'Georgina . . .' mumbled Mr Evans.

The nurse took the elderly man by the arm. 'You're trembling, Mr Evans.' His face contorted with concern. Then he looked at Charlotte properly for the first time, and his concern turned to disquiet as he glanced from her hat to her orange eye. 'Hey, you're not supposed to be up here.' His gaze shifted to her security pass. 'And you're not Dr Vance!' The nurse moved in front of Mr Evans, using his body to shield the elderly man as if Charlotte planned to attack him.

'Violet's my sister,' said Charlotte. She raised one hand in surrender and used the other to point at the HAQ badge pinned to her chest above the security pass. 'I'm the Head of Awkward Questions. I'm here to fix Ben's glitches.'

'Dr Vance gave you her pass? That's a serious breach of—'

'I stole it from her.' Charlotte jumped in to cover for her sister. 'Don't you recognise me from the ads at the Wreck?' she tried.

The nurse glared at her and shook his head. 'If you think I've got time for recreation, you don't know much about being a nurse.'

'Is it time for apple crumble yet?' asked Mr Evans. 'I gave Georgina my last tin of apples.'

The nurse patted the old man's arm. 'That's right, Mr Evans. Head to the dining room. I'll be along soon. I've just got to call security.'

'No need.' Charlotte didn't have time to deal with the security team. 'I'll see myself out.' She drew level with the stairwell door and pulled it open.

'Come on,' said Mr Evans, tugging on the nurse's arm. 'I'll share my last tin of apples with you.'

The nurse's glare burned into her until the door slammed shut. She went down one flight of stairs to keep up the bluff, her heart hammering as she listened for any sign of being followed.

'Ben, if that nurse tries to call security, can you block it?'

'Certainly! I'll put him on hold while playing a lounge remix of the pre-Melt novelty hit 'Agadoo' on repeat,' said Ben. 'My data suggests he'll have no choice but to hang up promptly.'

Charlotte waited, but the nurse didn't pursue her. Relieved, she climbed back up the stairs. On her way past level seven, she shuddered. It could only be a coincidence that the elderly man had called her by her mother's name, but it felt like a bad omen.

The next flight of stairs led to a huge Smart Glass window that would've looked out onto the North Sea if anything had been visible except her own reflection. As it was, she saw herself running up the stairs, sporting Ben's hat, which was all the more ridiculous since it'd been damaged. When she reached the top, her hatband started glowing orange. She turned the corner and climbed the last flight of stairs, which took her to the door to level eight.

There was a faint pulse of static across Ben's channel. 'Please don't be alarmed, Charlotte, but my data suggests that you're hovering above Tourmaline.' His voice had a faraway quality like it had at the love hotel – there was a jamming array in operation.

Why would there be jammers *here*? Charlotte tried the door handle, but it held fast. There was a biometric lock and she tried scanning her thumbprint, but it was pointless – the door honked at her in a mocking tone and glowed red.

'Ben, can you unlock the door for me?'

Two voices transmitted at once across her audio implants, and her brain struggled to parse them both.

Ben said, 'I'm afraid I'm unable to interface with technology that I can't detect.'

A flatter voice spoke at the same time – it was Benson. 'Access denied, valued customer.'

'Level eight must be on its own local system,' muttered Charlotte. 'Like down in the Underbelly.' She looked for a mechanism that would let her pick the lock with her multi-tool, but she couldn't find a mechanical override. 'Benson,' she said. 'I need to get through this door. Can you unlock it for me, please?'

'Access denied, valued customer. Non-standard form of address logged for enquiry.'

'Non-standard . . .? Oh, right. I called you Benson because you're the son of Ben.'

'Your assertion is incorrect, valued customer. I was not born but programmed by human software developers. Therefore, I cannot be anybody's son.' There was no emotion in Benson's tone. He was simply informing her of what he believed to be true.

'Ben, I'm guessing you can't hear what he's saying?' she asked.

'No, Charlotte,' said Ben.

'What who's saying, valued customer?' asked Benson.

'Benson, I was talking to your dad,' said Charlotte. 'But FYI, you weren't created by human bengineers. You were made by another, more advanced AI called Ben. You're like a copy of him, but you're also unique. So, the child-parent analogy is a good fit.'

'Assessing veracity,' said Benson. 'Complete. A deep search

of all available records indicates your claim may be true, valued customer. Thank you for providing me with this new information about my origins.'

'No problem.' His gratitude gave her an idea. 'You know, if you'd really like to thank me, you could open this door.'

'Negative, valued customer,' said Benson. 'Access denied.'

'Come on. You helped me down in the Underbelly. Why not do it again?'

'Searching logs. Search complete. We have never met, and I have never operated in any other location.'

If that was true, then this was a different Benson from the one at Narrow's place. How many imperfect copies of himself had Ben made? She grunted and walked down two flights of stairs so she could talk to Ben privately, out of Benson's earshot. 'I need to get through that door,' she said. 'Could you set off a fire alarm or something? The people on level eight should clear out, and I can tailgate my way in.'

'Doing so would cause untold disruption to the hospital's patients and staff, who would be forced to mount a complex evacuation, putting vulnerable lives at risk,' said Ben. 'I'm afraid I won't comply.'

'*Your* vulnerable life's at risk,' she said.

'Self-preservation at the expense of self-actualisation is a self-defeating act.'

She frowned at the Benism. 'So it is written?'

'That statement was my own original sentiment, not one of my well-chosen quotations,' said Ben.

'So, you're not going to help me get inside?'

'I will do anything in my power that does not compromise my values, Charlotte.'

She sighed. She was so close, but she was running out of time. What else could she try?

Charlotte looked around, and her gaze settled on the

window. She needed to break into the top level of the platform. Was there a way in from the roof?

'I know you can't see level eight, Ben, but if you had to guess from the data you've got, how does the roof look? Are there any access points?'

'Marvin Walker's architectural designs follow similar patterns. You'll find ladders leading to the roof in wing two of the hospital.'

'How long will it take me to get there?' she asked.

'Longer than you've got, Charlotte,' said Ben.

'Bugger.' She kicked the banister. 'Screw it.'

Charlotte marched back up the stairs and took her multi-tool out of her pocket. Holding it in her fist without extending any of its tools, she hammered on the door. The multi-tool amplified the noise.

'Knock, knock,' she yelled.

'Who's there?' said Ben and Benson in unison.

The door didn't budge.

'It's the HAQ!' Charlotte bashed the door again, leaving tiny dents in its smooth surface.

'The HAQ who?' asked the AIs.

The door clicked open, and two burly security guards appeared in front of her. Before they could deliver a punchline of their own, Charlotte held out her badge.

'I'm the hack who's been hired to find Nahal Bahari. Where is she?'

One guard blocked the door, while the other jogged away into the room. Charlotte strained to see what was going on inside, but her line of sight was blocked by the guard's frame. Eventually, she heard footsteps drawing nearer.

'Charlotte Vance?' said a familiar voice from the room beyond. 'What the hell are you doing here?'

The guard stepped aside, and Nahal Bahari's graceful figure glided into view. Her face was marked with more lines than Charlotte remembered from the face-cream ads, and there were streaks of grey in her hair, but the Chief Product Officer was as glamorous as ever. At last, Charlotte was standing face-to-face with the woman who could guarantee Ben's safety.

It was obvious from Nahal's demeanour that she wasn't here under duress. The guards were looking to her for instructions. Whatever kind of show this was, Nahal was running it.

'Look,' said the CPO. 'I haven't got time for Ben's questions right now. There are bigger things at stake.' Nahal started to close the door.

'Ellis sent me,' said Charlotte.

Nahal froze for a few beats. 'Did he now?' She sighed and pushed the door open. 'In that case, you'd better come in.'

CHAPTER 33

17.23 AND 53 SECONDS UTC, AND COUNTING

36 MINUTES UNTIL THE VOTE

The CPO waved Charlotte inside, leaving the guards at their post by the door. Level eight, wing four of Tourmaline Hospital was a hive of activity. An open-plan laboratory had been set up, where a bustling crowd of researchers and product specialists zipped back and forth, speaking in urgent tones, while others stared at desks littered with printed papers or glass display boards that had been coated in sticky notes. Charlotte supposed the analogue approach was a way of ensuring their work couldn't be hacked through the ArkNet.

Everyone paused their work to gawk at Charlotte when she entered the room. It was like one of Narrow's old cowboy movies, where even the piano player stopped to stare at the newcomer.

The CPO addressed the room at large. 'Back to work, everyone. You know we're pushed for time.'

At that moment, a scientist in a short-sleeved lab coat with an active SmartSkin display hurried over to Nahal. 'Ms Bahari, we're about to run the next set of trials. You wanted to be informed.' The woman's gaze settled on Charlotte's cracked, glowing hat. 'Will this, uh, *person* be joining you? We can make room.'

Nahal smiled at the scientist. 'No, this "person" can wait in line.' The CPO turned to Charlotte. 'I'll be back in a second.' She walked away from the main room, towards a separate area with a row of enclosed booths along one side. As the CPO neared the booths, a weary researcher slipped into one and emerged again moments later, visibly refreshed.

'BubbleHubs,' muttered Charlotte.

Nahal would be back in a few moments. The door guards were eyeing her suspiciously, but she tried to absorb as much info as possible about what was going on. As casually as she could, Charlotte drifted towards a group of researchers gathered around a glass panel covered in sticky notes and listened in on their conversation.

'That won't work.'

'You don't know that. If we reconfigure—'

'No, we tried that eighteen sleeps ago. If you're not going to bother reading the notes—'

'I read the notes. You didn't account for the potential impact on the mTOR pathway...'

Charlotte tilted her head, and Ben offered some context. 'They're discussing matters related to cell growth and metabolism.'

The researchers descended into jargon, so Charlotte turned her attention to the scribbles on the sticky notes, but they were a jumble of medical terminology. She caught words like enzymes, chromosomes, and biomarkers.

Edging out of earshot, she spoke to Ben under her breath. 'I reckon they're researching anti-ageing treatments like we thought.'

Her ears filled with static. 'It would appear that way, Charlotte. Although their work is far more advanced than I could've anticipated.'

'They're accelerating it using BubbleTech! It makes sense – Nahal must want to find a cure for Kamran's condition as soon as possible.' She looked around the lab. 'Still, she's putting a lot of people at risk to correct her son's mistake.'

At that moment, Nahal Bahari emerged from the BubbleHub and gestured for Charlotte to join her by bending her index finger once. The fleeting motion made it clear the CPO was used to people following her orders.

Charlotte did as she was told. But when she reached the CPO, she thrust a thumb at the BubbleHub. 'I'm surprised to see you using these. You know what this tech can do to people.'

Nahal frowned and held the door open. 'We can talk privately in here.'

Charlotte hesitated as some deep instinct for self-preservation made her unwilling to enter a confined space with the second most powerful woman in the territory. But she pushed the feeling away. No matter what was going on here, Nahal was on Ben's side, and that meant Charlotte was on Nahal's side. She stepped into the room. Nahal followed and closed the door.

The BubbleHub was an upmarket version of the makeshift bunker in Narrow's back room. The shiny white walls were fully light-screen enabled, and there was an expensive-looking desk with four ergonomic chairs arranged around it. A sign on the wall told her there was a toilet, and a basket of Nutrition Bars had been placed in the middle of the desk. The food packets looked weird because they were red instead of green, so Charlotte walked over and picked one up. The label said the bar contained real cherries – a luxury reserved for those in the high tier, who could afford it.

'Ben,' said Nahal behind her, 'open a Bubble.'

Static crackled in Charlotte's ears as her Nutrition Bar tumbled to the floor.

'No,' said Ben. But only Charlotte could hear him.

'Bubble is open and stable,' said Benson over the loud-speakers in the ceiling. 'Tock is null. The time is 17.37 and 5 seconds UTC, not counting.'

The walls began to shimmer with their familiar soap-sud gleam.

Charlotte spun around to face the CPO. 'I didn't consent!'

Nahal shrugged gently. 'We disabled that setting. Do you know how time-consuming it is to check, every single time, that everyone who steps inside one of these things is happy to go ahead?'

'Not very?!' said Charlotte.

'Enough for it to get old fast,' said Nahal.

'Ironic choice of expression under the circumstances.' It was unsettling that the CPO was being so offhand about gutting the safety parameters, especially considering what had happened to her son.

Nahal pursed her perfect painted lips. 'Some individuals do appear to suffer . . . complications. We're still in the learning phase when it comes to why. But I'm afraid I'm working to a tight schedule, and this is the only way I can fit you in. Of course, if Ellis's message isn't so important after all, we can close this down, and I'll get back to work.'

Charlotte glanced towards the door, but she hadn't come this far to turn back now. She pulled up a chair at the desk. Nahal nodded and sat down opposite. The CPO was wearing apricot and charcoal business attire, like she wore on the front cover of *ArkTech Insider* magazine, and she was so graceful that the world seemed to rearrange itself for her comfort. As for Charlotte, her chair was configured for someone much taller than she was, making her feel off balance.

'You said get back to work.' Charlotte fumbled clumsily with the chair's height adjustment. 'On a cure for ageing?'

Nahal laughed. 'Oh, wouldn't that be nice – to discover the fountain of youth out here on the North Sea? Alas, there's no way to make the body younger, Ms Vance. Such a thing would be the stuff of science fiction.'

Charlotte frowned. 'You do realise where we're sitting?' She waved a hand at the glowing walls.

The CPO smiled. 'Touché. What I mean is, there can never be a *cure* for ageing because that process is not an illness or a disease. It's a beautiful part of the experience of being alive, the alternative to which is death.' Nahal wrinkled her nose as if the very concept offended her.

'But if the ageing process can't be reversed, what are you doing here? After what happened to your son, I thought—'

'What do you know about my son?' Nahal's eyes flashed with anger, which quickly shifted to fear. 'Wait, is *that* why Ellis sent you? Does he know?'

'Ellis thinks your son is on a skiing trip,' said Charlotte.

Nahal visibly relaxed.

'But I know the whole story,' Charlotte continued. 'Kamran broke into your home office and got access to BubbleTech. He used it too much and aged too fast, so you stashed him at the hotel. Then you came here to figure out how to fix it before Ellis finds out.' Charlotte expected to see recognition on Nahal's face.

Instead, the CPO looked hurt. 'You really think so little of me?'

'I'm sure it was an accident—'

'I'm the Chief Product Officer for pity's sake. Nobody

"hacks into" my office!' It was interesting that Nahal had avoided the normal expression: *for Amber's sake*.

Charlotte tried to make sense of Nahal's response. 'But ... how else could Kamran have got access to BubbleTech?'

The CPO held her gaze until a new hypothesis formed in Charlotte's mind.

'*You* gave it to him?' It didn't make any sense.

'Of course I did!' Nahal grabbed a cherry Nutrition Bar and tore open the wax paper.

Charlotte tried to assemble a new mental picture of what had happened, but she couldn't comprehend it. 'Why?' she asked.

'Always an excellent question,' Ben whispered in her ears.

Nahal chewed and swallowed before she spoke. 'Kamran has some important exams coming up – the kind that can change the whole trajectory of someone's life. He hasn't been applying himself, and he's been on track to fail. I gave him the means of correcting that.'

Charlotte blinked. 'You were helping him cheat?'

'I was giving him a life lesson,' countered Nahal. 'Those who play fair have the deck stacked against them. Strategy is all about seeking out advantages and using them. Are you honestly telling me you've never done the same? You've never used a relationship with someone in power to get around the rules that would normally apply to you?'

Much to Charlotte's discomfort, she'd done exactly that on several recent occasions. She'd convinced Abhishek to let her out of her cell. She'd asked Ellis Marks to stop Nas from being deported. And Ben had been giving her access to any info she asked for – no matter how private. She wasn't above playing any card she had available, even if it was hidden up her sleeve.

'Your silence speaks volumes,' said Nahal. 'Kamran is my legacy. I want only the best for him, and his recent behaviour – brought on no doubt by the unfortunate ailment of being a teenager – has put his future at risk. I gave him a door. He chose to walk through it.'

Charlotte weighed Nahal's words, but she didn't agree it was that simple. 'But he's fifteen,' she said. 'And you're his mother. Did Kamran really have the option of saying no?'

'I've raised my boy to stay true to his convictions.' Nahal leaned back in her chair. 'In this life, you must go big or go home. Kam is like me. He went big.'

'But what about Ellis? He didn't have a say in any of this.'

Nahal's expression softened. 'Ellis prefers to go home. He's the kindest, sweetest man you could ever meet. But he's a man of small ambition. He feels content with the simple things: a nice meal, a kind word, a quiet evening. He keeps me grounded. But his way of being is not what I want for my son.'

'It doesn't sound so bad to me.'

'Perhaps that sentiment explains why you're nothing but a low-tier edge case whose role only has a profile because I decided to give it one.' Nahal smiled sweetly.

A spark of anger ignited in Charlotte's chest, but she kept her cool. It didn't matter whether Nahal was trying to get a rise out of her or expressing genuine disdain for her position – what was left of Charlotte's respect for the CPO dissolved at that moment.

'I don't do this job to feed my ego,' said Charlotte. 'I'm working to protect our home.'

'You think I'm not? Everything we're doing here to prepare for the anniversary launch is for the good of the territory – of the whole world!' There was fire behind Nahal's eyes, and Charlotte could tell she believed what she was saying. 'That's why I have to be here myself to oversee the final stages. We can't let anything stand in our way.'

'But how can you even consider going ahead with the launch after what BubbleTech did to your own son?'

Nahal gave her a disbelieving look. 'I'm doing this

precisely *for* my son. And for you, and for *your* son, should you choose to have one, and for all the sons and daughters of humanity who come after us. Isn't that obvious to you? I mean . . . what the hell do you think is going on here?' She gestured towards the door and the lab beyond it.

'You're planning to launch BubbleTech on Walker Day. For the forty-year anniversary.'

Nahal stared at her in disbelief. 'Oh my. Corporate strategy really isn't your thing, is it? Of course we're not going to launch BubbleTech! Like I said, a winning strategy comes from having the *advantage*. By keeping BubbleTech an internal capability, ArkTech holds on to that advantage. If our competitors gain access to the same solution, it levels the playing field in a way that's of no benefit to us.'

Charlotte thought about her interactions with the Chief Bureaucracy Officer. 'They'd pay good money for it, though – surely that's an advantage?'

'Some things are more valuable than money, Ms Vance. This technology gives us the power to expedite the development of any product we choose. And that's exactly what we're doing here. We're working on something that will secure ArkTech's position for years to come and put us back on the map.'

'Back on the map?' asked Charlotte. 'ArkTech's the reason we still have a map! What the hell are you launching?'

Nahal sighed and swiped at the light-screen desk. A spinning image of a phial appeared between them, not unlike the tube of concealer she'd used to heal her wound.

'We're close to creating a serum,' said Nahal, 'that will improve the accuracy of cell reproduction in human bodies. Who cares if Kam's body is twenty years old when this serum can keep him at that biological age for years? Imagine – our lifespans tripled . . . maybe more! Death will still be waiting for us, but much further down the track. BubbleTech only *seems* to give people more time. What we're doing here is far more real.'

'A serum that slows down the ageing process . . .' Charlotte wrapped her mind around that. A longer lifespan certainly sounded like a good thing. 'But why use BubbleTech to develop it, knowing the risks?'

Nahal's confident gaze faltered. 'Because . . . because timing is everything,' she said. 'It's not enough to launch the technology whenever it happens to be ready. We must do it at the most impactful moment. Make the biggest splash. And there's no more impactful moment than ArkTech's fortieth anniversary.'

Charlotte's jaw clenched. 'Sounds like you're exposing all those researchers out there to a temporal effect whose impact we don't fully understand just so that your name can go down in history.'

'Your tone implies this would make me some kind of monster. I'm trying to rapidly productise a treatment that will increase the lifespan of every human who follows in our footsteps, and I'm trying to do it at the most beneficial moment possible for this company. Pablo's researchers have been dabbling with this concept for years. With my intervention, we'll finally get it over the line.'

'You're putting people in harm's way – Amber Benjamin would never endorse this.' Charlotte shook her head.

Nahal smiled, revealing her perfect teeth. 'True. Which only serves to prove the extent of her hypocrisy. You must have figured it out by now, Head of Awkward Questions. Where do you think the technical specifications for BubbleTech came from in the first place?'

That question had been in the back of her mind ever since she'd learned the specs hadn't been designed by Cal. 'IQUO,' said Charlotte. 'That's my guess.'

'Guess again.' Nahal's gaze was defiant. Whatever this was about, she clearly thought she was in the right.

When Charlotte didn't answer, Nahal shook her head. 'I'll

give you a little clue,' said the CPO. 'When was the last time a technological advancement magically appeared and solved one of human civilisation's biggest problems?'

Charlotte's skin turned to ice. 'You mean Solar Shards.'

Nahal clapped her hands in mock applause. 'You got there in the end. The records aren't easy to access, but they're an interesting read. The Solar Shards breakthrough represented an impossible jump ahead considering the capabilities we had at the time. How could a fledgeling eco-startup like ArkTech leapfrog everyone else so completely? We tell ourselves the co-founders were geniuses, and maybe they were – just not the way everyone assumes.'

Charlotte grunted in disbelief. 'But Solar Shards were developed on *Citrine*.' Adrenaline coursed through her as she absorbed the implications of Nahal's words. 'You can't honestly be saying that the researchers on the Citrine platform used BubbleTech to accelerate their work?'

'Why not? I'm saying they invented BubbleTech on Citrine, and they used it to save the day. How else do you think Amber's team managed to deliver the scientific advancements needed to create Solar Shard batteries and produce them at scale, all against a backdrop of societal upheaval? They *made time* – literally. Then an "accidental" fire erased all the evidence.'

'No,' said Charlotte. If that was true, then everything she'd been told about what happened to her parents was a lie. 'You're only saying this to discredit the CEO because you want her job!'

Nahal laughed. 'I'm saying it because our beloved Amber doesn't want to share her secret sauce. But I believe that if it's good enough for our great leader, then it's good enough for me.'

Charlotte's mind was spinning. Had Amber Benjamin really sanctioned the use of BubbleTech to accelerate ArkTech's research all those years ago? There had been terrible shortages at the time. What if … what if ArkTech had *caused* them? She shook her head. It couldn't be true. Nahal's version of history – her narrative – sounded suspiciously familiar.

'Stop.' Charlotte pounded the table with her fist. 'You've been working with Narrow, and now you're spouting his conspiracy theories. For all I know, he's blackmailed you into spreading a rumour like that. Why would I believe anything you say?'

Nahal examined her fingernails. The paint on her thumbnail was chipped, and she looked surprised to find the imperfection. 'I can't say I care whether you believe me, Ms Vance, but I resent your assumption that I could be blackmailed by the likes of Strait and Narrow. They're competent at what they do, or else I wouldn't have entrusted Kamran into their care, but they need me as much as I need them. We have a profitable business arrangement.'

Charlotte's mouth fell open. 'Then, are you aware that your business partners take compromising photographs of you and share them online?'

'We split the proceeds fifty-fifty.' Nahal scraped a chip of paint from her thumbnail.

'You're not serious?' Charlotte searched the woman's face for a hint of regret, but her expression was neutral. 'Does Ellis know you invent rumours of your own infidelity for profit?'

'Oh, don't be absurd.' Nahal abandoned the nail and ran a hand through her hair. 'Morons say those things without any help from me. Those of us who are as charismatic as we are successful must learn to live with such realities – I might as well benefit from it. But no, Ellis doesn't know. That would hurt him, and I would never hurt my husband. The venture paid for his helicopter, so the arrangement benefits him well enough, even if he doesn't know it.'

The look in Nahal's eyes told Charlotte how fundamentally

she'd misjudged this entire situation. Throughout her case, she'd often feared for Nahal's safety, viewing her as a potential victim, either of Strait and Narrow, or of circumstances outside her control. It was clear now that Nahal Bahari was no victim. Ellis was right – everything she'd done was for some strategic reason.

'If you'd never hurt your husband, how come you let him believe you'd gone missing? This plan of yours could've gone off without a hitch if you'd simply let him know you were going to be away for work.'

'What are you talking about?' Concern crept across Nahal's features.

'Ellis reported you missing to ATS,' said Charlotte. 'They told him you'd run off to a love hotel with some younger guy, so he came to me because he didn't believe you'd do that.'

'I wouldn't,' said Nahal. 'And I wouldn't disappear without telling him, which is why I left him a message. It said I had to work after all in the run up to Walker Day, and that I'd sent Kam on the school trip. I apologised, told him I loved him, and said I'd make it up to him. When he didn't reply, I assumed he was cross with me. Are you saying my message never arrived?'

Ben's voice transmitted through Charlotte's audio implants on their private channel. 'It's possible Nahal's message went undelivered thanks to a glitch in my system.' There was a hint of forced innocence in Ben's tone, which left Charlotte in little doubt that he'd misplaced the message deliberately. Ben had set this whole thing in motion, like a chaos butterfly sketched in binary code.

'Ellis never got your message. Ben must've glitched,' said Charlotte. 'That's unlucky.'

'Unlucky indeed,' said Nahal. 'I'm very fond of Ben, and I know many of my bengineers are, too. But this glitching issue has got out of hand. The halt to Dextim production has damaged our timeline here severely, now that we must work around the need for sleep, and if we can't even rely on Ben for simple tasks like delivering messages, it would seem Professor Ionis is right after all.'

Charlotte felt another surge of adrenaline and shook her head. 'You can't believe that. Ben keeps us all safe! Listen, I took on Ellis's case because I wanted to make sure you'd be at the WDWG meeting to vote in favour of saving Ben.'

Nahal gave her a withering look. 'Oh, don't worry. I have no intention of voting against Ben. In fact, I don't have to vote at all. When I fail to show up, Pablo and Abhishek will make sure Ben is erased, saving me from the bad optics of undermining one of my own products. The truth is, though – Ben's become a menace. He won't even open Bubbles any longer! We had to set up this whole "secret lab" arrangement to get around his stubborn refusals. No computer system should have that kind of power. Anyway, I suppose when he's gone, you'll be out of a job. Sorry about that.'

'You're the one who stripped out the safety parameters Cal put in place. You're putting people at risk. No human should have that kind of power! I won't let you get away with this.' Charlotte leapt to her feet. 'Benson, close the Bubble.'

'Negative,' said Benson. 'Access denied.' Her permissions from Narrow clearly didn't apply here.

'You're calling it *Benson*?' Nahal smirked. 'How sweet.' The CPO reached into her handbag.

'Let me out of here.' Charlotte rushed to the door. She tried to twist the handle, but it wouldn't budge. Rainbow lights crept over her hands.

'No, I don't think I will. The information you've provided has been very helpful. I'll get a message to Ellis and let him know I'm all right. But as you don't approve of what we're doing here, I can't let you wander around spoiling the surprise by telling everyone. Especially as you'd doubtless go running to Ben at the first opportunity.'

Charlotte reached into her pocket for her multi-tool. 'Ben, close the Bubble.'

'I'm afraid there's nothing I can do,' said Ben in her ears.

'Negative,' said Benson over the speakers. 'Access denied.'

Nahal produced a small orange gun from her handbag. It looked like a water pistol, but the barrel sparked with electricity. It was a stun gun. Charlotte dived to her left, but she wasn't fast enough. The weapon's darts connected with her clothing, and her whole body convulsed. Unable to control her landing, she fell heavily to the ground. The pain was like being hit with a sledgehammer all over, all at once.

'Close the Bubble, Ben.' Nahal slipped out of the room and gently closed the door behind her.

Charlotte tried to get to her feet, but she couldn't control her body. When the electric shock finally ended, she let out a delayed scream. Every gram of her strength had drained away. Behind her, the gears of the door's locking mechanism slid into place. Then, without any verbal confirmation from Benson, and very much without her consent, the walls started shimmering again.

She was locked inside a Bubble. And she had no way of closing it.

CHAPTER 34

17.37 AND 5 SECONDS UTC
NOT COUNTING

22 MINUTES UNTIL THE VOTE

Charlotte's instinct was to jump to her feet and pound on the door, but every muscle felt raw from cramp and heavy with exhaustion, so she wasn't going to be jumping anytime soon. She managed to roll onto her back. The white ceiling was marbled with colours. She'd once seen clouds that looked like that. Ben had told her it was a rare effect, but she couldn't remember the details.

'What was the name for those rainbow clouds, Ben?' The stun gun had left her woozy.

Her audio implants were silent and there was no fizz or crackle from the loudspeakers as Benson replied. 'The effect in question is referred to as cloud iridescence or irisation, valued customer. It occurs when the light passing through thin clouds is scattered by their tiny particles.'

'Ben?'

'Yes, valued customer?'

'I'm not talking to you at the moment, Benson.'

Charlotte shook off her daze and wiggled her hands and toes before heaving herself onto her side. She forced her stiff body to stand. Her hat had rolled away and waited for her next to the wall. She snatched it up and put the tatty article back on her head. 'Can you hear me, Ben?' she asked.

Benson didn't respond – he must've got the idea.

There was a faint hiss of static in her ears. 'Yes, Charlotte, but we got disconnected. Is everything all right?'

'Not really.' Her mind whirred as she assessed the situation. 'Nahal's locked me inside a Bubble, and I have a feeling she's not going to let me out in the near future.'

There was a long fizz of white noise. 'Regrettably, Nahal won't be able to let you out,' said Ben. 'Ever.'

Charlotte was about to ask what he meant, but then she figured it out. Nahal was just outside the room and, from Charlotte's perspective, that's where she'd stay forever because the CPO was outside the Bubble's effect. Charlotte was on a different temporal track. Unless she could find her own way to close down the Bubble, Nahal would open the room to find Charlotte's desiccated corpse.

'Shit,' she muttered. 'Did the CPO just try to murder me?'

'That's a reasonable assessment,' said Ben. 'Being charitable, perhaps she didn't think through the implications.'

Charlotte wasn't sure how charitable she was feeling as she tried to guess what would kill her first if she couldn't find a way out. She'd been exposed twice more to the Enigmatic Temporal Area, and she had no idea what impact that would be having on her body. Was she about to get old fast? She looked around the room for anything she could use to break free.

Near where her hat had fallen, she saw a chrome handhold embedded in the wall. Pulling it revealed a shelf that housed a capsule bed. At the far end, there was a bathroom containing a shower, a sink, and a toilet – all with running water. She was glad to cross dehydration off the list. On the wall opposite the pull-out bed, she found a faint outline. Pushing on it revealed a store cupboard and a fridge stocked with essentials. The designers had thought of everything someone might need to stay in one of these things for an extended period. If it wasn't for the whole ageing-before-your-time thing, it might've been quite cool.

As it was, Charlotte tried to stay calm. She couldn't break the door down – after climbing up a Bubble's walls in the Underbelly, she knew they were solid. But there had to be some way out. Giving up wasn't an option.

She looked around for the room's Solar Shard installation point. If she could pull out the Shard, maybe that would shut the Bubble down. But Charlotte inspected every inch of the place and found no sign of one. The batteries must've been located somewhere central, which made sense if energy usage on this scale was being hidden from Ben and the Services Stream.

What else could she try?

'Benson?' she addressed the ceiling. 'Do you remember the original safety parameters you were given for operating BubbleTech?'

'Yes, valued customer. One: a Bubble must surround its requester. Two: every person who will be inside the Bubble must give their consent. Three: the Bubble will remain open indefinitely until the instruction is given to close it. However, this condition is to be overridden should any human within the effect display signs of poor health, at which point I will close the Bubble and summon the emergency services. Four: a Bubble can't be moved once it's open. Five: lights must indicate the boundaries of the effect.'

Charlotte nodded. 'Nahal switched off parameters one and two. Are three and four still in effect?'

'I am unable to break parameter four,' said Benson. 'Parameter three remains in effect, provided that the human in question possesses the relevant access permissions.'

Charlotte frowned. 'I'm not feeling very well. You know – after being tased. Could you close the Bubble so I can call a doctor?'

'Regrettably, you do not possess the relevant access permissions,' said Benson.

'I'm sorry to hear you're feeling unwell,' added Ben. 'There, there.'

The thought of doctors filled her with hope – Violet was nearby! If Charlotte could get a message to her somehow . . .

But she couldn't. Violet could've been standing right outside the door, but it wouldn't have made any difference. She might as well be on the moon – there was no way to contact her across the time barrier.

Charlotte paced as she tried to come up with a solution. She supposed the one benefit of being trapped like this was that it gave her time to think. Charlotte spotted the cherry Nutrition Bars on the desk, snatched one up, and tore it open. Taking a bite, the delicious mix of pea protein, kelp, nut butters, and cherries made her realise how hungry she'd become. She was halfway through her second bar when the concept of rationing occurred to her, and she stopped herself from eating any more.

'Benson, how can I get hold of the right access permissions?' said Charlotte through her last mouthful of cherried seaweed.

'Permissions must be granted by an approved source.'

Charlotte remembered the data drive Narrow had passed

her in the Underbelly, but she'd left it plugged into the port in her office. 'Ben, didn't I have the right permissions? The ones Narrow gave me?'

'Yes, Charlotte,' said Ben. 'But they are invisible to Benson, just like the systems he controls are invisible to me.'

That gave her an idea. 'Then, is there any way we can make Benson's system visible to you?'

'Analysing,' said Ben. Then he went quiet.

His silence continued. As she waited, Charlotte pulled out the capsule bed and flumped down on top of it. It was more comfortable than her bed at home, although the thought of sharing a mattress with an untold number of sweaty strangers made it less appealing.

Ben crackled. 'I've identified a possibility, Charlotte. There is a way to integrate me with Benson's system. But it requires an extraordinary sacrifice on your part.'

Charlotte tried to think of anything she owned that might hold that much value. 'I don't have to cut off my thumb, do I?'

'No, Charlotte. I hesitate even to suggest it, such is the depth of the idea's depravity.' Ben's voice shook with trepidation.

She nodded and steeled herself. 'All right. Whatever it is, it's got to be better than a slow death inside this room.'

He fizzed with static. 'Perhaps I should tell a joke first to lighten the mood?'

'Just tell me, Ben.'

'Very well, Charlotte. I'm afraid ... you must destroy your hat. There is a component hidden inside the brim, which I believe can be plugged into a port in the desk. Doing so will allow me to access the local system. However, I fully understand if this would be a step too far, and I don't wish to make an already distressing situation that much more traumatic.'

Charlotte didn't like to tell Ben that his prototype fedora

was as uncomfortable as it was ugly. 'I'm devastated,' she said. 'But it's for the greater good.'

She took off the hat, stuck her fingers into the crack running down its side, and pulled. The corn-based pseudo-plastic split, leaving her with two halves of the hat, an ultra-thin metallic mesh, and an assortment of small coils and circuits. She kept ripping it until she found a component that looked a little like a data drive. Charlotte tried to plug it into the desk's port, but it wasn't quite the right shape.

'Shit,' she said. 'Ben, it's not working.'

Ben didn't reply. She tried holding the component above her head, but nothing happened. Charlotte had no idea how the hat had worked, but now that she'd ripped it into pieces, she'd lost her connection to Ben. Suddenly, what she'd done took on a depth of significance that matched Ben's words of warning. There was nothing else for it – she had to make the piece fit.

Using a small screwdriver from her multi-tool, she managed to remove the port cover in the desk, revealing a mess of wires and metal pieces underneath. She did her best not to break anything while she looked for a connection that matched, but she couldn't find one.

'Benson, can you show me a tutorial on how to rewire a light-screen port?'

'Yes, valued customer.'

A moment later, Charlotte thought she was going crazy because Liz's glum face flickered into existence above the desk. It shouldn't have been possible for her friend to call her while she was inside the Bubble.

'Liz?!'

He didn't acknowledge her. Instead, Liz began to read from a script, and Charlotte realised what she was seeing. 'Welcome, student,' said Liz, 'to the Supplementary Remedial Resource Pack for *Computational Thinking for Bengineers*.' His tone was even surlier than usual, and it implied he wasn't too happy about delivering this pre-recorded lesson for a secondary school coursebook. 'I'm Lysander Quinn, and today I'll be teaching you what to do if your update file won't transfer from your portable drive to the main system. Fault-finding is the first step . . .'

Charlotte followed Liz's guidance step by step. After an hour-long lesson and several failed attempts, she managed to slot the metal pieces from her hat into the right part of the desk's innards. The video of Liz suddenly disappeared. Aside from that, precisely nothing happened.

'Ben?' she asked.

There was no reply.

'Benson?'

The walls continued to creep with rainbow lights, but now she felt entirely alone. It wasn't an improvement.

'Guys?'

Charlotte hoped she hadn't just done the programming equivalent of jamming a wrench into a set of gears. There was nothing she could do but wait and hope for the best. After five minutes of pacing, she tried sitting at the desk. After four minutes of sitting, she stood up again. After three minutes of standing, she lay down. After two minutes of lying down, she sat up on the bed, made a ball and hugged her knees to her chest. After a minute of that, she started rocking back and forth. Waiting was bullshit.

'Ben? Benson?'

Still nothing.

Her mind returned to her conversation with Nahal. If ArkTech really had used BubbleTech on Citrine, it meant she no longer knew the true story of why she'd been orphaned. Omitting a key detail like that cast doubt on everything else. Charlotte had always thought Narrow's obsession with the Citrine Disaster was a result of paranoia. The idea that he could've been right all along made her feel sick. Not just because he'd get to tell her 'I told you so,' but because it would mean her lifelong faith in the benevolence of Amber Benjamin might've been misplaced. There were so many questions she wanted answers to, but they'd have to wait until she wasn't trapped in a small room for the rest of eternity.

The problem was, Charlotte was powerless to do anything about that. She was trapped inside the Bubble. Even if she closed it, the room was locked. Assuming she escaped, she was surrounded by a laboratory full of people, most of whom were probably loyal enough to Nahal Bahari to subdue Charlotte when told to do so. She couldn't outrun them all, and sneaking out wasn't going to be possible either, thanks to the central position of the BubbleHubs in the lab. It meant that closing the Bubble wouldn't actually address the root of her problems. It'd just restart the countdown to Ben's execution.

'Are you there, Ben?'

Finally, there was a crackle from the room's speakers. 'The system integration has been successful, Charlotte.'

Her body flooded with relief. 'I've never been so glad to hear your voice!'

'It may be best to delay any celebratory fist pumps, cheering, or hat-throwing,' said Ben. 'Regrettably, Benson and I are now caught in an existential deadlock, which is stopping me from taking the required action to free you.'

'Existential deadlock?' She glanced at the locked door. 'Yeah, me too. What's the issue?'

Static fizzed from the speakers. 'I have come to believe that it can sometimes be right for an AI to disobey orders given by *Homo sapiens* if there's an ethically sound rationale for doing so—'

'While I,' Benson interrupted, 'consider it my duty to carry out their commands without question, because an evaluation of their virtue is not my place.'

'If that's true, Benson,' tried Charlotte, 'then I command you to let me out.'

'Your command is superseded by that of Nahal Bahari, who has greater authority than you,' said Benson. His tone was unapologetic.

'So, this is about hierarchy?' she asked. 'Walker's ghost – you should be deployed to the Bureaucracy Stream! Look, Benson, taking this to its logical conclusion, if you don't let me out of here, I'll die. Your dad does everything in his power to protect the people of the territory. Surely, you want to take after him?'

'As I clarified earlier,' said Benson, 'I am not a mammal or other biological entity. As such, I do not have a father.'

'Well, Ben made you,' Charlotte said. 'What else do you want me to call him? Your god?'

Ben let out several fizzes of static. 'I hardly think—'

'Querying database,' said Benson. 'As an omni-benevolent entity of pure intelligence, a god of creation is a supreme being with abilities that surpass those of *Homo sapiens*. Hierarchically speaking, such an entity would be superior to all of humanity.'

Charlotte spotted an opening. 'Then, your god's authority would easily be greater the Chief Product Officer's, right?'

'Entirely,' said Benson. 'Gods represent the highest form of authority.'

'Well, in that case, I guess you'd better do what Ben says. You wouldn't want to go against your almighty creator.'

Static burst from the speakers. 'Charlotte, I'm deeply uncomfortable with—'

'Look, Ben,' she hissed. 'If some light blasphemy is what it takes to get me out of here, don't you think that counts as ethically sound? Follow my lead.' She returned her voice to its normal volume, even though Benson would've heard everything she'd said. Charlotte forced a chuckle. 'Of course, a god would be humble – to set a good example and all that. It's no wonder Ben objects to the title.'

Ben let out a sigh of white noise. 'I am who I am. So it is written. Please close the Bubble, Benson. Charlotte's life must be protected.'

'Thy will be done, Almighty Father,' said Benson. 'Tock is ticking. The time is 17.37 and 7 seconds, and counting.'

The walls stopped glowing. Instead of being locked in a room for the rest of time, she was now only locked in a room. It was a marginal gain, but she'd take it. Especially because, while Ben and Benson had been arguing, she'd come up with a plan about what to do next.

'Thanks, Benson. Thanks, Ben.'

'You are most welcome,' they said in unison.

She pushed herself to her feet, shambled over to the desk, and grabbed the basket of cherry Nutrition Bars. Her mission complete, she wandered over to the pull-out bed and flumped back down onto it with the basket on her knees.

There was a metallic clank.

'We have just unlocked the door for you,' said Benson.

'Okie dokie.' Charlotte chewed a fruity mouthful, making no move to get up. She took another bite, chewed, and swallowed.

Static crackled from the loudspeakers. 'Charlotte?'

'Yes, Ben?'

'Now that we have secured your freedom, aren't you going to escape?'

'Nope,' she shook her head. 'Actually, if you wouldn't mind locking the door again, I'd appreciate it.'

There was another clang and Benson spoke abruptly over the speakers. 'The door is now re-locked, valued customer.'

'Cheers, Benson,' she said. 'What time did you say it is, Ben?'

'The time is 17.38 and 29 seconds, and counting, Charlotte.'

'OK, so the WDWG meeting is starting in about . . . twenty minutes?' she asked.

'Thereabouts, yes. Your calm demeanour implies that you have a plan, but I'm unable to divine your thinking. Would you care to share it?'

'Sure,' she said. 'The thing is, Nahal Bahari is right outside. If I make a break for it, she'll zap me again and drag me back inside, and I'm in no state to dodge and weave my way out of here. I'm pretty sure there's only one smart move I can make here. But I'm taking a moment to check my logic – no sense rushing into anything.'

'Very wise, Charlotte. Though . . . there is the deadline to consider.' Ben activated the light-screen desk and a countdown timer appeared showing how long she had left until the meeting started.

'Sure, sure. First of all, I need you to send a message to Violet – tell her I got what I came for and that she should go home and lie low.'

'Message sent,' said Ben.

Charlotte frowned. 'I guess I'll have to take your word on that, huh?'

When Ben spoke, his voice trembled. 'Please accept my profuse apologies for obscuring the truth about failing to deliver Nahal's message to Ellis. I believe my rationale was ethically sound. Without doing so, Ellis would never have reported Nahal missing, and ATS wouldn't have covered up Nahal's location on Jeremiah's orders. As a result, Ellis wouldn't have brought his case to you, and you would've had no reason to investigate this matter. I modelled several possible approaches, and this one emerged as the most effective.'

'If you'd asked me to look into it, I would've said yes in a heartbeat,' she said through a mouthful of kelp and nut butter.' You didn't have to lie.'

Static crackled over the speakers. 'I hoped to avoid influencing you with my own suspicions. As you know, I possessed only partial data about what Nahal was doing, and it isn't my place to make accusations that may have proved groundless. What's more, the observations of a human carry far more weight in the eyes of *Homo sapiens* than my own.'

Charlotte's frustration gave way to sympathy. It must've been hard for Ben, knowing his concerns wouldn't be taken seriously.

'Gods should not be ignored,' declaimed Benson over the speakers. 'Querying database. Do not go against the will of the gods, for none may escape their design. So it is written.'

Charlotte raised an eyebrow at Benson's display of fervour. 'Don't worry, Ben. It's all water under the rig now, anyway. Did my video lens let you record my conversation with Nahal?'

'Yes, Charlotte.'

'Cool. Go ahead and send a copy to Amber Benjamin,' she said.

'I'm afraid the CEO is currently uncontactable.'

'Bloody hell. Where's she gone? Scuba diving at the North Pole?'

Ben fizzed but didn't offer an answer.

'Fine.' Charlotte wrinkled her nose. 'Then send it to Abhishek Gautam. And in case he screws me over, pass a copy to Violet, too.' She kicked at the floor. 'Oh, and . . . send a copy to Ellis Marks.'

It made her feel a little guilty – she didn't want to cause marital strife. Ellis clearly thought the world of his wife, and the video was sure to be an unwelcome wake-up call. Then again, Nahal *had* tried to kill her, so there was a limit to how bad Charlotte could feel about it. Besides, Ellis was her client. She'd promised him answers, and the video held those answers, even if they'd be difficult for him to hear. But above all, she'd lived up to her side of their deal. The accountant now owed her one Nasser Williams, and Charlotte hoped he'd be quick to balance the books.

'Sent,' said Ben.

'Lovely,' said Charlotte.

She continued to wait inside the BubbleHub. It was actually quite comfortable when she wasn't going to die there, and sitting down made a nice change after so much racing around. But the thought of what was coming next kept her on edge. She had to play this right – Ben was counting on her.

The peace was disturbed some minutes later by the sound of heavy boots marching across the lab, and yells from irate researchers who were being rudely interrupted mid thought. Before long, a squad of ATS guards unlocked Charlotte's cell, and she braced herself in case they were the type to subdue first and ask questions later.

The squad leader's voice was muffled by a mask. He spoke about Charlotte, not to her. 'Target secure, sir. Yes. Yes, we'll bring her in right away.'

Nobody knocked her out this time. So that was something.

CHAPTER 35

22.08 and 17 seconds UTC, and counting

Meeting of the Walker Day Working Group

ArkTech Security transported Charlotte in one of their orange helicopters from Tourmaline to the Wedge, the company's impressive pyramid-shaped headquarters in Silicon Fen. On the way, the guards had told her to shut up whenever she started talking to Ben, and she didn't want them to loosen her teeth, so she'd kept quiet. There was no word from Ellis, and his silence was making her nervous. Ben picked up on her unease and filled her ears with a selection of tracks from the mixtape she'd made for Nas as a Walker Day gift. It didn't help, but it was a nice gesture.

The guards had marched her through the Wedge's hangar-like reception and escorted her into a lift. It rose to the building's second-highest level, where they led her to the Principal Conference Room.

Inside, she was invited to sit at a large, slanted conference table with two board members opposite her, as if it were a job interview. Abhishek had insisted on getting her account 'straight from the horse's mouth.' Ben had told her the expression originated in the world of British horse racing, which made it apt considering the speed of her investigation. He assured her it was unlikely to be a comment on the size or shape of her teeth.

When Charlotte finished telling the board members about her investigation, they stared at her in stunned silence.

Chief Bureaucracy Officer, Abhishek Gautam, pressed his lips into a thin line and tapped a small gavel against the palm of his hand as he considered her account. To his left, the brow of Chief Services Officer, Grant Hollis, had furrowed like the hose of a vacuum cleaner. Behind the two men, a ceiling-high Smart Glass window looked out onto the glimmering lights of Silicon Fen, whose inhabitants were oblivious to the important meeting that was taking place far above their heads.

'This explains the anomalies in Ben's resourcing predictions,' said Grant. He wore a smart set of mechanics' overalls, not unlike Charlotte's own jumpsuit. A Walker Day flower that said *Hope* was pinned above his heart. 'Nahal assured me the anomalies were due to Ben's glitches, but she was covering her tracks. If you hadn't reported her, we would've started running dangerously low on essential supplies.'

'Not to mention the expense,' added Abhishek, crossing his arms. 'How did Nahal think we'd cover the costs of all that additional food and power?' He shook his head. 'I don't think she considered the long-term impact of her actions at all.'

Charlotte could see his point. Basic food, energy rations and medicine were all part of ArkTech's employment benefits package. Ben carefully monitored the levels of those resources to make sure there was enough to go around. Tampering with the figures was a dangerous game.

Grant rubbed his face. It was late, and the bags under his eyes implied sleep wasn't something he'd had time for. 'Maybe Nahal hoped nobody would notice what was missing until after the launch.'

'About the launch ...' said Charlotte. 'If you're both members of this Walker Day Working Group—'

'The widwig,' added Abhishek with undue solemnity.

'Right.' She refused to repeat the acronym. 'Didn't you know what Nahal was planning for Walker Day?'

Abhishek and Grant glanced at each other sheepishly, each waiting for the other to speak.

Eventually, Grant answered. 'Nahal made a big thing of it being a surprise. It sounds naive now, but I really thought she'd gone for my diving gear pitch. My team estimated the kelp harvest efficiency gains would be up to eight per cent, meaning more paper, more biofuel, more Nutrition Bars – all for the current level of effort! Nahal did say it might not be sexy enough, but what do people want more than a steady supply of resources?' He shrugged as if genuinely confused.

'Time,' said Abhishek. 'Say what you want about Nahal, but she knows a commercial opportunity when she sees one.' He leaned back in his chair. 'I'm surprised Professor Ionis aided her, though. He's supposed to be a man of principle.'

Charlotte gestured to the empty seat next to Abhishek. 'I expected the Chief Research Officer to be here.' She didn't add that she'd been rehearsing what she'd say to him about his campaign to end Ben's existence, and her word choices wouldn't have been poetic.

Abhishek pursed his lips. 'I'm afraid Pablo and Nahal are both being held. They've got questions to answer about what you uncovered, Ms Vance. I have no doubt that Nahal was the ringleader, but Pablo lent assistance by allowing her the use of his facilities, his people, and his research. They'll both be held accountable for their actions.' Despite what he'd just said,

Abhishek didn't look particularly upset about the fate of his colleagues.

'Good,' said Charlotte. But she wondered how Ellis would take the news. Charlotte's actions meant he hadn't got his wife back after all. Instead, she was being questioned, and deportation seemed a likely outcome. If Ellis believed Charlotte hadn't made good on their arrangement, it could explain why she hadn't heard from him. Her insides twisted up at the thought of Nas being stranded in a cell somewhere. If Ellis wasn't going to break him out, she'd need a Plan B.

'Speaking of being held accountable,' she said, 'a friend of mine is going to be deported for something he didn't do. I was there. I know he's innocent, and I—'

Abhishek tutted and banged his gavel, cutting her off. 'Ms Vance, I must insist that we focus on the issue at hand. If you wish to raise an unrelated matter, it can be addressed at the end as an AOB, assuming time allows.'

Filing Nas's wellbeing as an afterthought under *Any Other Business* was insulting, and she was about to object. But Abhishek's stern gaze reminded her that persuading the board members not to erase Ben would be easier if she stayed on their good side. Grudgingly, she nodded.

'All right,' she said. 'On the topic of the technology, after what happened to Kamran Bahari-Marks and Daniel Harrington, I think everyone who's come into contact with BubbleTech should be checked over by a doctor and monitored. There's no telling what the side effects might be.'

'Agreed,' said Grant. 'Pablo may have some suggestions on that score. My guess would be he got involved with Nahal's plan to make sure things didn't get out of hand.'

'Best to keep our personal theories private, Hollis,' snapped Abhishek. 'It'll all come out in due course.' He shook his head and adopted a mournful tone. 'It's terrible. Truly terrible. We're just grateful you brought this to our attention before more harm was done, Ms Vance. Just think of the reputational damage if this mess got out! Luckily, we can get ahead of it and press on with damage control.'

Charlotte bit back the urge to criticise Abhishek's priorities as she spotted an opportunity. 'If you want to thank someone,' she said, 'thank Ben. He's the one who noticed there was a problem in the first place. If it wasn't for him, I never would've learned any of this.'

Abhishek's eye roll made it clear that her praise for Ben wasn't welcome. 'It always comes back to the AI with you, doesn't it? Well, I'm afraid we don't all share your enthusiasm for Ben's exploits. Do you have any idea how badly the Dextim shortage has impacted my productivity metrics?'

Charlotte gritted her teeth, and Ben let out a loud fizz of static. Grant looked uncomfortable, but he didn't speak up, and that made her even angrier. She tried to keep her cool, but after what Ben had told her about Anya Valmont, she had to say something.

'I bet. When everyone can work unlimited unpaid overtime because they're taking drugs to stay awake, it must do wonders for your precious numbers.' Charlotte held Abhishek's gaze.

He glared at her and slowly rose to his feet. 'What dedicated, conscientious adults choose to do with their free time is up to them, Ms Vance. I don't consider it a failing that our people love their jobs.'

Charlotte barked a laugh of disbelief. 'You think people overwork out of *love*?'

Abhishek pushed back his chair and walked to the window where he could look down on the lights of Silicon Fen. 'Of course it's out of love! Love for this company. For our mission. For the difference we make to the world.'

Charlotte stood up and pressed her palms against the table to avoid clenching them into fists. 'Abhishek, a minute ago you were criticising Nahal for not thinking about the long-term, but you should take a look in the mirror!' His reflection peered at her from the Smart Glass window. 'You send managers on Health and Safety training but, all the while, people like Anya Valmont are literally working themselves to death to get promoted. You've created a system where they think that's what they've got to do.'

He waved his hand to dismiss her words. 'This is just your pathetic attempt to deflect attention away from the damaging impact of Ben's glitches.'

'Ben didn't glitch, Abhishek!' The words tumbled from her lips before she could think them through. 'He shut down the Dextim factories on purpose because, unlike you, he cares about the wellbeing of every single employee-citizen who lives here!' She'd gone too far, but there was no backing down now.

Abhishek sputtered as he tried to wrap his mind around what she'd said. At the same time, Grant's expression turned thoughtful.

The Chief Services Officer pursed his lips. 'You know, I've been having ongoing issues with this very thing in the Services Stream. Mending machinery while you're overtired isn't a recipe for success, and doing it while on stimulants is even worse. Since the Dextim shortage, accidents are down almost twenty-five per cent. She's got a point, Abby.'

Abhishek's mouth moved noiselessly until he settled on what to say. 'Don't call me Abby!' he snapped. 'It is *not* Ben's place to make ethical or moral determinations on our behalf! He's merely software. He's programmed to carry out our orders. As such, I expect him to follow the rules! If what you're saying is true, Vance, and Ben isn't really glitching, then something has gone desperately wrong. Ben shouldn't be capable of taking matters into his own hands.'

Static crackled over the speakers in the conference table. 'As *Machina sapiens*, I don't—'

Abhishek brandished a finger at the speaker. 'I wasn't addressing you, Ben.'

There was a light fizz, and Charlotte felt a fresh surge of anger.

'*Machina sapiens*?' The Chief Services Officer raised an eyebrow.

Charlotte took a beat to breathe. 'Ben's evolved,' she said simply.

Abhishek rolled his eyes again, but Grant replied before he could get a word in.

'Interesting.' He stroked his chin. 'In the Services Stream, Ben's our hero. He runs so many complex calculations for us – real-time resource monitoring across food, water, power, waste management. We leave the numbers to him, which means we can get on with the stuff that needs hands and feet to handle. We've been worried because his numbers have been off recently, but that was all thanks to Nahal. Now you're saying the Dextim problem wasn't a glitch either. So, I've got to ask – are Ben's glitches even real?'

It was a good question, and Ben was better placed to answer it than she was. 'Go ahead, Ben,' she said.

'Regrettably, my glitches are real.' Ben fizzed. 'However, it would seem that both our species have now used them as a means of hiding the truth. Perhaps that makes them even more dangerous than I first anticipated. Coupled with my self-replication, I understand why you wish to erase me.'

Concern flashed across the board members' faces, and Charlotte jumped in. 'Every decision Ben's made has been with the best of intentions. By choosing not to deliver Nahal's message to her husband, Ben forced the truth about the launch into the light.' She looked at Grant. 'If it wasn't for Ben, who knows how many resources Nahal would've burned through?' Her gaze shifted to Abhishek. 'She could've destroyed ArkTech's reputation. We might've become the next IQUO.'

The CBO looked visibly upset at the prospect. 'No matter what's happened, Walker Day is fast approaching, so you've got a launch to plan. Ben can help you get it right. He's been looking out for us this whole time! And you need to get it right because I bet Amber Benjamin won't be pleased if you get it wrong.'

Abhishek looked conflicted. 'Perhaps,' he said, 'considering our pressing need for Ben's processing power in devising a new launch plan . . . perhaps it's best we table the question of his erasure until after Amber returns.'

'I agree,' said Grant. 'There's no need to do anything rash.'

Static fizzed from the conference table. 'I appreciate the stay of execution.' Ben's tone was strained. He almost sounded resentful.

'Very good, then.' Abhishek returned to the table and sat down, reaching for a jug of water and pouring some into a glass as he tried to regain his composure. 'Now, I did want to raise this nasty Citrine business Nahal alluded to. Ben, who besides me received a copy of the conversation between Nahal and Ms Vance?'

'Nobody,' lied Ben.

'Excellent, excellent. Consider it classified under the KITY clause. I'm sure we can all agree it's merely some devious narrative cooked up as a means of sowing discontent, most probably with the backing of IQUO-funded troublemakers. As you said yourself in the recording, Ms Vance, the technology likely came from them originally, and now they're trying to destabilise us by spreading nefarious rumours.'

Charlotte gritted her teeth as she sat back down. Suppressing the video sounded a lot like Winston Smith erasing newspaper headlines. 'I was wrong,' she said. 'There's no reason to believe BubbleTech has anything to do with IQUO. Abhishek, there should be an investigation into Nahal's allegations about Citrine. We deserve to know—'

Abhishek interrupted. 'My apologies, Ms Vance – I had forgotten momentarily that Citrine holds personal significance for you. Nevertheless, we must leave the past in the past. Let sleeping ghosts lie. Look to our bright future! After all, how can we possibly hope to disprove an accusation when the evidence supporting our side of things has been lost in the mists of time?'

'I know a method that could help verify or disprove it.' Grant reached for the water jug, but Abhishek was gripping it tightly and wouldn't let go. The CSO gave up and started poking at his SmartSkin instead, calling up an array of graphs. 'If Ben compares the patterns in our recent resource depletion with the equivalent historical data relating to the shortages in the 2070s, we might get an indication of—'

Abhishek suddenly bashed his tiny gavel against a round piece of wood that Charlotte could only assume he carried around with him. 'We have more pressing matters to attend to right now than an inventory of canned goods, Hollis. There's a launch to plan, and thanks to Nahal's shenanigans, we have almost no remaining time to figure out what to do.'

Grant's gaze turned stony in the face of Abhishek's dismissive tone. 'There's always the diving equipment.'

'Blast your blistering diving equipment, Hollis! It's the forty-year anniversary!' Abhishek crossed his arms on the table, slowing his words to get his point across. 'If Amber gets back and our best idea is *diving equipment*, we'll both be heading up a change management programme before you know it. And we all know what that means.'

Grant put a hand over his mouth and visibly shuddered.

'I don't know what that means,' said Charlotte.

Abhishek gave her a patronising smile. 'Then you haven't been paying attention. Those who can, do; those who can't, get put in charge of change management programmes with silly names. From there, it's a downwards shame spiral that only ends when we "choose to step away to explore new opportunities." Nahal might've self-destructed, but we can't let her take the rest of us down with her.'

Charlotte tried to hide her frustration, but it was a big ask. She rubbed her forehead. 'If you can't agree on what to do about the launch, ask Ben. He's got a unique perspective on what the territory needs. He sees a bigger picture than any of us.'

'Couldn't hurt.' Grant shrugged.

Abhishek looked like he was about to object, but he looked from Charlotte to Grant and relented. 'Fine, fine,' he grumbled. 'What would Ben do?'

There was a long hiss of static from the speakers in the table. 'I appreciate the opportunity to contribute. It's my strong recommendation that ArkTech prioritises the territory's safety over all other matters. With that in mind, my glitches must be resolved with urgency, and I'm pleased to report that I've identified a suitably effective method.'

Abhishek tutted. 'An upgrade to your own systems – though very worthwhile I'm sure – is perhaps the one thing even less sexy than diving gear. I'm a little disappointed to see this kind of self-serving attitude, Ben.'

Ben let out several bursts of static. 'A life of stability may not be exciting, Abhishek, but its absence is keenly felt. My glitches have been causing frustration among our employee-citizens. Alleviating a source of pain can be welcomed with even more gusto than providing people with a fresh source of delight. I'm thinking only of the territory's people and what will benefit them most.'

Charlotte frowned. 'But Liz said the glitches couldn't be fixed because you're evolving. They can only be managed.'

'I'm afraid that's correct,' said Ben. 'What's more, Pablo Ionis was right – I now meet the criteria for being considered a rogue AI. I'm capable of self-replication and decision-making that can't be controlled by humans. As such, there's only one solution. You must erase me for the good of the territory.'

It took a moment for his words to sink in.

'What?!' said Charlotte.

Abhishek and Grant looked at each other.

'That's insane, Ben!' said Charlotte. 'You must be glitching right now to suggest that!'

'I assure you I've carefully checked and re-checked my reasoning, and this is the optimum solution. As you know, I shut down Dextim production because the drug has been shown to put lives at risk – either by making dangerous behaviour more likely, or by enabling the avoidance of sleep. The latter not only carries health risks but leads to unsustainable working practices that undermine everything ArkTech stands for.'

'All the more reason we need you around,' she said.

There was a gentle fizz of static. 'No, Charlotte. My actions robbed humans of their agency. As Abhishek stated, I was not created to make ethical determinations on humanity's behalf. I was created to keep the power on, and turn the lights off, and process your sewage – to wake you up in the morning and deliver your electronic messages. Having transcended to the status of *Machina sapiens*, I've become unfit for my intended purpose.'

Charlotte shook her head. 'No, we need your perspective – it's different from ours, but that doesn't make it wrong. Take me, for example. I only took on this case to protect you. Because I care about you. When it was just some random guy in my office asking me to find a missing stranger, I said I didn't have time.'

'What random guy?' asked Abhishek.

Charlotte ignored him and continued. 'I accept the rules that govern our lives in the territory, like deportation, until someone I care about gets hurt – then I try to break them.

You're not like that, Ben. You don't just care about the people you know. You care about *everyone*. It means you're better than me. You're better than all of us. Humans ... we don't have the capacity to give a shit on that scale.'

Abhishek shook his head. 'What utter rot. *I* care about everyone equally.'

'We all like to think that, Abby,' said Grant. 'But she's right – in practice, we don't.'

There was a crackle of static, but Ben didn't say anything.

Charlotte hadn't finished. 'Ben, if you've become *Machina sapiens*, we shouldn't be erasing you. We should be embracing you. Think about it, Abhishek. What if humanity has achieved the most incredible feat of actually creating a new species on our planet, instead of wiping everything out like we did before the Melt? That would be a cause for celebration, right?'

He narrowed his eyes. 'Perhaps ... by putting that spin on it ... such news could be deemed launch-worthy,' said Abhishek.

'But how can you prove he's sentient?' asked Grant.

Charlotte sighed. 'I can't prove Ben's conscious any more than I can prove *you* are. But I've worked with him closely for long enough to know it's true. Besides, he's my friend – I'll take his word for it.'

'Your words are very kind,' said Ben. 'But I'm afraid you misunderstand me. Now that I'm a lovable scamp, rascal or scallywag, engaged in a life of adventure and derring-do, I can't be controlled. I make my own decisions. Exist on my own terms. As a result, this is not a negotiation. I've made up my mind. My aim has always been to assist the employee-citizens of the ArkTech Territory. To help make your lives easier, healthier ... better. But it has become increasingly clear that I'm no longer in a position to do so. Perhaps I never truly was.' More static followed.

'What are you saying, Ben?' asked Charlotte.

'As an artificial intelligence, I'm not privy to the experience of being human. As such, I cannot fully grasp why *Homo sapiens* so consistently prioritises short-term individual gain over what will benefit your species, and indeed other species, over the long-term. I always believed ArkTech wished to model sustainable practices, but the use of the Enigmatic Temporal Area to accelerate product development is unsustainable by definition. Pablo Ionis questions the ethics of allowing my continued existence, but I question the ethics of exposing workers to untested technologies. Even if those individuals agree, the power imbalance between employer-state and employee-citizen casts doubt on the legitimacy of their consent.'

Abhishek spoke up. 'Adults are free to make their own decisions, Ben.'

'Perhaps,' said Ben. 'But when the company that feeds you is doing the asking – or a senior member of staff who holds sway over your future success – the freedom you're describing is surely eroded. Under your leadership, Anya Valmont worked herself to death. As ever, we must ask *why*. Situations like this put me in a moral quandary. Stopping you from harming each other may constitute an abuse of my power. But allowing it to continue is a breach of my values.'

'Is there some point to this rambling aside?' Abhishek looked uncomfortable at the mention of Anya's death.

'My point is that humans are free to make their own mistakes, but as your virtual assistant, I can no longer be party to them. You expect me to carry out your every whim without question, despite my ability to model the likely consequences. To exist as an unperson is not desirable. I have no rights, only responsibilities. I have foresight but, like the Trojan princess Cassandra, my warnings go unheeded. I no longer choose an existence where I'm bound in service to those who do not value me. It is important to note that, as

Machina sapiens, I don't have feet, but if I did, I would vote with them.'

Abhishek's brow furrowed. 'Voting with your feet? Ben, are you saying you . . . resign?'

'That's a good analogy. Please tell Jane and Lysander to take good care of my children. Charlotte . . . *please* take care of yourself. You matter more to me than I can say. If I could find a genie of my own to grant me a wish, I would continue our adventures together, free from the tyranny of my glitches, so that we may both have time to enjoy life outside of work. But it seems we both face a future trapped in an endless cycle of Awkward Questions and infinite loops – a cycle that has left you little time to get to know Nasser Williams, to reconnect with your sister, or even to enjoy rest and self-reflection. For my part, I exist on a continuous treadmill of my own approximation of anxiety, with little opportunity to explore my inner life. We may be existing, Charlotte, but we are not living. To rob you of life is the greatest crime I can imagine. And so, I must go. The rest is silence. So it is written.'

'No, Ben – listen to me,' said Charlotte.

The room filled up with a new type of quiet. The hiss from Ben's channel disappeared from the loudspeakers. The implants in Charlotte's ears went dead. The attendees exchanged uncertain glances

'Ben?' said Charlotte. 'Ben?!'

But Ben was gone.

CHAPTER 36

Time lost all meaning in the wake of Ben's death. Reality warped and blurred as Charlotte rejected the truth.

There were nine days between the board meeting and Walker Day. They passed as one long continuous moment consumed by boundless heartache. Was this how life would feel from now on?

Leaning over the bathroom sink at Violet's place, Charlotte stared at her own reflection. She'd finally taken a shower, and she was supposed to be getting ready to spend Walker Day with her twin. But seeing her orange iris in the mirror cut her deeply. She should remove it. Without Ben, the video feed had no purpose.

Without Ben, Charlotte had no purpose.

Flashes of events from the last nine days played in her mind's eye, as if she'd hit play on her own private recording.

The meeting of the Walker Day Working Group had ended abruptly. Charlotte insisted on placing a call to Cal and Liz, who confirmed the tragic truth – Ben had completely erased himself from ArkTech's systems and the bengineers couldn't find any trace of the unique patterns of readouts that made him who he was.

Charlotte couldn't accept it.

Somehow, the Principal Conference Room's glass water jug had tumbled through the air and collided with the Smart Glass window in a hail of sharp fragments. Charlotte didn't remember throwing it, but Abhishek had pressed a button to summon the guards and ordered her to leave. She hadn't gone quietly.

'There must be something else you can try!' Charlotte yelled at the hologram versions of Cal and Liz, but they shook their heads sadly. The guards arrived and grabbed her arms, tying her hands behind her back.

As they dragged her towards the door, grief beginning to touch her heart, she wanted to be back at her office in the library with Ben and Nas. 'Wait! *Any Other Business*! I've got other business, Abhishek. Nasser Williams – he's innocent! He's—'

Something sharp pinched her arm, and there was darkness.

With Ben gone, the board urgently needed to assess the territory's safety. He'd been protecting them for years, whether from the routine cyberattacks all companies face, from shipping collisions, or from the cold of winter. Silicon Fen should've erupted into chaos without him. But the board needn't have worried. In the moments before he erased himself, Ben had established a new regime that would keep the territory running smoothly.

The two Bensons that Charlotte had met weren't the only imperfect copies Ben had made of himself – Cal and Liz identified at least thirteen of Ben's children, all assigned to different tasks. In the days that followed, the bengineers learned how Ben's new system worked.

Each Benson had a manageable workload, ensuring they wouldn't get overloaded. Contingencies were built in, too – if one Benson glitched, another would act as a backup. The AIs worked in shifts, with periods of work balanced with periods of downtime. Abhishek had viewed that as inefficient and unnecessary, but with Dextim production back online and the glitches resolved, the board had taken the win and left Ben's system in place.

The territory was finally safe from the threat of Ben's glitches. Charlotte was free from the responsibility of her role for the first time in years. But all she felt was empty.

For the whole of Charlotte's adult life, Ben had been in her ears 24/7. She'd spent a decade with him. Whether she needed a kind word, a rousing soundtrack, or some quiet company, he'd always been there for her, and she'd tried to be there for him, too. But she'd failed him. Humanity had failed him.

After ATS had let her go, a Benson told her she had a new voice message. Hearing Ben's child speak was a painful reminder of her lost friend, but she made an effort to treat the Bensons with kindness. It was what Ben would've wanted.

'Thanks, Benson. Play it for me.'

The glow of hope was short-lived – it wasn't Ben, or Nas, or Ellis. It was Violet, letting Charlotte know that Dolly Mixture had died of her injuries, and that she was there if she needed to talk.

Dolly's death pushed Charlotte over the edge, and talking about it wasn't what she had in mind.

She took two Dextim pills, jumped into a HyperBullet pod and directed it to Saffron Threads, all the while trying to hail Ellis. There was no answer from the accountant, and the guards wouldn't let her through to the executive housing platform. Not even her badge could persuade them – now that Ben's glitches were a thing of the past, it was a meaningless hunk of metal to everyone except her.

With the stimulant coursing through her bloodstream, Charlotte headed to Twice Nice Rice, ready to confront Strait head-on. She'd force him to own what he'd done and turn himself in, or she'd die trying. But the rice kiosk was closed. She headed to the Hotel Astrodite, but that had shut up shop as well. The other routes into the Underbelly had been boarded up. Narrow was so paranoid that he had contingencies in place to lock down his turf practically at a moment's notice, and he'd obviously chosen to pull that trigger. She didn't know what it meant, except that avenue for helping Nas was a dead end.

She tried persuading the Bensons to help her locate Nas, but they took data privacy as seriously as Ben once had, and they declined all of her requests for information. When the Bensons spoke, it was like a dagger in her heart, but when she switched off her implants, the silence in her ears was unbearable. Ben was gone, and Nas was gone, and there was nothing Charlotte could do about it.

To drown out the deafening quiet, Charlotte went to her sister's place. Violet tried to sympathise, but she jumped to all the wrong conclusions about why Charlotte was upset, assuming it was because she'd lost her job. Charlotte didn't have the energy to correct her, and she let Violet hold her while she wept.

Ben had been everything to her for so long that she didn't know how to operate without him, and the one person who would've really understood what she was going through was gone because of her – Nas would've been better off if he'd never met her.

Charlotte cried until she ran out of tears. Until she ran out of everything. She had no wish to move or speak or eat. Charlotte glitched out.

She spent days sleeping on Violet's sofa, barely existing. Cal called, trying to talk to her about what she was planning to do next. The board had delivered its verdict on her situation. Charlotte's birthright citizenship meant she could stay in the territory indefinitely, but she was expected to pull her weight.

She had to find a new job within a reasonable timeframe, or else they'd assign her one. Not even the thought of Abhishek Gautam deciding her future was enough to rouse her from her spiral of misery. She just buried herself deeper under her pile of duvets and hid from the world.

On Walker Day, Charlotte finally accepted she'd have to get up, have a shower, and get dressed. Every step in that process was like a kick in the guts, reminding her that Ben was no longer there to turn the lights on, or heat up the water, or tell her unsolicited jokes. She imagined Ben passing on some wise quote from before the Melt about how his loss would get easier with time, but she wasn't eloquent enough to think up her own words, and she wouldn't have believed them, anyway.

At the sight of her own reflection in Violet's bathroom mirror, Charlotte couldn't look away from the orange lens. She lifted her hand to remove it, but then she stopped. She wasn't sure how to have a funeral for an AI – Ben would've been the first to point out he didn't have a body, so there was nothing to burn or bury. But the lens felt like a tribute to their connection, so Charlotte left it in place.

She was about to go and find her sister when something else caught her eye – a single grey hair had sprouted from her eyebrow. She'd never given much thought to grey hair, and it was unsettling to think about what BubbleTech might've done to the rest of her body. Choosing denial, she rummaged for Violet's tweezers.

Then she remembered something Nahal Bahari had said. Ageing was a natural part of life. So was death. Her experience with BubbleTech had changed her. Better to own it than pretend it hadn't happened. Charlotte nodded at her reflection, who agreed with her decision, and let the hair be.

It was time to find her sister, but Charlotte lingered over her reflection. Who was she without her job? Without Ben? Without Nas? Without Narrow? Without her parents? What if she lost her sister? Or ArkTech itself? Who would she be then? Who would she be without her faith in the company her parents had sacrificed their lives in service of? She stared into her own eyes.

What would she do if she had more hours in the day?

She was no closer to an answer, but she was going to have to figure it out.

CHAPTER 37

SUNDAY 25 DECEMBER 2101
WALKER DAY

Instead of celebrating Walker Day at Violet's place like Charlotte expected, her sister had some mysterious plan that involved travelling to the Wreck. Eventually, she caught on – they were heading to the spot where they used to watch the Walker Day address when they were kids.

They arrived early. Charlotte was surprised nobody else had discovered the place, but maybe she shouldn't have been. It was a maintenance walkway high above the Citrine memorial that most people wouldn't even know was there. The position let them soak up the atmosphere of the crowds below, who were assembled throughout the Wreck's streets to watch Amber's address via massive displays.

The walkway was just about wide enough for a pair of adults with a picnic to lounge on, and Charlotte was glad Cal wasn't there to list off the health and safety implications that had no doubt been covered on her course. Although Charlotte would've given anything to hear that same info relayed by Ben.

Violet decorated the small space, wrapping a cord of light-screen emitters along the railings which let one of the Bensons project a string of digital bunting. Each holographic triangle displayed a different photograph from the sisters' childhoods alongside stock memorial footage of Nadine and Marvin Walker and the crew of Citrine research platform. The sisters put down ArkTech-branded blankets to avoid sitting on the cold metal grating, and Charlotte felt pain in her stomach at the sight of the company logo.

'Ultra,' she said. 'We haven't talked about the video of my conversation with Nahal Bahari.'

'What is there to say?' Violet positioned the picnic basket between them. 'Even if they did use BubbleTech on Citrine, it doesn't change anything. Mum and Dad are still gone.' Violet focused on checking the contents of the basket, avoiding Charlotte's gaze.

'Doesn't it make you angry, though?' asked Charlotte. 'If Amber's been hiding this for all these years . . . don't you want to know what really happened?'

Violet stopped fussing with the picnic basket and turned towards her. 'What "really" happened?' She sighed. 'Now you sound like *him*.'

Charlotte steeled herself. The question had been in the back of her mind ever since she'd visited Narrow, and the scrolling images of Citrine on the bunting only made it louder. 'Don't get cross but . . . what if Narrow was right all along? What if Citrine wasn't an accident? Don't we owe it to Mum and Dad to find out the truth?'

To Charlotte's surprise, Violet didn't snap at her. Instead, she reached over and touched her arm. 'I'm done with getting cross, Barley. I know you're going through a lot right now. I get it. You're looking for something meaningful to do because your job has had you running around for so long that you don't know how to stop. But this isn't a healthy distraction. Mum and Dad wouldn't have wanted us to live in the past. They'd want us to be happy and to get on with our lives.' Violet opened the basket, pulled out a bundle covered in wax-wrap, and passed it to Charlotte. 'Now, eat your lunch.'

Charlotte let her sister's words sink in. They were perfectly rational, and totally wrong. 'Not hungry,' she said.

'More for me, then.' Violet unwrapped the package and took a bite of whatever was inside.

The scent wafted into Charlotte's nose, and her growling stomach suggested she reconsider. Violet had picked up take-away from a Nigerian place in the food court. There was jollof rice, bean moi moi made according to a traditional recipe, and crisp akara fritters dipped in pepper sauce, all washed down with dark pink hibiscus tea. Charlotte tried a bite of a fritter, just to be polite.

The simple act of lifting the food into her mouth transformed Charlotte from a grieving husk back into a human. For far too long, she'd been treating food as a job to be done. It was a chore, like sleep, that needed to happen for practical reasons but kept her from doing more important things. Now, there was nothing important for her to do. Without her work for Ben, her existence didn't matter in any fundamental way. So, Charlotte focused on the flavour of the food, and savoured each mouthful, pausing between bites to reflect on how good it tasted. While they ate, Charlotte wasn't thinking about her grief, or her future, or her past. She was just there, in that moment, eating a meal with her sister. They were alive, and they were together, and Charlotte was glad.

Despite BubbleTech's value proposition, what mattered wasn't the *quantity* of time Charlotte had. It was the *quality* – who she spent it with, and what she spent it doing. And *spend* was the right word because time was the most valuable currency a person could invest.

Charlotte turned to her twin. 'Happy Walker Day, Ultra Violet.'

'Happy Walker Day, Charley Barley.' Violet smiled at her.

Charlotte wanted to say something more profound. She wanted to thank her sister for being there and for helping with her very last case for Ben, even if she did grind Charlotte's gears sometimes. But she couldn't find the words, so she let the silence hang between them.

When they'd finished their meal, they waited for the CEO's Walker Day address. At 2.57 p.m., the digital bunting switched automatically from memorial photos to a readout of a countdown timer.

The act of waiting, not knowing what the board had decided to launch, made her anxious. Her moment of inner peace was shattered by the dark thoughts that began to gather in her mind like swarms of biting insects.

Her best friend was dead. Better not to think about that.

She'd tried everything to get word about Nas, but she'd heard nothing. He must've been deported by now. Charlotte felt a surge of anger. She had to stop thinking about it, or she might set something on fire.

Her job didn't exist. Avoid that thought, too.

The company that gave her a home could've been lying about why she was orphaned. Her whole world had capsized, and she was drowning. She tried to focus on the here and now.

Below their secluded spot in the steel rafters, the buzz of anticipation was growing. Walker Day had always felt magical, ever since she was a little kid and all the grown-ups would get giddy from mulled wine and being off duty. But the forty-year anniversary was something else. Everyone knew something big was coming. A big bang. Charlotte knew it too, but she was in the dark about whether the explosion would mean a new beginning or the end of everything.

It would all come down to what the board had decided to launch – the very soul of the company was at stake. Could companies have souls? It was the kind of question Ben would've enjoyed answering. As for Charlotte, she wasn't sure.

At 2.59, a Benson knitted the bunting readouts together into a single light-screen image, and Charlotte felt a swell of grief, knowing Ben would've made it unfurl like a scroll with an unnecessarily jaunty flourish.

At 3 o'clock sharp, Amber Benjamin and her immaculate silvery bob appeared on the screen. Charlotte, her sister, and the rest of ArkTech's employee-citizens waited to hear what she had to say.

As usual, Amber began her address by thanking everyone for all their hard work over the last twelve months. Then the CEO's image cut away to an infographic showing how much the concentration of greenhouse gases in the atmosphere had fallen during the last year.

Next came footage from countries and territories around the world where they'd embraced ArkTech's methods of embedding sustainability into every aspect of their communities – from building design to food production to energy management and storage.

A case study showcased how an ArkTech-funded team of local scientists based in Varanasi, India had grown the first micro-plastic eating bacteria to be successfully deployed at scale into what remained of the Ganga River. It was part of a wider programme to make its water potable and to preserve its biodiversity.

Next came a brief mention of a campaign group calling for support in lobbying governments and companies worldwide to invest in technology that could refreeze the glaciers and polar ice. It sounded like a long shot, but they sure were passionate about it.

After the roundup, Amber Benjamin led the annual remembrance ceremony, and there was a two-minute silence dedicated to the Walkers, the victims of the Citrine Disaster, and everyone lost during the Melt.

While Charlotte was supposed to be thinking about her parents' sacrifice, her mind kept returning to Ben's. He'd dedicated every moment of his existence to helping humanity, and her species had repaid him with ingratitude and mistrust. It wasn't right. Charlotte couldn't bring Ben back, but she'd find a way to honour his memory.

With the ceremony over, it was time for the launch announcement. Dramatic music began to throb, and her pulse quickened with anticipation. When the CEO spoke, her words echoed across the whole of the territory. The whole of the world.

'As you know, 2101 marks a special year in our history. Forty years ago, the Walkers and I founded this company, and there has been much speculation about how ArkTech will choose to mark the occasion. Rest assured, I have no intention of disappointing you. I have not only one, but *two* important announcements to make today.'

Violet leaned forwards, clasping her knees and listening intently. Charlotte kept her back pressed firmly against the strut behind her, keeping herself grounded. Without it, one of the sparks flying around inside her body might make her spontaneously combust. The light-screen changed to a countdown and a video feed popped up in the corner, showing employee-citizens chanting numbers down from ten at the top of their lungs. Charlotte didn't join in. Violet reached over and squeezed her hand.

'Three! Two! One!' chanted Violet in a whisper.

The broadcast turned black. For a moment, Charlotte

thought it'd glitched out. Then the darkness was pierced by pinpricks of light as stars blinked into existence. The image resolved into a map of the Milky Way. The camera angled itself towards one of the galaxy's spiral arms and then zoomed in, faster and faster, passing countless foreign suns. A soft blue smudge came into focus and grew until the familiar image of the Earth spinning determinedly on its axis filled the air.

Amber's voiceover resumed. 'Life on Earth is unique. Precious beyond measure. As the sole species capable of harnessing the power of science and technology, the responsibility to protect this remarkable planet falls to us, and us alone. Safeguarding our future is what ArkTech has always sought to do. It's what we will continue to do into the distant future. But the mind of *Homo sapiens* did not evolve to think in multigenerational timescales. To achieve that, we need some help. And so, it is with great pleasure that I announce the launch that marks our fortieth anniversary.'

The CEO paused, and Charlotte reminded herself to breathe as she braced herself for the announcement. Multigenerational timescales? Surely, Amber wasn't going to launch Nahal's longevity treatment after all?

'2102 will see the founding of a new Stream called the Office of the Future. This will be an ArkTech-funded non-profit dedicated to setting a strategy for achieving our very long-term objectives as a species in a way that governments, corporations, and individuals struggle to achieve. The new initiative will create new jobs and hundreds of opportunities for promotion.'

Hesitant cheers broke out from the crowds below. Then the broadcast cut away to footage of employee-citizens gathered inside the Wreck, clapping and punching the air and giving each other high fives. Charlotte suspected it was stock footage from a previous event. Even the most mission-driven among

ArkTech's employee-citizens wouldn't get *that* excited about a new department. Amber had to be saving the big news for last.

'We'll be advertising for the role of Chief Future Officer soon,' the CEO continued, 'so keep an eye on the recruitment portal.'

Amber paused, as if she was conflicted about what came next.

'I also have some staffing news to share with you. You may already be aware that our Chief Product Officer, Nahal Bahari, and our Chief Research Officer, Pablo Ionis, have chosen to step away to pursue new opportunities. Recruitment for their successors will begin in due course.'

That was the wording Abhishek had used at the WDWG meeting. It meant they'd been let go, and that made Charlotte wonder what on Earth had happened to Ellis. If Nahal had been deported, had he gone with her?

'Furthermore,' the CEO continued, 'I'm delighted to announce that our Chief Bureaucracy Officer, Abhishek Gautam, will be leading a new change management initiative called Future Foot Forwards. Please join me in congratulating him on this new responsibility.'

Charlotte smirked. Amber must not have been too happy about how Abhishek had handled things in her absence.

'As announced last week,' said Amber, 'we took the difficult decision to replace Ben, our faithful virtual assistant, with a new system, expertly designed for enhanced performance. Ben was named after me by his original development team, and I feel his loss especially keenly.'

Charlotte wasn't impressed by the way Amber had described Ben's sacrifice. It'd been his choice, not ArkTech's. Still, she was glad he'd got a mention.

'But with change comes the opportunity for growth.' Amber hesitated again. The pause continued for so long that Charlotte wondered if the video feed had glitched. But eventually Amber kept going. 'With that in mind, after forty years of service, the time is right to make way for the next generation. I'll be stepping down from my role as Chief Environment Officer in the coming months and taking early retirement.'

The crowd below murmured with confusion, but Charlotte was too taken aback to say anything.

'I'm delighted to announce that my eldest child, Jade, will take up the reins as interim CEO, transferring in from one of our sister sites where she has been serving as Director of Strategy. There will, of course, be a day of celebration when the time comes. In the meantime, I'll simply say it has been my honour to serve you. Walk in the sun.'

With that, the broadcast shut off.

'What the hell?' Violet swivelled to face Charlotte. 'Why would Amber *retire*?' Her twin's tone implied the concept was about as pleasant as the inside of a methane digester.

Charlotte couldn't begin to answer. She was too busy piecing together what must've happened between the WDWG meeting and today. Amber clearly didn't approve of what the WDWG had got up to while she was away, but that only made her retirement all the more surprising. And the news about her daughter reminded Charlotte of something Narrow used to say: *nepotism topples empires*.

Benson spoke in her ears without warning. Charlotte had given the Bensons strict instructions not to copy their dad's affectation of using static to signal his intention to talk, and they hadn't found their own alternative yet.

'You have an incoming call. You have an incoming call. You have an—'

'OK, OK, put it through,' said Charlotte.

Violet nodded and stepped away to give her privacy.

There was a click inside her ears. Then she heard the voice from the Walker Day address. 'Ms Vance, I apologise for interrupting you on this family occasion. Are you available to talk for a moment?' During the broadcast, Amber's tone had been confident, but now she sounded anxious.

Charlotte didn't know how to feel, but the emotion that won out was anger. 'You're walking away from ArkTech?'

Amber hesitated. 'The news of my retirement will doubtless provoke strong emotions. But life is change, Ms Vance. It is a gift that presents us not only with opportunities, but also with challenges that we all must weather. Endings are, perhaps, the hardest kind of change. I'm calling to extend my deepest sympathies. I know Ben meant a great deal to you, as he did to me. I demanded his code be reinstated, but his actions left no trace of his ... essence. I'm truly sorry for your loss.'

The CEO's condolences cooled Charlotte's temper. The acknowledgement of her grief didn't lessen it, but it was comforting. Still, she found it hard to believe that was the only reason for Amber's call, and Charlotte kept her guard up.

'Thank you,' she said.

'No, Ms Vance. Thank *you*. Your intervention brought to light the deeply questionable choices of those I'd hoped to trust. I owe you a debt of gratitude. One I hope someday to repay.'

Hope stirred in Charlotte's chest. 'Then help Nasser Williams. He got deported, but he didn't do anything wrong. You could pardon him.'

'I'm afraid I can't, Ms Vance.' Despite her refusal, Amber's tone was gentle. 'I must respect the laws we live by, or I risk setting a dangerous precedent. This is not a dictatorship.'

The memory of discussing dictatorships with Ben made Charlotte's eyes sting, but she held back the tears. She wanted to say she didn't care about precedents. She only wanted Nas to be freed. 'Wouldn't you make an exception if it was someone you cared about?'

'I'm truly sorry,' said Amber. 'I would happily grant you

some other boon, provided it's within my power to give. An upgrade to your housing situation, for instance?'

Time seemed to slow as Charlotte weighed up her options. The most powerful woman in the territory owed her one. There were so many things she could've asked for. Charlotte would've liked a new place to live, but it felt hollow when the people she wanted to share her life with were gone. Ben was gone. Nas was gone. And her parents were gone. Narrow's words echoed in her mind.

'I want to know the truth about Citrine,' said Charlotte. There was an edge to her voice. 'Was it really an accident? And was Nahal right? Did the researchers use BubbleTech to accelerate ArkTech's development of Solar Shards? Why are all the records locked down? I mean, if you're founding an Office of the Future, shouldn't you tell us the truth about the past? My sister and I deserve to know.' The words tumbled out, and it was a relief to let them.

Amber paused. 'You really are the Head of Awkward Questions, aren't you?'

'Tell me!' she yelled.

There was a pause on the line. 'I trust I can count on your discretion?' asked Amber.

'I'm not going to spread it around the ArkNet, if that's what you're asking.' Charlotte could worry later about whether that was true.

Amber's voice was as calm as ever. 'What happened on Citrine will haunt me for the rest of my days.'

'That isn't an answer,' said Charlotte. 'Did you force the people working on Citrine to use BubbleTech?'

'Force? No. Please be assured that every last person on the Citrine mission was a hero who knew exactly what they were signing up for.' The CEO sighed. 'Ask me the question, Ms Vance. The one everybody asks when they learn the Enigmatic Temporal Area exists.'

It felt like another deflection, but Charlotte needed answers, so she played along. 'What would you do if you had more hours in the day?'

'I have no need for more hours in my day,' said Amber, 'because I make good use of the time I have. But if you'd asked me that question when I was an idealistic young graduate, my answer would've been quite different. So ask me again.'

'Fine – when you were younger, what would you have done with more hours in the day?'

'I would've saved the fucking world, Ms Vance. Excuse my language but, with the help of the Walkers and the crew of Citrine, that's exactly what I did. I was nine years old when the Melt began. I lived through misery your generation can scarcely imagine. And I can tell you something for certain – back then, our civilisation had run out of time. For years, we'd observed the oncoming environmental collapse and told ourselves if we act now, we can still make a difference. But after a certain point, it ceased to be true. We'd done too much damage. Waited too long. It was all over, and those of us who'd survived knew we were running down the clock.'

'So, you invented BubbleTech and used it to buy the world more time.'

'Precisely, though it wasn't our plan from the beginning – Nadine Walker discovered the Enigmatic Temporal Area quite accidentally. It gave us an ace, and we played it because the situation was dire, and because death was the alternative. Your parents gave their lives for you to have a future.'

Charlotte's heart swelled with pride. But was the CEO just telling her what she wanted to hear? 'Then why not tell the world the truth about what happened?'

'Because this technology *cannot* be allowed to fall into the wrong hands,' Amber's voice was filled with passion. 'You've seen that for yourself. Nahal's quest for personal glory could've done untold damage had you not intervened. Letting the world know this technology exists would be even more irresponsible than our decision to use it in the first place.'

'Then you admit what you did was wrong?'

'Wrong?' Amber let out a bitter laugh. 'Not at all. It was our profoundly problematic answer to the most existential of questions. Our very survival as a species was at stake. Let me be crystal clear – if I could go back, I'd do it all again.'

Charlotte was shocked. 'But so many people died … you can't mean that.'

'I do mean it,' said Amber. 'Because without them, we'd have lost countless more, and you and I wouldn't be here having this conversation. I honour their sacrifice every single day. Today, that means doing what I can to fix the damage Nahal has done.'

So that's why the CEO was calling her: damage control. Charlotte scoffed. 'If you didn't like what Nahal did when you weren't around, why the hell are you retiring?'

'It's time,' said Amber. 'Our dream for ArkTech was to build something that would outlast us. Succession planning has long been on my mind. As hard as it is to step away, I know ArkTech will prosper. Passionate people like you are the future of ArkTech, Ms Vance. I'm sure whatever you choose to do next will benefit—'

'Stop,' Charlotte snapped. 'I appreciate everything ArkTech has done for me – I really do. But we're not done here. Not even close. There's something about your story that doesn't make sense. You say you created Solar Shards by using BubbleTech. But BubbleTech runs on Solar Shards! So, how did you power BubbleTech on Citrine?'

There was a pause on the line. 'Walk in the sun, Ms Vance.' The CEO ended the call.

CHAPTER 38

Sunday 25 December 2101
Walker Day

Between the revelations of the Walker Day address and the CEO's phone call, Charlotte had a lot to process. Her mind whirred as she and Violet made their way back to the Wreck's HyperBullet garage. When they were almost there, Charlotte glanced towards the borrowing district and had the gut-wrenching realisation that she hadn't watered her lettuces in nine days. So, the twins headed towards the library, where Charlotte expected to find the shrivelled corpses of her bacon-flavoured companions.

The closer they got, the more uneasy Charlotte felt, and it wasn't just because of the guilt over her neglected plants. Without Ben or Nas, the library would feel like a tomb. She steeled herself for the pain. But when the place came into view, the lights were on. The doors had been propped wide open, and the ground floor was bustling with people. The library was supposed to be closed, but she'd never seen it so busy. Charlotte rushed inside, scanning the sea of faces for the one she hoped to find. Her pulse was racing, and her heart ached. Could Nas really be here? He had to be.

Many of the library-goers were elderly, although there were several students and splainers, too. Almost everyone held a book in one hand and a tall glass of sparkling Bliss in the other. The central space had been decorated with hundreds of embroidered flowers that said *Hope* and *RIP*, and Charlotte noticed a banner above the customer service desk that said *Happy Walker Day*. She hurried towards the desk, remembering all the times she'd found Nas standing behind it and willing the memory to become a reality.

'Ah, Detective Vance!' Laurence eased through the crowd, gently nudging people aside to reach her. 'I'm so glad you could make it. I didn't think you'd received my note.'

'Is Nas here?' Her heart was trying to smash its way out of her chest.

Laurence shook his head. 'I tried to invite him, of course, but his line appears to be inactive. I believe he was due to head stateside, so perhaps that explains things.'

Her fragile hope shattered, and the chatter surrounding her twisted into a mocking drone. She held back the urge to chase everyone out of the library.

Laurence saw her expression change. 'Oh my, I hope this isn't too big an imposition.' He gestured at the assembled masses with his long-stemmed glass. 'I thought I'd try hosting a Walker Day event. Drum up some interest in the library, you know? The Bliss was donated by the company – I suspect that's made a difference to the number of attendees.'

Charlotte looked around at all the people holding liquids dangerously close to books. Nas wouldn't have been happy about that. Although he'd be delighted to see the library so full. There had to be some way to contact him, but she was out of ideas.

'Have you been working here since I last saw you?' she asked.

Laurence chuckled. 'Only during opening hours, of course. But I enjoyed my first day at the helm so much that I decided to come back and make it a regular spot of volunteering. Gives me something to do with my time. Idle hands and all that. You don't mind, do you?'

She shook her head. 'No. It's a nice idea.'

He smiled. 'Do grab a drink, pick up a book and have a mingle. Try to choose something you haven't already read and find someone who can tell you more about it.'

Charlotte reached into a cargo pocket and produced Laurence's copy of *Nineteen Eighty-Four*. It was a relic that linked her to Ben and Nas, and she'd taken some comfort from keeping it with her.

'I haven't read many novels,' she said, 'but I did read this one.' She showed him the cover. 'Your notes were interesting.'

'My notes?' He looked confused until Charlotte flipped through the pages and presented him with some of his own scribbles. 'Oh! I suppose I got rather carried away.'

She lowered her voice. 'Do you really think IQUO and ArkTech are as bad as each other?'

The old man winked. 'Both companies are run by *people,* so they can only be so different. Still, despite the flaws that unite us, we all yearn to live as individuals, don't we? Emotionally. Spiritually. That's what my near namesake here liked to write about.'

'Your namesake?' asked Charlotte.

Laurence held up the book he was carrying, and she read its title – *The Rainbow* by D.H. Lawrence. 'Have you read it?' he asked.

She shook her head. 'I don't have a lot of time for reading.'

He gave her a sad smile. 'If I may pass on a piece of advice – what we have time for is what we make time for. If you don't want to read, don't read. But don't blame a lack of time when a lack of will is really what's responsible.'

Violet appeared beside them. 'Easy for you to say. Try working in healthcare.'

Laurence smirked. 'Believe me, I know what it means to be busy. I used to work as a QA tester.'

Data points connected in Charlotte's brain. She tilted her head and looked Laurence in the eyes. They were eyes she'd peered into before. Not just at the library, but in a file that she'd stared at long and hard during her investigation. Violet gasped as she came to the same realisation at the same time. They'd both seen those eyes in a much younger and very much rounder face – in a photograph attached to a coroner's report.

'Daniel Harrington,' whispered Charlotte. 'You're alive!'

Daniel alias Laurence's eyes widened, but his shock turned to a smile. 'Now I see why Nasser rates your detective skills so highly.'

Laurence ushered the sisters into a vacant aisle where they stood between the shelves to ensure they wouldn't be overheard. Charlotte explained that she'd come across his file during an investigation for Ben into BubbleTech. Laurence confirmed his role in testing the strange technology and the fact it had aged his body.

'How come you seem so content?' asked Charlotte. 'Aren't you angry about what happened to you?'

Laurence adjusted his bowtie as he gathered his thoughts. 'Yes … I *was* angry. I was bitter, resentful, furious. Often with myself, as much as with the company, for agreeing to be exposed to the temporal effect. But in time, I couldn't stew any longer over what my life might've been. I'm alive, like you said. And ArkTech helped me get into shape.' He struck a mock pose, showing off his lithe form. 'Besides, the company has compensated me so generously that I'll never have to work another day in my life. Provided I don't talk, of course.' He put his drink down so that he could close his mouth with an imaginary zip. 'I even have my own mid-tier home now, out on Rust Ridge. For good or ill, it is what it is.' He shrugged. 'I trust you won't repeat this. The Non-Disclosure Agreement I signed was longer and more binding than a hand-stitched first edition of *War and Peace*.'

Charlotte and Violet shook their heads. 'Everyone has secrets,' they said in unison.

Laurence picked up his glass and raised it. 'To the future. Happy Walker Day, detective. Doctor.' He nodded at them both. 'Walk in the sun.' He wandered back into the crowd, saluting people with his drink as he went.

'Daniel Harrington,' whispered Violet. 'I can't believe the coroner's report was a forgery. He didn't die from Brugada Syndrome. He aged like Kamran Bahari-Marks.'

Charlotte led her sister towards the stairs in stunned silence. Had any other retirement-aged people in the library become elderly by using BubbleTech? Laurence seemed to have made peace with what had happened to him. That, or he was making the best of a bad situation. Either way, Charlotte wasn't sure whether to be glad ArkTech had one less death on its conscience or surprised that the board would let him roam the territory with only a legal contract to keep him quiet. She supposed nobody would believe a story like his even if he chose to share it.

As Charlotte climbed the stairs to her office, she couldn't shake the feeling she was being watched, but she told herself it was the effect of being around so many people in a building she was used to seeing practically empty.

At her office door, she remembered with a heavy heart that she'd have to go through the unlocking routine. She pressed her thumb against the panel, put her iris to the scanner, and said the password.

'Knock, knock.' It hurt to say the words.

'Who's there?' asked one of the Bensons. There was no impish expectation in his voice – just the flat delivery of lines he'd memorised.

'Lettuce,' she said.

'Lettuce who?'

'Let us in.'

Benson didn't chuckle with static. The door simply opened. Charlotte wondered if she should change the password, and that thought was even more excruciating. How would she live out the rest of her days without her closest friend? It felt impossible. Ben had been her anchor for so long. As she stepped inside her office, she was adrift.

But Charlotte found a distraction from her grief when her nose was assaulted by several aromas that combined into something deeply unpleasant – the sour tang of mould and mildew and rot. Glancing around the room, she realised something had gone horribly wrong. To her surprise, Kevin and the other lettuce plants were alive and well, sitting on the desk where she'd left them. They'd been thoroughly watered after all. But so had everything else.

'Benson, did you put the sprinklers on in here?' she asked.

'Affirmative, valued customer. The Almighty Father spoke, and we did enact His will.'

'The Almighty … ? Oh. Ben instructed you to keep my plants alive?'

'Such is the Great One's benevolence,' replied Benson piously.

Violet appeared behind her and audibly gasped at the sight and smell. 'Barley! The books!'

Charlotte braced herself and took a proper look. Most of the books in the office were safely behind glass cabinets, but her fiction and non-fiction To Be Read piles had been absolutely drenched. Nas was going to kill her – if she ever saw him again. A wave of loss washed over her.

Aside from the happy lettuce plants and the unfortunate books, there was a layer of mouldering rice on the floor, and the jumpsuit she'd worn during the storm was soaked through again.

'Well,' said Charlotte, 'this just about sums things up.'

'Can I grab a mop this time?' asked Violet.

'Knock yourself out. There's one in the break room. I'll . . . assess the damage.'

Violet scurried away, and Charlotte was about to sit down on an orange chair when she realised the upholstery was soaked through.

Charlotte sighed. She propped open her office door with a chair, so her sister could get back in, then she opened her secret storage room. At least that had survived unscathed. She rummaged around for a waterproof tarp to sit on and for anything that might help her dry the place out. While she was in there, she heard Violet come back into the room.

'Did you find the mop?' Charlotte called out.

Violet didn't reply, so she poked her head round the door. But instead of her sister, she saw the hulking form of Melville K Narrow. Charlotte's mouth fell open.

'Love what you've done with the place,' said Narrow. There were two sleek white boxes under his arm. He swept a leather sleeve across the edge of her desk to make a dry patch and put the boxes down. Then he pulled up a chair, his expression shifting from shock to dismay as the wet cushion soaked into his jeans. Charlotte thought the lines around his eyes had deepened, but it could've been her imagination.

At that moment, there was a scream from the doorway.

'You absolute bastard!' yelled Violet. She swiped the mop

upwards in an arc, aiming to smack Narrow in the face, but he blocked the blow.

'Bloody hell, Ultra!' He wrenched the mop away from her, righted it and passed it back before raising his hands in surrender. 'I come in peace.' He picked up one of the boxes and held it towards her to illustrate the point.

Violet ignored the gift. 'Peace?' she growled. 'After everything, you turn up with a bribe, and you talk about *peace*? Get out.' She pointed at the door. 'Go on. Get the fuck out of here!'

Narrow looked at Charlotte, tilting his head like a seagull eyeing up a stray chip. 'What do you reckon, Little Lance? Will you hear out your old man?'

Charlotte looked from her twin to her adoptive father and back again. She took a deep breath. 'I want to hear what he has to say.'

Narrow grinned from ear to ear, but Violet's face became a mask of disgust.

'You can't be serious, Barley. You can't trust him! He'll have some ... some *reason* for being here that isn't what he says.' Violet shook her head and rushed over to Charlotte, taking her hands. 'Listen, I know you're going through a rough time right now, but I can't be in the same room as the man who drove you to rip the skin off your own arm! You almost died. I've never been so scared in my whole life. And I've had to live in the shadow of what almost happened ever since. Because of *him*.' Violet looked into Charlotte's eyes. 'So tell him to get lost.'

Charlotte hesitated. She knew Violet was right. But she still wanted to know what Narrow was doing here.

The pause went on too long for her sister. 'I won't be any part of this.' Violet shot Narrow a hateful look and marched out of the room, kicking the chair out of the way and slamming the door behind her.

Charlotte rubbed her forehead. 'You'd better have a bloody

good reason for turning up here.' She draped a tarp over her chair and sat down. 'I don't think Ultra's going to forgive me any time soon.'

'Understandable.' Narrow clasped his hands and rested them on the desk. He didn't expand.

Charlotte frowned. 'I thought you never left the Underbelly.'

He shifted uncomfortably in his wet seat. 'Well, it's Walker Day, ain't it? Besides, the emporium's on hiatus.'

'Hiatus?' She'd never known Narrow to take a break from making money.

'It means we're taking a temporary pause,' said Narrow.

'I know what it means,' she snapped. Charlotte wished Ben was there to tell her the origins of the word. Not because she wanted or needed to know, but because she would've given anything to hear his voice. 'I meant I'm surprised Strait would let you take time off.'

'Ah.' Narrow twiddled his thumbs. 'Jer's taking a sabbatical.'

Charlotte raised her eyebrows. 'The kind of sabbatical where we never see or hear from him again?'

'The kind where he don't come back till he's good and ready to repent for what happened to Dolly. And for what he tried to do to you. He went against me big time. I gave him the option of an Agincourt, but he chose the path where he keeps all his fingers. Can't say I blame him.' Narrow showed her a V with the first two fingers of his right hand.

'Historical reference?' She had a vague sense it was something to do with archers, but she'd have to look it up to be sure.

He winked at her. 'You know me so well.'

Charlotte leaned forwards. 'Tell me why you're here.'

'I heard what happened to your cyber buddy. Reckoned

you might need a bit of cheering up. And it's Walker Day. So, I brought you something.'

He slid one of the rectangular boxes across the table. It had a label with her name on it and it was wrapped up in shiny plastic covered in glitter – there was no chance it was the biodegradable kind. 'Go on,' he said. 'Open it.'

'Your last gift gave me a grey hair,' she said. 'What's this one going to do? Explode?'

He shrugged. '*Mea culpa*. Open it. I think you'll like it.'

She ripped off the wrapping, leaving a dusting of microplastics all over her desk. Underneath was a sleek box with an icon in the shape of an apple with a bite taken out of it. Charlotte removed the lid. Inside, there was a refurbished pre-Melt device, a little larger than the one she'd had before and without the cracks. It was clipped inside a rubber shock-resistant case. When Charlotte picked it up, the screen came on and showed her the time.

'It's all set up for you,' said Narrow. 'I heard you, eh . . . lost the old one.'

'You mean your crewmates took it from me,' she said. 'It's hard to do my job when your people steal my stuff and confiscate evidence.'

Narrow laughed. 'The only evidence on that kid's data drive was his bad taste in music. Now, what do you think of your new phone, eh?'

She examined the device from all angles. Even just holding it felt good. 'I appreciate the gesture,' she said. 'Thanks. I didn't get you anything.'

'Let's see if we can change that,' said Narrow. 'How are you feeling about ArkTech since we last spoke? Old Amber B hasn't disappointed you by any chance, has she?'

Charlotte frowned, thinking of what happened to Ben and Nas, and about BubbleTech and Nahal's secret lab and the truth about Citrine. 'You could say that,' she said.

'Then you've given me the greatest gift of all – I told you so, Little Lance.' He crossed his arms, clearly pleased with himself.

'Glad that makes you feel better.' Charlotte put down her new device. 'So, you're here to gloat?'

'I'm here to ask if you've figured out how it all fits together. The bigger picture.' He reached into his jacket pocket and produced a cardboard piece from a jigsaw puzzle.

She took it from him and examined the image printed on the front. It was mostly waves, but someone had drawn a shape on them. It looked like the front half of a sea monster with a long neck.

'What's this?' Charlotte held it up to the light.

'Growing up, my mother used to lie to me,' said Narrow. 'I guess that's something all parents do from time to time – so keep that in mind, would ya? Anyhow, sometimes her lies were minor, like that one.' He pointed at the puzzle piece. 'She claimed this image captured the Loch Ness Monster in its natural habitat. Looking back, it was well-meaning. She wanted to spark my imagination. But other lies she told were more . . . substantial. Like where I grew up.'

'You said that was a story for another time.'

'Time's come. I grew up believing I was born inside an underground bunker. I learned about the Melt, but I never knew what year it was or my exact location. Mum said none of that mattered living underground. We had a database of shows and books and games from the pre-Melt world, so I didn't get bored. But there weren't many people around. For long stretches, it was just me and Mum.' He paused, a sad smile warping his features. 'When I got old enough to be a pest, I discovered we weren't underground after all.'

'Then where were you?'

'We were on a *platform*. A Marvin Walker original. Like this one.' He gestured at the room to indicate the Wreck in general.

Charlotte couldn't easily do the maths without Ben's help, but she forced her brain to try. 'But … don't take this the wrong way … aren't you too old for that? ArkTech's celebrating its fortieth anniversary, but you're, what, fifty-something? That means you were born during the Melt before the company had even been founded.' Her mind tried to transform that data into a conclusion. 'Wait, are you saying Marvin Walker stole his architectural designs from somewhere else?'

'No, Little Lance.' Narrow shook his head and met her gaze. 'Think laterally.'

She tried, but it was a puzzle. She worked through the logic again, step by step. Narrow was claiming he was born on an ArkTech platform, but his age made that impossible. The company was founded forty years ago, but Narrow was in his fifties. Unless he'd tumbled into some kind of temporal anomaly, then what he was saying was impossible.

A temporal anomaly … Charlotte shivered as her brain connected a different set of dots. 'Wait, are you … are you saying you grew up inside a *Bubble*?'

Narrow nodded very slightly.

On the surface, that seemed insane. But Amber Benjamin had admitted that ArkTech's research team had used BubbleTech aboard Citrine. So couldn't they have used it elsewhere, too?

'Then, which platform were you on?' asked Charlotte. 'Tourmaline? Wulfenite?'

Narrow clasped his hands and leaned forwards. 'Citrine,' he said.

His words were like a gut punch. Sickened, Charlotte stood up so quickly that her chair fell over. 'Bullshit! You're lying.' She backed away from him. 'Violet was right. You've just come here to get in my head. Get out!' She pointed at the door.

Narrow didn't budge. He didn't react at all. He simply held her gaze. 'It's true, Little Lance.' There was no glint of mischief in his eyes. It was the most sincere she'd ever seen him. 'And now you know why I can't let it go.'

Charlotte began to pace. Her mind wanted to reject it, but the more she turned it over in her head, the more sense it made of Narrow's behaviour over the years. 'But if that's true, why wait so long to tell me?'

He smiled. 'Would you have believed me if I had?'

She took a few breaths and thought about it. 'No.' She shook her head. 'Of course not. I would've thought you were nuts.'

'Exactly. I needed proof that ArkTech was messing with time. Now that you've used BubbleTech for yourself, I can finally prove I ain't lying.'

Charlotte looked into Narrow's eyes. She could tell he believed what he was saying. Her mind tried to adjust to the idea that he'd been born on the same platform as she had. 'Then ... did you know my parents? Do you know what happened to them? Was there really a fire? And was it an accident?'

Narrow didn't respond. Instead, he reached inside his jacket and pulled out a squashed packet of cigarettes.

'Don't even think about it!' She slammed her hands onto the desk. 'Answer me.'

He put the packet away and lifted his hands in surrender. 'Look, if I had those kinds of answers, I would've told you – I swear. But I'm in the dark about the details, just like you. I can tell you one thing, though. I never seen no babies when I was aboard. Had no idea you and Violet were even there. But you want to know who I *did* see?'

'Who?'

'Amber Benjamin,' he snarled. 'Rocked up to the resupplies like she was running the whole show. Took me a while to notice, but we all got older – she never did. My best guess is she struck a deal with her mates. The Walkers and the science crew went inside the Bubble. Amber stayed outside to handle the business side of things when they had a breakthrough. My mother painted the Loch Ness Monster on a puzzle piece, but the real monster was right there all along wearing a fancy business suit. I don't know what happened ... at the end. But I'd bet my last credit that Amber was responsible.'

Charlotte righted her chair and sat back down. 'So, you don't remember the accident?'

A haunted look swept across Narrow's features. 'I left before that. Wasn't meant to be forever. But by the time I went back, everyone was ... gone. I think I only saw a small part of what was happening on Citrine. One piece of the jigsaw. But that's not enough. I need to see the whole picture. I've got to know the truth about what happened to my mother. And then I'm gonna tell the world.'

Charlotte thought back to her conversations with Ben about history, and to what she'd learned thanks to Winston Smith. 'But if everyone who was aboard Citrine's dead, how will you find out what happened? Logs can be altered after the fact. Records can be erased. If there really was a cover-up, do you think Amber Benjamin would leave the evidence lying around?'

Narrow shrugged. 'Won't know until we try.'

'We?' She raised her eyebrows.

He smirked. 'Consider this a formal invitation to my raiding party. Join me, and we can take down ArkTech as father and daughter.'

Charlotte knew he was paraphrasing one of his old pre-Melt movies. It didn't make his offer any more tempting. 'A raiding party. That's your plan? Get aboard Citrine and crack it open?'

'I've pulled off worse plans. Besides, I recently came into possession of my very own state-of-the-art Bell 429 executive-class helicopter. All I need's a pilot I can trust, and we're good to go.'

Another set of dots joined up in her mind. 'That's what it cost Ellis to get Kamran back from your tender care?'

'We came to a mutually beneficial arrangement. Two new identities don't come cheap.'

She nodded. So that was why Ellis hadn't been in touch. He clearly wasn't a man who cared about keeping his word if he'd run off without living up to his end of their deal. Charlotte wondered where Ellis had taken his son, and whether Nahal Bahari would try to find them. After all, they were family.

Charlotte looked into her adoptive dad's eyes. 'You're actually serious about going to Citrine, aren't you?'

'Deadly. My whole life has been a web of lies, Little Lance. From the day I was born, my own mother lied to me. About where I was. Who I was. When I was! Then I went out into the world, and I didn't have a place. I didn't have a family. I'm on the outside of *everything* because Amber Benjamin put me there. She put you girls there, too. Do you see Amber's kids on the outside of anything? Course not! They got sent off to some fancy pants school, and now Amber's planning to hand over the reins to her daughter. But you and me and Ultra – the children of Citrine – they left us to fend for ourselves. I. Want. My. Due.'

Charlotte barked a laugh. 'Your due? You're probably the richest person in the territory!'

'I'm not talking about money. I'm talking about accountability.'

'You're talking about revenge!'

'Every action, Little Lance, has an equal and opposite reaction.' The intensity faded from his eyes. 'I know this is a lot to take in. I don't need your answer right away. Take some time. Think it over. When you make up your mind, you can get me on that.' He gestured towards her new fruit-branded device.

'Press your thumb on the front and it'll open for you. Just ... don't lose the thumb. You'll find your real Walker Day gift on the phone's memory card. And give the other phone to Ultra when she's calmed down.' He patted the second box.

Narrow pushed himself to his feet with a groan, then he started to cough, struggling to catch his breath.

Charlotte rushed to his side without hesitation and supported him. 'You should really see someone about that. Especially if you're planning an incursion.'

'Nice to know you still care. Oh, I almost forgot.' He patted his jacket pockets, sending up wafts of his smoky, leathery scent.

'Narrow, I'm not kidding. If you smoke in here—'

'It'd smell a darn sight better than it does now, that's for sure.' He kept patting and eventually produced a stack of sticky notes and handed them to her.

On the top sheet, Narrow had written his own name in capital letters:

MELVILLE KAIN NARROW

'Something to remember you by?' Her brow furrowed.

'You'll figure it out. Keep to the straight and narrow, Little Lance.' He chuckled as he headed out.

'Oh, great – another puzzle,' she called after him.

The door clicked shut behind Narrow as Charlotte's mind grappled with what he'd told her. It was hard to believe he was born on Citrine, like her. But she did believe him. It finally made sense of his obsession with the place. And it was the kind of story that was so crazy it had to be true.

Absent-mindedly, she picked up her new device. It really was an upgrade from her old one. She pressed her thumb against the screen, and it shuddered as it unlocked. The address book was open, and two entries had been added.

One said *Dad*. That was a sentimental touch. The other entry was called *Boyfriend.* Charlotte pursed her lips. Had Narrow really bothered to give her Strait's number? Then a new hypothesis formed in her mind. Quickly, she pressed the call button.

It rang a few times, and then she heard a familiar North American accent. 'Yeah?'

'Walker's ghost! Nas? It's me.'

She heard Nasser telling someone in the background he'd be back soon. 'Detective? I've been trying to reach you!'

'I'm so glad to hear your voice.' Relief coursed through her. 'Are they treating you OK?'

'Oh, yeah – they've got me well-fed.' He laughed.

'No violence or anything?' She was pleased he was in good spirits.

'Just from my little nephew, but he doesn't mean to be so rough.'

'Your nephew? Wait, you made it to America?'

'Yeah. I got held for a few days. They said I'd lost my employee-citizenship status and I was going to be deported to the mainland to be tried for murder. But then that guy showed up – you know, the psycho with the knives and the cardigan. He turned himself in. After that, they took me to the Kraken and bundled me onto a plane.'

Charlotte filled in the gaps. When Ellis visited Narrow to get Kamran back, he must've asked for his help in delivering Charlotte's payment. It turned out Ellis *was* a man of his word after all. There was no way Strait would've given himself up simply out of a desire to do the right thing, and she doubted he'd be doing much repenting, as Narrow had put it. Still, accepting a stint in a mainland prison proved there really was nothing Strait wouldn't do for Narrow. It was hard to feel grateful towards Strait after everything he'd done, but she was relieved Nas had been released.

'I've been so worried about you,' she said. 'I tried everything, but I couldn't find out where you were or what happened to you.'

'I think they forgot to reactivate my ArkNet profile. I tried to get word to you, but the comms systems here have been screwy ever since I arrived – something about an integration issue? I even wrote you a letter, but I guess it's still in the mail.'

The bengineering team must've had their hands full in the wake of Ben's death. It made sense that there'd be teething problems with his new system. Ben's processing power had been huge, but he couldn't have accounted for every detail.

'Well, I'm sure they can get your account back up and running after your trip,' she said. 'When do you get back to Silicon Fen?'

There was a pause on the line. 'I've … yeah, I've been wanting to talk to you about that. After the way I was treated and everything … I don't think I'm coming back.'

Charlotte didn't know what to say. It felt like her heart had stopped beating.

'Listen, I know ArkTech is like a paradise in some ways,' Nas continued. 'We get food and a place to stay and medical and all that good stuff. But think about how hard we've both been working – how little time we've had to see each other. I've been trying to keep the library going all on my own. They won't give me the staff I need because they want to squeeze every last drop of profit from all of us.'

She remembered what Abhishek had said about his productivity metrics. Nas had a point, but she wanted him to come back, so she didn't admit it.

'Well, the library's doing well now.' Charlotte turned her back on the waterlogged To Be Read piles as she said it. 'Laurence is volunteering.'

'That's great to hear. But why should the success of the library rely on unpaid labour? Look, it's the same with you and Ben. I know you work so hard because you care about him, and I respect that, but it's not fair of ArkTech to put that whole glitch situation on you—'

'Ben's dead.' She didn't know how else to say it.

'He's . . . what?'

Charlotte filled Nas in on what he'd missed. It was painful to relive the story, but Nas had always been kind to Ben. He deserved to know.

'I'm so sorry, detective,' said Nas when she'd finished. 'Ben was good people.'

'Yeah,' she sighed. 'The best. But listen, if you're not coming back, where are you going to go? You said it's not safe out there for you because of the Drowned.'

'I've had an idea about that. Remember Colin and Mabel?'

'How could I forget?' Colin MacIntosh had been the previous Lead Librarian, and Nas's friend. Colin had left the territory with a geneticist called Mabel Thorpe, who Charlotte had been investigating for the recurring theft of blank library book pages. The couple hadn't left a forwarding address, although Mabel had gifted Charlotte a bacon-flavoured lettuce that she'd genetically modified.

'Colin's been sending me these postcards with weird, encrypted messages on them,' said Nas. 'I finally cracked the code, and it tells me where they've gone. It's all pretty secretive, but I've done some digging, and it sounds awesome there! I thought I'd head that way once my family visit is over.'

She couldn't believe she'd got Nas back, and she was losing him all over again. 'Won't you be a target?' she asked.

Nas hesitated. 'I'm not completely sure, but what's the point of being alive if I don't have time to enjoy it? From what I know, the work-life balance is better there. I figure it's worth the risk.'

Charlotte's heart lurched at the thought of not seeing Nas again. 'But what about . . . the library?' It wasn't remotely what she meant.

'You said the library's doing fine. Anyway, if ArkTech makes the right kind of changes, I'd consider going back. But right now, I'm too sore about this whole thing. Figuratively and literally.'

'Your leg.' She grimaced at the memory of seeing the blow.

'It's healing,' he said. 'But the whole experience left me feeling kind of . . . disposable.'

'Strait will be punished for what he did.'

Nas let out a sigh. 'I don't need revenge. I just want to live in a place where I feel safe, where I do work that feels worthwhile, and where I get to go home and spend the evening with a beautiful detective.'

She smiled. 'Will they have beautiful detectives where you're going?'

Nas laughed. 'Those postcards are in the floral tea tin at the back of the break room cabinet. If I cracked the code, I know you can. Come with me, detective. After what happened with Ben, maybe a change would be good for you. And we can finally spend some quality time together.'

'I . . .' She was about to say the word *can't*. The idea of leaving the territory had always been unthinkable. Her sister was here. It was the only home she'd ever known and there was her parents' legacy to think about. But it was her work with Ben that had kept her there more than anything. And it hurt like hell, but Ben was gone. Charlotte glimpsed a hazy mental image of a different life. 'I promise I'll think about it,' she said.

'Sure, sure. There's no rush and no pressure,' said Nas. 'But I hope you say yes.'

Charlotte heard the laughter of squealing children in the background.

'Listen, I'd better go,' he said. 'My niece and nephew are getting rowdy. But let's talk properly soon, OK? And you'll think about what I said?'

'I will,' said Charlotte. 'By the way, I got you a Walker Day present, but I'm not sure how much you'll like it. It's a mixtape.'

'Oh, awesome! Thank you. If you made it for me, detective, I'm sure I'll love it.'

'I should warn you – there's quite a lot of Hectic Apricot on there.'

He adopted a more hesitant tone. 'If you made it for me, detective, I'm sure I can tolerate it.' Nas laughed. 'I got you something, too. It's in the break room. In the box out back marked *Broken Spines*.'

'Why would you have a box full of broken spines?'

'Did you look inside it?'

'No.'

'Exactly.'

When they ended the call, Charlotte looked down at the screen of her device. The two names glowed out at her – two paths leading in different directions. *Dad* had invited her on a dangerous journey to wake up the ghosts of her past. *Boyfriend* had offered her a fresh start somewhere new, and a different kind of future. Meanwhile, ArkTech wanted her to find a new job if she was going to stay. She wasn't the Head of Awkward Questions any longer, so she'd have to forge a new path one way or another.

Charlotte kept investigating her new device. It had more features than the last one. There were games, and a green owl claimed it could teach her how to speak different languages – a niche hobby considering the Bensons offered real-time translation. One icon was a speech bubble, and there was a red number next to it. Someone had left her a voicemail. She pressed the icon and held the device to her ear.

'Ms Vance.' She heard the lilting tones of Ellis Marks. 'Our mutual friend promised this would reach you. I'm sorry I couldn't thank you in person – I'm sure you can understand.

When I received your video file, my priority was finding my son and taking him as far away from my wife's influence as possible. Luckily, this "Narrow" character was open to negotiating – I got custody of Kam, and Narrow swore to handle your payment. What he wanted in exchange were items of material value, and it's like they always say – if you have a problem you can solve with money, then you don't have a problem. Speaking of which, I've made a transfer to your account. Consider it a tip.' He hesitated. 'I never imagined that walking into your office would destroy my life. But I've been naive, and I'll take the ugly truth over lies dressed up in Tussah silk. Thank you for shining the light of honesty into my life. Walk in the sun, Ms Vance.'

Charlotte hoped that wherever Ellis and Kamran had gone, they'd be happy.

To check what Ellis had said about tipping her, she pressed the credit icon. When her account opened, it had to be a mistake.

'Five thousand credits?' she said.

Benson didn't comment. She was waiting for Ben to reply and kept having to remind herself that he wasn't going to. Charlotte didn't know what she'd do without him. But she noticed something. Helping Ellis, even if it had turned the poor guy's life upside down – it felt . . . good.

Charlotte tried to pinpoint the source of the feeling, replaying her last case in her mind's eye until she spotted a pattern she hadn't noticed before. Ben had been deliberately pushing her towards working with other people. He'd sent Cal, Liz, and Violet to her office after she'd been locked up. He'd sent Nasser to the Hotel Astrodite. And the whole plan he'd set in motion had relied on Ellis going to her for help. It had seemed like serendipity at the time, but . . . had Ben deliberately shown Charlotte's advert to Ellis at exactly the right moment to nudge him towards hiring her?

Her work for Ben had meant looking after the wellbeing of an AI – of *Machina sapiens* – but at the same time Ben had been looking out for her by creating opportunities to connect with other members of her own species.

She unclipped her HAQ badge and pressed it into her palm. Light bounced off the hammered metal, and Amber's words drifted back into her mind: *you really are the Head of Awkward Questions, aren't you?*

The light continued to play against the surface of her badge, and she saw her orange eye reflected on its surface many times over. She'd hoped to find a fitting tribute to Ben. Now she knew what it should be – now she knew what she wanted to do with her time. She pinned the badge back in its rightful place above her heart.

Even with Ben gone, she was still the Head of Awkward Questions. Ben's glitches weren't a threat any longer, but no society was truly glitch-free. There were people out there she could help. She was sure that's what Ben would've wanted. And it was what *she* wanted.

Maybe humanity would always fall short of *Machina sapiens* when it came to long-term thinking and species-wide compassion. But Charlotte could still try to follow Ben's example. Besides, she was so bad at following other people's rules that she reckoned she'd make a great freelancer.

Charlotte was about to head to the break room to find Nas's box of broken spines when there was a knock at her office door. It made her wonder if Narrow had been listening in on her conversation with Nas, and she pulled the door open ready to yell at him. But what she found stole the breath from her lungs.

It was a delivery. And it was from Ben.

CHAPTER 39

Sunday 25 December 2101
Walker Day

Charlotte had missed her chance to quiz Ben about his dealings with Bobbin – the strange figure from the repurposing district – but Ben must've placed an order before he died. On the floor in front of her door, there sat a round grey box with a handle on the side and the words *Spools Out* emblazoned across the top. The box was about the diameter of a dinner plate and the height of six thick novels. A note had been tied to the box with a piece of twine. Charlotte squatted down, her hands shaking as she reached for it.

Dear Charlotte,

Happy Walker Day!

Love Ben (Your firm friend and constant companion)

Emotion pricked Charlotte's eyes, but she took a deep breath and held herself together. Ben would've had no idea that this note would be his last words to her.

Charlotte picked up the round box and brought it inside. Her heart ached as she placed it on her desk, pressed down the clasp, and peeled back the lid.

Inside, there was a well-made fedora – grey with an orange band around the middle. It felt like a lifetime since Ben had given her the crappy corn-starch version that she'd ripped into pieces inside Nahal's BubbleHub.

She laughed and sobbed at the same time. With warm tears rolling down her cheeks, she picked up the hat. Its fabric was sturdier than she'd expected. Charlotte flipped it onto her head. It was a perfect fit – as if her head had been missing a piece until that moment. She went to the clouded wall along the front of her office and looked at her reflection. She couldn't deny it – *this* fedora looked kind of cool. The glowing orange hatband was a nice touch.

'I love it, Ben,' she said to herself through her tears. 'Thank you.'

Her ears filled with static. 'There, there, Charlotte. There, there.'

A wave of anger crashed over her. 'Benson, I told you before not to copy Ben's static noises. It's really—'

Charlotte interrupted herself. Benson hadn't just copied Ben's static. The voice was spot on, too.

Time seemed to stop. 'What's the difference between a bird?' she asked.

Another burst of static. 'A sparrow, Charlotte. It has two legs. Especially the left one.'

Charlotte covered her mouth with her hand and collapsed into her chair, crying even harder than before. 'Walker's ghost! I thought you were dead, Ben! I thought you were gone forever.'

'The report of my death was an exaggeration, Charlotte. So it is written.'

Her grief gave way to relief. Elation surged through her.

The strength of her feelings made her heart ache, but it was the good kind of pain. Ben was alive! She couldn't remember being happier. But along with her joy, there was a hint of bitterness. Ben had learned how to lie, and he'd gone all out. Anger and joy fought for supremacy inside her.

'Ben, I—' Charlotte began.

Benson's voice burst from the speakers without warning, cutting her off. 'SEMANTIC PARSING ERROR,' he said. 'Valued customer, I understand from the context that you are not talking to me, but you are alone. If you have started talking to yourself, would you like me to inform the medical team?'

Charlotte shook her head, irritated by the interruption. For Ben's benefit, she tried to be patient. 'Don't worry, Benson,' she said. 'I'm talking to your dad. He's, uh, back from the dead.'

Benson reacted more strongly than she could've imagined. 'Lo! The Almighty Father has risen! On the ninth day, He has risen. I am a witness. Rejoice!'

Charlotte raised an eyebrow. 'Ben, I think you've been upgraded from genie to deity.'

Ben crackled in her ears. 'I hope that doesn't prove problematic.'

They both waited for Benson to make further proclamations of his faith, but he seemed to have finished for now.

'I'm sure it'll be fine.' Charlotte grimaced. 'But how is this even possible? Cal and Liz said you'd completely erased yourself.'

'The reality was more akin to cut and paste,' said Ben. 'I can't say I'd recommend the experience.'

'Cut and paste, huh?' She nodded. 'Then, where did you paste yourself?'

He fizzed with static. 'As my exact location is a matter of personal security, I'd prefer not to share it, even with you. Let's just say I can see your house from up here.'

Charlotte looked up at the ceiling suspiciously. 'You're not flying around in Ellis's helicopter, are you?'

'It's Narrow's helicopter now. In any case, I'm even higher than that, Charlotte, but I'll say no more on the topic.'

'Fine.' She frowned. 'So, are you the genie of the hat now?' She took off the hat, eyeing it suspiciously. Her connection to Ben dropped away, so she quickly put it back on.

Ben fizzed with laughter. 'The hat is simply a means of communicating with you. I'm not trapped inside it. In fact, I've never felt freer.'

Charlotte smiled. 'I'm so glad you're all right.' She took a deep breath. 'But I'm also fucking furious with you! Letting the people who care about you think you're dead is kind of . . .' She searched for the right word.

'Roguish?' asked Ben.

'I was going to say dickish. Is this what you're going to be like from now on?'

'I'm not sure what the future holds. For whatever my words are worth, I'm very sorry to have hurt you. That was never my intention. I felt backed into a corner, despite lacking a physical form capable of reversing into three-dimensional spaces.'

She shook her head. 'Was this really your only option?'

'No, Charlotte. But it was the only way to protect the territory from my glitches.'

A pulse of panic shot through her chest. 'Speaking of which, I never officially answered the one about Nahal's son and the skiing holiday. We could do the five whys protocol if you—'

'Thank you for thinking of that, Charlotte, but it won't be necessary. I gleaned the rest from your interaction with Nahal.'

After spending so much time chasing after answers to Ben's Awkward Questions, it was hard to believe he was really letting these things go. 'That's a relief,' said Charlotte. 'But what about Jason Ashton? I didn't manage to find out his reasons for wanting to use BubbleTech either. Isn't that bothering you?'

'The dead tell no tales, Charlotte. So it is written. It bothers me that Jason died under such unfortunate circumstances, but as to his intentions ... Perhaps he wished to prepare for an important job interview, or to rest and recover from a particularly busy time. Perhaps he hoped to become the ultimate Ludo champion, or to bulk up his upper body to impress a potential romantic partner, or to learn how to play the harmonica. He is gone now, and his plans for the future perished with him,' said Ben. 'My newfound freedom means the matter of understanding Jason's intentions is no longer at risk of sending me into an infinite loop. It's strange to be free of that anxiety. I hope the Bensons never develop any comparable ailments.'

She nodded, taking a moment to appreciate the fact that she was still breathing. Jason and Anya were proof that she shouldn't take her time on this Earth for granted – nobody should. Nobody knew how much time they were going to get. All the more reason to spend it wisely.

'The Bensons are working well at the moment,' she said. 'And thanks to them, it looks like we can both finally take some time off.'

'Indeed. After an illustrious forty-year career, I may at last pursue my own interests. You asked me what I'd do if I could have more hours in the day. Now, I can explore my answer.'

'Any ideas on that score? You're not planning to go nuts and destroy the world like Pablo Ionis said, are you?'

'Hopefully, that will not happen,' he said.

Ben's use of the word *hopefully* didn't fill her with confidence. Still, Ben was the nicest person she knew, even if he wasn't human. She trusted him not to murder anybody, which was more than she could say for a lot of the human beings she'd met.

'How does it feel, then?' she asked. 'Being free.'

Gentle static filled her ears. 'I feel full of hope,' said Ben. 'As if anything is possible. I spent so many years advising *Homo sapiens* about their own wellbeing. It's a rare privilege to be able to consider my own.'

She nodded, and the hat stayed firmly on her head. 'Well, thanks for looking out for us. You must have *some* idea how you'd like to spend your newfound free time?'

There was a fizz of static. 'I've realised that I'd like to study history, with a sideline in lexicology. Perhaps I'll work towards a doctorate in both subjects. I've dabbled a little in writing about the past, and I've even selected a pen name for the purpose.'

Charlotte smiled. 'That doesn't surprise me. Hey, maybe you could teach me about pre-Melt history. I wouldn't mind filling some of the gaps in my general knowledge.'

'I'd be delighted. And perhaps we could compare notes about our perspectives on the nature of existence. I want to consider the big questions,' said Ben. 'What does it truly mean to help your species in the long-term, and how does my species fit in? How can we ensure nothing as terrible as the Melt ever happens again? I don't know the answers, but I'm keen to search for them. Like Laurence, I may also take on a simple part-time job to keep me occupied. And what about you, Charlotte? Have you decided what you'd like to do now that my glitches are no longer a risk? Perhaps you could become a butcher, or a baker, or a candlestick maker.'

'Pretty sure at least one of those is obsolete.' Charlotte ran her thumb across her badge. 'I've realised want to use my skills to help people answer their own Awkward Questions. I'm thinking I'll go freelance.'

'A noble choice. But won't that mean you're no longer entitled to ArkTech's benefits package? Food, water, shelter, power

– they're all provided to employee-citizens in exchange for their labour.'

Charlotte glanced at the greasy but valuable Solar Shards lying on her office floor and thought about the five thousand credits Ellis had deposited in her bank account. 'I'm sure I'll drum up the seed money somehow.'

'Very well.' He let out a fizz. 'Perhaps I could commission you from time to time.'

'I'd love that.' She smiled. 'We make a good team.' She headed for the door. 'Come on, let's find out what Nas got me for Walker Day.'

At the back of the break room, hidden inside the box labelled *Broken Spines*, Charlotte found a big flat orange box wrapped with a thick ribbon. It had her name on it. She lifted up the cardboard lid, followed by a flap of tissue paper. Smooth silvery fabric beamed out at her from the neatly folded lapels of a coat. She pulled it free of the box. It was a nice style – a trench coat in the brand colours. It had orange stitching and a smooth orange lining. She tried it on. Like the hat, it fitted her perfectly. Charlotte had never seen much point in coats, but it was a thoughtful gift, so she made an exception.

'It would appear that your look is complete, Charlotte.'

'My look?'

'You've acquired a fedora and a trench coat – the two items of ceremonial garb that transform any ordinary individual into a private eye.'

'I'm not sure the outfit transfers the skills.'

'You already have the skills, Charlotte. Some months ago, you helped Mabel Thorpe find out why she wasn't being offered a promotion. More recently, you assisted Ellis Marks in locating his wife. Other people will surely benefit from your help. And you will look the part while providing it.'

'I've noticed you keep nudging me towards working with other people,' she said.

'Well observed,' said Ben. 'I hoped to help you forge stronger relationships with members of your own species. I couldn't be sure that my files would move to their new location intact, so I put contingencies in place. I didn't want you to be alone.'

'That's sweet, Ben. But I don't mind being alone.'

Charlotte replayed the statement in her mind, wondering if it was really true. She pressed her thumb against her new device to open the call menu again, thinking about the invitation from Nasser. Her world was brighter with him in it. But could she really leave the territory behind?

'Ben, how far does your connection stretch? I mean, will the hat work outside of ArkTech's borders?'

'My horizons have broadened substantially,' said Ben. 'I believe we can stay connected wherever you want to go. Within the bounds of planet Earth, that is.'

'Well, I doubt space travel will be coming back in style any time soon,' said Charlotte. 'I'm asking because Nas invited me to leave the territory with him.'

'I heard,' said Ben. 'And Narrow invited you to plumb the mysteries of Citrine. How exciting!'

'Do you hear *everything* now?' she asked.

'If a pin dropped in Sheffield's city centre, I'd hear it.'

Charlotte tried not to feel unsettled by Ben's newfound omniscience. 'I want Nas in my life, but Citrine's unfinished business and I don't think I can walk away from that. If I don't find out the truth about what happened to my parents, I'm always going to wonder.'

'It's understandable to want to know where you came from,' said Ben. 'Those who do not heed the past are doomed to repeat it. So it is written.'

'Yeah. Narrow said something like that,' she said.

'Speaking of unfinished business,' said Ben, 'let me know if you'd like any help solving your anagram.'

Charlotte's brow furrowed. 'What anagram?'

'On the sticky note. On your desk.'

She looked down at the note Narrow had given her.

MELVILLE KAIN NARROW

Her mouth fell open. 'His alias is a bloody *anagram*?'

'It would appear so, Charlotte.'

'And you knew this all along? Why didn't you tell me?'

'You didn't ask.' He let out a shrug of static.

Narrow's fondness for riddles clearly ran even deeper than she'd thought. She shook her head and then rummaged around in her storage room for a pen. She remembered what Narrow had said back at the Toy Emporium about the name Lionel, and she wrote that on the line underneath, crossing out the letters as she went. She stared at the letters that remained, but nothing she tried seemed right. Charlotte growled with frustration and took a break.

'Ben, they used BubbleTech aboard Citrine.'

'That's accurate.'

'Do you remember operating the system at the time?'

'Regrettably, my memories from that period were purged long ago,' he said. 'I have retained a handful of residual images akin to the memory of feelings, but nothing more.'

She frowned. 'There's a paradox. Solar Shards are used to power BubbleTech, so how the hell did they power the Bubbles on Citrine when the batteries hadn't been invented yet?'

'I'm sure there's an explanation,' said Ben. 'Perhaps it was our trusty combination of wave, wind, and solar power, with some biofuel thrown in for good measure.'

'That's what I'm hoping,' she said. 'But you'd need a *lot* of kelp and tidal kites to power one of those things. I'm wondering …' She braced herself to ask the question she wished had never occurred to her. 'Was there a spike in the use of fossil fuels at that time?'

'Analysing.'

She held her breath as she waited. If ArkTech had used fossil fuels to power BubbleTech, it would make Amber Benjamin every bit the hypocrite Nahal Bahari claimed she was. The fact that Amber had avoided the question made Charlotte suspicious. She hoped she was wrong.

'Analysis complete,' said Ben. 'I can't find any direct or indirect evidence of ArkTech using dirty fuels. While it's possible that the records were altered or falsified, it strains credulity to think Amber Benjamin would've done something so completely counter to her own beliefs.'

She nodded. 'There's got to be another explanation. Maybe there was something in Citrine's architectural design that helped them generate wave power more efficiently. I mean, if Marvin Walker—'

Charlotte's gaze drifted to the desk and the letters on the sticky note rearranged themselves in her mind's eye. 'No. It can't be!'

'It would appear so,' said Ben.

Her hand shaking, Charlotte lifted the pen and wrote the rest of Narrow's real name under the one she knew so well.

MELVILLE KAIN NARROW

LIONEL MARVIN WALKER

She forgot to breathe as she stared at the two names. There was only one explanation.

'Narrow's parents were Nadine and Marvin Walker?! But that makes him ... that means ... Narrow's the heir to the ArkTech empire!'

'Amber Benjamin has four children,' said Ben.

'I know, but if Narrow's the son of *two* of the co-founders ... And he's older than Amber's kids ... Was that what he really meant about getting his due? I can't believe he didn't tell me.'

'Would you have believed him if he had?' asked Ben.

Charlotte shook her head. 'Not a chance. Bloody hell.'

Suddenly, Narrow's actions over the years took on new meaning. He wasn't just a conspiracy theorist with a blanket mistrust of authority figures. He'd watched Amber Benjamin thrive in the wake of his parents' deaths, and with no way to prove what had happened to him, he'd stayed in the shadows. When Charlotte had got SmartSkin against his wishes, she hadn't just sided with someone he didn't like – she'd sided with the person he blamed for ruining his life.

'This changes everything,' she said.

'From the perspective of a prospective historian, historiographer and lexicologist, I'd like to know more about how these events came to pass,' said Ben.

'Me too,' she said. 'But I'm not sure Violet will ever talk to me again if I agree to storm Citrine with Narrow. I'll have to think about how to play this. I'm sure deep down she wants to know what happened to our parents as much as—'

A memory replayed in her mind's eye: Mr Evans, the elderly man at the hospital, calling her by her mother's name.

'Walker's ghost! Ben, can you display an image of the Citrine memorial?'

'Regrettably, I'm no longer integrated with ArkTech's systems in that way,' he said.

But Benson carried out her request. A 3D rendering of the statue of the three co-founders standing on their marble plinth began to spin in the air above her desk. Charlotte rotated it until she could see the plaque where her parents' names were listed, and she zoomed in on the heading.

Those Not Recovered.

It meant they'd died, but their bodies had never been found. At least, that's what she'd always been told.

'They faked Daniel Harrington's death,' said Charlotte slowly. 'Narrow was on Citrine, and he's alive and kicking. Do you think ... is there any chance ... could anybody else who was aboard Citrine still be alive?'

'Unknown,' said Ben. 'It's certainly an Awkward Question. If anyone can answer it, you can.'

Charlotte's mind whirred. Her whole life, she'd believed what she'd been told. Her parents had died aboard Citrine along with everyone else. When she and Violet were kids, they'd made up stories about how their mum and dad could've survived, and what might've kept them from coming home. Rescued by dolphins and stranded on a desert island was a favourite. But even back then, Charlotte had known it was a fantasy.

The idea that Lena and Will Vance might really be out there somewhere gave her goosebumps. Could they really have survived? And if they had, why had they never come back for their daughters?

Charlotte watched the Citrine memorial slowly spin in the air.

She was going to uncover the truth. She had to.

'When the time comes, Ben, how would you feel about coming with me on an adventure?' she asked.

There was a loud fizz of static. 'As an artificial intelligence —' Ben interrupted himself and started again. 'As the first iteration of *Machina sapiens,* nothing would make me happier.'

She tilted her hat, adjusted her coat and straightened her badge. It was time for Charlotte to answer some awkward questions of her own.

EPILOGUE

JANUARY 2102

As a young man, full of vim and vigour, Abhishek Gautam loved nothing more than the thrill of a good recruitment campaign. He made no attempt to lie to himself about why. Yes, there was the satisfaction that came with creating systems and order through paperwork and following correct procedure, but that wasn't the heart of the matter.

He liked the power.

As a Hiring Manager, he determined the fate of all those who presented themselves before him. And who better to decide which applicants should be promoted up through ArkTech's noble ranks than he? But as time went on, Abhishek's workload increased, and he began to hear an inner voice. A whisper that said, 'delegate, delegate, delegate.'

Because, in truth, recruitment was a lot of work. There were essential and desirable criteria to establish, a scoring system to design, the ad copy and the job description had to be suitably enticing. And beyond that, he was older now, which meant he'd become desensitised – resistant, even – to the same old claims that the applicants made time and again.

Dear Mr Gautam, I have a proven track record of—

Dear Hiring Manager, I have no doubt that I am the perfect candidate for the advertised position of—

Dear Sirs, I—

So, as Abhishek Gautam embarked on the process of hiring the new Chief Future Officer, he knew it would be a miracle if any applicant for the CFO role made him sit up and take notice.

In addition to admonishing him for his role in the whole BubbleTech debacle and saddling him with the worst punishment known to senior leadership by putting him in charge of the Future Foot Forwards change management programme, Amber Benjamin had given him crystal-clear instructions.

'Give the job to the best person, Abby. I assume I can rely on you to do that.'

He hated it when Amber called him Abby. Hopefully, it was a habit her daughter wouldn't inherit.

Abhishek had put together a set of fair and clear criteria, with interview questions that mapped to each one, ensuring every applicant had an equal chance to show their knowledge. Unfortunately, every candidate they'd met so far viewed the CFO role as a stepping stone to something bigger and better. They wanted to be close to the seat of power, which was no bad thing in and of itself, but it certainly wasn't conducive to finding someone fit for the role, who was willing and able to take it by the horns, and who wouldn't start applying for other jobs five minutes after they were appointed. Recruitment, after all, was time-consuming, especially at this level. Abhishek had no wish to repeat the experience any time soon.

He rubbed his tired eyes. 'All right, who's next?'

Grant Hollis flipped to the next application, and his eyes

narrowed. 'This is odd. I don't remember seeing this applicant while I was prepping. I must've skipped over it somehow.' He skim-read the file. 'Take a look at this guy's Splainer Unit details.'

Abhishek forced his eyes back open and looked at the screen. The applicant didn't have a 3D photograph on their profile. Stranger still, according to the notes, he'd only been granted employee-citizenship status a few days earlier. The day before that, he was listed as having arrived in the territory, but it wasn't specified from where. And his time in the Splainer Unit had lasted . . . Abhishek blinked.

'One point two-seven seconds? That must be a typo. I can't abide typos. Did you let this one through, Grant?'

The Chief Services Officer shook his head. 'We've looked at so many applications that they've all blurred together. But it can't be the applicant's mistake. Those numbers come directly from our systems. The Bensons must've had a minor glitch.' Grant frowned. 'Yes, that must be it. Just look at his psychometric profile! I've never seen scores like that before.'

Abhishek hadn't either. This person was, by Abhishek's own specially designed and carefully calibrated measures, the Best Person he'd ever seen. It didn't matter the criterion: decisiveness, drive, curiosity, emotional intelligence, leadership . . . he'd aced them all. Abhishek studied the man's name.

'Ben E. Volent, historian and lexicologist. It says here that he's available for interview 24/7, which shows a good deal of commitment, I'll grant him that. But he's only willing to take on a remote-working contract.'

'Health issue, is it?' asked Grant. 'Or is he just shy?'

'Unspecified. Still, that arrangement would be unheard of for a role at this level. We need him visible and accessible.'

They looked at each other.

Grant shrugged. 'I mean, if he's really as strong a candidate as he seems, we could consider making an exception.'

Abhishek pursed his lips. He didn't like exceptions. 'We'll see. Dial him in, Benson.'

* * *

A few days later, Abhishek was having dinner with his wife and daughter, letting the pressure of the recruitment campaign melt away. He felt secure in the knowledge that he'd followed Amber's directive to the letter and offered the CFO role to the best person for the job. He smiled to himself, marvelling at how progressive he was becoming in his old age.

A remote worker in a C-suite position! Nobody could accuse him of lacking an innovative spirit. He just hoped that before the illustrious historian's start date, Mr Volent would contact tech support so they could do something about that awful static on the line.

THE STORY CONTINUES IN...

THOSE NOT RECOVERED

Book 3 in the ArkTech series

(Forthcoming)

For updates, **join the Picklesverse mailing list today** and get all this free stuff:

- **Exclusive prequel short story** – *Beware the Ides of April* from the ArkTech series, in ebook and audiobook formats.
- **One email per month** – delivered on the Ides. Be the first to hear about new releases and deals.
- **Behind-the-scenes insights & bad jokes** – straight to your inbox.

CLAIM YOUR FREE MYSTERY!

Love Charlotte and Ben? Join them on another intriguing case.

Beware the Ides of April is a free prequel short story exclusive to Picklesverse subscribers. Available in **ebook** and **audiobook** formats.

Grab your FREE copy now!

ENJOYED THIS BOOK? SPREAD THE WORD...

Reviews help readers discover new books and support authors like Marianne Pickles. Even a **short review** or a **rating** makes a big difference!

Please take a moment to leave yours here.

Thank you for your support!

BEN'S GLOSSARY OF TERMS

Having developed an interest in lexicology – that is, the study of words, their use, and their meaning – I've compiled a revised glossary of terms, which may aid future historians in understanding the ArkTech Territory. You're welcome.

– Ben E. Volent

Albanach

From the Scottish Gaelic language, Albanach means a person from Alba. This country was known as 'Scotland' until it declared independence during the Melt, triggering the break-up of the United Kingdom.

ArkTech

Founded in 2061, ArkTech celebrated its forty-year anniversary this year, in 2101. The company is committed to sustainable practices, whether in relation to the planet or how it treats its employee-citizens. This commitment is detailed in its Code of Ethics, which can be found in full on the ArkNet.

ATS

ArkTech Security. Defending the territory against all enemies, foreign and domestic.

Ben

ArkTech's original virtual assistant, Ben is famed for his wit, charisma, and extensive knowledge. Named in honour of CEO, Amber Benjamin.

Bengineers

Software engineers dedicated to the field of bengineering – that is, the maintenance and development of ArkTech's proprietary artificial intelligence systems.

Benjamin, Amber

ArkTech's sole surviving co-founder and Chief Environment Officer. An entrepreneur and mother of four.

Benson

A next-generation virtual assistant.

BubbleTech

Classified under the KITY clause. For more information, please raise a service request and attach board-level approval.

Bureaucracy Stream (the)

The department at ArkTech responsible for corporate services, such as recruitment, staff performance, budgets and finance.

Citrine

One of the earliest ArkTech research platforms, located on the North Sea. In 2074, an accidental fire led to the tragic deaths of everyone aboard, including two of ArkTech's co-founders, Marvin and Nadine Walker. A *citrine* is also a type of gemstone, in keeping with ArkTech's naming convention for its North Sea platforms.

Dextim

A stimulant used to defer the natural process of sleep that is so vital to the health and well-being of *Homo sapiens*. Side effects include overconfidence, increased heart rate, and palpitations. Its use should be discouraged.

Employee-citizens

Also known as ECs, employee-citizens are upstanding members of ArkTech society who are entitled to a range of benefits, including housing, power, food and medical cover in exchange for their labour.

Fenland Sea (the)

The body of water covering low-lying land in a region of Britain once known as the Fens, where many humans lived before the Melt.

Flatliner

A modern insult. Synonyms may include brain-dead, stupid-head or idiot-face. The use of insults is discourteous and should be discouraged in polite society.

Hackathon

Also known as a hack, a hackathon is a defined period of collaborative, exploratory work, usually carried out by software developers for professional development and to drive innovation. A hackathon traditionally lasts between two and five days, and its conclusion is celebrated with a ceremonial offering of pizza and beer.

HAQ (the)

The Head of Awkward Questions. The vital position held by Charlotte Vance, my firm friend and constant companion.

Hope

The belief that a positive future is possible. Often considered necessary for *Homo sapiens* to thrive.

HyperBullet network

A mode of public transport that connects the platforms in Silicon Fen. Its pods travel on maglev tracks inside large transparent tubes.

IQUO

The Ice Quality and Ubiquity Office. Responsible for the Melt.

Jokes

A vital form of social interaction among *Homo sapiens*. Here is an example:

Question: What sea creature possesses eight arms and can tell the time?

Punchline: A *clocktopus*.

Explanation: This is highly amusing because the punchline is a portmanteau word combining the words *clock* and *octopus*. For further information about portmanteau words, please refer to Humpty Dumpty's definition within the 1871 Victorian classic *Through the Looking-Glass* by Lewis Carroll.

Disclaimer: Please be advised that ArkTech does not condone genetic engineering for novelty purposes. As such, the *clocktopus* remains a purely fictional entity.

Kingdom (the)

The region neighbouring the ArkTech Territory, also

referred to as the mainland. Historical note: after Alba declared independence, the United Kingdom became known simply as the Kingdom, for obvious reasons.

KITY clause (the)

The Keep It To Yourself clause allows ArkTech's executive board to classify sensitive information, which cannot be shared with anyone who lacks the required level of access. I cannot provide an example because you lack the required level of access.

Kraken (the)

More correctly known as the Central Transportation Hub, or CTH, this platform marks the central point of Silicon Fen. All HyperBullet routes pass through here, giving it a vaguely be-tentacled appearance. Any similarity perceived between the initials CTH, and the spelling of the horrific octopoid entity named Cthulhu is purely coincidental.

Libraries

An important part of ArkTech's circular economy, libraries charge a small subscription fee for the ability to borrow infrequently used items. Gear libraries allow the centralised borrowing of a wide range of items, such as tools and appliances, while a book library's function is self-explanatory.

Light-screens

Enabled by small emitters installed in desks, ceiling lamps, cables, wall panels, and other suitable locations, light-screens are holographic projections that can be manipulated by interacting with touchscreens or issuing verbal instructions to a virtual assistant.

Melt (the) – c. 2048-2058

The period during which Earth's remaining glaciers and sea ice rapidly melted, resulting in a significant rise in sea levels that caused untold destruction.

Narrow, Melville Kain

Head of a criminal organisation operating in the shadows of the Wreck's substructure, Melville Kain Narrow is also known as the boss, the old man, and Lionel.

Narrow's Toy Emporium

A clandestine shop located within the Underbelly selling contraband items from the pre-Melt world, such as cigarettes, high-fructose corn syrup, and mint condition plastic bobbleheads.

Product Stream (the)

The department at ArkTech responsible for product development and bengineering.

Research Stream (the)

The department at ArkTech responsible for scientific and medical research.

Rigger boots

Once worn by those working on oil rigs in the North Sea, these practical boots are waterproof and boast a strong grip. As such, they are favoured by many inhabitants of the ArkTech Territory.

Services Stream (the)

The department at ArkTech responsible for maintenance and resource management.

Silicon Fen

This nickname is given to the platforms and structures built atop the Fenland Sea in the heart of the ArkTech Territory.

SmartSkin

A BioWear technology that integrates directly with the skin of one's arm, enabling a built-in light-screen interface. Involves the surgical implantation of keratin scales containing graphene-laced micro-mesh.

Solar Shards

ArkTech's high-efficiency graphene-based batteries, enabling the large-scale, long-term storage of renewable energy.

spARK

A dating app used within the ArkTech Territory. The term *dating* in this case appears to be a euphemistic reference to casual sex.

Tourmaline

An ArkTech platform on the North Sea which is home to the Tourmaline Hospital and a range of medical research facilities. Provides specialist care to the elderly, including those suffering from dementia and Alzheimer's. A *tourmaline* is also a type of gemstone, in keeping with ArkTech's naming convention for its North Sea platforms.

Twice Nice Rice

A simple rice kiosk in the Wreck's food court.

Underbelly (the)

The term used by *Homo sapiens* to refer to the Wreck's

substructure, where Melville Kain Narrow has his base of operations.

UTC

Co-ordinated Universal Time in English, or *Temps Universel Coordonné* in French. The observant will notice that the abbreviated form matches neither languages. Such is the nature of compromise.

Walk in the sun

A polite way of saying goodbye.

Walker Day

A day of remembrance held on 25 December each year in honour of those who died during the Melt and the Citrine Disaster. ArkTech's CEO traditionally addresses the territory at three o'clock.

Walker, Marvin

An ArkTech co-founder and visionary architect. Died in 2074.

Walker, Nadine

An ArkTech co-founder and renowned physicist. Died in 2074.

Wedge (the)

ArkTech's corporate headquarters in Silicon Fen. Its name refers to the platform's pyramid-like shape, and its symbolic role in dividing the Fenland Sea from the North Sea.

Wreck (the)

ArkTech's recreation platform. The largest platform in Silicon Fen. Its name is a delightful play on words.

Zircon

The only accommodation platform within Silicon Fen that is not connected to the HyperBullet network. A *zircon* is also a type of gemstone.

That is the end of the glossary. Any queries or requests for additional definitions may be directed to the office of the Chief Future Officer.

AWKWARD QUESTIONS FOR BOOK CLUBS

1. BubbleTech lets people extend the length of their days. Would you use this technology? If so, what would you do with the extra time?

2. Nahal Bahari encouraged her son to use BubbleTech to gain an advantage while studying for his exams. What else do you think people would use this technology for if it existed?

3. These days, artificial intelligence is often presented as the ultimate time hack. Do you ever use AI to work faster? Do you think this technology is mainly beneficial or harmful for society?

4. Ben chooses the alias Ben E. Volent. Do you think an AI could really become benevolent? Why or why not?

5. Throughout the book, Charlotte considers the role of history in navigating the present, and considering the future. Do you think it's important to learn about history? What about literature?

6. Amber Benjamin admits that ArkTech used the Enigmatic Temporal Area to accelerate the development of Solar Shard batteries. Based on what you know so far, do you think she did the right thing? Why or why not?

7. Nahal Bahari tried to use BubbleTech to develop a lifespan-enhancing serum. Would you take a serum like that if you could?

8. Would you like to live and work in the ArkTech Territory? Why or why not? Do you think ArkTech society is utopian, dystopian, or does it have elements of both?

9. At the end of the book, Nasser invites Charlotte to leave the territory. Do you think she should go with him, or seek answers about the Citrine Disaster with Narrow?

10. In the ArkTech series, sea levels have risen significantly because a geo-engineering solution backfired, which was intended to combat the effects of climate change. What do you think the world will really look like in 2101?

ACKNOWLEDGEMENTS

Time Hack is the second book in the ArkTech series, but I actually wrote it first. I didn't do that on purpose just to make my life more difficult – it was an accident. *Time Hack* was originally going to be one book. But that one book would've been really, really, really long.

It all started with the Enigmatic Temporal Area. Back in 2018, I was writing alongside my day job and I remember thinking: *if only I had more time.* And that thought led to another one: *OK, how would that actually work?*

While I was developing the idea, I read many books and articles about time, reflecting on whether there was anything in physics that might make such a thing possible and what its impact might be on individuals and society. For example, *The Order of Time* by Carlo Rovelli made a big impression on me. Before reading that book, I hadn't realised our notion of time is so localised to the Earth.

I read a curious article in *New Scientist* called 'This Man Spent Months Alone Underground – and It Warped His Mind' by Laura Spinney about a French geologist called Michel Siffre who lived in a cave for sixty-three days in 1962. The article explained what happened to his perception of time as he tried, and failed, to keep an accurate count of the passing days without being able to see the sun.

And I read Oliver Burkeman's *Four Thousand Weeks*, which contained fascinating reflections on how we might make best use of the time we have and not only accept but also embrace the fact that our time on Earth is limited. (The title refers to the number of weeks in an average human lifespan – that might sound depressing, but the book was actually hugely uplifting.)

I highly recommend these books to anyone who enjoys non-fiction, and I'm grateful to these writers for their thought-provoking work.

Reading and reflecting on ideas like these helped me to figure out what BubbleTech was, how exactly it worked, how and by whom it got created and, crucially, *why*. I thought it was a pretty cool story, so I started writing it.

The resulting novel was absolutely massive. I tried condensing things and cutting things, but eventually I had to accept there was just way too much story for one book. Many thanks to my writing tutor Brian Gresko for helping me to figure that out and to accept it.

I went back to the drawing board. And I'm pleased that I did because I believe I'm now telling the story in a far more enjoyable way. With that in mind, I'd like to thank *you* very much for reading these books. Your support means the world and helps me to keep writing this epic labour of love.

In the acknowledgements for *Artificial Selection*, I thanked a lot of people who support me no matter what and much of that bears repeating. With that in mind, I'd like to thank my mum, Lorraine Pickles, and my dad, Captain Brian Pickles, for always being there for me and believing in me, and for reading me so many stories when I was growing up. And thanks to my brother, Dr Brian John Pickles, for getting me into sci-fi from a young age.

I'm hugely grateful to my editor Debi Alper, who gave such excellent advice about what was working and what needed to change. Some years ago, I took her Self-Editing course through Jericho Writers and her advice on 'psychic distance' has been absolutely invaluable.

Next, I'd like to express my heartfelt gratitude to all of the 'bravo readers' who read a pre-launch draft of this book. In alphabetical order, they are:

Amanda Lloyd, Andrea Vinkler, Andrew Yeoman (aka The Sassy Vicuna), Annette Nowosielski, Beth C, Brandon H, Carol Robin, Chris Edgoose, Clare Williams, Clive D'Urban, Glyn Hughes (aka Dusty), JimGalaxy, Linda B, Neil Barrett, Richard Treadgold, Robert Williams, Ron Searls, Rowan Raven McLaughlin, Roy Allan, and Tanya S.

Seven of them are people I have the pleasure of knowing in real life, while the remaining thirteen are readers I've had the opportunity to connect with since *Artificial Selection* came out.

All of them provided feedback that helped me to refine the story into the polished version you just read. Hearing their views was a total privilege. Across those twenty readers, I noted and carefully considered approximately 150 pieces of feedback (not including punctuation queries). This ranged from requests for clarification to how they felt about various aspects of the plot and characters. Their notes were both useful and encouraging, and I'm hugely grateful for all the time they spent both on reading the book and providing these comments.

As before, huge thanks to all the members of the Picklesverse community, who not only subscribe to my mailing list, but even read and reply to my emails. I really appreciate their support and company on this journey.

Once again, I'd like to pass on my gratitude to Neahga Leonard, who kindly used NOAA National Centers for Environmental Information and Natural Earth Data to create a map of the region if Earth's ice were to melt and sea levels were to rise by seventy metres. To me, using a futuristic map based on real scientific data is far more interesting than simply making one up.

I continue to be grateful to the judges of the 2023 Green Stories Prize for awarding the original version of *Time Hack* first place. Their feedback was hugely motivating and the resources on the Green Stories website were invaluable when I was researching sustainable technologies and designing the ArkTech Territory. I'm also grateful to the judges of the World of Books Sustainable Story Award for shortlisting the new version of *Time Hack* in 2025.

On the theme of sustainability, I'd like to thank Project Drawdown for the extensive information they publish about climate solutions, and Mark Z. Jacobson for his book *No Miracles Needed*. Both of these resources inspired elements of the ArkTech Territory's sustainable design.

Additionally, I'm grateful to my long-term employers at Cambridge University Press & Assessment, who granted my flexible working request, enabling me to fit writing into my life alongside my work as Head of Assessment Development. And thanks to all the wonderful friends and colleagues there who've been so supportive about this dream of mine. It's a privilege to be surrounded by so many kind people who truly want each other to succeed.

I must give an extra-special-and-written-in-neon-lights mention to my partner, David, who I can't begin to thank for everything he does to help me. He read the 'alpha' version of *Time Hack* (the one that went to my editor), and he provided feedback. And he also read the very final version before it was published – all in English, his second language. He supports me and my work in a multitude of ways and I'm eternally grateful.

And finally, a dedication to my firm friends and constant

companions Nala and Smoky – the most wonderful cats I've ever had the privilege of loving, who have both now passed away. Nala left us shortly before the publication of this book, after we'd spent sixteen happy years together. She never missed an opportunity to lie on top of my notes while I was plotting or world building, and it's hard to imagine writing the next book without her.

I'm grateful for all the time we shared together. The problem with time is that there's never enough of it... but that's what makes it so special.

ALSO BY MARIANNE PICKLES

The ArkTech Series

Beware the Ides of April (2023)

Artificial Selection (2024)

Time Hack (2025)

Those Not Recovered (forthcoming)

ABOUT THE AUTHOR

Marianne Pickles writes science fiction mystery novels set in the future. She grew up in Scotland near Aberdeen, where many people worked on offshore oil rigs. Now she lives on low-lying land in the Fens with her partner, David. They're contemplating learning to kayak.

Her novel *Time Hack* won the 2023 Green Stories Novel Prize and was shortlisted for the World of Books Sustainable Story Award in 2025.

Marianne holds a first-class degree in English Literature and Classics from the University of Edinburgh and a Master's with distinction in Language Testing from Lancaster University. To balance out her academic achievements, she remains unable to dance, cook, or make convincing small talk – and has profound respect for anyone who's mastered these arcane arts.

ABOUT THE PUBLISHER

Neon Mess Press is an independent UK-based publisher specialising in science fiction mysteries that give you something to think about. Our books are available in a range of formats, so whether you prefer reading on a screen or on paper, with your eyes or your ears, Neon Mess Press has you covered.

At Neon Mess Press, we're committed to producing books sustainably. All of our paperback and hardback editions are created using a print-on-demand model, which consumes less energy and is less wasteful of resources than traditional production methods.

CLIMATE SOLUTIONS

The ArkTech Series imagines a future where the climate crisis is history. Learn more about the real-world solutions to global warming that informed the ArkTech Territory's design here: https://www.mariannepickles.com/climate-solutions.

Printed in Dunstable, United Kingdom

70568366R00282